ALSO BY JEFFERY DEAVER

EDGE

A NOVEL

JEFFERY DEAVER

DOUBLEDAY LARGE PRINT HOME LIBRARY EDITION

SIMON & SCHUSTER

NEW YORK · LONDON · TORONTO · SYDNEY

This Large Edition, prepared especially for Doubleday Large Print Home Library, contains the complete, unabridged text of the original Publishers' Edition.

Simon & Schuster
1230 Avenue of the Americas
New York, NY 10020

This book is a work of fiction. Names, characters, places, and incidents either are products of the author's imagination or are used fictitiously. Any resemblance to actual events or locales or persons, living or dead, is entirely coincidental.

SIMON & SCHUSTER and colophon are registered trademarks of Simon & Schuster, Inc.

Manufactured in the United States of America

ISBN: 978-1-61664-756-8

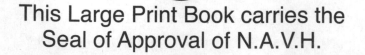

This Large Print Book carries the Seal of Approval of N.A.V.H.

For Shea, Sabrina and Brynn

EDGE

June 2004

THE RULES OF PLAY

The man who wanted to kill the young woman sitting beside me was three-quarters of a mile behind us, as we drove through a pastoral setting of tobacco and cotton fields this humid morning.

A glance in the rearview mirror revealed a sliver of car, moving at a comfortable pace with the traffic, piloted by a man who by all appearances seemed hardly different from any one of a hundred drivers on this recently resurfaced divided highway.

"Officer Fallow?" Alissa began. Then,

as I'd been urging her for the past week: "Abe?"

"Yes."

"Is he still there?" She'd seen my gaze.

"Yes. And so's our tail," I added for reassurance. My protégé was behind the killer, two or three car lengths. He was not the only person from our organization on the job.

"Okay," Alissa whispered. The woman, in her midthirties, was a whistle-blower against a government contractor that did a lot of work for the army. The company was adamant that it had done nothing wrong and claimed it welcomed an investigation. But there'd been an attempt on Alissa's life a week ago and— since I'd been in the army with one of the senior commanders at Bragg—Defense had called me in to guard her. As head of the organization I don't do much fieldwork any longer but I was glad to get out, to tell the truth. My typical day was ten hours at my desk in our Alexandria office. And in the past month it had been closer to twelve or fourteen, as we coordinated the protection of five high-level organized crime informants, before handing them over to Witness Protection for their face-lifts.

It was good to be back in the saddle, if only for a week or so.

I hit a speed dial button, calling my protégé.

"It's Abe," I said into my hands-free. "Where is he now?"

"Make it a half mile. Moving up slowly."

The hitter, whose identity we didn't know, was in a nondescript Hyundai sedan, gray.

I was behind an eighteen-foot truck, CAROLINA POULTRY PROCESSING COMPANY painted on the side. It was empty and being driven by one of our transport people. In front of that was a car identical to the one I was driving.

"We've got two miles till the swap," I said.

Four voices acknowledged this over four very encrypted com devices.

I disconnected.

Without looking at her, I said to Alissa, "It's going to be fine."

"I just . . ." she said in a whisper. "I don't know." She fell silent and stared into the side-view mirror as if the man who wanted to kill her were right behind us.

"It's all going just like we planned."

When innocent people find themselves in situations that require the presence and protection of people like me, their reaction more often than not is as much bewilderment as fear. Mortality is tough to process.

But keeping people safe, keeping people alive, is a business like any other. I frequently told this to my protégé and the others in the office, probably irritating them to no end with both the repetition and the stodgy tone. But I kept on saying it because you can't forget, ever. It's a business, with rigid procedures that we study the way surgeons learn to slice flesh precisely and pilots learn to keep tons of metal safely aloft. These techniques have been honed over the years and they worked.

Business . . .

Of course, it was also true that the hitter who was behind us at the moment, intent on killing the woman next to me, treated *his* job as a business too. I knew this sure as steel. He was just as

serious as I was, had studied procedures as diligently as I had, was smart,
IQ-wise and streetwise, and he had ad-
vantages over me: His rules were unen-
cumbered by *my* constraints—the Con-
stitution and the laws promulgated
thereunder.

Still, I believe there is an advantage in
being in the right. In all my years of doing this work I'd never lost a principal.
And I wasn't going to lose Alissa.

A business . . . which meant remaining calm as a surgeon, calm as a pilot.

Alissa was not calm, of course. She
was breathing hard, worrying her cuff as
she stared at a sprawling magnolia tree
we were passing, an outrider of a or
chestnut forest, bordering a huge cotton
field, the tufts bursting. She was uneasily
spinning a thin diamond bracelet—a treat
to herself on a recent birthday. She now
glanced at the jewelry and then her
palms, which were sweating, and placed
her hands on her navy blue skirt. Under
my care, Alissa had worn dark clothing
exclusively. It was camouflage but not
because she was the target of a professional killer; it was about her weight,

which she'd wrestled with since adolescence. I knew this because we'd shared meals and I'd seen the battle up close. She'd also talked quite a bit about her struggle with weight. Some principals don't need or want camaraderie. Others, like Alissa, need us to be friends. I don't do well in that role but I try and can generally pull it off.

We passed a sign. The exit was a mile and a half away.

A business requires simple, smart planning. You can't be reactive in this line of work and though I hate the word "proactive" (as opposed to what, anti-active?), the concept is vital to what we do. In this instance, to deliver Alissa safe and sound to the prosecutor for her depositions, I needed to keep the hitter in play. Since my protégé had been following him for hours, we knew where he was and could have taken him at any moment. But if we'd done that, whoever had hired him would simply call somebody else to finish the job. I wanted to keep him on the road for the better part of the day—long enough for Alissa to get into the U.S. Attorney's office and give him sufficient information via deposition so that she would no longer be at risk. Once the testimony's down, the hitter has no incentive to eliminate a witness.

The plan I'd devised, with my protégé's help, was for me to pass the Carolina Poultry truck and pull in front of it. The hitter would speed up to keep us in sight but before he got close the truck and I would exit simultaneously. Because of the curve in the road and the ramp I'd picked, the hitter wouldn't be able to see my car but would spot the decoy. Alissa and I would then take a complicated route to a hotel in Raleigh, where the prosecutor awaited, while the decoy would eventually end up at the courthouse in Charlotte, three hours away. By the time the hitter realized that he'd been following a bogus target, it would be too late. He'd call his primary—his employer—and most likely the hit would be called off. We'd move in, arrest the hitter and try to trace him back to the primary.

About a mile ahead was the turnoff.

The chicken truck was about thirty feet ahead.

I regarded Alissa, now playing with a gold and amethyst necklace. Her mother had given it to her on her seventeenth birthday, more expensive than the family could afford but an unspoken consolation prize for the absence of an invitation to the prom. People tend to share quite a lot with those who are saving their lives.

My phone buzzed. "Yes?" I asked my protégé.

"The subject's moved up a bit. About two hundred yards behind the truck."

"We're almost there," I said. "Let's go."

I passed the poultry truck quickly and pulled in behind the decoy—a tight fit. It was driven by a man from our organization; the passenger was an FBI agent who resembled Alissa. There'd been some fun in the office when we picked somebody to play the role of me. I have a round head and ears that protrude a fraction of an inch more than I would like. I've got wiry red hair and I'm not tall. So in the office they apparently spent an hour or two in an impromptu contest to find the most elf-like officer to impersonate me.

"Status?" I asked into the phone.

"He's changed lanes and is accelerating a little."

He wouldn't like not seeing me, I reflected.

I heard, "Hold on . . . hold on."

I would remember to tell my protégé to mind the unnecessary verbal filler; while the words were scrambled by our phones, the fact there'd been a transmission could be detected. He'd learn the lesson fast and retain it.

"I'm coming up on the exit. . . . Okay. Here we go."

Still doing about sixty, I eased into the exit lane and swung around the curve, which was surrounded by thick trees. The chicken truck was right on my bumper.

My protégé reported, "Good. Subject didn't even look your way. He's got the decoy in sight and the speed's dropping back to the limit."

I paused at the red light where the ramp fed into Route 18, then turned right. The poultry truck turned left.

"Subject is continuing on the route," came my protégé's voice. "Seems to be working fine." His voice was cool. I'm pretty detached about operations but he does me one better. He rarely smiles, never jokes and in truth I don't know much about him, though we've worked together, often closely, for several years. I'd like to change that about him—his somberness—not for the sake of the job, since he really is very, very good, but simply because I wish he took more pleasure in what we do. The endeavor of keeping people safe can be satisfying, even joyous. Especially when it comes to protecting families, which we do with some frequency.

I told him to keep me updated and we disconnected.

"So," Alissa asked, "we're safe?"

"We're safe," I told her, hiking the speed up to fifty in a forty-five zone. In fifteen minutes we were meandering along a route that would take us to the outskirts of Raleigh, where we'd meet the prosecutor for the depositions.

The sky was overcast and the scenery was probably what it had been for dozens of years: bungalow farmhouses, shacks, trailers and motor vehicles in terminal condition but still functioning if the nursing and luck were right. A gas station offering a brand I'd never heard of. Dogs toothing at fleas lazily. Women in stressed jeans, overseeing their broods. Men with beer-lean faces and expanding guts, sitting on porches, waiting for nothing. Most likely wondering at our car—containing the sort of people you don't see much in this neighborhood: a man in a white shirt, dark suit and tie and a woman with a business haircut.

Then we were past the residences and on a road bisecting more fields. I noted the cotton plants, shedding their growth like popcorn, and I thought of how this same land 150 years ago would have been carpeted with an identical crop; the Civil War, and the people for whom it was fought, were never far from one's mind when you were in the South.

My phone rang and I answered.

My protégé's voice was urgent. "Abe."

Shoulders tense, I asked, "Has he turned off the highway?" I wasn't too concerned; we'd exited over a half hour ago. The hitter would be forty miles away by now.

"No, still following the decoy. But something just happened. He made a call on his mobile. When he disconnected, it was odd: He was wiping his face. I moved up two car lengths. It looked like he'd been crying."

My breath came quickly as I considered possible reasons for this. Finally one credible, disturbing scenario rose to the top: What if the hitter had suspected we'd try a decoy and had used one of his own? He'd forced somebody who resembled him—just like the elfin man in *our* decoy car—to follow us. The call my protégé had just witnessed might have been between the driver and the real perp, who was perhaps holding the man's wife or child hostage.

But this, then, meant that the real hitter could be somewhere else and—

A flash of white streaked toward us as a Ford pickup truck appeared from the driveway of a sagging, deserted gas station to the left and bounded over the highway. The truck, its front protected by push bars, slammed into our driver's side and shoved us neatly through a tall stand of weeds into a shallow ravine. Alissa screamed and I grunted in pain and heard my protégé calling my name, then the mobile and the hands-free flew into the car, propelled by the deploying airbag.

We crashed down a five-foot descent and came to an undramatic stop at the soupy bottom of a shallow creek.

Oh, he'd planned his attack perfectly and before I could even click the seat belt to get to my gun, he'd swung a mallet through the driver's window, shattering it and stunning me with the same blow. My Glock was ripped off my belt and pocketed. Dislocated shoulder, I thought, not much blood. I spat broken glass from my mouth and looked to Alissa. She too was stunned but didn't seem hurt badly. The hitter wasn't holding his gun, only the mallet, and I thought that if she fled now she'd have a chance to tumble through the underbrush and escape. Not much of a chance but something. She had to move immediately, though. "Alissa, run, to the left! You can do it! Now!"

She yanked the door open and rolled out.

I looked back at the road. All I could see was the white truck parked on the shoulder near a creek where you might hunt frogs for bait, like a dozen other trucks I'd seen en route. It perfectly blocked anyone's view from the road. Just like I'd used a truck to mask *my* escape, I reflected grimly.

The hitter was now reaching in to un-latch my door. I squinted in pain, grate-ful for the man's delay. It meant that Alissa could gain more distance. My people would know our exact position through GPS and could have police here in fifteen or twenty minutes. She might make it. Please, I thought, turning to-ward the path she'd be escaping down, the shallow creekbed.

Except that she wasn't running any-where.

Tears rolling down her cheeks, she was standing next to the car with her head down, arms crossed over her round chest. Was she hurt more badly than I'd thought?

My door was opened and the hitter dragged me out onto the ground, where he expertly slipped nylon restraints on my hands. He released me and I sagged into the sour-scented mud, beside busy crickets.

Restraints? I wondered. I looked at Alissa again, now leaning against the car, unable to look my way. "Please." She was speaking to our attacker. "My mother?"

No, she wasn't stunned and wasn't hurt badly and I realized the reason she wasn't running: because she had no reason to.

She wasn't the target.

I was.

The whole terrible truth was obvious. The man standing over me had somehow gotten to Alissa several weeks before and threatened to hurt her mother— to force Alissa to make up a story about corruption at the government contractor. Because it involved an army base where I knew the commander, the perp had bet that I'd be the shepherd to guard her. For the past week Alissa had been giving this man details about our security procedures. He wasn't a hitter; he was a *lifter*, hired to extract information from me. Of course: about the organized crime case I'd just worked. I knew the new identities of the five witnesses who'd testified at the trial. I knew where Witness Protection was placing them.

Gasping for breath through the tears, Alissa was saying, "You told me. . . ."

But the lifter was ignoring her, looking at his watch and placing a call, I deduced, to the man in the decoy car, followed by my protégé, fifty miles away. He didn't get through. The decoy would have been pulled over, as soon as our crash registered through the mobile phone call.

This meant the lifter knew he didn't have as much time as he would have liked. I wondered how long I could hold out against the torture.

"Please," Alissa whispered again. "My mother. You said if I did what you wanted . . . Please, is she all right?"

The lifter glanced toward her and, as an afterthought, it seemed, took a pistol from his belt and shot her twice in the head.

I grimaced, felt the sting of despair.

He took a battered manila envelope from his inside jacket and, opening it, knelt beside me and shook the contents onto the ground. I couldn't see what they were. He pulled off my shoes and socks.

In a soft voice he asked, "You know the information I need?"

I nodded yes.

"Will you tell me?"

If I could hold out for fifteen minutes there was a chance local police would get here while I was still alive. I shook my head no.

Impassive, as if my response were neither good or bad, he set to work.

Hold out for fifteen minutes, I told myself.

I gave my first scream thirty seconds later. Another followed shortly after that and from then on every exhalation was a shrill cry. Tears flowed and pain raged like fire throughout my body.

Thirteen minutes, I reflected. Twelve . . .

But, though I couldn't say for certain,

probably no more than six or seven passed before I gasped, "Stop, stop!" He did. And I told him exactly what he wanted to know.

He jotted the information and stood. Keys to the truck dangled in his left hand. In his right was the pistol. He aimed the automatic toward the center of my forehead and what I felt was mostly relief, a terrible relief, that at least the pain would cease.

The man eased back and squinted slightly in anticipation of the gunshot, and I found myself w—

SATURDAY

The object of the game is to invade and capture the opponent's Castle or slay his Royalty. . . .

—FROM THE INSTRUCTIONS TO THE
BOARD GAME FEUDAL

Chapter 1

"We've got a bad one, Corte."

"Go ahead," I said into the stalk microphone. I was at my desk, on a hands-free. I set down the old handwritten note I'd been reading.

"The principal and his family're in Fairfax. There's a go-ahead order for a lifter and seems like he's under some time pressure."

"How much?"

"A couple of days."

"You know who hired him?"

"That's a negative, son."

It was Saturday, early. In this business, we drew odd hours and workweeks of varying lengths. Mine had just begun a couple of days ago and I'd finished a small job late yesterday afternoon. I was to have spent the day tidying up paper-

work, something I enjoy, but in my organization we're on call constantly.

"Keep going, Freddy." There'd been
something about his tone. Ten years of
working with somebody, even sporadi-
cally, in this line of work gives you clues.

The FBI agent, never known for hesitating, now hesitated. Finally: "Okay,
Corte, the thing is . . . ?"

"What?"

"The lifter's Henry Loving. . . . I know,
I know. But it's confirmed."

After a moment, in which the only
sounds I could hear were my heart and
a whisper of blood through my ears, I
responded automatically, though point-
lessly, "He's dead. Rhode Island."

"*Was* dead. Was *reported* dead."

I glanced at trees outside my window,
stirring in the faint September breeze,
then looked over my desk. It was neat
but small and cheaply made. On it were
several pieces of paper, each demand-
ing more or less of my attention, as well
as a small carton that FedEx had delivered to the town house, only a few blocks
from my office, that morning. It was an
eBay purchase I'd been looking forward

to receiving. I'd planned to examine the contents of the box on my lunch hour today. I now slid it aside.

"Go on."

"In Providence? Somebody else was in the building." Freddy filled in this missing puzzle piece, though I'd almost instantly deduced—correctly, from the agent's account—exactly what had happened. Two years ago the warehouse Henry Loving had been hiding in, after fleeing a trap I'd set for him, had burned to the ground. The forensic people had a clear DNA match on the body inside. Even badly burned, a corpse will leave about ten million samples of that pesky deoxyribonucleic acid. Which you can't hide or destroy so it doesn't make sense to try.

But what you can do is, afterward, get to the DNA lab technicians and force them to lie—to certify that the body was yours.

Loving was the sort who would have anticipated my trap. Before he went after my principals, he'd have a backup plan devised: kidnapping a homeless man or a runaway and stashing him in the warehouse, just in case he needed to escape. This was a clever idea, threatening a lab tech, and not so far-fetched when you considered that Henry Loving's unique art was manipulating people to do things they didn't want to do.

So, suddenly, a man a lot of other people had been content—I'd go so far as to use the word "happy"—to see die in a fire was now very much alive.

A shadow in my doorway. It was Aaron Ellis, the head of our organization, the man I reported to directly. Blond and fiercely broad of shoulder. His thin lips parted. He didn't know I was on the phone. "You hear? Rhode Island—it wasn't Loving after all."

"I'm on with Freddy now." Gesturing toward the hands-free.

"My office in ten?"

"Sure."

He vanished on deft feet encased in brown tasseled loafers, which clashed with his light blue slacks.

I said to the FBI agent, in his office about ten miles from mine, "That was Aaron."

"I know," Freddy replied. "My boss

briefed your boss. I'm briefing you. We'll be working it together, son. Call me when you can."

"Wait," I said. "The principals, in Fairfax? You send any agents to babysit?"

"Not yet. This just happened."

"Get somebody there now."

"Apparently Loving's nowhere near yet."

"Do it anyway."

"Well—"

"Do it anyway."

"Your wish, et cetera, et cetera."

Freddy disconnected before I could say anything more.

Henry Loving . . .

I sat for a moment and again looked out the window of my organization's unmarked headquarters in Old Town Alexandria, the building aggressively ugly, 1970s ugly. I stared at a wedge of grass, an antique store, a Starbucks and a few bushes in a parking strip. The bushes lined up in a staggered fashion toward the Masonic Temple, like they'd been planted by a Dan Brown character sending a message via landscaping rather than an email.

My eyes returned to the FedEx box and the documents on my desk.

One stapled stack of papers was a lease for a safe house near Silver Spring, Maryland. I'd have to negotiate the rent down, assuming a cover identity to do so.

One document was a release order for the principal I'd successfully delivered yesterday to two solemn men, in equally solemn suits, whose offices were in Langley, Virginia. I signed the order and put it into my OUT box.

The last slip of paper, which I'd been reading when Freddy called, I'd brought with me without intending to. In the town house last night I'd located a board game whose instructions I'd wanted to reread and had opened the box to find this sheet—an old to-do list for a holiday party, with names of guests to call, groceries and decorations to buy. I'd absently tucked the yellowing document into my pocket and discovered it this morning. The party had been years ago. It was the last thing I wanted to be reminded of at the moment.

I looked at the handwriting on the

faded rectangle and fed it into my burn box, which turned it into confetti.

I placed the FedEx box into the safe behind my desk—nothing fancy, no eye scans, just a clicking combination lock—and rose. I tugged on a dark suit jacket over my white shirt, which was what I usually wore in the office, even when working weekends. I stepped out of my office, turning left toward my boss's, and walked along the lengthy corridor's gray carpet, striped with sunlight, falling pale through the mirrored, bullet-resistant windows. My mind was no longer on real estate values in Maryland or delivery service packages or unwanted reminders from the past, but focused exclusively on the reappearance of Henry Loving—the man who, six years earlier, had tortured and murdered my mentor and close friend, Abe Fallow, in a gulley beside a North Carolina cotton field, as I'd listened to his cries through his still-connected phone.

Seven minutes of screams until the merciful gunshot, delivered not mercifully at all, but as a simple matter of professional efficiency.

Chapter 2

I was sitting in one of our director's scuffed chairs next to a man who clearly knew me, since he'd nodded with some familiarity when I entered. I couldn't, however, place him beyond his being a federal prosecutor. About my age—forty—and short, a bit doughy, with hair in need of a trim. A fox's eyes.

Aaron Ellis noticed my glance. "You remember Jason Westerfield, U.S. Attorney's Office."

I didn't fake it and try to respond. I just shook his hand.

"Freddy was briefing me."

"Agent Fredericks?" Westerfield asked.

"That's right. He said we have a principal in Fairfax and a lifter who needs information in the next few days."

Westerfield's voice was high and irritatingly playful. "You betcha. That's what we hear. We don't know much at this point, other than that the lifter got a clear go-ahead order. Somebody needs information from the subject by late Monday or all hell breaks loose. No idea what the fuck hell is, though. *Pardonnez moi.*"

While I was dressed like a prosecutor, ready for court, Westerfield was in weekend clothes. Not office weekend clothes but camping weekend clothes: chinos, a plaid shirt and a windbreaker. Unusual for the District, where Saturday and Sunday office hours were not rare. It told me he might be a cowboy. I noted too he was also sitting forward on the edge of his chair and clutching files with blunt fingers. Not nervously—he didn't seem the sort who could be nervous—but with excitement. A hot metabolism burned within.

Another voice, female, from behind us: "I'm sorry I'm late."

A woman about thirty joined us. A particular type of nod and I knew she was Westerfield's assistant. A tight hairstyle that ended at her shoulders, blond.

New or dry-cleaned blue jeans, a white sweater under a tan sports coat and a necklace of impressive creamy pearls. Her earrings were pearls too and accompanied on the lobes by equally arresting diamonds. Her dark-framed glasses were, despite her youth, trifocals, I could see by the way her head bobbed slowly as she took in the office and me. A shepherd has to know his principals' buying habits—it's very helpful in understanding them—and instinctively I noted Chanel, Coach and Cartier. A rich girl and probably near the top of her class at Yale or Harvard Law.

Westerfield said, "This is Assistant U.S. Attorney Chris Teasley."

She shook my hand and acknowledged Ellis.

"I'm just explaining the Kessler situation to them." Then to us: "Chris'll be working with us on it."

"Let's hear the details," I said, aware that Teasley was scenting the air, floral and subdued. She opened her attaché case with loud hardware snaps and handed her boss a file. As he skimmed it I noted a sketch on Ellis's wall. His corner office wasn't large but it was decorated with a number of pictures, some posters from mall galleries, some personal photos and art executed by his children. I stared at a watercolor drawing of a building on a hillside, not badly rendered.

I had nothing on my office walls except lists of phone numbers.

"Here's the sit." Westerfield turned to Ellis and me. "I heard from the Bureau's Charleston, West Virginia, field office this morning. Make a long story short, the state police were running a meth sting out in the boonies and they stumbled on some prints on a pay phone, turned out to be Henry Loving's. For some reason the homicide and surveillance warrants weren't cancelled after he died. Well, *supposedly* died, looks like.

"They call our people and we take over, find out Loving flew into Charleston a week ago under some fake name and ID. Nobody knows from where. Finally, they tracked him down to a motel in Winfield this morning. But he'd already checked out—a couple of hours ago, around eight-thirty. Clerk doesn't know where he was going."

At a nod from her boss, Teasley continued, "The surveillance warrants are technically still active, so the agents checked out emails at the hotel. One received and one sent: the go-ahead order and Loving's acknowledgment."

Ellis asked, "What would he be doing in West Virginia?"

I knew Loving better than anybody in the room. I said, "He usually worked with a partner; he might be picking somebody up there. Weapons too. He wouldn't fly with them. In any case, he'll avoid the D.C.-area airports. A lot of people up here still remember what he looks like after . . . after what happened a few years ago." I asked, "Internet address of the sender?"

"Routed through proxies. Untraceable."

"Any phone calls to or from his room in the motel?"

"Mais non."

The French was irritating. Had Westerfield just gotten back from a package

vacation or was he boning up to pros-
ecute an Algerian terrorist?

"What does the order say exactly, Jason?" I asked patiently.

At a nod from him, Chris Teasley did
the honors. "Like you were saying, it
was solely a go-ahead. So they'd have
had prior conversations where they laid
out the details."

"Go on, please," I said to her.

The woman read, " 'Loving—Re: Kessler. It's a go. Need details, per our discussion, by Monday midnight, or unacceptable consequences, as explained.
Once you get information, subject must
be eliminated.' End of quote. It gave an
address in Fairfax."

Unacceptable consequences . . . all
hell breaking loose.

"No audio?"

"No."

I was disappointed. Voice analysis can
tell a lot about the caller: gender, most
of the time, national and regional roots,
illnesses, even reasonable morphologi-
cal deductions can be made about the
shape of the nose, mouth and throat.
But at least we had a confirmed spelling

of the principal's name, which was a plus.

"Kessler's a cop in the District. Ryan Kessler, detective," Westerfield explained.

"Loving's response?"

"'Confirmed.' That was it."

"The primary wants the 'details'"— Westerfield did air quotes—"by late Monday. Details . . ."

I asked to see the printout. Noted a slight hesitation on Teasley's part, then she passed it over when Westerfield gave no reaction.

I read through the brief passage. "Grammar, spelling and punctuation are good. Proper use of 'per.'" Teasley frowned at this observation. I didn't explain that "as per," what most people say, is redundant; she wasn't *my* protégée. I continued, "And matching commas around the appositive, after 'details,' which you hardly ever see."

Everyone stared at me now. I'd studied linguistics a long time ago. A little philology too, the study of languages from analyzing texts. Mostly for the fun of it, but the subject came in useful sometimes.

Ellis toyed his neck sideways. He'd wrestled in college but didn't do many sports nowadays that I knew of. He was just still built like an iron triangle. He asked, "He left at eight-thirty this morning. He probably has weapons so he's not going to fly . . . and he doesn't want to risk being seen at an airport here, like you were saying, Corte. He's still about four hours away."

"His vehicle?" I asked.

"Nothing yet. The Bureau's got a team canvassing the motel and restaurants around town."

Ellis: "This Kessler, what does he know that the primary's so interested in extracting from him?"

"No clue," Westerfield said.

"Who exactly is he, Kessler?" I asked.

"I've got some details," Teasley said.

As the young attorney dug through a file, I wondered why Westerfield had come to us. We're known as the bodyguards of last resort (at least Aaron Ellis refers to us that way in budgetary hearings, which I find a bit embarrassing, but apparently it plays well on the Hill). The State Department's Diplomatic Security and the Secret Service guard U.S. officials and foreign heads of state. Witness Protection cloaks the noble or the infamous with new identities and turns them loose in the world. We, on the other hand, handle situations only when there's an immediate, credible threat against a known principal. We've also been called the ER of personal security.

The criterion is vague but, given limited resources, we tend to take on cases only when the principal is involved in matters like national security—the spy I'd just delivered to the CIA gentlemen yesterday— or public health, such as our job guarding a whistle-blower in an over-the-counter tainted-drug trial last year.

But the answer became clear when Teasley gave the cop's bio. "Detective Ryan Kessler, forty-two. Married, one child. He works financial crimes in the district, fifteen years on the force, decorated. . . . You may've heard of him."

I glanced at my boss, who shook his head for both of us.

"He's a hero. Got some media coverage a few years ago. He was working undercover in D.C. and stumbled into a robbery in a deli in North West. Saved the customers but took a slug. Was on the news, and one of those Discovery Channel cop programs did an episode about him."

I didn't watch much TV. But I did understand the situation now. A hero cop being targeted by a lifter like Henry Loving . . . Westerfield saw a chance to be a hero of his own here—marshalling a case against the primary, presumably because of some financial scam Kessler was investigating. Even if the underlying case wasn't big—though it could be huge—targeting a heroic D.C. police officer was reason enough to end up on Westerfield's agenda. I didn't think any less of him because of this; Washington is all about personal as well as public politics. I didn't care if his career would be served by taking on the case. All that mattered to me was keeping the Kessler family alive.

And that this particular lifter was involved.

"*Alors,*" Westerfield said. "There we have it. Kessler's been poking his *nez* where it doesn't belong. We need to find out where, what, who, when, why. So, let's get the Kesslers into the slammer fast and go from there."

"Slammer?" I asked.

"Yessir," Teasley said. "We were thinking Hansen Detention Center in D.C. I've done some research and found that HDC has just renovated their alarm systems and I've reviewed the employee files of every guard who'd be on the friendly wing. It's a good choice."

"C'est vrai."

"A slammer wouldn't be advisable," I said.

"Oh?" Westerfield wondered.

Protective custody, in a secluded part of a correctional facility, makes sense in some cases but this wasn't one of them, I explained.

"Hm," the prosecutor said, "we were thinking you could have one of your people with them inside, *non*? Efficient. Agent Fredericks and you can interview him. You'll get good information. I guarantee it. In a slammer, witnesses tend to remember things they wouldn't otherwise. They're all happy-happy."

"That hasn't been my experience in circumstances like these."

"No?"

"You put somebody in detention, yes, usually a lifter from the outside can't get in. And"—a nod toward Teasley, conceding her diligent homework—"I'm sure the staff's been vetted well. With any other lifter, I'd agree. But we're dealing with Henry Loving here. I know how he works. We put the Kesslers inside, he'll find an edge on one of the guards. Most of them are young, male. If I were Loving, I'd just find one with a pregnant wife—their first child, if possible—and pay her a visit." Teasley blinked at my matter-of-fact tone. "The guard would do whatever Loving wanted. And once the family's inside there're no escape routes. The Kesslers'd be trapped."

"Like *petits lapins*," Westerfield said, though not as sarcastically as I'd expected. He was considering my point.

"Besides, Kessler's a cop. We'd have trouble getting him to agree. There could be a half dozen cons he's put inside HDC."

"Where would you stash them?" Westerfield asked.

I replied, "I don't know yet. I'll have to think about it."

Westerfield gazed up at the wall too, though I couldn't tell at which picture or certificate or diploma. Finally he said to Teasley, "Give him Kessler's address."

The young woman jotted it in far more legible handwriting than her boss's. When she handed it to me I was hit by another blast of perfume.

I took it, thanking them both. I'm a competitive game player—all sorts of games—and I've learned to be humble and magnanimous in victory, a theory I'd carried over to my professional life. A matter of courtesy, of course, but I'd also found that being a good winner gives you a slight advantage psychologically when you play against the same opponent in the future.

They rose. The prosecutor said, "Okay, do what you can—find out who hired Loving and why."

"Our number-one priority," I assured him, though it wasn't.

"Au revoir. . . ." Westerfield and Teas-

ley breezed out of the doorway, the prosecutor giving sotto voce orders to her.

I too rose. I had to stop at the town house and pick up a few things for the assignment.

"I'll report from the location," I told Ellis.

"Corte?"

I stopped at the door and glanced back.

"Not sending the Kesslers to the slammer . . . it makes sense, right? You'd rather get them into a safe house and run the case from there?" He'd backed me up—Aaron Ellis was nothing if not supportive of his troops—and would go with my expertise on the question. But he wasn't, in truth, asking for reassurance that it made tactical sense not to put them in protective custody.

What he was really asking was this: Was he making the right decision in assigning me, and not someone else, to the job of guarding principals from Henry Loving? In short, could I be objective when the perp was the one who'd murdered my mentor and had apparently escaped from the trap I'd set for him several years before?

"A safe house's the most efficient approach," I told Ellis and returned to my office, fishing for the key to unlock the desk drawer where I kept my weapon.

Chapter 3

Many governmental agencies are wedded to initials or acronyms to describe their employees or departments, but in ours, for some reason, nicknames are the order of the day, as with "lifter" and "hitter."

The basic bodyguards in our organization are the close protection officers, whom we call "clones," because they're supposed to shadow their principals closely. Our Technical Support and Communications Department is staffed by "wizards." There are the "street sweepers"—our Defense Analysis and Tactics officers, who can spot a sniper a mile away and a bomb hidden in a principal's cell phone. The people in our organization running surveillance are called, not surprisingly, "spies."

I'm in the Strategic Protection Department, the most senior of the eight SPD officers in the organization. We're the ones who come up with and execute a protection plan for the principals we've been assigned to guard. And because of the mission, and the initials of the department, we're known as shepherds.

One department that doesn't have a nickname is Research Support, to me the most important of all our ancillary divisions. A shepherd can't run a personal security job without good investigative research. I've often lectured younger officers that if you do research up front, you'll be less likely to need tactical firepower later.

And I was lucky to have as my protégée the person I considered the best in the department.

I called her now.

One ring. Then: "DuBois," came the voice from my earpiece.

It was the woman's secure mobile I'd called, so I got her work greeting. With its French origin, you'd think the name would be pronounced *doo-bwah* but her family used *doo-boys*.

"Claire. Something's come up."

"Yes?" she asked briskly.

"Loving's still alive."

She processed this. "Alive? . . . I'm not sure how that could happen."

"Well, it has."

"I'm thinking about it," she mused, almost to herself. "The building burned. . . . There was a DNA match. I recall the report. There were some typos in it, remember?" Claire duBois was older than her adolescent intonation suggested, though not much. Short brunette hair, a heart-shaped and delicately pretty face, a figure that was probably very nice— and I was as curious about it as any man would be—but usually hidden by functional pantsuits, which I preferred her wearing over skirts and dresses. The practicality of it, I mean.

"It doesn't matter. Are you in town? I need you."

"Do you mean did I go away for the weekend? No. Plans changed. Do you want me in?" she asked in her snappy monotone. I pictured her having breakfast as the September morning light slanted through the window of her quiet town house in Arlington, Virginia. She might have been in sweats or a slinky robe but picturing either was impossible. She might have been sitting across from a stubble-bearded young man looking at her curiously from over a sagging *Washington Post*. That too didn't register.

"He's after a principal in Fairfax. I don't know the details. Short time frame."

"Sure. Let me make some arrangements." I heard a few brief clicks—she could type faster than any human being on earth. Half to herself: "Mrs. Glotsky, next door . . . Then the water . . . Okay. I'll be there in twenty minutes."

I suspected duBois had a bit of attention deficit disorder. But that usually worked to my advantage.

"I'll be on the road with the principals but I'll call you with the assignments."

We disconnected. I signed out a Nissan Armada from our transportation department and collected it in the large garage beneath the building. I drove up King Street and then through the quaint and narrow avenues of Old Town Alexandria, on the Potomac River, the Virginia side, not far from Washington, D.C.

The SUV wasn't tell-all black but a light gray, dusty and dinged. Cars are a big part of the personal security business and, like all of ours, this Nissan had been modified to incorporate bullet-resistant glass, armor on the doors, run-flat tires and a foam-filled gas tank. Billy, our vehicle man, had lowered the center of gravity for faster turning and fitted the grille with what he called a jockstrap, an armored panel to keep the engine protected.

I double-parked and ran inside the brownstone town house, still smelling of the coffee I'd brewed on a one-cup capsule machine only an hour earlier. I hurriedly packed a large gym bag. Here, unlike at my office, the walls were filled with evidence of my past: diplomas, certificates of continuing-education course completions, recognitions from former employers and satisfied customers, including the Department of State, the CIA, the Bureau and ATF. MI5 in the UK too. Also, a few photos from my earlier years, snapped in Virginia, Ohio and Texas.

I wasn't sure why I put all of this gingerbread up on the walls. I rarely looked at it, and I never socialized here. I remembered thinking a few years ago that it just seemed like what you were supposed to do when you moved into a good-sized town house by yourself.

I changed clothes, into jeans and a navy windbreaker and a black Polo shirt. Then I locked up, set the two alarms and returned to the car. I sped toward the expressway, dialing a number then plugging the hands-free into my ear.

In thirty minutes I was at the home of my principals.

Fairfax, Virginia, is a pleasant suburb with a range of residential properties, from two-bedroom bungalows and row town houses to sumptuous ten-acre lots ringed with demilitarized-zone barriers of trees between neighbors' houses. The Kesslers' house, between these extremes, sat in the midst of an acre, half bald and half bristling with trees, the leaves just now losing their summer vibrancy, about to turn—trees, I noted, that would be perfect cover for a sniper backing up Henry Loving.

I made a U, parked the Armada in the

driveway, climbed out. I didn't recognize the FBI agents across the street personally but I'd seen their pictures, uploaded from Freddy's assistant. I approached the car. They would have my description too but I kept my hands at my sides until they saw who I was. We flashed IDs.

One said, "Nobody paused in front of the house since we've been here."

I slipped my ID case away. "Any out-of-state tags?"

"Didn't notice any."

Different answer from "No."

One of the agents pointed to a wide four-lane road nearby. "We saw a couple of SUVs, big ones, there. They slowed, looked our way and then kept going."

I asked, "They were going north?"

"Yeah."

"There's a school a half block away. They've got soccer games today. It's early in the season so I'd guess it was parents who hadn't been to the field yet and weren't sure where to turn."

They both seemed surprised I knew this. Claire duBois had fed me the information on the way over. I'd asked her about events in the area.

"But let me know right away if you see them again."

Up the street I saw homeowners mowing late-season grass or raking early leaves. The day was warm, the air crisp. I scanned the entire area twice. I'm often described as paranoid. And I probably am. But the opponent here was Henry Loving, an expert at being invisible . . . until the last minute, of course, at which time he becomes all too present. Thinking of Rhode Island again, two years ago, when he'd just materialized, armed, from a car that he simply couldn't have been inside.

Except that he was.

Hefting my shoulder bag higher, I returned to the Nissan and noted my reflection in the window. I'd decided that since Ryan Kessler was a police detective, what it took to win his confidence was looking more like an undercover cop than the humorless federal agent that I pretty much am. With my casual clothes, my trim, thinning brownish hair and a clean-shaven face, I probably resembled one of the dozens of fortyish businessmen dads shouting encouragement to their sons or daughters at the soccer game up the street at that moment.

I made a call on my cold phone.

"That you?" Freddy asked.

"I'm here, at Kessler's."

"You see my guys?"

"Yes. They're good and obvious."

"What're they going to do, hide behind the lawn gnomes? It's the suburbs, son."

"It's not a criticism. If Loving's got a spotter on site, I want him to know we're on to him."

"You think somebody's there already?"

"Possibly. But nobody'll make a move until Loving's here. Anything more on his position or ETA?"

"No."

Where was Loving now? I wondered, picturing the highway from West Virginia. We had a safe house, a good one, out in Luray. I wondered if he was driving near it at the moment.

Freddy said, "Hold on, just getting something . . . Funny you asked, Corte.

Got some details from the team at the motel. Okay, he's in a light-colored sedan. No year, no make, no model that anybody saw."

Henry Loving stimulates the amnesia gene. But it's also true most people are simply extremely unobservant.

Freddy continued, "I say at least three hours before he's even in the area. And he's going to spend some time staging before he gets to the Kessler place."

I said, "Are you owed any favors—the Virginia State troopers?"

"No, but I'm such a lovable guy, they'll do what I ask."

I have trouble with Freddy's flippancy. But whatever gets you through the day in this difficult business.

"Can you get his picture to the state police? Have it sent to all the cars between here and West Virginia on an orange notice." The officers on patrol would get a flash on their computers and they'd be on the lookout for light-colored cars and a driver who fit Loving's description. The orange code meant he was dangerous.

"I'll do it but I know you're a math wizard, Corte."

"And?"

"Divide a million cars by forty troopers. Whatta you get?"

"Thanks, Freddy."

We disconnected and I called Ryan Kessler.

"Hello?"

I told him who I was and that I'd arrived. I'd be at his door in a moment or two. I wanted him to call Freddy and check on my appearance. This was a good security measure but I also did it to increase his paranoia. I knew Kessler, as a cop—and a decorated street cop at that—would be a reluctant principal and I wanted him to sense the reality of the danger.

Silence.

"Are you there, Detective Kessler?"

"Well, sir, I told Agent Fredericks and those men outside . . . I see you out there too, Agent Corte. I told them this isn't necessary."

"I'd still like to talk to you, please. If you don't mind."

He made no attempt to mask his irritation. "It's really a waste of time."

"I'd appreciate it," I said pleasantly. I tend to be overly polite—stiff, many people say. But a calm, structured attitude gets people's cooperation better than bluster, which I'm not very good at anyway.

"All right, fine. I'll call Agent Fredericks."

I also asked him if he was armed.

"Yes. That a problem?" Testy.

"No," I said. "Not at all."

I would rather he wasn't, but as a police officer he was entitled, and asking a cop to give up his weapon was a battle rarely worth fighting.

I gave him some time to call Freddy, while I considered the house.

Nearly all single-family residences are indefensible.

Visibility, permeable construction, susceptibility to fire. They're naked to thermal sensors and have limited escape routes. Tactical cover is a joke. A single bullet can take out the power. A proudly advertised five-minute response time by central station security companies simply means the lifter knows he has a guaranteed window for a leisurely kidnapping. Not to mention that the paper trail of home ownership, automobiles and financial documents will lead the perp directly to even the most reclusive citizen's front door in no time at all.

Principals, of course, always want the security blanket of their homes but I remove them from their beloved residence as fast as possible.

Seeing Ryan Kessler's house I was determined to spirit him and his family away from the insubstantial two-story colonial as soon as I could.

I walked to the front door, checking windows. Ryan opened it. I knew what he looked like from personnel files and my other research. I glanced past him at the empty downstairs and moved my hand away from the small of my back.

He moved his from the holster on his hip.

I introduced myself. Shook his hand. I showed him my ID, which has my picture, name and a federal government logo on it, eagle included like the Justice Department's but our own brand of bird. There's nothing specific about our organization. I'm described simply as a "United States officer."

He took a fast look and didn't ask the questions I would have.

"Did you call Agent Fredericks to check on me?"

"No." Maybe he felt his cop's intuition could verify my credibility. Maybe it didn't seem very macho.

Ryan Kessler was a solid man, broad shoulders and black hair, looking older than his years. When he tilted his head down, which he had to do because I was shorter and a step below, a double chin rolled outward. A round belly above tapering thighs and hips. His eyes were inky and focused. It was as hard to imagine a smile on his face as on mine. He'd be good at interrogation, I surmised.

"Well, Agent Corte—"

"Just Corte's fine."

"One name? Like a rock star."

My ID has two initials but I never use them or anything more than Corte. Like some people, Ryan seemed to consider this pretentious. I didn't explain to him that it was simply a wise strategy; when it came to my business, the rule was to give people—good people, bad or neutral—as little information about myself as possible. The more people who know about you, the more compromised you are and the less efficiently you can do your job protecting your principals.

"Agent Fredericks is on his way over," I told him.

A sigh. "This is all a big mixup. Mistaken identity. There's nobody who'd want to threaten me. It's not like I'm going after the J-Eights."

One of the most dangerous Latino gangs in Fairfax.

"Still, I'd like to come in if I could."

"So you're, what, like protection detail?"

"Exactly."

He looked me over. I'm a little under six feet and weigh about 170, a range of five pounds plus or minus depending on the nature of the assignment and my deli-sandwich preference of the month. I've never been in the army; I've never taken the FBI course at Quantico. I know some basic self-defense but no fancy

martial arts. I have no tattoos. I get outside a fair amount, jogging and hiking,
but no marathons or Iron Man stuff for
me. I do some push-ups and sit-ups, inspired by the probably erroneous idea
that exercise improves circulation and
also lets me order cheese on my deli
sandwich without guilt. I happen to be a
very good shot and was presently carrying a Glock 23—the .40—in a Galco
Royal Guard inside-the-pants holster
and a Monadnock retractable baton. He
wouldn't know that, though, and to Ryan
Kessler, the protection package would
be looking a little meager.

"Even them." His eyes swung toward
the FBI car across the street. "All they're
doing is upsetting my wife and daughter. The fact is, they're a little obvious,
don't you think?"

I was amused that we'd had the same
observation. "They are. But they're more
a deterrent than anything."

"Well, again, I'm sorry for the waste of
time. I've talked it over with my boss."

"Chief of Detectives Lewis. I spoke to
him too on the way over here."

Ronald Lewis, with the District of Columbia's Metropolitan Police Department. Squat, with a broad face, dark brown skin. Outspoken. I'd never met him in person but heard he'd done a good job turning around some of the more dangerous neighborhoods in the city, which was one of the more dangerous cities in the country. He'd risen high in the MPD from street patrol in South East and was a bit of a hero too, like Ryan Kessler.

Ryan paused, registering that I'd been doing my homework. "Then he told you he doesn't know any reason I'd be a target. I really will have to ask you to leave now. Sorry you wasted your time."

I said, "Mr. Kessler, just do me a favor? Please. Let me come in and lay out a few things. Ten minutes." I was pleasant, not a hint of irritation. I said nothing more, offered no reasons—arguments held in doorways are hard to win; your opponent can just step back and close the door. I now simply looked up at him expectantly. My eyes never left his.

He sighed again. Loudly. "I guess. Come on. Five minutes." He turned and, limping, led me through the neat subur-

ban house, which smelled of lemon furniture polish and coffee. I couldn't draw
many conclusions about him or his family from my observations but one thing
that stood out was the framed yellowing
front page of *The Washington Post*
hanging in the den: HERO COP SAVES TWO
DURING ROBBERY.

A picture of a younger Ryan Kessler
accompanied the story.

On the drive here Claire duBois, as
efficient as a fine watch, had given me
a backgrounder on Ryan. This included
details of the officer's rescue. Some
punk had robbed a deli downtown in the
District, panicked and started shooting.
Ryan was en route to meet an informant
and happened to be in the alley behind
the deli. He'd heard the shots, drawn his
weapon and sped in through the back
door, too late to save the husband and
wife who owned the place, but he had
rescued the customers inside, taking a
bullet in the leg before the robber fled.

The story ended with a curious twist:
The woman customer had stayed in
touch with him. They'd started going
out. She was now his wife, Joanne. Ryan

had a daughter by his first wife, who'd died of ovarian cancer when the girl was six.

After delivering the bios, duBois had told me in the car, "That's pretty romantic, saving her life. Knight in shining armor."

I don't read much fiction but I enjoy history, medieval included. I could have told her that knight's armor was the worst defensive system ever created; it looked spiffy but made the warrior far more vulnerable than a simple shield, helmet and chain mail or nothing at all.

I also reflected that getting shot in the leg seemed like a rather *unromantic* way to get a spouse.

As we moved through the cluttered family room, Ryan said, "Here it is, a nice Saturday. Wouldn't you rather be hanging out with your wife and kids?"

"Actually, I'm single. And I don't have children."

Ryan was silent for a moment, a familiar response. It usually came from suburbanites of a certain age, upon learning they're talking to an unmarried, family-less forty-year-old. "Let's go in here." We entered the kitchen and new smells mingled with the others: a big weekend breakfast, not a meal I'm generally fond of. The place was cluttered, dirty dishes stacked neatly in the sink. Jackets and sweats were draped on the white colonial dining chairs around a blond table. Against the wall the number of empty paper Safeway bags outnumbered the Whole Foods four to one. Schoolbooks and running shoes and DVD and CD cases. Junk mail and magazines.

"Coffee?" Ryan asked because he wanted some and preferred not to appear rude, only discouraging.

"No, thanks."

He poured a cup while I stepped to the window and looked out over a backyard like ten thousand backyards nearby. I observed windows and doors.

Noting my reconnaissance, Ryan sipped, enjoying the coffee. "Really, Agent Corte, I don't need anybody to stand guard duty."

"Actually I want to get you and your family into a safe house until we find the people behind this."

He scoffed, "Move out?"

"Should just be a matter of days, at the most."

I heard sounds from upstairs but saw no one else on the ground floor. Claire duBois had given me information on Ryan's family too. Joanne Kessler, thirty-nine, had worked as a statistician for about eight or nine years, then, after meeting and marrying widower Ryan, she had quit to become a full-time mother to her stepdaughter, who was ten at the time.

The daughter, Amanda, was a junior at a public high school. "She makes good grades and is in three advanced placement programs. History, English and French. She's on the yearbook. She volunteers a lot." I'd wondered if some of the organizations were hospitals or devoted to health care because of her mother's death. DuBois had continued, "And she plays basketball. That was my sport. You wouldn't think it. But you don't have to be that tall. Really. The thing is you have to be willing to bump. Hard."

Ryan now said, "Look, I'm just a cop

handling some routine nonviolent cases. No terrorists, no Mafia, no conspiracies." He sipped more of the coffee, snuck a look at the doorway and added two more sugars, stirring quickly. "Agent Fredericks said this guy needed the information, whatever it is, by Monday night? There's nothing I'm working on that has a deadline like that. In fact, I'm in a down period now. For the past week or so, I'm mostly on some departmental administrative assignment. Budget. That's all. If I thought there was something to it, I'd let you know. But there just isn't. A mistake," he repeated.

"I had a principal last year I was protecting." He hadn't invited me to sit but I did anyway, on one of the swivel stools. He remained standing. "I spent five days playing cat and mouse with a hitter—a professional killer—who'd been hired to take him out. It was all a complete mistake. The hitter had been given the wrong name. But he would have killed my principal just the same. In this case, it isn't a hitter who's after you, it's a lifter. You ever heard that term?"

"I think. An interrogator, right? A pro."

Close enough. I nodded. "Now, a hitter's one thing. Mistake or not, you'd be the only one at risk. But a lifter . . . he'll target your family, anything to get an edge on you—some leverage to force you to tell him what he wants. By the time he realizes it's a mistake, someone close to you could be seriously hurt. Or worse."

Considering my words. "Who is he?"

"His name's Henry Loving."

"Former military? Special ops?"

"No. Civilian."

"In a gang? Organized crime?"

"Not that we could find."

In fact, we didn't know much about Henry Loving, other than he'd been born in northern Virginia, left home in his late teens and had maintained little contact with most of his family. His school records were missing. The last time he'd been arrested was when the sentence involved juvenile detention. A week after he was released the magistrate in the case quit the bench for reasons unknown and left the area. It might have been a coincidence. But I, for one, didn't think so. Loving's court and police files vanished at the same time. He worked hard to hide his roots and protect his anonymity.

I looked out the window once more. Then, after a brief conspiratorial pause and a glance into the still-empty hall, I continued, speaking even more softly, "But there's something else I have to say. This is completely between us?"

He gripped the coffee he'd lost his taste for.

I continued, "Henry Loving has successfully kidnapped at least a dozen principals to interrogate them. Those are just the cases we know about. He's responsible for the deaths of a half dozen bystanders too. He's killed or seriously injured federal agents and local cops."

Ryan gave a brief wince.

"I've been trying . . . our organization and the Bureau have been trying for years to collar him. So, okay, I'm admitting it: Yes, we're here to protect you and your family. But you're a godsend to us, Detective. You're a decorated cop, somebody who's familiar with tactical response, with weapons."

"Well, it's been a few years."

"Those skills never go away. Don't you think? Like riding a bicycle."

A modest glance downward. "I do get out to the range every week."

"There you go." I could see a change in his dark eyes. A bit of fire in them. "I'm asking for your help in getting this guy. But we can't do it here. Not in this house. Too dangerous for you and your family, too dangerous for your neighbors."

He tapped his pistol. "I'm loaded with Glasers."

Safety bullets. Powerful rounds that can kill, but they won't penetrate Sheetrock and injure bystanders. They're called suburb slugs.

"But Loving won't be. He'll come in with M4s or MP-5s. It'll be carnage. There will be collateral damage."

He was considering all that I'd said. His eyes took in the dirty dishes, seemed to notice them for the first time. "What're you suggesting?"

"You, another officer and I'll form the guard detail. We'll get you and your family into a safe house that'll give us a defensive advantage over Loving. My people and the Bureau'll try to take him on the street or his hidey-hole, if they can find him. But if he gets through, and he could, I'll need you. I have a safe house in mind that'll be perfect." I was speaking very softly now, making clear that what I was asking was off the record.

"You sound like you've been up against this guy before."

I paused. "I have, yes."

As he debated, a female voice came from the hallway: "Ry, those men're still out there. I'm getting—"

She turned the corner and stopped quickly, glancing at me with narrowed brown eyes. I recognized her face immediately from the photos duBois had uploaded to me. Joanne Kessler. In running shoes, jeans and a dark zippered sweater sprouting a few snags, Joanne had a handsome, though not pretty or exotic, face. She got outside a lot, sun wrinkles and tan, gardening, I guessed, from the short nails, two of which were broken. She didn't seem athletic, although unlike her husband she was slim. The hair was dark blond, frizzy and long, pulled into a ponytail. She wore glasses, which were stylish, but the lenses were thick, a reminder of her prior career. If anybody looked like a statistician for the Department of Transportation, it was Joanne Kessler.

Her face had registered a moment of shock seeing me—apparently she hadn't heard me arrive—and then went completely blank. Not stony or cold in anger. She was numb—a bookish woman, I guessed, who'd been thrown by these events.

"This is Agent Corte. He works with the Justice Department. He's a bodyguard."

I didn't correct Ryan about my title or employer. I shook her limp hand and offered a momentary smile. Her eyes remained uninvolved.

"Mrs. Kessler—"

"Joanne."

"You're familiar with the situation?"

"Ry told me there's been some mixup. Somebody thought he was being threatened."

I glanced at Ryan, who tipped his head in response.

I kept a calm visage and said to Joanne, "There may be a mixup, yes, but the fact is that there's no doubt a man has been hired to get information from your husband."

Her face deflated. She whispered, "You think we really might be in danger?"

"Yes." I explained about lifters and Henry Loving. "A freelance interrogator," I summarized.

"But you don't mean he tortures people or anything like that, do you?" Joanne asked softly, her eyes eerily emotionless as she stared at her husband.

I said, "Yes, that's exactly what I mean."

Chapter 4

"Some lifters bribe, some threaten, some blackmail with embarrassing information," I explained. "But the man who's after Ryan, yes, specializes in physical extraction."

"'Physical extraction,'" Joanne muttered. "'Specializes.' You make it sound like he's a lawyer or doctor."

I said nothing. In this line you look for anything to help you do your job. It's like the games I play—board games exclusively. I like to see my opponent. I learn a lot, noting body language, verbal language, eye contact, clothing. Even breathing patterns. I had to convince the Kesslers that *they* needed *me.* I made a decision based on what I'd learned just now. I spoke to them both, though directed most of my attention to the wife.

I said evenly, "Loving's low-tech. Usually he uses sandpaper and alcohol on sensitive parts of the body. Doesn't sound too bad but it works real well."

I tried not to picture the crime scene photos of the body of my mentor, Abe Fallow. I wasn't very successful.

"Oh, God," Joanne whispered and lifted her hand to her narrow lips.

"A lifter's basic technique is 'getting an edge,' as in getting the advantage over you. In one job where I was protecting someone from him, Loving was going to break in and torture a child right in front of the father he wanted information from."

"No," Joanne gasped. "But . . . Amanda. We have a daughter. This is . . ." Her eyes swung from one part of the room to another, then settled on the sink and the dirty dishes. Almost urgently, she stepped forward, grabbed a pair of yellow kitchen gloves, pulled them on and twisted the hot water faucet open wide. This happened a lot, principals focusing on—sometimes obsessing over—the little things. Things they can control.

Ryan said, "We should do what Agent Corte says. Get out of the house for a little while."

"Leave?"

"Yes," I said. "Just a precaution."

"Now?"

"That's right. As soon as possible."

"But where? A hotel? One of our friends' . . . We're not packed. Leave now?"

"You just need to take a few things. And you'd go to one of our safe houses. It's not far away. It's a nice place." I wasn't more specific about the location. I never was. I didn't blindfold principals before I drove them to a safe house and they could probably figure out some general idea of where it was located but I never told anybody the address. "Now, if I could ask you to pack your—"

"Amanda," Joanne interrupted and, perhaps forgetting she'd mentioned it before, said, "We have a daughter. She's sixteen. Ry! Where is she? Is she back from school yet?"

Principals often slipped into a hyperactive mode, and their minds jumped from thought to thought. At first I guessed she'd forgotten it was Saturday morning but it turned out the girl was taking a computer course for extra credit at a nearby community college on week-ends.

"I heard her come in a half hour ago," Ryan said.

Joanne was staring at the bright yellow gloves. She tugged them off, twisted the faucet closed. "I'm thinking . . ."

"Yes?" I prompted.

"I don't want her there, Amanda, I mean. I don't want her with us at that safe house."

"But she's as much at risk as Ryan is. So are you . . . what I was saying earlier, about the edge Loving wants."

"No, please," she said.

It seemed important to Joanne that the girl be separated from them. I recalled that Amanda was Ryan's alone and I wondered why the Kesslers had not had any children. Maybe he'd had a vasectomy during his first marriage or maybe Joanne had been unable to conceive or maybe they'd simply chosen not to have a family together. Preferring to know all I can about my principals, I consider information like this. It can make a difference. Joanne stared at the dishes and put down the gloves.

Ryan was considering this too. "I agree. Let's get her someplace out of harm's way." I realized he'd be thinking of what I'd mentioned—about the possibility of a firefight to take Loving.

Joanne said, "*We'll* go to the safe house. But she goes somewhere else. It's the only way I'll agree."

Then Ryan said to his wife, "You and Amanda go."

"No," she said adamantly. "I'm staying with you."

"But—"

"I'm staying." She took his hand.

I stepped to the window once more and looked out. Joanne noted this, the same way her husband had earlier, and she was uneasy with my apparent concern. I turned back. "I don't mind in theory but I don't have enough people to put your daughter in a separate safe house. Can you send her away somewhere? As long as the place she goes to has no connection to you or your family at all and her name isn't on travel records or credit-card purchases."

Loving and other expert lifters managed liberal access to data-mined information.

"Bill," Joanne said suddenly.

"Who?"

Ryan said, "William Carter. He's a family friend. He was in the department with me. Retired about ten years ago. She could stay with him."

I wondered if Loving could track him down because of his past association with Ryan. "Was he your partner, were you ever assigned together? Is he Amanda's godfather?"

"No. Just a friend. We were never on the same detail. He's got this place on a lake in Loudoun County, near White's Ferry. They could go there. Amanda likes him. He's sort of her uncle." He reiterated, "And he's a former cop."

"You're absolutely sure nobody could place you two together? You don't own anything together, a fishing boat, a car? Ever loaned each other money that was part of a public filing, bought property from each other?"

"No. Nothing."

"Can he be here in ten minutes?"

"Five. He lives a neighborhood away. He was going to the game this afternoon but he'll change his plans on a dime for something like this."

I opened my bag and withdrew my laptop. I booted it up and began typing commands into a new window. I examined the information scrolling past on our organization's secure database. Nothing about William Carter or his career or life circumstances gave me any concern. My next search was about the girl. Amanda Kessler was a typical teenager, active on Facebook, MySpace and blogs but the personal information was minimal. I was relieved at that. Social networking sites have made our jobs as shepherds nightmares, given all the personal details people threw out into the ozone. I noted too that Amanda had never posted anything about William Carter or his vacation house or Loudoun County.

I was satisfied that it would be virtually impossible for Loving to find any connection. "Call him." I handed Ryan a mobile, a flip phone, black, a little larger than your standard Nokia or Samsung.

"What's this?"

"A cold phone. Encrypted and routed through proxies. From now on, until I tell you otherwise, use only this phone." I collected theirs and took out the batteries.

Ryan examined the unit—Joanne stared at it like it was a poisonous snake—then he made the call and had a conversation with Carter.

He disconnected. "He's on his way." Then the detective paused for a moment, framing what he was going to say, and turned toward the doorway, calling, "Amanda? Come on down here, honey. We want to talk to you."

A moment later a shadow appeared in the doorway and their daughter entered the kitchen. The girl was wearing red-framed glasses, her dark hair long and moppy. She had her father's physique: narrow hips and broad shoulders. A basketball player.

Her eyes were quick, and though she'd probably heard something about what the agents were doing outside she seemed unafraid. She looked me over carefully.

Her stepmother said, "Amanda, this is Agent Corte. He works with the government. Like the FBI."

"Hi, Amanda," I said easily.

"Hello." She seemed more interested in my impressive laptop than me personally.

Telling children they're in danger is an art (girls, I'd found, do better with the bad news than boys). I'm skilled at having the discussion but I generally prefer to let the parents talk to them first. Ryan took over. "Mandy, we've got a little problem."

The girl nodded, eyes growing sharper yet.

"Looks like somebody's not too happy about a case of mine and some of the boys at the department and the FBI are going to arrest him. But until they do, we're going to get out of the house for a while."

"Somebody you busted?" Amanda asked matter-of-factly.

"We're not sure."

"You said you weren't working many cases lately."

Ryan paused before saying, "It could be from the past. We don't know yet."

I told the girl, "We aren't sure what he's up to but we know he's dangerous."

"Your mom and I are going with Agent Corte to talk about the case. Try to help them figure out who's behind it."

"A lockdown?"

Ryan smiled. I wondered what TV show she had gotten the term from.

"Not quite, but it's better if we leave the house. While we're helping out the feds you're going to spend a few days with Uncle Bill at the lake house."

"Dad, come on," she whined. Her pretty, round face, dusted with a bit of mild acne, screwed up in disappointment, which seemed exaggerated to me. "I can't miss school." She recited the reasons: the first quiz of the term in her biology class, basketball practice, her assignment at a student counseling center hotline, a homecoming parade committee. She shot them out fast, hoping one would stick. "I mean, I just *can't*."

Children . . . invulnerable, immortal. And, by their own reckoning, the center of the universe.

"You'll be out of school for a few days, tops. Like a vacation."

"Vacation? Aw, Jo, come on."

"Go pack some things. Now."

"Now?"

I gave her a cold phone too and collected hers. She was reluctant to part with it. I added to the girl, "And until I say it's all right, I'm afraid you can't go online."

"What?" To a teenager, the worst deprivation possible.

"It won't be for very long. But this man probably knows how to trace your computer."

"That, like, sucks."

"Amanda," her father said sternly.

"Sorry. But I *have* to go online. I mean, Facebook and Twitter, at least. And I write my blog every day. I've never missed—"

Joanne said, "Not until Agent Corte says it's okay. You can rough it at Uncle Bill's. Watch TV, read, play games. You can go fishing. You like to fish."

"Oh, that totally . . ." The teen's face crinkled into well-honed exasperation.

"You'll have fun. Now go pack. Bill'll be here any minute."

"Fun," she muttered sarcastically. As the daughter left, I asked the Kesslers, "Any other close relatives in the area?"

Joanne blinked in surprise. "Oh, my God. My sister. I forgot about Maree." It was an odd name, *Marr*-ee. "She's been staying here for the past month. She'll have to come with us."

"Is she out?" I asked. I'd seen no other signs of life in the house.

"No, she's still asleep."

"My sister-in-law's a night owl," Ryan explained.

"Wake her up," I said. "We have to leave. . . . Oh, and don't let her use her mobile."

Joanne blinked at the urgent instructions. She nodded to a tray on the island. "That's her phone there." I shut it off, removed the battery and slipped it into my bag. Joanne stepped into the hall and I heard her footfalls on the stairs.

Ryan went into the den and began fill-ing a large briefcase and a shoulder bag with paperwork. The Metropolitan Police logo was on many of the documents. I continued my inquiry about other relatives who could be used as an edge. Ryan's parents had passed away. His brother was in Washington state. Joanne's father and his second wife—he was a widower—lived in the area but they were on vacation in Europe. Maree was her only sibling. Joanne had never been married before.

"Does Joanne have children?" I asked.

He hesitated for a weighty second. "No."

The Kesslers would have friends, of course, but lifters usually had little success using people who weren't blood kin for edges.

Another glance outside, across the backyard. Two doors down a man coiled up a green garden hose, wrapping it leisurely under his elbow and between finger and thumb. Another neighbor was taking down screens. One house nearby was quiet, though a window shade moved slightly.

"That house behind you, kitty-corner,

to the left? Are the residents home today, as far as you know?"

Ryan looked where I pointed. "Yeah, I
saw Teddy this morning on his way to
Starbucks." Then he glanced at the
doorway to see if his wife was out of
earshot. "You know, Corte, this world . . .
what you and I do? Joanne can't handle
it well. Things freak her out, things we
don't even think about. Sometimes she
even leaves the room when the news
comes on. I'd appreciate it if you'd keep
that in mind."

"Sorry. I'll make sure of it."

"Thanks." Ryan smiled and went upstairs to pack.

In fact, I'd been much more blunt with
sensitive Joanne than I needed to be—
so that Ryan would do what he just had:
asked for that very favor, which I'd
agreed to. Solely for the purpose of getting him more on my side.

My phone buzzed and my audible
caller ID said through my earbud, "Fredericks."

I hit ANSWER. "Freddy."

"I'm pulling in the driveway, Corte.
Don't shoot me."

Chapter 5

I never understood the FBI agent's compulsive joking. Perhaps it was to protect himself, the way not joking is some kind of shield for me. I found it irritating but I didn't have to live with him, the way his wife and five children did, so I tried not to let it bother me.

I told him, "Come in the front," and disconnected.

At the door I greeted the tall, white-haired agent. Claire duBois, whose quirky mind had a habit of prodding her to make odd but accurate observations, once said of Freddy, "Did you ever notice that the best FBI agents look like TV Mafia dons and the best Mafia dons look like TV agents?" I hadn't but it was true. Solid and columnar, ever in low gear, the fifty-five-year-old Paul Anthony Xavier Fredericks was a long-timer in the Bureau; he'd worked nowhere else after his graduation from college. He stepped into the house, accompanied by a younger agent. Both followed me into the kitchen.

Special Agent Rudy Garcia was in his late twenties. Scrubbed and reserved, he'd clearly been military before the Bureau. Quick eyes, unsmiling and married, he wasn't, I judged, the sort to have a good time going out for a beer with. But, then, I've heard the same about me.

"The Kesslers're packing. Any word from West Virginia?"

A shrug said it all. I hadn't expected much. An unidentified vehicle, an unknown route. Loving was invisible.

"What do you think, Freddy, about his ETA?"

"At least two hours plus till he gets to Fairfax, at the earliest," the agent said, reading the framed news story about Ryan the hero. "I remember that. Sure."

Garcia was walking around the ground floor, glancing out the windows. He was good, careful not to give anything away to anybody outside.

And not presenting any target himself.

Joanne and Ryan came down the stairs, two suitcases in the cop's beefy hands. They stopped in the hallway and he set them down. They joined us in the kitchen and I introduced them to the agents.

"Messing up your weekend," Freddy said. "Sorry about that."

I asked, "Is Maree up? We have to go."

"She'll be down in a minute."

I suggested, "Amanda might feel more comfortable if her aunt goes with her to your friend's place in Loudoun."

For some reason Ryan replied, after a hesitation, "Probably not." Joanne agreed.

Freddy's radio clattered. "SUV approaching. Registered to William Carter."

I told him, "The friend. The Kesslers' daughter's staying with him."

A moment later Bill Carter was at the door. He entered without knocking and joined us, hugging Joanne hard, then he shook Ryan's hand warmly. The white-haired man was in his early sixties, tanned and fit, six-two or so. His face grave and gray eyes sharp, he looked me over through large, clear aviator glasses as he gripped my hand. He greeted Freddy and Garcia too, carefully examining all the IDs. I caught the crown of a holster and shiny butt of a pistol under his jacket.

"This is for real, then," he muttered.

"It's terrible, Bill," Joanne said. "One day everything's fine and then . . . this."

I handed Carter another of the cold phones and explained it to him.

"Who's after you?" he asked Ryan.

"The devil incarnate" was the dry response.

I replied to Carter's very nonrhetorical question—the former cop would want details: "His name's Henry Loving. He's white, midforties, about two hundred pounds, dark hair. Had a scar, his temple. Probably doesn't anymore." I typed on the computer. "Here's an old picture. He's good at changing appearances but it'll give you a rough idea." My principals and Carter had fallen silent, looking at the benign face of Henry Loving. Put a white band of collar on him and he could have been a minister. A navy blue suit, an accountant or salesman at Macy's.

His face was as placid as mine, merely a little fuller. He didn't look like a killer, torturer and kidnapper. Which worked to his advantage.

I said to Carter, "I think we're on top of things and he doesn't know about you. But be alert. You have wireless in your house in Loudoun?"

"Yessir."

"Can you disable it?"

"Sure."

I added, "And make sure Amanda doesn't configure your computer for dial-up."

"She'd know how to do that?"

"She's a teenager," I said. "She could *build* a computer out of kitchen appliances."

"Suppose you're right about that." He looked at the Kesslers. "How much did you tell her?"

Ryan said, "Pretty much everything. But I didn't overdo it."

"She's got some grit, your daughter. It'd take a lot to get her rattled. But I'll keep her distracted."

"Thanks, Bill."

"And when you leave," I told him,

"keep her down. Have her look for something you lost under the front seat. Just for a block or two."

Maybe Carter thought this was excessive but he agreed.

Amanda bounded down the stairs, clutching a pillow in a red-and-white gingham case. It seemed teenagers couldn't travel without pillows, girls at least. Security blankets maybe.

"Uncle Bill, hi!" She hugged the man and sized up Freddy and Garcia, the new arrivals.

"Hey, this's some weird adventure, honey," Carter said.

"Yeah."

"We better hit the road," the former cop said.

I was amused; the solidly built teenage athlete had around her shoulder a purse in the shape of a plush bear, with a goofy smile and a zipper down its back.

Joanne grabbed the girl and hugged hard, to her stepdaughter's embarrassment.

Then her father did the same. He too was treated to a stiff return embrace.

"Come on, humor your old man," Ryan said affectionately.

"Dad . . . okay." She stepped back, though her father kept his hands on her shoulders.

"You call us anytime. About anything."

"Yeah, okay."

"It's going to be fine, honey." Then the bulky detective released his grip, apparently worried that his coddling might give his daughter more cause to worry. He smiled.

"Like, bye." Lugging her pillow, backpack and bear purse, Amanda ran to Carter's SUV.

Again the former cop hugged Joanne and then gripped Ryan's hand with both of his. "I'll take really good care of her. Don't worry. God bless."

Then he was gone.

Ryan returned to the den and came out with his briefcase and another backpack. It was heavy and I assumed it contained ammunition and possibly another weapon.

Freddy called his men outside on the radio. We heard one of them respond,

"Carter's gone. Nobody following. The girl wasn't visible."

Then I heard footsteps on the stairs, and a woman, quite attractive, appeared in the kitchen doorway. She was blinking, as if she'd just awakened, though she was dressed in a nice outfit and her face was made up. She bore a faint resemblance to Joanne and was six, eight years younger. She was taller but willowy, not as solid.

"This is Maree," Joanne said.

"Well, lookit this," she said. It seemed that she hadn't quite believed what her sister had been telling her. Sure enough: "I thought you were kidding, Jo. I mean," looking at Freddy and Garcia, "didn't I see you in *The Sopranos*?" She poured some orange juice and added an herbal powdered concoction to it. She drank it down and made a face.

The agents regarded her blankly.

Maree had longer and straighter hair than her sister's and it was mostly but not completely, or authentically, blond. She wore a full suede skirt and a gossamer floral blouse of yellow and green. Silver jewelry. No wedding ring. I always look, not for availability, of course, but because marital status gives me information about a lifter's options in getting an edge on the principal.

A fancy camera dangled over her shoulder, and I could see in the foyer her luggage. She had a large wheelie, a heavy backpack and a laptop case, as if she were going away for two weeks. Maree picked up a stack of mail on a table near the kitchen door. The pieces had been sent to her but the printed address—in the North West quadrant of the District—had been crossed out and the Kesslers' penned in, forwarded here. Maybe she'd lost her job and been forced to move in with her sister and brother-in-law.

As she flipped through the mail, I noted the woman give a slight wince; she moved her left arm more gingerly than her right. I thought I saw a bandage near the elbow, beneath the thin cloth. She took a jacket from a coat rack, tugged it on and turned to her sister. "This looks like it's shaping up to be a great party but I'm out of here. I'm going to stay in the District tonight."

"What?" Joanne asked. "You're coming with us."

"I don't see a lot of fun in that option. I'm choosing door number three."

"Mar, please . . . You've got to come. Where would you go?"

"I called Andrew. I'm going to stay with him."

"Called him?" I was concerned she had another mobile. "From the house phone?"

"Yeah."

This didn't trouble me; while monitoring and tracing mobiles was a piece of cake, tapping into a landline was very difficult, and even if an associate of Loving had done so, Maree couldn't have given away anything crucial to the job.

She was looking around. "I couldn't find my cell. You know where it is?"

"I've got it." I explained about the risks of tracing.

"Well, I need it."

She wasn't happy when I told her that she was incommunicado. I didn't have any more cold phones to hand out.

"Well . . . I'm still going downtown."

Joanne said, "No, you don't want to do that."

"I—"

I said, "I'm afraid you're going to have to stay with your sister and brother-in-law. And I want to leave now. We've waited too long as it is. I mean, right now."

Maree waved a hand whose fingernails ended in glittery white crescents, French tipped, I thought they were called, though I could have been wrong. She said to me, nodding at her sister, "I don't want to stay with *her*. My God, she's no fun." Then laughed. "I'm kidding. . . . But really, I'll be fine."

"No," I said firmly. "You're coming with us and—"

"You guys go on. Let me borrow the Honda, you don't mind." She looked at me. "My car's in the shop. Do you know what they want for a new fuel pump? . . . Hey, what're you doing?"

Garcia was taking the luggage out to the Armada. He returned to the kitchen and nodded at me, meaning the yard was clear.

To Maree, Freddy said, "You'll have to listen to Corte. You need to leave. Now."

Maree opened her eyes wide. "Wait, wait . . . I know you." She regarded me with a frown.

I must have blinked in surprise. Had we met?

The woman added, "You're on that reality show. *The Vacation from Hell.* You're the tour guide."

"Please, Mar," Joanne said.

Her sister pouted. "He's mean. He stole my phone."

At that moment I was looking out the kitchen window again into the backyard, trying to figure out what was different from when I'd looked earlier. There was something visible now that hadn't been a half hour ago, because of the shifting angle of the late morning September sun. I called Ryan over and pointed. "Is that a path?"

A line of trampled grass lay between the Kesslers' house and the one I'd mentioned earlier, kitty-corner to the left. It was Teddy's, I recalled, the man who'd gone out for coffee.

"Yeah, to the Knoxes. They're our, I

guess, best friends in the neighborhood. We hang out with them all the time."

The path had been created over the summer, from trekking back and forth for barbecues, borrowing cooking ingredients and tools, birthday parties.

"What is it?" Joanne asked. "You're making me uneasy."

"Wow, he *does* look totally intense," Maree said.

"Corte?" Freddy grunted.

Grimacing, I nodded.

"Shit," the agent muttered. He sighed and unbuttoned his jacket. "Garcia!"

"Go dark," I said.

Freddy and Garcia pulled shades and drapes in the den, TV room and kitchen.

Ryan tensed and Joanne, eyes wide, blurted, "What's going on? Tell me."

I could see the palm of Freddy's hand tap the butt of his Glock. We do this to reorient our muscles and nerves so we know exactly where our weapons are. Like I noted the pressure of the Baby Glock, in the small of my back. I left it in the holster for the moment.

Ryan stepped forward to the window.

"No," I said firmly. "Get back. Loving's

here." I herded everyone into the windowless hallway between the kitchen and the front foyer.

"How'd he do it?" Freddy asked. "He should still be halfway from West Virginia."

I didn't answer. There were several possible explanations, though none relevant to our goal at the moment: to keep the principals alive and get out of the area instantly.

"What do you have, sir?" Garcia asked me.

"The house that path leads to? The window closest to here? The blinds were down ten minutes ago. They're about six inches up now. Makes no sense for them to be open only that far, except for surveillance."

"A spotter?"

"No," I said. "A spotter would've picked the house with the best view. That's the one directly behind here, or to the right. Loving's in the left house because he noticed the path and figured the family who lives there'd be good friends with the Kesslers." I added, "They'd have the best information about you and might know what my SUV was doing in your drive and the sedan parked in front."

"Teddy and Kath!" Joanne blurted. "You mean he's there with them?"

"You sure, Corte?" Freddy asked. Meaning, we push the button on this, it's going to get expensive and possibly messy.

"I'm sure enough. . . . I want people here now. Fairfax County and your folks, whoever's nearby."

"Call it in," Freddy ordered Garcia, who pulled his cell phone out of a holster and hit a speed dial button.

"I'm sorry, this is too weird for me," Maree said with an edgy laugh. "The tour guide's freaking us out because somebody opened a window? Good luck, guys." Maree lifted car keys from a dish on a table nearby. "I'm going downtown." She started for the front door.

"No," I told her firmly. "And everybody, get—" The rest of my instructions were cut off at the sound of a huge crash from the street.

Joanne screamed, Maree gasped and stood frozen in front of the door.

I strode forward fast, gripped the

young woman by the collar of her jacket and yanked her backward and we fell together onto the tile floor, as the bullets began crashing through the front picture window in the living room.

Chapter 6

The numbness vanished from Joanne's face and she scrabbled forward on her knees, grabbing her sister and sliding her farther into the foyer, away from the windows.

The younger woman had dropped her forwarded mail in a white spill on the floor. Her camera too had fallen and she cried out, reaching desperately for it.

"Leave it!" Joanne muttered, restraining her.

Ryan had his weapon out now and was crouching.

I still didn't draw because there was no target yet and I was busy flinging my computer into my shoulder bag. Besides, as the shepherd, I tend to let people with more tactical experience handle the firepower.

Two or three more shots into the living

room. The slugs slammed into a lamp, a picture frame, the wall. The gunshots were soft, the sound of shattering glass loud.

Freddy was on the phone, calling his agents out front but getting no response.

Were they dead?

"Garcia!" I called. The young agent had instinctively gone to the side windows overlooking the trees, covering our flank. "What do you see?"

"Clear," he shouted. "Only incoming's from the front."

I gestured everyone farther back into the dim hall and then slipped into a small guest bathroom in the front and glanced through a window. A silver Ford had slammed into the rear of the agents' vehicle, knocking it forward ten feet or so. The men, without their seat belts on, had been thrown back then forward and were slumped in the front seat. I couldn't tell if they were dead or alive.

The Ford was immobilized but the driver, who'd been belted in and protected by the airbag, was firing a pistol at us through the open window. I couldn't see the face clearly. He was hunkered down and taking careful aim. I stepped out of the bathroom to find Ryan Kessler taking a deep breath and then bursting forward, breaking the window next to the front door with his pistol barrel, like Clint Eastwood in a spaghetti western. He was aiming toward the car.

"No!" I shouted, grabbing him and pulling him back.

"What're you doing?" the cop cried. "I've got a target!"

"Wait," I replied as calmly as I could. "Garcia, monitor the side yard. Stay on it."

"Roger that."

"Freddy, the back?" I called to the senior agent, who was in the kitchen.

"Clear so far."

Two more shots slammed into the living room.

Maree screamed again.

Ryan said, "Out the back! We can flank him. Why didn't you let me shoot, Corte?"

Maree started crawling toward the back kitchen door, sobbing, her flippancy turned to raw panic. "I'm scared, Jesus, I'm scared."

"Get back," I said to her, grabbing her shoulder to stop her once more.

Joanne had gone catatonic again, staring at the broken glass, saying nothing. Eyes unfocused. I wondered if we'd have to carry her, as sometimes happened.

I said calmly, "Nobody go anywhere."

Freddy took a call. "Corte! Five minutes ago, somebody called in two shooters at George Mason University. Ten students down. All of Fairfax County Tactical is on the way. I'm trying to get a team here but there's nobody available for us."

"A school shooting? No, no, it's fake. Loving called it in. . . . Garcia?"

"Clear on the flank still."

"Okay, we're moving. Out the front."

"He's out there!" Ryan cried.

"No, he's not," I said. "The couple behind you, the Knoxes—what do they drive?"

"A Lexus and a Ford." He glanced out quickly, ducked back. "That's their car! He killed them! Oh, shit."

"God, no . . . no," Joanne whispered, clutching her sister, who was sobbing, her own arms around her camera, which she'd retrieved and was cradling like a baby.

"It's Teddy Knox in the car, not Loving," I said.

"What do you mean?" Ryan asked. "He's a hostage?"

"No, he's the one shooting."

"Teddy wouldn't do that. Even if Loving forced him to."

"Loving *is* forcing him. He's threatened his wife, who's back in the house. But Teddy's not supposed to hit anybody. He's just shooting at random, to drive us out the back. That's where Loving's waiting for us. In their house, or maybe the bushes. He'll have a partner. He wouldn't try an open assault alone. We go out the front. Freddy, you and Garcia stay in the house and cover the side yard, the one with the trees, and the back. Ryan, when we go, you cover the field on the other side. Don't shoot unless you see somebody engaging with a weapon. We're going to be getting neighbors on the street any minute. I don't want collateral damage."

Ryan hesitated, looking toward the

front of the house. He was debating: follow my orders or not?

Joanne said, "Do what he says, Ry!
Let's do what he says. Please!"

"Go to my SUV fast but not so fast
you hurt yourself falling. Okay?"

"Hurt ourselves *falling*?" Ryan blurted,
at my bizarre concern.

The delay from a twisted ankle could
kill us all.

"What if Loving's in the car, the backseat?" Freddy asked.

"Wouldn't be logical," I called, then
turned to Ryan. "The side yard? Loving
could be prone and crawling up. You
saw his picture. If you can confirm it's
him, try for a nonlethal shot. We need to
know who hired him."

"I can park one in his shoulder or ankle," Ryan said.

"Good. Better to aim low. Avoid the
femoral. I want him stopped but not bled
out."

"Got it."

I hit the button on the key fob that
started and unlocked the Nissan, then
opened the front door to the house a
few inches, drew a target on the driver

of the silver Ford, which was sitting half on the parking strip, half in the street. He was in a baseball cap and sunglasses, tears running down his cheeks. He appeared to be mouthing, "I'm sorry, I'm sorry." A black pistol was secured to his hand with duct tape. The slide was back; he'd run out of ammunition.

"Teddy!" Joanne called.

Miserable, the man shook his head. Thinking of his wife, the edge, at home— with Loving holding a gun on her, or so he thought. Loving had likely killed her the moment her husband pulled out of the driveway. The lifter's plan was good. It was what I would've done had I been in Loving's position, limited personnel attempting to snatch a principal who was an armed cop, with several other law enforcers inside, in daylight, no less.

I looked around and ushered Ryan, Joanne and Maree out. We moved steadily toward the Armada, about twenty-five feet away.

Though I was convinced that Loving and any backup were waiting behind the house I checked the garage first. It was clear. We continued on.

Like a hungry wolf, Ryan kept his eye on the far side yard, weapon up and finger outside the trigger of his revolver.

We arrived at the Armada and I got everybody inside and locked the doors.

Maree was still crying and shivering, Joanne was blinking, her eyes wide, and Ryan was scanning for prone soldiers crawling up on our flank.

"Seat belts!" I called. "It'll be rough for a few minutes."

I skidded in a wide circle through the yard that Ryan had been guarding, then over a neighbor's lawn and into the street, redlining the big vehicle up to sixty, sitting forward and watching carefully for pedestrians, bicyclists and backing-out cars.

I wasn't surprised that I heard no gunshots from either the hostiles or from Freddy and Garcia. The lifter and any associates would have noted the plan didn't work and would get away as fast as they could. Had Loving not called in the fake school shooting announcement, we'd have had more than enough Fairfax County Police in the area to set up roadblocks and interdict them but that wasn't going to happen now.

I slowed the vehicle, to keep attention off us; I wouldn't want Loving to circle around in this direction, flash a fake badge and ask if anybody had seen a gray Nissan SUV.

Ryan sat back and holstered his weapon. "You're sure it was Loving?"

"Yes. That's exactly the kind of strategy he'd choose. There's no doubt it was him."

I was aware of the corollary to that conclusion: Loving would know too— because of the escape strategy—that *I* was the opponent he was now playing against.

Chapter 7

Thirty minutes later—it was about half past noon—I was eyeing a beige car some distance behind us, moving at about our speed, as we cruised along surface roads in Prince William County, a place with a multiple personality. The populace included politicos, business people, farmers, proud rednecks, entry-level strivers and plenty of recent immigrants.

Most of the meth in the Northern Virginia area got cooked in PW.

I couldn't tell the make or model of the car but was well aware that it had made the same turn we had a couple of miles back, a pointless trip down a bleak, blue-collar side street, a shortcut to nowhere. You either lived on Heavenly Lane or you detoured along it to see if somebody was trailing you.

Whoever was in the beige car didn't live there; it was still behind us.

Light sedan. No year, no make, no model . . .

I guessed that Loving had probably switched wheels. Yet it was possible that he would keep the same car . . . because it wasn't what we'd expect. I debated but decided not to radio for assistance, not yet; again, I didn't want to call attention to us.

I'd just keep an eye on our beige shadow.

The Kesslers were calmer now, not much, but some. In the front passenger seat Ryan was playing lookout and Maree's pendulum had swung eerily from hysterical back to cute and coy. She kept calling me "Tour Guide," which I found more irritating than her panicked screaming a half hour before. Joanne had gone into withdrawal again and was staring blankly out the side window. I wondered if she'd always been this timid or if the incident at the deli six years ago—facing her own death and seeing Ryan and the owners shot—had affected her fundamentally. The degree of

Joanne's emotional state might have been extreme but the frame of mind itself wasn't. The response of principals when a lifter or hitter is after them often follows the stages of grief: denial, anger, bargaining, depression, acceptance. Joanne's detachment was a form of denial.

Once we'd sped out of the Kesslers' neighborhood, via an evasive route, Joanne had said only two things. First, she'd made the accurate observation that at least her stepdaughter and Bill Carter were safe, since it was obvious where Loving and any partners had been hiding. Then she offered the speculation that it made sense that Teddy Knox's wife was all right too. If Loving had killed her, that would lessen the leverage—the edge—he'd have over Teddy to discourage him not to testify against him. That was a possibility, yes. It was also possible, however, that Loving didn't care what Teddy knew and could testify to and he'd just killed the wife for convenience. That was my opinion but I said nothing.

Ryan asked me to call Freddy and find

out if the wife was all right, but it was possible that he, Garcia and the other agents—if they were alive and functioning—had engaged Loving or were in pursuit and I didn't want to distract them. Freddy would call when he had something to say. I told Ryan this and he nodded, though he seemed irritated I wouldn't make the call. He returned to his impromptu surveillance.

I made a sudden turn into a Burger King parking lot and paused.

Startling me, Maree said quickly, "Hey, can I escape for a minute? There's a pay phone."

"No. Stay in the vehicle."

"Please?" Sounding like a teenager begging for a trip to the mall.

"No," I repeated.

"But it wouldn't be traced or anything. Really, I know all about it."

"About what?" her sister asked.

"Surveillance. I saw this episode on *NCIS*? Spies use pay phones to be safe. Off the grid. That's what they say."

"Sorry, no calls," I said.

"Oh, you're no fun. I demand a lawyer!" She fell into a juvenile pout. It irritated me all the more and I ignored her.

I waited for the beige car to pass us. Which it didn't do. After ten minutes, I returned to the road and sped up, trying to catch the lights, incurring a horn or two. An extended middle finger, as well. But we saw no beige cars.

My hands-free announced Freddy was calling.

At last . . .

I asked, "Your guys in the car out front, they're okay?"

"Yep. Battered. Should've had their belts on. They learned their lesson."

"And how about the shooting at the school?" I'd *believed* it was fake but I wasn't sure. I would have been troubled by casualties, certainly; I was, however, more interested to learn if false alarms were a technique Henry Loving was adding to his repertoire. Something else to file away about him.

"You were right, son. Three-dollar bill. Nothing at all. But it kept sixty troopers and agents busy for close to an hour."

"Okay, Loving?"

"Got clean away. No leads. No vehicle."

"Anybody see anything beige that was there and then wasn't? Sedan."

"Beige? No, and we canvassed. But one of my guys across the street got a look at his partner. In the side yard, the trees, where Garcia was covering. Tall, thin, sandy hair, wearing a dark green windbreaker or army jacket."

"Weapon?"

"Black autoloader. Couldn't tell what kind. He was running out of the woods fast, after you left."

We were past densely populated areas and were surrounded by fields and houses and some commercial lots with businesses limping along or abandoned to banks. I now eased up the speed of the big SUV steadily.

"Did Teddy Knox ID Loving?"

"Yep."

Abe Fallow had refused to use that trite line about making an ass of you and me with careless assumptions but he beat into our heads the same principle. Though Loving might have been identified in West Virginia as the man

hired to target Kessler, we'd had no independent proof that in fact he was the
attacker. Until now.

Freddy added, "We also got some
prints on the tape he'd used on Knox
and his wife. Just a partial but it's him."

My principals, I could see or sense,
were all staring at me, wanting information.

"The Knoxes?" I sure didn't want to
deliver the news that the wife was dead.

"Both'll be okay, if that's what you're
asking."

"It is."

I told the Kesslers this.

"Oh." Joanne exhaled and lowered
her head. She whispered, "Thank you."
The household hadn't seemed religious
but I got the impression she herself
might be and was sending aloft a prayer.

"And?" I asked Freddy, meaning: Did
either of them say anything more?

"Other than the ID, squat. We could
put 'em in a room with speakers blaring
wall-to-wall Captain and Tennille and
they wouldn't talk."

"Impression?" I asked, ignoring the
pointless quip.

"They really don't know diddle. We could maybe find out what he's wearing but how helpful would that be? I submit, not very."

I asked him if the weapon in Knox's hand could lead us anywhere.

He gave a sour laugh. "Stolen years ago. Evidence Response's been over, under and through the car, the yard, compost heaps and recycling bins in the whole goddamn neighborhood. The woods where the partner was spotted too. No leads. Zero, zip. They don't even know where Loving and his boyfriend parked. Not a single fucking tire tread or fiber. And here I *swore* he couldn't be there for another couple of hours. Did I get this one wrong or what?"

I believed I had the answer to Loving's early arrival in Fairfax. "I'm guessing he got an edge on the clerk at the motel in West Virginia and had him say Loving'd checked out at eight but he'd really left around four or five this morning."

"You win the cee-gar, Corte. All he had to do was mention the name of the clerk's daughter and what middle school she was in."

Loving did the same amount of homework as Claire duBois did. And, as I had years before, I felt a perverse admiration for his methodology and meticulousness.

I continued, "But the light-colored sedan was his, legit, because there were other witnesses at the motel who'd seen it earlier."

"Yup squared." He then added that the Charleston field office had gone through the room carefully. "Nothing."

I looked behind me and then executed another series of evasive turns.

No beige car. Nothing out of the ordinary. Locals doing what they did on Saturday. Driving to stores, fast food restaurants for a treat after errands, movies, kids' soccer games and tae kwon do lessons.

"What do you think, Freddy? Real or a diversion?" I couldn't decide what Loving's strategy at the house had been. Did he really want to kill us and take Ryan and his family hostage? Or was it a feint? Did he have something else in mind, something I couldn't figure out?

Freddy mused, "Real? . . . I'd say so.

I think he wanted to get in fast, get Ryan and get out. He could've pulled it off too. If we'd gone out the back, like he wanted, that'd be it. They'd be writing our eulogies right now and Kessler'd have bamboo under his fingernails. Or more likely his wife's. . . . Oh, and I'll give you my opinion about the sister, son. She gives blondes a bad name."

"Next step?"

"Find the primary." I'd told Ryan that he'd possibly been targeted by mistake but I didn't believe it. Henry Loving wouldn't make an error like that. I wanted to find who'd hired him and what information Ryan had that was so important to him . . . or them.

I told Freddy I'd start looking into that when we landed and I disconnected the call.

As soon as I did, my phone buzzed and I listened to the numbers read off by the caller ID voice. It was the federal prosecutor, Jason Westerfield. He would have heard the news—that his hero cop, a star witness in a case that didn't exist yet, had nearly been kidnapped amid a shootout in Fairfax County. Westerfield was the last person in the world I wanted to talk to at the moment. I didn't hit AN-SWER.

I noted Ryan was staring into the side-view mirror.

I said, "Detective Kessler?"

"Call me Ryan."

"Okay, Ryan. Thanks for covering our flank at the house. Were you ever SWAT?"

"Never. Just worked the street. You pick things up." He was subdued—he'd come close to shooting his neighbor. He continued to look behind us. He kneaded the grip of his revolver the same way I held tight to the wheel.

The atmosphere in the car was somber, quiet. I was calmer now too, reflecting on the operation, trying to step into Henry Loving's mind and determine his next strategy. I noted that in a relatively short period of time he'd made a clandestine trip from another state, found a trusted partner, obtained weapons, successfully masked his travel to the target location, conducted thorough surveillance of the area where his victim lived, targeted the most knowledgeable neighbors and attempted a risky daylight assault after calling in a fake school shooting to divert backup. He had executed a "friendly feint"—getting one of your allies to assault you, either because he's mistaken or because he's been forced to, while the real opponent comes at you from another direction. He wasn't afraid to give up weapons to a potential risk—Teddy Knox.

This analysis was helpful but, like looking over a chessboard in the early stages of a game, gave me only a flavor of his plan; there was still an infinite variety of strategies he could choose.

Joanne was shaking her head, clutching her purse closely, which I'd also noticed happened frequently with principals. Familiar objects gave comfort. She said to me, in a soft voice, "If you hadn't been there . . ." She was, I imagined, speaking in general of the family's fate but then realized, as I did, that the comment was also a criticism of her husband, who'd resisted our help at first, and she fell silent on the subject. If Ryan noticed, he didn't react.

He looked toward me a moment later. "I want to call Amanda."

"Sure. Just don't mention our location."

He pulled out the cold phone. I explained the unit and he placed the call. He got through at once and, keeping his voice completely calm, asked about her trip. Finally he explained that there'd been a little problem at the house. Whatever she heard on the news stories, everybody was fine.

"Little problem," Maree said and laughed cynically. "That's what the captain of the *Titanic* said." The young woman opened her large shoulder bag and pulled out and began sorting black-and-white photographs. Good, I reflected. Keep her busy. Count cows. Look for out-of-state plates.

Ryan handed the phone to his wife. Joanne too downplayed the incident to her stepdaughter, though it seemed more difficult for her to put on a cheery face. A pause as she listened. "I don't know why, honey. We'll find out. Mr. Corte . . . Agent Corte's going to find out. . . ." She listened some more and they fell into a meaningless conversation about high school, some friends, a ski vacation they had planned for Christmas.

I made a fast turn. Another scan in the mirror; nobody was following. I saw too Maree wince and I thought she'd been hurt in the escape. But then I recalled seeing an Ace bandage wrapped around her arm. She rolled up her sleeve and examined it.

"Maree, are you all right?" I asked.

"Just bumped my arm last week."

"Is it bad?" I sounded sympathetic but I was asking because I needed to know if the injury would affect my guard job. Lifters, like wild animals, go right for the wounded. Breaks take at least six weeks to heal.

"No. The orthopod says it's just a bad hematoma. That's a great word. Sounds so much sexier than 'bruise.'"

"Hurt much?"

"Some. Not too bad. But I milk it for all it's worth." She laughed then explained, "I was shooting some images in downtown D.C. and this asshole on his mobile knocked into me and I slipped down some steps. He didn't even apologize, not really. It was like, oh, what're you doing taking pictures when people're trying to get to *real* jobs?"

I wasn't interested in the source of the injury, just her state of wellness, but Maree continued, loud and indignant, "I couldn't take pictures for a few days afterward, I was so dizzy. I should've gotten his name. And sued him." Her voice faded. Then she looked my way. "Hey, Mr. Tour Guide? Can I call my friend? Please? Pretty please?" Singsong again.

"Who?"

"The guy I was going to be staying with. Before the Terminator screwed up my plans. I was going to meet him at six. If I don't show up, he'll be worried."

Joanne asked, "Mar, don't you think it's better if you don't? Andrew'll figure it out. I mean, Agent Corte didn't want you to call from that pay phone."

"No," I said, "that was just because I didn't want to spend any time there. But if you want to call, go ahead. It's not a bad idea. We don't want him getting curious and coming to the house, now that Loving knows where it is."

I handed her my cold phone. "Just keep it short. Don't say anything at all about where we are or what's happened. Understand?"

"Sure."

With that, Maree dropped the giddy persona and suddenly grew reluctant—because, I guessed, she realized the conversation would be overheard by us all. Or maybe she just really didn't want to change plans. Finally she called. I glanced into the mirror and saw that her shoulders were knotted with tension. After a moment, though, her body language changed—she relaxed—and I deduced she'd got Andrew's voice mail. Her voice became that of a teenager again: "Hey, it's me . . . Um, I feel so bad. I really, really want to see you but I can't come over after all. . . . Like, something's come up. Kind of serious. With the family. It's totally important, so I can't make it tonight. I'll call you as soon as I can. Okay, have a good day. I'm sorry."

She disconnected and handed the phone back to me. Her hand seemed to

be trembling. She asked Joanne something about plans for Thanksgiving, a
non sequitur, and they had a conversation that I stopped listening to.

Traffic thinned and I sped up—but
now that we weren't being pursued I
kept the needle no more than six miles
an hour over the limit. My organization
doesn't use government license plates—
all the vehicles were registered to one of
a dozen corporations, commercial and
nonprofit—so if a cop were to speed-
gun us, he'd pull us over, which could
be inconvenient and dangerous.

A whisper from Ryan: "Ask you a
question?"

"Sure."

"It was two of them there at the house?
Loving and his partner?"

"Probably. Could have been three or
even more but Loving's profile is working mostly with one partner."

"Well, it's just that . . . there were five
agents there, plus me. We could've
taken him."

He was thinking of the plan I'd laid out
earlier, to nail Loving.

I gave him a knowing look, then back

to the road. "The agents in the car? They were out of commission."

"True. But . . ."

I continued, "I considered a takedown but it wasn't an advantageous playing field. I was worried he'd involve Mrs. Knox or maybe some other hostages from the neighborhood. He puts innocents into play all the time. It's one of his trademarks."

He said slowly, "I guess. I didn't think about that."

Ryan went back to riding shotgun. I glanced his way and concluded that he had no clue he was being conned.

As my mentor taught me and I teach duBois, you always ask yourself: What's my goal and what's the most efficient way to achieve it? Nothing else matters. That's the rule in the business world, medicine, science, academia. And it's the rule in the protection field, which is a business like any other, Abe Fallow regularly had said. Frustration, hurt feelings, vindictiveness, elation, pride . . . they're all irrelevant.

You disappear. You don't have feel-

ings, you don't have lust, you don't get insulted. You're nothing. You're vapor.

Part of being efficient as a shepherd was calmly picking the best strategy to get your principals to do what you wanted. Some you have to order around; they're more comfortable that way. Some you reason with.

Others you just plain trick.

The story I'd given Ryan Kessler about having him help me capture Henry Loving was nonsense. Though rooted in the truth—of course, I wanted Loving collared—it was just a strategy I was playing to win Ryan over. I'd decided on my approach after meeting him and learning, from duBois, details of the incident at the deli, from which he'd emerged a hero. The rescue of the customers and the ensuing love story were in themselves irrelevant to me; what was important was how the event had affected Ryan. A formerly active man, he was now off the street he loved, with a bad leg and relegated to investigating financial crimes, mostly from a desk, I supposed, and poring over balance sheets.

I needed to play to where his heart was: his macho, cowboy side.

So I'd given him the role of partner. Since I'd make sure he'd never have to act out that part, you could make the argument that my strategy was condescending, even mean. In a way it was.

But: What's the goal, what's the most efficient way to achieve it?

I had to make him believe that I couldn't take Loving on my own. I thought I'd been overacting but apparently he'd bought the whole story. This trick—exploiting the desires and weaknesses of the principals to get them to do as we wish—was called bait-and-switch. Abe Fallow had taught me the technique. It was, of course, inconceivable to enlist a principal to help us engage a hostile but the difference between the Detective Ryan Kessler I'd met at the front door just an hour and a half ago and the man sitting beside me was significant.

Just then I sensed him tense. I glanced in the rearview mirror. The, or *a,* beige car was behind us once again. It was going about our speed, which was only three miles over the limit now.

Maree saw us both looking backward as much as toward the road ahead. "What?" she asked, her addled voice resurrected as she sat up, eyes wide.

"There was a car that might have been following us earlier. Vanished for a while. It's back now."

Ryan was regarding me impatiently.

It was time for a decision.

I made one. Easing off the gas, I slowed, so that the beige car moved closer. Then, glancing behind me, I said firmly, "Go ahead, now! Shoot!"

Chapter 8

Ryan Kessler blinked, drawing his pistol. "Should I aim for the wheels? The driver?"

"No, no!" I said quickly. I hadn't been speaking to him but to the woman who'd been looking into my eyes in the rear-view mirror. "Maree, with your *camera.* Shoot the license plate."

The woman had a serious telephoto lens mounted on her Canon. I wanted the tag of the car. It was too far behind to get a visual with naked eyes.

"Oh." Ryan sat back. He seemed disappointed.

Maree played with the camera's controls, spun around and shot, with the *click-buzz* of single-lens reflex cameras. I wondered, with the digital models, like they all were nowadays, if that was just sound effects and speakers.

A moment later she was looking at the screen. "I can read the plate."

"Good job. Hold on a minute." I called Freddy and told him I needed a tag run immediately.

Maree gave me the letters and numbers and I recited them into the phone.

Ryan was looking around, gripping his gun again.

Fewer than sixty seconds later, Freddy came back on. He was laughing. "Registered to one Jimmy Chung. Owns a restaurant in Prince William. His son's driving around, dropping off flyers for the restaurant. I got his number and talked to the kid. He said he's behind a gray SUV—that needs washing, by the way—and it looks like somebody just took his picture, which he's not too happy about. They have a good menu, Corte. The General Tso's chicken is a specialty. Was there really a General Tso?"

"Thanks, Freddy."

I disconnected and noted the passengers were staring at me.

"It's safe, there's no problem. Chinese food delivery."

After a moment Maree said, "Let's order out."

A fragment of a laugh from her sister. Ryan seemed not to hear.

Now that the vehicle had turned out to be harmless, I relaxed somewhat and fell into the rhythm of the road. I enjoyed driving. I never had a car as a teenager. But my father, a lawyer for an insurance company and a good one, made sure I learned to drive safely and well. Once you realized that most of the other people on the road were idiots—he knew this firsthand from his job—and took appropriate precautions you could enjoy the process of tooling around the roads quite a bit.

He himself drove a Volvo, claiming it was the safest thing on the highway.

In any event I liked the act of driving. I wasn't sure why. It certainly wasn't speed. I was quite a cautious driver. Maybe it was that, as a shepherd, when I was driving, my principals and I were moving targets and therefore, incrementally at least, safer. Though not always, of course. Abe Fallow had been captured by Henry Loving and killed during a convoy transport. The chicken truck incident in North Carolina.

I pushed the thought away.

At the moment we were on a road heading west, dancing in and out of Fairfax and Prince William counties. We moved past the Tudor turrets of strip malls with their assembly-line chain outlets and busy fast food franchises, manned by teen clerks counting down the hours, the glistening humps of used cars in rows, their features touted with exclamation points, doctors' offices and insurance agencies, the occasional antiques store in a fifty-year-old single-story building, gun shops, ABC stores. A sagging barn or two. Some high-rise wannabes in office parks.

Northern Virginia could never decide whether it was a suburb of New York or a part of the Confederacy.

I checked the time. It was a little after 1:30 p.m. We'd been on the road for less than two hours. I'd decided not to go directly to the safe house but to stop at a way station—a nearby motel—to confuse the trail and switch cars. I often moved my principals in stages. We'd stay there for three or four hours, then continue to the safe house. My organization had a list of about a dozen hotels or motels in the area that were secure and out of the way; the one I had in mind was perhaps the best.

Checking traffic, I hit SPEED DIAL.

"DuBois."

I asked her, "Who are we at the Hillside?"

We have different covers for the various halfway houses we use. Even if I'm sure I know, I always ask.

There came the clatter of a keyboard, the jingle of her charm bracelet. The young woman said, "You're Frank Roberts, sales director of Artesian Computer Design. You were there eight months ago for two days with Pietr Smolitz and his friend." The last word was delivered frostily; duBois had formed an indelible opinion about the whistle-blower's condescending mistress, who'd accompanied him. "Roberts, that is, *you,* was making sales calls in Tysons and Reston, along with your associate from Moscow. The bullet hole in the wall got repaired before they knew about it."

"That, I remember." We hadn't been attacked. The crazy Russian had a hidden gun that had emerged after significant consumption of equally clandestine vodka. The discharge of the silenced weapon was accidental but the Taser hit to his back, compliments of me, had not been.

I told duBois, "I'm checking in now. I'll call in twenty."

"In twenty. Okay."

In a few miles I slowed, signaled and turned into the long drive of the Hillside Inn. The white colonial buildings, stuccoed and gabled, squatted in the middle of five acres of attractive landscaping: geometric lawns, trimmed trees, English gardens, roses still in abundant bloom. Though I doubted she was in the mood to appreciate it, I hoped Joanne would enjoy a brief glance at the grounds, given her interest in gardening. Despite Maree's sarcasm earlier, I *am* a bit of a tour guide, in that it works to my advantage to keep my principals occupied and content.

The Hillside Inn was indeed situated on an incline, though more at the bottom than the side, and was backed by naked farmland. There was an anemic forest to the right but a lifter or hitter would have a tough time approaching from a distance without being seen.

I headed up the drive, then cut right and through the parking lot to the back of the motel, avoiding the large windows in the lobby. I parked and told everyone to stay inside. I walked through an archway between two wings of rooms at the back and headed for the office. There were twenty-two cars in the lot. I have a scanner with a direct uplink to a national DMV database but to scan that many cars would take some time and look suspicious. Besides, in all my years of this business, I'd never known a lifter or hitter to park at a halfway or safe house in a vehicle with tags that would give him away.

I fished in my wallet from among the ten credit cards in various personal and company names and found the Artesian MasterCard, issued in the name of Frank Roberts. Artesian is a real company—well, it's incorporated, that is—and has an impressive Web site. Had we ever decided actually to go into computer software design, we had a lengthy list of potential customers who'd emailed us. My organization has a number of cover companies like this, and research specialists like duBois have fun writing up a briefing sheet on each of them, incorporating all sorts of information like bios of chief executives, exotic locations for sales conferences and even ad campaigns. Shepherds spend hours memorizing the data so we can have credible, if brief, conversations on the subjects of computer design, aircraft hydraulics, deli meat and cheese and a number of other products and services—I've been told my recitation of these cover stories is unsexy, if not boring, and discourages further inquiry. Which is, of course, the point.

I checked in, noted nothing out of the ordinary with the desk clerk and a bellboy, then returned to the SUV, seeing nothing that aroused suspicion in the parking lot either.

I opened the driver's side door and announced, "Bring your things with you."

"I thought we weren't staying here," Maree said.

"For a little while. We're switching vehicles."

"You think that's necessary?" Ryan asked.

"Just a precaution." If there's a mantra in the personal security field, that's it.

"There a hot tub?" Maree asked. "Preferably with a cute masseur named Raoul?"

"I'm afraid you'll have to stay inside," I repeated.

Maree's look silently reiterated her comment about my attitude as a tour guide.

I ushered them quickly into the two-bedroom suite, tactically the best in the Hillside Inn for defense since there was no sniper vantage point outside. Joanne looked around blankly. Her sister seemed genuinely disappointed at the small, sparse place. Maybe she thought the federal government should put some stimulus money into her accommodations. Like a SWAT officer Ryan opened doors to bathrooms and closets. Then he went to the window and carefully pulled back the curtain to look outside at a blank wall about thirty feet away— the side of the banquet hall. There was something defiant about this gesture, as if he half expected to see Loving on the other side of the glass.

He seemed disappointed to find gray cinder block rather than a target he could gun down. Still, he said, "Good choice. Defensible."

I nodded.

"Oooh, can I have that room?" Maree asked, pointing to the larger. I shrugged. The rooms were just for showers and a nap, if they wanted. I wasn't going to be using one. The others agreed and the young woman stepped toward it.

I said, "The phones in there don't work."

Her step slowed. I'd had a feeling that she'd wanted to have a longer, and private, conversation with her friend Andrew. But she gave an exaggerated pout and said, "Then *you'll* have to arrange for my masseur, Mr. Tour Guide." She winked and vanished.

With a tired glance after his sister-in-law, Ryan lifted his cold phone. "My boss?"

"Sure. Just nothing about the location."

A nod. He took his backpack and stepped into the other bedroom, dialing. He swung the door closed with his foot.

Leaving me in the living room of the suite with somber Joanne. She clicked the TV on, flipped through the channels. There was nothing about the assault on her home, only a report about the false alarm of a shooting at George Mason University.

"How did they keep it out of the news?" she asked.

"I don't know," I told her.

Though I did: Aaron Ellis, my boss. He had never been a shepherd, like me. His background was administration in federal security agencies and he was experienced at congressional liaisons, budgetary infighting . . . and media relations. When Abe Fallow died, six years ago, there was some talk of me taking over the organization; I was Abe's protégé. But it would have meant less time in the field and I didn't want that. So the powers that be shopped around and found Ellis, who'd been doing some good work at Langley.

He didn't completely get the subtleties of what shepherds did but when it came to gutting a news story that might work to our disadvantage, he was the man for the job. Though he couldn't completely eradicate accounts of an assault in a quiet suburban neighborhood he could delay the report and turn it into something like a break-in gone bad.

Of course, Ellis's skills were as mysterious to me as mine were to him and I never quite figured out his magic. I supposed part of his talent was rooted in finding an edge too, the same sword that Henry Loving used. And I did that too, on occasion.

As does nearly everyone, of course, from time to time.

Joanne stared unseeing at the screen, her shoulders slumped. Her face was free of makeup. She wore only a watch and her wedding and engagement ring, while Maree, I recalled, was decked out in a flare of funky jewelry. Joanne examined one of her broken nails.

I stepped to a window, gazed out through the curtain at the cinder blocks and placed a call to Aaron Ellis. I gave him an update on our progress, though I didn't share with him where we were and which of the three or four dozen government safe houses in the area we were going to. That was need-to-know only. If a fellow shepherd or an agent from Freddy's office was providing backup or—as was about to happen— our transport man was bringing a new vehicle, I'd part with the information. But I always tried to minimize the number of people who knew where the principals were.

It's not that I didn't trust colleagues but there was no doubt in my mind that if Henry Loving got to my boss, he'd do anything he could to find the location of my principals. Ellis had a charming wife, Julia, and three children, exactly four-teen months apart, the oldest being eight. Loving would get Ellis to give up my principals' location in about ten min-utes.

I didn't blame him one bit. I'd give them up too, in circumstances like that.

Abe Fallow himself said to me when I joined our organization, "Corte, listen. Rule number one, and it's a rule we don't mention to anybody but ourselves, is at the end of the day your principals are packages. They're a dozen eggs, they're crystal vases, lightbulbs. Consumer goods. You risk your life to keep them safe. You don't *sacrifice* your life for them. Remember that."

Ellis asked a few questions but I sensed he had something else on the agenda, so I preempted, saying, "Westerfield called."

"I know. He said you didn't pick up. . . . Or was it a missed call?"

"I didn't pick up. I decided I can't add him to the mix right now, Aaron. Can you keep him off me?"

"Yes." But it was a yes with the flu. My boss added, "Just let him know from time to time what's going on."

"Can I let *you* know and you let *him* know?"

"Just give him a fast call. What can it hurt?" he chided, like one brother reminding another to phone Mom on her birthday.

I relented and agreed.

"No word on Loving's location?" Ellis asked.

"No," I said.

"And an accomplice?"

"He's got one, we've confirmed. We have a rough ID." I described the tall, sandy-haired man who'd been spotted flanking the Kesslers' house. "We don't know anything more about him. I should go, Aaron. I'm going to talk to Ryan about his caseload. With the lifter out of sight, I really want to move forward on finding the primary."

After we hung up, Joanne asked for my cell phone and called her stepdaughter. She continued to put on a good facade for Amanda. She said she was going to call the school on Monday and have the girl's absence excused. It seemed the girl was genuinely upset to be missing school and her various extracurricular activities.

Amanda reminded me of myself at that age. I actually enjoyed going to class. I liked the precision of study, taking exams. I got bored easily—still do—and school was a chore originally. But

when I began to look at classes as a
series of increasingly complex games, I
devoted myself to the courses inten-
sively. Once, my father wanted me to
come to his office with him, some holiday party. I was happy he wanted me to
go. But I told him I was sick. After he
left, my mother still in bed asleep, I
tossed off the blankets—I was fully
dressed—and headed off to school. The
only instance I ever heard of where a
student played sick to *attend* class. I
nearly went into academia. Only through
some veering of circumstance did I end
up in personal security work.

I whispered to Joanne, "Let me talk to
Bill."

She nodded and when she concluded
her conversation with her stepdaughter
she asked to speak to him. She then
handed the phone to me.

"It's Corte."

"Hi. Talked to a friend downtown,"
Carter said. Meaning, I assumed, some-
body at MPD had told him what hap-
pened at the Kesslers' house. He added,
"On my fancy new phone—don't worry.
Sounds like we just missed an interest-

ing party." He was speaking euphemistically because the girl would be listening.

"He got close. Nobody was injured."

Carter said, "What I heard. Nobody knows where our friend is."

"Correct."

He gave a laugh. Sometimes I was chided for using stiff or old-time language. I prefer to think it's being precise. Besides, by the time you get to twenty or so—when I graduated from college—you talk the way you've learned to talk. No sense in trying to change it. That doesn't work. And why should you anyway?

I added, "Our information is that he's in the dark about you."

"That part's good."

"How was the drive?" I asked.

"Uneventful. I got lost. Saw the same scenery three or four times."

His way of telling me he'd used evasive driving techniques.

"Good. Keep Amanda busy and don't let her near your landline."

"Oh, about that. I just remembered it's broke."

I liked the old detective. "Thanks."

"Keep 'em safe, Corte."

"I will."

A mysterious chuckle. "I wouldn't want your job for any money."

Chapter 9

Ryan stepped out of the bedroom, carrying his shaving kit. He'd washed up. He'd changed his shirt.

And he'd had a drink. Bourbon, I thought. A fair amount.

I like some wine or beer occasionally but you can't deny that alcohol makes you stupid and careless. I can prove it. When I'm playing a board game that involves skill not chance—like chess or Arimaa or Wei Chi—and I'm not in a seriously competitive mood, I might have a glass of wine. The occasional successes due to some bold, unforeseeable strategy on my part, inspired by a nice Cabernet, are vastly outnumbered by the mistakes I make, thanks to the grape.

Ryan's drinking was something else I'd have to factor into the protection equation, along with his eager pistol and his role as protector of his family. I assessed the situation: an armed, drinking cop with a hero complex; a woman in shock—though she didn't know it yet—and furious with her husband for bringing this tragedy on the family (also in the dark about that); and a giddy, irresponsible sister with no self-esteem, who whipsawed back and forth between panic and grating giddiness.

Of course, every principal I've ever protected has had some glitch or foible—Lord knows I do too—and if their quirks affect your job you simply note them and compensate; if they don't, forget the issue and get on with your business. We're shepherds; we're not parents.

Joanne too noted the real purpose behind her husband's fake mission to the bedroom but didn't acknowledge it. Much less share a look with me.

I made some coffee and poured a good dose into a Styrofoam cup. I stepped into the corner and asked Ryan to join me, cop to cop, and we sat down together. Before I could speak, Ryan said, "Look, Corte. I was wrong. I mean, what Jo was saying: If you hadn't been there, it could've been . . . well, I don't even want to think about it."

So he had heard his wife after all.

I acknowledged the gratitude with a nod and noted that booze made him agreeable and sentimental, not hostile. If it weren't for the gun on his hip, I might have encouraged him to have another drink.

His comments had been spoken loudly enough for Joanne to hear and I decided he was apologizing to her too, indirectly.

I said, "I know you think this is a mistake but on the off chance it isn't, I want to find who hired Loving."

"The primary," he said. "I overheard you. That's what you call them?"

"Right."

"At first, I was thinking it was all bullshit. But after what happened at the house . . . I mean, it doesn't make sense that anybody'd go to that kind of trouble if they didn't think I knew something."

"No, not Henry Loving," I said. Then I explained that we always try to get to the primary. "We do that, and arrest him, then usually we get information that leads to the lifter. Or the lifter will just vanish, since their only interest is getting paid. With the primary in custody, the lifter isn't going to be collecting the balance of his fee. He just takes off."

"There're only two major cases I've got at the moment."

That was all? I wondered, surprised. A cop of his age and experience, in a city like D.C., would normally be inundated with open case files. I asked, "Give me the details. I'll have somebody check them out. Carefully. They won't disrupt your investigation."

"But I must've collared a hundred perps in my day. No, more. It might be revenge."

I was shaking my head. "I don't think so."

"Why?"

"For one thing he doesn't want to clip you. He wants information. Besides, you worked street crime."

"Yeah."

"How often was revenge a motive? And who was behind it?"

Ryan considered this. "Only a dozen times. Usually jealous lovers or a gangbanger after another one for diming him out. You're right, Corte, nothing like this."

"Tell me about the cases."

The first, he explained, was a forged check, written on the account of a man who worked for the Pentagon.

"The victim's name is Eric Graham. Civilian analyst." Ryan went on to explain that the man's checkbook had been stolen from his car in downtown D.C. The perp had been smart. The forger had noted Graham's balance and written a check in nearly the full amount and sent it to an anonymous online payment account. Once it cleared, he'd used the money to buy gold coins from a dealer. They were delivered to a post office box and he picked them up and, presumably, sold them for cash. A clever money laundering scheme. The perp had never had to present the check in person anywhere, only collect the coins at the private mailbox operation.

"Poor bastard," Ryan said. "Know how much was in the account? He'd just deposited forty thousand."

Joanne was sitting nearby, staring at the TV screen, the volume low. She'd been listening apparently. "That much in a checking account? That's a little suspicious, don't you think?"

I recalled that she'd been a statistician, so that numbers would come easily to her, which suggested that she probably was the one who ran the household finances. I noted too that it seemed she'd never heard about the case. This struck me as odd, since my experience was that husbands and wives often talked about their careers. But then I recalled her sensitivity to the seamier side of life; maybe pillow talk about even nonviolent crimes was discouraged.

But her husband said he'd looked into that question. "It seems he'd just sold some stock and put the money into the account to pay his son's tuition at an Ivy League school. It was due a week after the forgery."

"Any leads?" I asked.

"I just drew the case ten days ago. I hadn't gotten very far. The P.O. box where the coins were picked up was in

New Jersey. The man who collected them was Asian, in his twenties. I followed up with Newark PD but . . . well, you can guess: They've got more serious things to worry about than bad paper." Newark had one of the biggest drug and gang problems on the East Coast.

"Did you look into what he was working on?" I asked.

"Who?"

"The victim, guy whose checkbook got boosted."

Ryan examined the shag carpet for a moment. "At the Pentagon?"

"Right."

"Not really. Why?"

I noted the defensive tone was back.

"I was wondering if it was a random crime or if he was targeted."

"Well, random, it looked random. Smash and grab. They got a gym bag, some clothes, nothing classified or sensitive."

I asked for details, names, phone numbers, addresses. He opened his large briefcase, which was filled with hundreds of papers, and found a manila folder. He gave me the information I'd asked for. I reassured him again that we wouldn't jeopardize his investigation.

"Appreciate that."

"What's the other big case you're working on?"

"A Ponzi scheme," he answered.

"Like Madoff?"

"Lot smaller. But the theory's the same. It looks like he could be causing just as much damage, relatively speaking. Madoff ruined a lot of rich people's lives. My suspect could ruin a lot of poor folks'. You ask me, that's even worse. They don't have anything to fall back on."

He explained that the investment advisor under investigation was accused of preying on people in a lower-income, primarily minority quadrant of the District.

"What's the suspect's name?"

"Clarence Brown. He's a reverend."

I lifted an eyebrow.

"I know. Could be legit but it's also a good cover to win over investors, especially in that part of the city. He got his divinity degree mail-order." Ryan added that he'd been surprised to find that the man had nearly a thousand clients, so that, although the amounts each contributed were small, the total in the portfolio was significant.

He explained that over the past month several of those clients had tried to get their money out but Brown kept stalling, making excuse after excuse—the classic symptoms of a Ponzi scheme. The clients complained to the police and the case landed on Ryan's desk. He'd just taken a dozen victims' statements and was starting to piece together Brown's operation. The delays in getting the money were just technical problems, because of some of the particular investments he'd picked, Brown had explained to Kessler. The advisor didn't live the sweet life. The office was modest and based out of a storefront in South East D.C. Brown lived up the street in a tenement.

"I'm just curious," I said. "If it's a securities violation, why's Metropolitan Police handling it?"

Ryan gave a tight smile. "Because it's

small potatoes: the crime, the victims. So a small-potato cop gets the case."

An awkward silence.

Another excavation of the big brief-case. Documents appeared and I took down relevant details on this investigation too. "No other cases it could be?"

Another shrug. "Like I said, it's a quiet time. The other cases're small. Credit-card scams, identity theft. Low-dollar amounts. Mostly misdemeanors." He pulled out a pad and wrote the details. "Penny-ante stuff." A shrug. "That's it."

I gave him a nod of thanks. "This is helpful. I'll get somebody on it right now."

I took my notes to a table in the corner, clicked on the light—it was dim inside with the shades and curtains drawn—and made a call.

"DuBois."

"Claire. Got some info on Kessler's cases. I want to find out if anybody connected to them—suspects, witnesses, victims, *anybody*—could be the primary who hired Loving. I want you to start backgrounding all the players."

"Okay, I'm ready."

DuBois never calls me anything. She's about twelve years younger than me, which puts her squarely between "sir" and "Corte."

I gave her the details of the cases Ryan Kessler was running.

She said, "The forgery case? The guy works for Defense. That can be tricky. Sometimes you're dealing with military, sometimes civilian government, sometimes private contractors. If there's one thing they don't like to do, it's talk to outsiders. Even inside outsiders like us. Do you have any contacts there?"

"No," I told her.

She was silent a moment. One of her habits was tucking and retucking her brunette hair behind her ears. I pictured her doing this now. It never stayed in place but then neither did she. "I know somebody who dated a friend of mine. He was wacky. Played games a lot. Not your kind of games. And not boyfriend or husband games. I mean he'd run scenarios for the Pentagon and CIA. Like World War Three scenarios. And World War Four scenarios. There really is such a thing. Now, that's pretty scary, don't you think? I always wondered if there was a Five. Anyway, I'll call him. And I'll get on the Ponzi scheme too. I myself don't invest. I like the mattress theory."

As we disconnected I heard a jangle I was sure came from her bracelet.

I knew that if there was any connection, however slim, between Ryan's cases and Henry Loving's primary, duBois would find it. Despite her youth, she was better than I at the investigation side of our job—tracking down leads. She didn't have a game player's mind, which I seem to have been born with, so the deadly chess match between me and lifters and hitters didn't come naturally to her. But she was persistent as a terrier, sharp and wily when the script called for it. Because of her frenetic nature and dancing mind, she chatted up a storm with the subjects she interviewed, who ended up overwhelmed or intimidated. Or captivated. (She'd actually gotten a marriage proposal from a principal we'd protected about a year ago, after she'd spent some hours interviewing him. Since he was a former organized crime enforcer, duBois had declared him "not prime dating material.")

About a year ago Barbara, the personal assistant I share with another shepherd at the office, caught me gazing at duBois with what was apparently a smile, an uncharacteristic expression for me. It was only a look of admiration after the woman had poured out a flood of helpful details she'd unearthed about a potential primary. That smile, though, was enough for Barbara, a single mother of fifty and a regular in the online dating world. She assumed my gaze was romantic and had later asked why I'd never asked duBois out. (She mentioned something about "May–September," which seemed to me a little harsh for a mere twelve-year difference.)

In any case, of course, I deflected the suggestion. But my professional enthusiasm for my protégée was unrelenting and I didn't pull back from expressing it, though admittedly in my typically subdued way.

I now typed my own notes into my laptop, encrypted the file and saved it.

Maree joined us; for some reason

she'd changed clothes and renewed her makeup. A flowery scent of perfume surrounded her. She seemed even more attractive than earlier. Interestingly, though she and her sister resembled each other in many ways, only Maree was what I'd call sexy, and this had nothing to do with the age difference. She walked to the coffee station and poured some. She then set the cup down, cocked her head as she looked at an arrangement of flowers on the dresser. Lifting her camera, she shot a dozen or so fast pictures. I made a mental note to review all the photos she'd taken since the family had come under my care; I'd make sure she deleted any that depicted me or anyone else on the team.

Then she returned to the coffee, glanced my way and refilled my cup.

"Thanks."

"Anything in it?"

"No, this is fine."

She looked at me as if she wanted to say something else but kept silent.

I received a text message, read it and then sent a reply. I turned to my principals. "The new SUV's here. We'll be leaving soon."

Ryan joked, "Just about to take my shoes off and put the game on." His attitude was completely different from when we'd first met. The mission I'd given him and the liquor helped, I assessed.

I rose. "Stay here." I looked at Ryan. "Don't open the door for anybody but me."

He nodded and adjusted his holster.

I stepped outside and circled our wing to the parking lot behind the motel. A dark green GMC Yukon pulled up, trailed by a Ford Taurus. I gave a wave and the two vehicles stopped nearby. Two men emerged from the SUV.

A young officer in my organization, Lyle Ahmad, was a solid, olive-skinned former marine with a trim crew cut. He was a clone, a close protection officer. I had met Ahmad when he was a marine guarding the U.S. embassy in Warsaw and I was an agent with the State Department's protection and investigation arm, Diplomatic Security, where I worked before joining my present outfit.

He was quiet and sharp and boasted impressive multiple-language skills. He was a rising star in our organization.

Driving the SUV was our transport man, Billy. The gangly man, whose age I couldn't begin to guess, had shaggy hair and a crooked incisor you had to force yourself not to look at. He absolutely loved cars, trucks, motorcycles, anything that moved by what he called "dead dinosaur"—gas or diesel fuel. He not only maintained the fleet but he would play Rubik's Cube with the three or four dozen vehicles we use—swapping them and shuttling personnel and principals around the area. We had quite a collection—after salary and safe houses, transportation was the biggest item on our budget. Vehicles are like fingerprints. Along with cell phones and credit cards, there's probably no better way to trace somebody than through his car. So we made sure to swap vehicles often.

Billy nodded at the Nissan. "She ready to go?"

"Yep." We swapped keys and he drove off.

The man who had emerged from the Taurus was Rudy Garcia, the young FBI agent Freddy had brought with him to the Kesslers' house.

I shook his hand and introduced him to Ahmad and we started back to the motel room.

I introduced the new arrival to the Kesslers and Maree, who whispered to her sister, "He's cute," drawing a blush— but no other reaction—from the unmarried Ahmad. I noted dismay behind the nod Ryan gave, as if the presence of other guards might rob the D.C. cop of his chance to see some action as my wingman in the operation to take down Loving.

It was then that my phone rang. The caller ID was from my organization but I wasn't expecting this particular individual.

"Hermes," I said. That was the real name—pronounced without the *H*—of our technical director, the man in charge of surveillance devices, computers and communication systems.

"Corte," he said urgently, his voice tinted with an indiscernible accent. "Believe it or not, we got a hit on the squawk box, the one connected to the Armada. Then fifteen minutes ago somebody made a call to the North East D.C. trap."

I felt my heart begin to thud quickly.

"All right, thanks, Hermes."

I disconnected. I thought for a moment. Yes? No?

Then I told my principals, Garcia and Ahmad that there was a slight change in plans.

"You'll be staying here a few hours longer. If you want some food, Lyle or Rudy can order room service. Nobody leave the room. I won't be long."

Ryan asked, "Corte, what's this all about?"

I gave what I thought was a nonchalant shrug. "I have a meeting with somebody about the job."

I headed out the door fast, not explaining that that somebody happened to be Henry Loving himself.

Chapter 10

There's some debate about exactly what the role of a shepherd should be in personal security work.

The nickname itself is telling. "Shepherd," to me, doesn't refer to a motley farmhand with a hooked staff, but to a very big dog.

I'm not a canine person myself but I know there are herding dogs that move sheep around a field and then there are herding dogs that both guard the flock and attack predators, however big and however numerous. Which of those two roles should we personal security officers have? Abe Fallow used to say, "A shepherd's job is to protect the principals. That's it. Let somebody else catch the lifter and hitter and their primaries."

But—one of the few areas in which I disagreed with my mentor—I didn't subscribe to that theory. I think our task is both to move the herd to safety and rip out the throats of any wolves who're threats. Protecting the principal and neutralizing the lifter or hitter and the person who hired him are, to me, inextricably joined.

Driving fast toward the District in Garcia's Taurus, I was speaking with Freddy, who would lead up the hunting party. The one department my organization doesn't have is tactical. I've always wanted one (and had the nickname, "gunslinger," all ready to go) but Ellis got shot down, so to speak, in committee; tac departments are surprisingly expensive. So we rely on the FBI and, in some cases, local SWAT.

After I laid out the plan that I hoped would snare Henry Loving, Freddy said, "You think this is gonna work, Corte? Sounds like Santa Claus meets the Tooth Fairy."

"Are you there yet?" Based out of Ninth Street, in the District, he had a shorter drive than I did.

"Make it twenty minutes."

"Move fast. How many do you have?"

"Plenty, son. Peace through superior firepower," he said, a quote from somewhere, I believed. We disconnected. I sped on, toward Washington, D.C.

Hermes's call had been about a fly-trap, a ploy we regularly use to lure the bad guys to a takedown location. They work once in twenty, thirty times but that's no reason not to try. All of our cars and most shepherds' mobile phones have inside them an electronic device we call a squawk box, which periodically transmits a fake phone call that's encrypted but traceable. A lifter or hitter with the right equipment can pick up the number that these phones call, a landline whose location they can track down through your basic commercial reverse look-up.

According to Hermes, Loving had picked up one of these automated calls from the Armada, when it was parked at the Kesslers' house. He'd called the landline, a phone in a warehouse in North East D.C. The message he would have heard was that the place was no longer in business. The kicker was that I had recorded that message myself, so

that anyone with a print of my voice, as
I imagined Loving had, would think that
it was indeed the place where the Kesslers were being kept.

Given the pressure to get information
from Ryan by Monday night—and avoid
the "unacceptable consequences" mentioned in the email Loving had received
in West Virginia—and given Loving's unrelenting drive to finish his assignments
I thought it was likely that he and his
partner would at least conduct some
surveillance at the warehouse.

The contest between Loving and me
was now about to begin in earnest.

I often put my job in terms of something that I (an otherwise dispassionate
person, I've been told) *am* passionate
about: board games, which I not only
play but collect. (The FedEx package
that had arrived that morning was an
antique game I'd been looking for for
years.) One of the reasons I picked the
town house in Old Town Alexandria is
that it's about two blocks from my favorite gaming club, just off Prince Street.
The membership is reasonable and you
can always be sure of finding somebody

inside to play chess, bridge, Go, Wei Chi, Risk or dozens of other games. The members are a great mix: all nationalities, levels of education, ages, though most are male. All manners of dress and income. Politics vary but are irrelevant.

In the town house are sixty-seven games (and I have even more, 121, in a house near the water in Maryland), all arranged alphabetically.

Naturally I prefer the more challenging games. My present favorite is Arimaa, a recent invention and a variation on chess but so elegant and challenging that the creator's prize to anybody who can write a program so a computer can play is as yet unclaimed. Chess itself is certainly a good game and I enjoy it. It has, though, been so written about and studied and deconstructed that when I sit down across from an experienced player I sometimes feel that I'm not playing against him but against a crowd of stuffy, eccentric ghosts.

What do I like about board games as opposed to, say, computer games, which certainly offer the same mental challenge?

For one thing I like the art. The design of the board, the playing pieces, the cards, the die, the spinners and the wooden or plastic or ivory accoutrements, like sticks and pins. The aesthetics are pleasing to me and I like it that they also serve a functional purpose, if you can call playing a game utilitarian.

I like it that a board game has longevity and is tangible, it doesn't go away when you shut off a switch or pull a plug from the wall.

Most important, though, I like sitting across from a human being, my opponent. Much of my life involves playing a match of life and death against people like Henry Loving, who are invisible to me, and I can only imagine their expressions of consideration as they pick their strategies to capture or kill my principals. Playing chess or Go or Tigris and Euphrates—a very good game, by the way—I can watch people as they choose their strategy and note how they respond to something I've done.

Even über-techie Bill Gates is a devout bridge player, I've heard.

In any event, playing games has honed my mind and helps me as a shepherd.

So does game theory, which I became interested in while I was getting one of my graduate degrees, in math, also for the fun of it, lolling in academia and delaying entry into the real world.

Game theory was first debated in the 1940s, though the ideas have been around for years. The academics who formulated the theory originally analyzed games like bridge and poker and even simple contests like Rock, Paper, Scissors or coin flipping, with the goal not of helping win leisure-time activities but to study decision-making.

Simply put, game theory is about trying to make the best choice when presented with a conflict among participants—either opponents or partners—when neither knows what the other will do.

A classic example is the Prisoners' Dilemma, in which two criminals are caught and held in separate cells. The police give each one a choice: to confess or not. Even though each doesn't know what the other will pick, they do know—from the information the police give them—it will be for their mutual good to confess; they won't go free but they'll get a relatively short sentence.

But there's also the chance that by *not* confessing, they will get an even shorter sentence, or none at all, though that's riskier . . . because they could instead receive a much longer one.

Confessing is the "rational" choice.

But not confessing is acting with what's called "rational irrationality."

In the real world, you see game theory applied in many situations: economics, politics, psychology and military planning. For instance, customers might know that it's better not to withdraw all their savings from a troubled bank, because if they do they'll contribute to a panic, the bank will fail and everybody will lose. On the other hand, if they're the first to get their money out, they won't lose anything; to hell with the common good. By withdrawing all their funds fast, rational irrationality might save them individually, even though it will start a run on the bank and ruin it.

How does this affect my job as a shepherd?

Since neither I nor opponents like Henry Loving know what moves the other will make, I continually apply game theory in trying to pick the best strategy to win—strategy being not an overall approach to a contest but a specific move, like "Pawn to Rook Seven" or selecting a fist in Rock, Paper, Scissors.

Here, my strategy was to play the flytrap, believing that Henry Loving was more likely than not to make a rational choice: to go for the bait.

But game theory exists because of uncertainty—on gaming boards and in real life. Perhaps Loving would sense this was a trap and, knowing that I was preoccupied there, would use this opportunity to find the real safe house the Kesslers were in, while I was busy here.

Or would he try a different strategy altogether, something I couldn't figure out but which was even now brilliantly outmaneuvering me?

I was getting closer to the nation's capital. I noticed behind me a black SUV

I might have seen earlier. Westerfield? Someone else? I called Claire duBois again. "I need a crowd. Festival, parade. In the District. I don't think I have a tail but I want to make sure of it. What do you have for me?"

"A crowd. Okay. How big a crowd? There's the game at the stadium—but, sorry to say, *that*'s not going to be much of a crowd, given how they're playing this season. Then there's a romance author and the cover model of her books—they're signing at a Safeway in North West."

How did she know this without looking anything up?

"How many people go to romance book signings at grocery stores?"

"You'd be surprised."

True. "But I want bigger. And downtown. Make it a thousand people, plus."

"Too bad it's not spring. I don't go for the cherry blossoms myself," she told me. "If the blossoms *did* something while you were there, that would be one thing. But I never quite understood going to look at trees. Let's see, let's see. . . ." I heard typing, I heard tinkling charms.

DuBois said, "There's not much. A gay rights march up Connecticut in Du-Pont Circle. Preaching to the converted. Estimate four hundred . . . A Mexican-American parade in South East but it's just winding down now. Oh, here we go. The biggest thing is the protesters outside of Congress. That's about two thousand strong. I never know why they say that. 'Strong.' As opposed to 'two thousand weak.'"

"That sounds good."

The crowds were there to protest against, or support, a Supreme Court nominee, she explained. I was vaguely aware that the jurist—projected to be confirmed by one or two votes in the Senate—was conservative, so the left was busing in folks to protest, while the Republicans had marshaled their own troops to show support.

"Where exactly?"

She told me—near the Senate Office Building—and I disconnected and steered in that direction. In five minutes, with the sanction of my federal ID, I was easing

in and around the demonstrators and
past barricades that would stop anyone
tailing me. The supporters of the nominee were on one side of a line, the protesters on the other. I noted the vicious-
ness of the insults and even threats they
flung back and forth at each other. The
police were out in force. I recalled reading a recent series in the *Post* about the
increasing polarization and aggressive
partisanship in American politics.

My phone buzzed. "Freddy."

"Where are you?"

"Trying not to run over Supreme Court
nominee protesters."

"Hit a few of 'em for me."

"You're on site?"

"We're here, in the staging area."

"Anything?"

"Nothing so far."

"I'll be there soon." I now emerged on
the other side of the demonstration, assured that I had no tail, and sped to a
small garage we sometimes used, just
north of Union Station. In five minutes
I'd swapped Garcia's official car for another fake one and was heading out a

different doorway from the one I'd driven into.

Ten minutes later I was at the flytrap.

A new round of the game against Henry Loving was about to begin.

Chapter 11

We'd picked this location, a scruffy portion of North East D.C., because it was a perfect takedown site.

Some industrial parts of the District of Columbia, like this one, are as breathtakingly grim as anything Detroit or Chicago's South Side can offer. The warehouse we leased for a song was in a marshy, weed-cluttered landfill crisscrossed with rusting railroad tracks (I'd never seen a train), crumbling access roads and a couple of sour-smelling canals. Our property was three acres of overgrown lots, filled with trash, clusters of anemic trees, pools of water the color of a sickly tropical lizard. In the center was an ancient warehouse with just enough evidence of habitation to make it seem like a credible safe house. Nearby were two small crumbling outbuildings, where tactical teams could wait for the bad guys; they offered perfect crossfire positions. The warehouse itself had bulletproof brick walls and few windows. We've used it a number of times, though only twice successfully. The most recent was last January, when I'd sat in a snowstorm for four hours, sipping increasingly chilly coffee from a flabby cup clutched in my stinging red fingers, until the hitter finally made his bold and, for him, unfortunate move.

I now drove through back alleys and fields, largely invisible to any surveillance from the perimeter. I parked some distance from the warehouse, beside the other federal cars, out of sight of the nearby driveways and roads. Then, my shoulder bag bouncing on my back, I walked through a stand of brush and beneath a rusting railroad bridge that was graffiti-free; even the gangbangers had no interest in this prime example of urban decay. I surveyed the area again, saw no sign of hostile surveillance and slipped through tall weeds toward the staging area. A glance at the ground—the broken twigs, overturned leaves and stones—told me that Freddy had brought with him at least six agents (all of them seemingly unconcerned that they left such clear evidence of their presence; I spent some time obscuring the most obvious signs).

Surrounding me was a world of trash and abandoned vehicles and rusting machinery and outright garbage piles. On my right, I could see a glimpse of a narrow canal, filled with bile green water and dotted with refuse and a dead squirrel or two, which I suspected had ended up there after taking a sip. Improbably, a small recreational power boat floated in the current toward the Potomac. Then the strip of foul water vanished from sight; a moment later I got to the command post and greeted Freddy and his people: six male agents in their thirties, large and unsmiling, and one younger woman, equally somber. The mix of these law enforcers was like the city itself: black, Latino, the minority white— the woman and an older, weathered male agent. People tend to think that the FBI is all dark suits and white shirts or the scary tactical outfits that make them look like science fiction movie soldiers. In reality, most agents dress informally: windbreakers, baseball caps and blue jeans. In the case of the woman, make that *designer* jeans, which I couldn't help but notice fit very closely. All were in body armor.

Which I myself now donned.

Everyone seemed tense, though I could tell from their eyes that they were looking forward to engaging.

As I slipped on my com device earpiece and stalk mike, Freddy gave me their names and I paid attention, since I might need to differentiate them if the situation heated up. I nodded to each in greeting. I asked if there'd been any contact. The woman said, "We had a light sedan, gray or tan, go by the west perimeter, that road over there, five minutes ago. Didn't pause but it was going slow. I'd guess ten miles an hour."

Gray or tan could have been beige. Loving's car from West Virginia? I suggested this and they took note.

The slow transit in itself might not be suspicious. A lot of roads in the District were riddled with potholes, the asphalt was crumbling and traffic signs were missing. Kids stole them for souvenirs. Which could explain the car's leisurely pace. But then the bad conditions would also provide a good excuse for Loving to drive slowly and be less suspicious.

"You have a sniper?" I asked Freddy.

He snorted a laugh. "Sniper? You've been watching too many movies, Corte. Best we have is Bushmasters."

"Accurate is what we want, Freddy. It's not about size."

"Was that a joke, Corte? You never make jokes."

"A map?" I asked.

"Here, sir." The woman agent produced one.

I looked it over carefully, though I was keenly aware we didn't have a lot of time. Either Loving would move fast or he wouldn't try for the assault at all. I turned to the agents and explained my plan for the takedown, then pointed out the best placement for everyone and for the hardware. Freddy made a few suggestions, which I thought were good.

I looked at the building that was supposedly our safe house. A few lights were on inside. And there was a machine that Hermes had developed, a nice little toy, like a slow-motion fan whose blades cast shadows randomly on shades and curtains, giving the impression that somebody was inside and walking occasionally from room to room. It also produced a light that mimicked the glow of a TV screen. You could program voices to sound like people having conversations. There was even a mode selector: argumentative, humorous, conspiratorial—to make any eavesdropping lifters or hitters believe the warehouse was populated by principals under guard, and not workers.

"How're the Kesslers?" Freddy asked.

"Calmer than a lot of my principals." But, I told him, Joanne was a zombie and would be in therapy for a year; her husband was drinking and wanted to shoot anything that moved, and Maree—when she wasn't hysterical—was more concerned about boyfriend trouble than professional killers.

"I warned you about that sister, Corte. You know, you get tired of this job, you should think about doing some kind of Dr. Phil show."

Then I said, "I'm going into position."

He gave me one of his looks. It was a container of a dozen messages that I read instinctively. Freddy, whom I'd met years ago under unusual circumstances, was the only person in the world I could be partnered with in operations like this. Of the two of us, I'm the strategist—I pick the moves—and he's the tactician, figuring out how to implement my choices.

In terms of games, I decide rock . . . and Freddy makes the fist.

I trekked through a long weedy gully, bordered by a thick stand of trees to my right, the smelly canal beyond and, on the left, grass and piles of machinery. At the end, under cover of the sad foliage, I set up a Big Ear unit—a twelve-inch parabolic dish that was an ultrasensitive microphone—and slipped on a headset. I turned this toward the warehouse, aiming the device below the window, which had purposely been left open.

I focused beyond the warehouse and noted in the middle of our property two civilian vehicles up on blocks. A Chevy sedan and a Dodge van, rusty and covered with graffiti, some of which I myself had helped spray on a few years ago.

Alone now, feeling *very* alone, I looked around once more, as a trickle of excitement and anticipation danced down my spine.

Fear too, of course.

As Abe Fallow had told me and I told my protégés, you have to be afraid in this business. If you don't get scared, you can't be effective.

Ten minutes passed, a long, long ten minutes.

"Team One to Command Post," a voice clattered through our earphones. "Got some movement north."

"Command Post to One. Go ahead."

"Be advised. Unknown person moving slow. Dark clothing, male probably. Gone from sight now. He's in grid eighteen."

"Weapon?"

"Not obvious."

I strained, leaning forward to look where the subject had been spotted—

the opposite side of the property from where I was. After a moment of staring at blond and green weeds, I too noted some motion. The subject was moving furtively from a dead end road toward the warehouse.

"I've got him," the woman agent said. "No weapon. Doesn't appear to be Loving."

"Probably the partner," I radioed, "but he's not alone. Loving'll be here too."

The others called in, reporting what they saw—or, mostly, *didn't* see—from their respective positions. The figure tentatively approaching the warehouse had stopped.

Then a whisper: "Team Two. He's noticed the Dodge, he's interested in it."

I kept quiet. I'd be getting the details as soon they were verified. It was inefficient to waste time by asking professionals for more information. It was like urging, "Be careful" as you're moving in for a takedown. I wiped my hands on my slacks.

"This is Team One. He's on the move again. Slow."

"Team Two. Copy that. He's real interested in the Dodge." One of the agents asked, "Any equipment in there?"

"No," Freddy said. "It's clean. Let him poke around. . . . Team Four, you see anything more? Any sign of Loving?"

"Negative."

"Three?"

"Negative."

Then: "This is Team Two. The partner's getting closer . . . hand in pocket . . . looking behind him . . . has something in his hand. A mobile."

I pulled out my Alpen 10x32 Long Eye binoculars and scanned the area but couldn't see him.

Working on calming my breathing—which was shallow and fast. I tried thinking one of my mantras. Rock, paper, scissors. Rock, paper, scissors.

It was then that I heard: *Snap.*

Directly behind me.

I froze and turned my head slowly.

Holding his silenced pistol steadily on me, Henry Loving glanced down briefly, his mouth curling with faint disappointment at not having avoided the dry branch he'd just stepped on.

Chapter 12

Loving noted a bit of body armor pro-truding from beneath my jacket. He lifted his gun and aimed at my exposed neck.

Then his pale left hand moved slightly, delivering instructions.

I stood. I was to remove the radio mike bud from one ear and the listening de-vice earpiece from the other. And to pull my weapon from the holster with thumb and index finger.

I complied with all of his requests, as-sessing him calmly.

The way the game was moving was now clear. Loving had guessed that this was a trap and had decided to engage me personally. A rational decision. Which explained why he'd ordered the partner to hold back, near the Dodge, and not approach the warehouse itself, which he would have done if Loving had fallen for the setup.

He'd known it was a trap but he'd taken the risk. Not to get Ryan Kessler, of course, but to kidnap me. Who, after sufficient coercion, would tell him where exactly the Kesslers were. I had suddenly become a principal.

Loving's murky eyes in the fleshy, nondescript face of a businessman approaching middle age took in the scene quickly and noticed no threat around him, here at a distance from the command post and the warehouse.

I realized that this was the closest I'd ever gotten to the man who'd tortured and killed my mentor. In Rhode Island, in the botched takedown, I'd never been nearer than a hundred feet or so. Close enough to see him squint slightly as he pulled the trigger—an instant before realizing that he'd walked into a trap and the principal was really an undercover agent, behind an invisible bulletproof shield.

Neither of us said anything now. His plan was that we would talk, of course, but later and in the back of his vehicle or in another grim abandoned warehouse somewhere far away. He'd be thinking how long I could last before I told him where Ryan Kessler was.

Because, Henry Loving knew, I would talk. Everybody talks sooner or later.

With my weapon, the radio and cell phone on the ground and knowing he had limited time, Henry Loving gestured me toward him.

Walking forward, I lifted my hands to shoulder level to show I was no threat, my gaze riveted to his. I couldn't look away. This was not because his eyes were intense or focused, though they were, but because they were the last thing that Abe Fallow had seen as he died. I knew this because the bullet had been fired from close range and had struck Abe in his forehead. The men would have been looking at one another. I often wondered, sometimes for hours before I fell asleep, about Abe's last moments. He'd given up the locations of the five principals he'd been guarding. But I'd been listening on the still-connected mobile. Between the moment Abe whispered the address of the last

witness and the fatal gunshot thirty seconds or so had passed. What had happened during that time? What had their
expressions been?

This was perhaps the reason I was so
obsessed with catching Henry Loving:
not only because he'd killed Abe Fallow,
but because he'd forced the man to
spend his last few moments in agony
and despair.

Hands submissively out to the sides, I
began to wonder what shepherds always wonder under such circumstances:
How long can *I* hold out under torture?

*Loving's low-tech. Usually he uses
sandpaper and alcohol on sensitive
parts of the body. Doesn't sound too
bad but it works real well.*

This question, though, was merely
theoretical, something that popped into
my mind as I stepped forward.

Because, despite appearances, I wasn't
the losing player at the moment.

Henry Loving was.

The real bait here wasn't the warehouse and the suggestion that Ryan
Kessler was inside.

The real bait was me.

The trap was something altogether different from what it appeared to be.

And the moment had come to spring it.

Squinting, I lifted my hands over my shoulders. This was the signal to the two FBI teams hiding nearby, my backup.

And, as I dropped to the ground, I caught a glimpse of the shock in Loving's face as the explosions began. They were stunning. I felt the blast wave and heat slam into my face as I rolled on the dirt to retrieve my weapon, radio and phone. The powerful remote-controlled flash-bang grenades continued to detonate along the line I'd ordered them set up fifteen minutes before by the agents covering me, Teams Three and Four. They'd been told to set them off when I raised my hands above the level of my shoulders.

Or if Loving shot me.

"Move in, move in!" I shouted from the ground, plugging the earbuds in and grabbing my weapon. "He's headed for the canal."

I heard Freddy's voice, "Team Two, take down the partner!"

The agents on Teams Three and Four—the ones who'd been with me the whole time, hidden only thirty or so feet away—were on the move now, heading after Loving. I joined them, sprinting. We ran in pursuit, through the brush and weeds, around tires and abandoned washers and refrigerators. The lifter was ignoring us, concentrating on speed, not turning to fire.

I'd decided that Loving would probably guess that this was a trap but I also believed that he'd figure I'd be present and he'd take the risk to kidnap me. And extract the location of Ryan Kessler.

Then kill me afterward.

I am, of course, the Henry Loving of *his* life.

My strategy had been to put the agents around me and rig explosive charges nearby, then set up the microphone and turn my back to where I believed he'd come at me. I became the most obvious target I could be. Like a suspect in the Prisoners' Dilemma, I'd made a risky choice. Rational irrationality. I'd bet that Loving wouldn't kill me outright but would try to extract infor-

mation about the Kesslers' whereabouts.
I wondered if he'd arrived by that boat
in the canal and possibly he had, but he
was now heading the other way—toward an open field. There was very little
cover and it seemed a strange choice.
But then I spotted, a hundred yards
away, an embankment on top of which
was a road. He had a getaway car there
waiting, I saw.

We'd stop him easily before he got
halfway there, though. The four agents
who'd been guarding me were gaining
on him—I was holding my own. I called
Freddy to tell him that Loving was heading for the road and to send a car to
intercept him.

The radio transmissions were flying
like shrapnel, as our voices stepped on
each other.

Gasping, I continued to race after our
prey.

We got some good news.

"Team Two. Got one in custody. Loving's partner."

That was something, I reflected. We
could learn valuable information from

him, his phone, forensics. He might even confess.

The Prisoners' Dilemma . . .

But then an agent from Team Two said, "We've got him down. No weapons."

Not armed? I wondered. He'd had a semi-automatic pistol at the Kesslers'.

Oh, no . . .

I stopped fast as the stark under-standing came home. I forced myself to speak clearly as I radioed the message, meant for the four agents ahead of me: "Teams Three and Four; get down! Find cover immediately. The man in custody's not the partner! It's a setup!"

I dropped to the ground like a rag doll.

Which was probably what saved my life.

As I landed in a stand of brush, I heard a snap over my head and nearby dirt and rocks flew up. A moment later the rolling boom of a distant rifle shot filled the field.

I called, "Incoming sniper fire!"

"What?" somebody transmitted.

The agents ahead of me similarly rolled to the ground as dirt and bits of trash leapt up around them.

Loving's partner was a talented shot but the agents managed to find suitable cover. Nothing would protect them from a direct hit but the weeds were tall enough so that the partner couldn't spot them.

Loving was now only about forty feet from the embankment and the car. The agents tried a few shots his way but the moment they rose, the partner would let go with three shot bursts—he had an automatic weapon—and the teams dropped again to cover.

I looked for a target and saw nothing.

The car Freddy had sent was speeding along the embankment and would get to the escape vehicle about the same time Loving did.

I sighed and hit TRANSMIT. "Freddy, get the car back! Now!"

"It's our only chance, Corte."

"No, no. Call it back. They're sitting ducks."

"Shit. . . . Okay."

Would it be in time?

Then I saw the car swerve and I was watching bits of asphalt and debris pop up on the road beside the vehicle as the partner turned his long gun their way. The driver steered off the road fast; the car disappeared down the embankment on the other side and I heard a crash.

Loving reappeared and jumped into his car, which sped off.

A light-colored sedan.

Tan or gray . . .

I heard Freddy radioing the Bureau and the MPD to order a search for the car.

The sniper fire ceased.

But we knew the drill and duck-walked back toward the staging area, low, presenting no target, as we assumed the partner might be holding in shooting position.

Finally, with no more shots fired, we arrived at the command post. I looked over the man that Team Two had collared. I didn't have much hope that this scared kid could be helpful but still, you go through the motions. The diversion was a young meth head. He explained that somebody—Loving, to hear his description—had picked him up near a club in South East and asked him to help score some drugs at the warehouse. Loving had explained that he wanted some heroin but was too scared to buy it himself. There was a dealer operating out of an old derelict Dodge van on the premises here. He'd slipped him cash and told him to buy four hundred dollars' worth for Loving and a hundred for himself. He was to be careful—"Go up slow"—because sometimes the cops checked it out.

"I'm going to go to jail, aren't I?"

There was something almost humorous about the kid's wide-eyed lament. Though it occurred to me I wasn't sure he'd actually done anything illegal.

I asked him a few questions but Loving had known the kid would be caught; the decoy had been told nothing that might be helpful to us. Freddy went over him for evidence but, while I certainly appreciate forensic science, in these circumstances the only connection between Loving and this kid was the hundred-dollar bills. If there'd been any trace evidence exchange, through shaken hands and the money, it wasn't going to lead to Loving's hidey-hole.

We tried to reconstruct where the real partner had been shooting from. There were dozens of high-ground vistas that would have been perfect. Nobody had seen a muzzle flash or leaf reaction from the powerful gun. The agents in the car that had crashed were all right. One of them radioed that he was canvassing some workers on the other side of the embankment who'd heard the shots. A man reported seeing somebody running to a dark blue four-door sedan. "Buick, they thought."

I clicked TRANSMIT. "This is Corte. Ask them what he looks like."

After a moment: "Tall, thin, blond. Green jacket."

"Yes, that's the partner."

"Nobody got the tag number. Or anything else specific."

"Thanks," I said.

Calls came in about the search, which included a Metropolitan Police chopper. But Loving had left the immediate vicinity without being spotted.

"We gave it a try," Freddy said.

We had. But Loving had outthought

me and negated my strategy. We were playing a game, yes, but that didn't mean it might not end in a draw.

Rock-rock. Paper-paper . . .

For me, though, a draw was as good as a loss.

I walked up to the car I'd driven to the warehouse and took a handheld scanner from my shoulder bag.

Freddy said, "You think the partner got to the staging area?"

I didn't answer—why guess?—but apparently he had. I found the first tracker in my car's wheel well in about fifteen seconds and, just after that, the second one, hidden six inches from the first, in hopes that I might stop the search after finding number one. I kept going but I didn't find a third. At least not a third one that had switched itself on yet. I noted that removing them switched off the power, alerting Loving that they'd been found. We couldn't use them as bait to lure him to another trap.

I searched a second time with an explosives sniffer and didn't come up with any bombs. I hadn't really thought that was a risk, though. Loving wanted me to lead him to the principals. He didn't want to kill me.

That would come later.

Chapter 13

I swapped the borrowed car for Garcia's Taurus and drove it to Old Town Alexandria, parking in our garage next to the office.

The D.C. area is peppered with operations like this, units of various government agencies. Sometimes it's a question of space; Langley, for instance, is extremely crowded. For meetings at the CIA I sometimes have to park a hundred yards or more from the entrance. Sometimes it's security. Everybody, from the writers at Slate.com to the Mossad to al Qaeda, know where the NSA, NRO and CIA are located; other operations, like ours, prefer to stay off the grid as much as possible.

In the garage I greeted Billy and told him to run a full scan of Garcia's car. It had been unattended in the garage near

Union Station for several hours while I was at the flytrap.

"I stopped halfway here and ran a scan. Nothing active. But you'll have to give it a thorough check."

A lot of trackers have timers that turn on hours or weeks into the future. You need very sophisticated equipment that can detect not radio signals but tiny electrical sources.

"You bet, Corte," the scrawny man said. "I'll call a sweeper." Billy would look right at home in the cab of a Peterbilt tractor-trailer.

I made a detour outside and bought a roast beef on whole wheat, extra mustard and two pickles, and black coffee. I returned to the office. The boring and uninviting lobby featured an unhealthy tree, a poster of a smiling man and woman who'd apparently just been approved for a loan and a black sign containing white adhesive-letter names of a half dozen companies, all fake. I nodded at the two guards, both seriously and subtly armed, then did the eye and thumb thing at the wall panel and walked through the door. I went up a flight of stairs.

Outside my office my shared personal assistant, Barbara, lifted her head and handed me some message slips. The slim, middle-aged woman purposefully didn't look at my coffee and I knew she was thinking, why didn't I like hers, which she made daily for the floor? I didn't like it because it was reliably bad.

Her hair was grayish dark and frozen into shape. I sometimes thought she got the hairdo about where she wanted it and then pushed it into position with gusts of hair spray.

Since our organization never closed we had support staff all the time, though no one assistant was required to work more than forty hours a week. I hadn't done the math but I believed Barbara was working on her second forty.

"I like weekends," she sometimes said. "It's quieter."

Apart from lying in polluted mud and getting shot at by a talented sniper.

I sat down at my desk and ate a pickle spear and a large bite of sandwich, a

Heimlich bite. I then sipped hot and strong and very good coffee.

I called Lyle Ahmad at the Hillside Inn.

"What's the status?"

"Quiet. Garcia and I make rounds every twenty or so."

"Any calls? Anybody from the front desk? Anything?"

"No," he said crisply. Ahmad's ancestry was Middle Eastern of some sort and he might or might not be a Muslim. Unlike some people of that faith in this country, he didn't seem the least self-conscious or defensive about it. Nor should he have been. The vast majority of people who've tried to kill me have been of Christian or Jewish or agnostic leaning.

"The principals?"

"Doing fine," he assured, though with a certain tone in his voice that meant they were probably impatient, bored and uneasy but he didn't want to say so while ten feet from them. I heard the sound of a baseball game in the background and Joanne saying to her sister, "Well, sure. I just wonder. . . . If you think that's the best idea, though, sure."

My mother would often sound like that.

"I'll be back for the move to the safe house in about forty-five."

"Yessir."

After we disconnected, I ate two more large bites of sandwich, thinking of the FedEx package I'd received, the antique game I'd been looking forward to examining on my lunch hour. I wondered if it was in good shape, if it had all the pieces and cards, as the seller had promised. I glanced at the safe behind my desk but left it where it was.

I didn't have it locked away because I was afraid it would be stolen. No, it was simply that I didn't share my personal life with anybody here, even those I worked closely with. Yes, there were some security reasons for this; in reality, though, I just felt more comfortable being secretive. I couldn't really say why.

I reached for the phone to call duBois and have her brief me about what she'd found out so far about Ryan's case but it buzzed first. My boss's extension.

"Corte."

"It's Aaron. Could you come in for a moment?"

Tone often tells more than content and I noted the uneasiness in Ellis's voice, making the otherwise innocuous request. I expected to find Westerfield sitting in his office when I arrived but in fact it was somebody else altogether. A slim man, balding, in a suit and powder blue shirt. No tie. He looked at me with eyes that didn't look at me. As if he was seeing what I represented, rather than who I actually was.

We shook hands. He identified himself as Sandy Alberts.

Ellis seemed to have met him before, but then my boss knew almost everybody in Washington, D.C. He said to me, "Sandy's chief of staff to Senator Lionel Stevenson."

Moderate Republican from Ohio. I thought he'd been on the cover of *Newsweek* or something recently.

"I'm not really here," Alberts said jokingly, referring to the secret nature of our organization. We heard this a lot. I'm sure you're busy. I'll tell you what's going on, sir."

"Corte."

"Officer Corte, then. The senator is on the Intelligence Committee."

Which explained the security clearance allowing him inside. I'd been wondering.

"The committee'll be holding hearings next month on domestic surveillance issues, Patriot Act, FISA warrants. It's looking into possible privacy abuses and I'm doing some research for the senator." He held up jovial hands. "We're not suggesting anything's wrong *here.* Just interviewing as many people as we can in federal law enforcement. Gathering information. You're the senior protection officer in your organization and we'd like to interview you to see if you've been aware of instances in which there's been, let's say, carelessness in failing to apply for warrants for wiretaps on phone lines and emails in any agencies you've dealt with. The Bureau, the CIA, DEA, NSA, NRO, local law enforcement."

"I'd be happy to help but . . . well, I need to run this job now."

Alberts was nodding. "We know what you do here. The senator's a friend of

Aaron's." A glance toward my boss. "We don't want to jeopardize any of your great work. It's just that there's a bit of time pressure."

"Why?" Ellis asked.

"Any time committees start looking into things, the press invariably catches on and if they preempt us everybody loses."

I couldn't disagree with that. "There are plenty of other people you could talk to here," I suggested.

"Oh, we want the star," Alberts replied.

My boss backed me up. "I'm afraid I agree it'll have to be after this case is concluded."

Alberts wasn't pleased but he took it in stride. "Three, four days, you think?"

"Probably something like that," I said. "But I can't commit. It's a very critical time for the family in my care. I'll let you know as soon as I'm free."

"Sure, I understand," Alberts said. Looking through me again, smiling that nonsmile of his. "Appreciate it." He rose. With a nod to Ellis the man collected his briefcase. "And I meant that—about the good job you folks do."

After he left I asked Ellis, "The senator's a friend of yours?"

Ellis scoffed, shrugging his huge shoulders. "If you call going to somebody with hat in hand a friend, then I guess. Stevenson usually comes through with most of what I want for the budget. He's to the right but it's a thinking right. He's smart and he'll listen to the other side. We need more pols like him. Too much screaming in Congress. Too much screaming everywhere."

I recalled the turbulent demonstrations I'd just driven through. Each side really looked like they wanted to kill the other. I believed that was the gist of the *Newsweek* article, Senator Stevenson's efforts to encourage bipartisanship in Washington.

Good luck, I thought.

I regarded my boss's children's artwork on the wall. A river dominated by a very large fish. A purple airplane. Rabbits.

"And Alberts?"

"Only met him once or twice. Typical

Beltway pro: political action committees, fund-raising, aide for senators on
the Finance Committee, Armed Services
and now Intelligence, with Stevenson."
Ellis was shifting in his chair. "You'll follow up?"

"With Alberts? I suppose."

"I need you to, Corte. Keep the purse-
string people happy . . . though *you*
don't look too happy about it."

"I can't testify in a hearing. I'm only
good because I don't exist."

"Alberts knows that. He only needs
leads to other agencies, the public
ones."

"You know what 'lead' translates into
in this line of work, don't you, Aaron?"

"Snitch?" my boss suggested.

The very word I had in mind.

Chapter 14

I returned to my office.

Barbara said, "Your coffee was cold so here's a new one. I just made it."

Ah. I thanked her and sipped. It was even worse than I'd remembered.

I punched SPEED DIAL.

"DuBois," the voice chirped. "You're in the building."

"For ten minutes or so. Can you come over here?"

She appeared a moment later and I wondered how the job had disrupted her plans for the weekend.

She had two cats and a boyfriend, who seemed like a regular, I deduced from snippets of conversation, but whom she didn't live with. I'd never met him; I don't socialize with colleagues. Her boyfriend was apparently always ready to come over to feed the animals and change the litter. I sometimes felt sorry for him. On the other hand, I wondered if he wasn't better off in that sort of relationship with Claire duBois, rather than living with her, which might be an exhausting proposition.

She sat across from me.

"Principals' phones." I handed her the bag containing the Kesslers' Nokias and Samsungs and BlackBerrys and their respective batteries, which I'd removed. She'd put them in the sealed room up the hall, in Hermes's work area. If Ryan or Joanne absolutely needed a number from their phones in an emergency and had no other way to get it, Hermes or a wizard in Technical would go inside, power up the phone and get the information, without any risk of a telltale signal escaping.

"Loving?" duBois asked.

"His partner was there but no further description or lead except a blue four-door, probably Buick. Nothing else."

A raised eyebrow. "Light or dark? Blue, I mean. There're about twenty-five shades of green for current passenger vehicles, I happen to know. Eighteen red. I haven't looked at blue, sorry, but it's probably the same. Oh, and they typically fade one degree of color temperature every six months. Depending."

"Darker."

She jotted this down in her ubiquitous notebook.

"Now, there's this." I handed her the plastic bag containing the trackers.

DuBois lifted a thick, dark eyebrow. "Two. Okay. You were telling me they do that sometimes. Sometimes three. In your car at the flytrap?"

I nodded. "Loving's partner did it. I need prints. And source of origin."

"I'll track them down," she said, without any irony at her choice of verb.

I asked, "Now, Ryan's cases?"

DuBois didn't need to glance at her notes. "First, the forgery. Graham, Eric. Forty-nine. Civilian employee of the DoD. Here's the background. They call it the Inner Circle, where he works. I think it's Ring E or something like that. Inside the center of the Pentagon. I couldn't find out exactly what he does, even with my ID and pulling strings, but we can go with it's classified and it involves weapons development."

"How'd you find that?" Weapons developers are very careful to make sure they never say they develop weapons.

"Checked his résumé, his clearances, correlated some times and places of meeting with a defense contractor or two. You know, sometimes you can tell more about somebody from what he doesn't tell you than what he does. I put it all together."

DuBois was really a gem.

She tucked away strands of hair, and the charms on her bracelet jingled. I saw a sterling silver dog, an armadillo, a baguette and a tiny silver King Wenceslas, which she'd bought in Prague when we'd been on assignment there. She continued, "No security incidents involving Graham. But something's come up, something odd. I don't know what to make of it." She was looking at my sandwich. "Is that dinner?"

I looked at my watch. It was a little after 4:30 p.m. I said, "It's more lunch. Go on. What else did you find, you were saying?"

"I went back to the Detective Bureau at the Metropolitan Police—to find out more—and it seems Graham's decided to drop the case."

"Dropping it?"

"He called the chief of detectives, Lewis, on Friday and told them he's not going to pursue it. He wants it dropped."

"Any reason?"

"Because of his job is what he's saying. Security issues. He doesn't want to be public."

"Seems odd. What does getting robbed have to do with national security? Ryan told me the perp didn't get anything sensitive, no computers or files from work."

DuBois agreed, "That's right."

"Why now?" I wondered. "Wouldn't he have been worried about that from the beginning and not even reported the theft in the first place?"

"You'd think. And there's something else. I checked the law. He's to blame. It seems if you're careless with your checkbook or your signature, if you're negligent, then the bank doesn't have to cover a forged check. It's your own insurance company that has to pay. Which isn't going to happen unless there's a police report."

I tried to understand this. "So essentially, he's taking a forty-thousand-dollar hit. Walking away."

"Is the government going to reimburse him? Now, that's not likely. I've been trying to get to talk to him. Which is *not* easy, I'll tell you. Go ahead. Eat. I saw you looking at the sandwich. You ever notice in restaurants if people are with somebody, they look at their food more than at the other person? If they're not with somebody, they watch people more than the food."

I said, "But Ryan didn't say anything about the case being dropped. I just talked to him about it at the Hillside."

"He probably didn't know. His assistant told me he was working out of the office all Thursday and Friday on some administrative thing. There's some big meeting next week about revamping accounting procedures in the department."

I recalled that Ryan had mentioned an internal assignment of some sort.

She asked, "So does that cross the Graham case off our primary list?"

"No. Just the opposite. Nobody ignores forty thousand dollars, unless they're being forced to." I ate some more of my sandwich.

"Dunch or linner," duBois was saying. "There's no meal in the afternoon corresponding to brunch." She wasn't making a joke.

I asked, "Your impressions of him, of Graham?"

DuBois considered. "Upset, evasive."

"Somebody's leveraging him to drop the case?"

"Possible. They don't make a lot of money, the Graham family. Without the forty K, his kid's not going back to Princeton. If that was me, I'd go all-out to nail the perp."

Some scenarios unfolded in my mind. "Okay, the primary forges the check, buys the gold and launders himself some cash. He spends it on something compromising—donation to a radical mosque, a big coke buy, prostitution, who knows? Maybe fronts that he's Graham. The money can be traced back.

The primary says, Give me access to secure files or sabotage the system you're working on, or I ruin your life forever and get you arrested. Graham agrees. Only Ryan's still on the case. The primary hires Henry Loving to find out what he knows."

"Plausible," duBois said.

"Now the other case. The Ponzi scheme."

Her azure eyes, framed by shiny dark hair, now dipped to her notes.

I'd Googled "Ponzi." I knew a bit about the scams from the Madoff thing, of course, you couldn't watch the news without learning something. The theory was that a scam artist would pose as an investment advisor and take people's money, which he would claim to invest. He'd keep the money for himself but would send out statements reporting that the fund had increased in value. If the early investors wanted to cash out, the thief would pay them off with more recent investment money—a scam that works fine as long as not all the investors want their money at the same time. They were usually discovered when customers got nervous and there was a run on the fund. In the Prisoners' Dilemma analysis of the depositors: acting with rational irrationality.

DuBois explained, "Now, the suspect, Clarence Brown—"

"The mail-order reverend."

"Not exactly. I checked his online church and—"

"Online?" That was a new one.

"Yep. Mail's not involved at all. You can download and print out your divinity degree. New Zion Church of the Brethren dot com. Anybody can do it. You could, I could. I wanted to see if it was as much of a scam as it seemed, and I got halfway to being a priest. Well, priestess, I guess. They wanted big money, though, and I logged off." On her bracelet were cross, Star of David and Islamic crescent charms. A cat with an excessively arched back and a witch's hat too. DuBois was not easy to define.

"Go on, Claire."

"He's a fake reverend but that's not the most interesting part. What I found out is that 'Clarence Brown' is an alias. He's really Ali Pamuk."

"He have a record?"

"Don't think so. Nothing in the standard databases. But I've got some friends looking into his history a little more closely. I'm particularly interested in doing-business-as records. I've got to correlate social security number, address, phone records, accounting statements, SEC filings."

I'd noted the reference to "friends," hardly an official U.S. government designation for an investigator. But, however duBois was doing this, it would be by the book. You could break all the rules you wanted in bodyguarding your principals—my job. But the task of finding the primary required us to be cops like any other, marshalling evidence and not giving the defense attorneys any windows through which the bird could escape.

"Any more details?"

"Turkish father, mother from Nigeria. Both naturalized. A few years ago he seems to have converted to Christianity, before he became a reverend. But he contributed a lot of money to a mosque in Virginia last year and the year before.

Not on any watchlists. He's kind of a player," duBois said. "Has that small place in the South East tenement, sure. But he also lives in the Watergate. Which he doesn't talk about much. State tells me he's been to Dubai, Jeddah and Jordan in the past two years."

This was a portrait very different from the one Ryan Kessler had uncovered.

"That's helpful." It was my highest compliment. "What about those smaller cases Ryan was running?" The cop had dismissed these but I'd asked her to talk to Chief of Detectives Lewis and check them out anyway.

"Oh, the stolen credit cards?" duBois continued. "They were all pretty small. Most of them got pled out. The identity thefts were bigger, low-class felonies. Most were pled. The big one was some kids ordering electronics online. They picked the wrong vic—a computer security expert with Advanced Circuit Design."

One of Intel's big competitors.

"The victim traced the perp and turned them in. But they got off with probation and fines. That's pretty neat. Somebody who got hacked got revenge by hacking in after the hackers. Rough justice."

I finished my sandwich, reflecting: some leads, yes, but nothing golden. I was frustrated. "Keep digging."

"Got my shovel."

"Both cases."

"Got my Indian clubs."

I gave her a smile. I hoped Cat Man treated her right.

Flipping through my phone, I jotted some information. "A few more things to look into." I slipped the note to her and gave her some more instructions. "A priority," I added.

"Sure."

"I've got to get the Kesslers to the safe house."

She rose. Hesitating.

I glanced at her, a gaze of curiosity.

"I heard, at the flytrap . . . Loving got pretty close."

She fell into a rare bout of silence.

But there was nothing to talk about regarding the topic of my brush with mortality. It was in the past, and what might have happened—Loving's death or mine—hadn't. There were no lessons to be learned from it, nothing for me to file away for future strategies, nothing to impart to her.

Speculation about the past is ineffi-cient. And therefore irrelevant to achiev-ing your goal.

So I simply regarded her with a neu-tral gaze.

"I'll get right on these, Corte," she said, using my name for what I believed was the first time in all the years we'd worked together.

Chapter 15

I collected Garcia's car, to which Billy had given a clean bill of surveillance health, and I piloted it back onto the highway. I made several bizarre but legal route changes and, when I was convinced nobody was following me, returned to the highway and drove toward the Hillside Inn.

At a little after 7:00 p.m. I arrived at the motel and parked behind it once more, in about the same spot as when I'd left, several spaces down from the Yukon.

I looked to the north and saw in the haze the distant hints of housing developments. I was probably looking at two or three thousand people . . . such a tiny sliver of the population in the county, and a smaller portion yet of the region. I couldn't help but think, as I often did on a job, that the lifter was out there somewhere. But where?

How close?

Thirty miles away, lost in the same speculation about where the principals and I were?

Or was he very close, a mile or less, with knowledge of our whereabouts and a clear strategy for killing the shepherds and kidnapping Ryan Kessler?

I returned to the room, calling Ahmad on the phone to announce my arrival. We don't use secret knocks, though it probably wouldn't be a bad idea. He let me in and I got a cup of black coffee from the kitchenette. The smell of room-service food—onions and garlic mostly—permeated the air. Two plates, one clean, one picked over, sat on a tray near the sink.

"We're going to be leaving soon, for the safe house."

Everyone was looking at me in anticipation and I realized that I'd left under mysterious circumstances. But keeping with need-to-know, I didn't explain about where I'd been, just told them they

should pack up anything they'd un-
packed when we arrived.

While Maree and Joanne were doing
this, I pulled Ryan aside. He'd had more
liquor, I could tell, but he didn't seem
any more inebriated than when I'd left.
"We've found out something about the
Graham case. He dropped the charges."

"He did what?" The cop was surprised. "That doesn't make sense. Are
you sure?"

I told him I was.

He continued, "When I first interviewed Graham he was furious about
the forgery. . . . Man has a temper, I'll
tell you. How was he going to pay for
his kid's tuition? The boy'd have to drop
out. All his dreams for his son were ruined. He was practically bullying me to
nail the perp. And now this?"

"When did you talk to him last?"

"Probably Tuesday."

"So something significant happened
between then and yesterday."

"That's when he dropped the charges?"

"Right."

Ryan said, "I was in meetings all day.
That accounting crap." He thought for a

moment. "So it's looking like that could be the relevant case."

"That's what I'm thinking. Something you found during the investigation could be a key to whoever's targeted him."

He sighed and said defensively, "It's tough to get information about people like that, the DoD, I mean. They don't talk to us little guys."

I had an idea he wouldn't like what I was about to tell him next—a significant fact about his other investigation that he hadn't uncovered. "And the Ponzi scheme?"

"Yeah?"

"Clarence Brown is a fake name. He's really Ali Pamuk." I explained what Claire duBois had found, then added that she was continuing to look into his background. But if Ryan was upset that a federal government sleuth had uncovered more information than he'd been able to find, he didn't show it. He was mostly confused by the turn the case had taken, it seemed.

"Legal name change?"

"We don't know yet. Now, is there anything that suggests you've uncovered facts in the investigation that some-body would want to have?"

He lowered his head and looked over my shoulder. I wondered at what. His wife, his sister-in-law, the armed guards? His hidden bottle of Wild Turkey or Mak-er's Mark? "I'm sorry, Corte. No, I can't think of anything. I'll keep looking. I'll keep thinking."

I glanced at my watch. I wanted to get everyone up to the safe house. I stepped outside and walked to the front desk, recalling again who I was.

I'm Frank Roberts. My company is Ar-tesian. We do kick-ass computer soft-ware designing.

I smiled at the man behind the desk and said, "We're going to be heading off. I'd like to settle up."

"Sure thing, Mr. Roberts," the man said. He was fidgeting, acting the way a clerk sometimes does when things weren't going quite by procedure. "Ev-erything okay?"

Meaning, why would you check out after just three or four hours?

"Oh, it's great, as always. We just needed the rooms for a sales meeting.

We finished up early and I'm taking the gang to a play downtown."

"Sure, sure. Tough, you gotta work on Saturday."

"Well, the company's paying for a night out, so there you go."

I looked over the bill and noted that someone had ordered a bottle of wine with the food they got from room service. Ryan, of course; no one else seemed to be drinking. I was a little irritated. It was always a pain to get liquor expenses approved. And didn't he have an entire bar in that backpack of his?

I thanked the clerk and I returned to the room.

When Rudy Garcia opened the door I glanced inside and saw Maree, laughing as she spoke to her sister. I frowned as I examined the scene. The women weren't in the common living area; they were in a bedroom to the side and I was watching them in the mirror.

I asked him, "Did you get the Kesslers and Maree into the bedroom when the room service got here?"

"Oh, sure."

"Was the door open? To the bedroom there?"

He was looking back. "Well, I don't know. I made sure they were out of sight."

I was grimacing. "From the reflection too?"

The agent studied the mirror. "I . . . oh, shit."

"Did the bellboy act odd?"

"He was pretty nervous, now that you ask."

I closed the door behind me and pointed Ahmad to the back windows and Garcia to the front. Without a word, they drew their side arms and moved fast into defensive positions. I swept the lights out throughout the room.

I called to Joanne and Maree, "Bedroom lights out. Now."

A pause and then that room went dark too.

"What's going on?" Joanne asked, alarmed, stepping into the doorway.

"I think Loving's found us and's on his way."

Or more likely, I reflected, he was already here.

Chapter 16

My mind had done something that occasionally happens when I'm playing certain types of games against a skilled opponent.

Via instinct, I understand exactly what their strategies are. This usually occurs in games with what's called perfect information, like chess or tic-tac-toe. Perfect information means that all of a player's past moves—his strategies—are accessible to his opponent. Both see every move made from the beginning of the game. (Unlike the Prisoners' Dilemma, say, which is a game of *imperfect* information, since Prisoner One doesn't know what Prisoner Two's choice will be.)

For some reason, at times, all the past moves the opponent has made coalesce in my mind into a clear understanding—

for me it's almost a graphic or picture—
and I know what his next strategy will
be.

Now, the pieces falling into place were
the clear view of my principals in the
mirror, the manager's uneasiness in the
front lobby a few minutes earlier, the
bellboy's nervousness.

Though I didn't know all the details, I
believed almost to a certainty that Loving had posed as a law enforcement officer and sent faxes or emails to dozens
of hotels and motels in the area—maybe
the ones he felt might be good safe
houses. He'd included a picture of Ryan
Kessler, claiming perhaps that he was a
fugitive. Loving would have given a
phone number and instructions to call
but warned the managers not to take
any action on their own in the event the
suspect was spotted. The manager
would have shown the picture to the
wait staff. When the food was delivered
to our room, the employee would have
gotten a glance in the mirror at Ryan
and probably seen the man's damn Colt
on his hip.

The manager wasn't fidgety because I

was unhappy with the service and checking out early; it was that two women and
I were hostages of Ryan Kessler and the
men with him—tough, unsmiling and
dangerous-looking.

The big question as far as I was concerned was when exactly the manager
had called Loving. Ten minutes earlier,
we probably would be fine. An hour,
Loving was already nearby.

"Clear," each of my colleagues reported in his own accent.

I called Freddy. He picked up at once.
"Corte."

"We have a situation."

"You just had one, at the flytrap."

"Loving's on his way here. The Hillside
Inn." I rattled off the address.

"Okay, hold on. I'm scrambling our
people—and Prince William County
too."

"Try them. But I'll bet he's going to
call in a fake incident, like he did in Fairfax."

"Sure. Right."

"Just concentrate on getting your folks
here. Fast."

I ignored the frantic looks my principals sent me as they threw together their personal items. I did, however, gesture at Ryan Kessler to put his pistol away. With that much liquor he could shoot his wife, or me, or himself. Thank God his weapon was a revolver, which meant the trigger had a heavy pull. I noticed him looking at me with a broad shrug and I realized his meaning: Isn't this what we're supposed to be doing, luring Loving here and then taking him out, like I'd told him earlier?

Bait-and-switch . . .

Reluctantly he slipped the gun back into the holster.

Freddy came back on the line. "Cavalry's on the way. ETA probably twenty or thirty. You going defense? Or rabbiting?"

"I don't know yet. Patch me through one of your public lines to the motel lobby here. And don't mask it. I want the clerk to see Justice Department or the Bureau on caller ID."

"Yeah, hold. I lose you, call me back. I don't know this technical shit."

As the people in the room gathered jackets and suitcases, and my colleagues moved efficiently from window to window to door, signaling that they spotted no threat, I waited tensely, listening to clicks on the line.

Finally, ringing.

"Hillside Inn, may I help you?" It was the man I'd spoken to before. I'd just have to hope that he wouldn't recognize my voice.

I said briskly, "Yessir, this is Special Agent Hugh Johnston. We're following up on that report about the suspect at your motel."

"I was just about to call back about that. They're fixing to leave!"

So I was right.

"A hostage came in—Mr. Roberts," the clerk continued. "He looked pretty beat up. He's been here before, works for a company and they use our place some. He paid. Tried to act like nothing was going on but it's weird, them checking out after only four or five hours or so."

"I'm coordinating the rescue efforts," I told him. "Which agent did you speak to before?"

"Said his name was Special Agent Jonathan Corte, with an *e.*"

My stomach did a little flip at Loving's perverse sense of humor, if that was what it was. Jonathan was his own middle name.

"And," I asked, "when did you call him exactly?"

"Had to be forty-five minutes ago, just after Benny got a look at the kidnapper when he delivered the food. He's got a gun but I guess you know that. You have to move fast, they'll be leaving any minute."

"All right. Now listen," I said seriously. "The MO of this man—you know MO?"

"Modus operandi. The wife and I watch *Criminal Minds.*"

"His MO is that he sometimes leaves somebody behind to stop pursuers. You understand what I'm saying? I want you to try to keep everybody inside their rooms for the next hour or so. I don't want any innocents caught in a cross fire."

"God . . . Sure. Okay. I'll do what I can. God."

I disconnected and rubbed my fore-

head as I debated, considering the tim-
ing. Loving had heard forty-five minutes
ago that we were here. He and his partner would have to rendezvous, ditch the
car Loving had collected on the embankment near the flytrap. They'd switch
wheels, which would take a little time.

But not much.

Rock, paper, scissors . . .

Defense or rabbit?

I thought for a moment. "Okay, we're
going. Now, fast."

"Still clear," Garcia said, peeking out
through a splinter of window.

Ahmad echoed him.

Then Ryan limped closer to me, the
skin around his drunken eyes crinkled.
"Corte, come on, we can take him. We
can do it. There's four of us. Jesus
Christ, we're running from one man."

"Two," Joanne corrected. "His partner. And he could have more."

Ryan ignored her and said to me, "You
just called for backup. Look, it's perfect.
He doesn't know we know about him.
He'll walk into a trap. Get him in a cross
fire!"

I said, "No. My job is to get you away."

"I'm tired of running. I'm tired of this crap. Fuck it, Corte. You get Joanne and Maree out of here. Take 'em to that safe house. I'll stay. Him too." He looked at Ahmad, who wore two weapons.

"We don't do last stands, Ryan. Too many innocents."

"There're always innocents around, Corte. There're always excuses for not doing what you should."

"Ryan," Joanne snapped. "Please! I'm scared."

I calmly said, "*This* is not the time or place for a firefight. It's not the rational choice to engage." Implying: The safe house we're headed for is better.

"Honey," she begged. "Please."

With the obligatory look of disgust, Ryan grabbed his belongings. "Fuck."

I gazed over Ahmad's shoulder into the courtyard of the hotel. What troubled me were the dozens of black windows facing us across the parking lot and garden. We would have to exit the suite, turn to the left and traverse about fifty feet, exposed to those windows, before we got to the alley that would lead us behind the building where the Yukon was parked.

I regarded the windows of those rooms facing us. You couldn't open them but every hitter or lifter in the world knows the two-shot technique of firing through windows—first bullet aimed way off target into the sky or ground to take the glass out without letting your target know he or she is under fire and then the money shot a moment later.

Still, we'd have to take the risk. I knew the Yukon was safe; it had a security system that called the key fob in my pocket if somebody so much as breathed on the bumper. I decided to break us up into separate groups. That way Loving or his partner—a good shot, I now knew from experience—couldn't hit all of the personal security officers at once. "We're going to the SUV, behind the building, three groups. Garcia, you're with Maree. Ahmad, Joanne. Ryan's with me." In the air I drew a letter U on its left side, explaining, "Garcia, you first. Out the door, down the sidewalk to the left. Hold at the alley to the parking lot and cover us.

Ahmad, you next. Go all the way to the lot and hold there. You cover the back."

"Roger."

"We'll go next and cover your retreat to the lot," I said to Garcia.

Her pretty jaw trembling, Maree looked like she was going to cry. The flippancy was gone completely. In many ways she was a child in a woman's body.

"I'll start the SUV remotely. Jump in and get your belts on. Okay. Now."

Garcia and Maree moved slowly along the sidewalk as I crouched in the doorway, looking for threats. I saw no obvious ones.

My phone buzzed.

"Freddy."

"Just for the record, he tried the same thing—false alarms. Prince William's had ten assault-in-progress calls. Just like you guessed."

I hadn't guessed. I was learning Loving's strategy.

"But our guys are en route. Make it fifteen minutes now."

"We're leaving. He found out about us forty-five minutes ago. He's got to be

close by now. I can't talk." I disconnected.

Garcia and Maree were behind a pil-
lar, the agent scanning those black, leer-
ing windows looking down on us. The
rooftops too.

Ahmad went next with grim-faced
Joanne, again clutching her purse to her
chest and wheeling her suitcase. They
hurried past Garcia and turned left down
the alley to the parking lot.

I got a sign from Garcia.

"Let's go," I whispered to Ryan.

I started one of the longest walks of
my life.

I was close to Ryan and knew that
Loving wouldn't risk killing him to take
me out, despite the partner's skill as a
sniper, but they might have sprayed our
legs and kept Garcia and Ahmad pinned
down while they dragged Ryan away.

But we joined Garcia without incident
and, as I covered the troubling windows,
he and Maree slipped to the back lot.
When they'd made it, Ryan and I moved
out. My pistol in one hand, the key fob
in the other, I pressed the start button
for the Yukon. I hadn't expected an ex-

plosion but I still felt relieved when there wasn't one. We hurried forward and scrambled inside the vehicle, belting up and locking the doors.

No incoming shots, no diversions—screams or collisions—to take our attention.

In ten seconds I was out of the space fast and we were heading around the back of the wing on the right of the motel, the way we'd come in. I eased to the front and merged onto the main driveway, which led to the highway via a hundred yards of winding asphalt. I was trying to narrow down the time calculation to gauge how likely it was that Loving was close.

I was angry with myself. Most shepherds used the two-part transport to get their principals to the ultimate safe house. It makes sense—to organize your escape, to make sure nobody's following, to change vehicles. I reflected that my strategy, however, had backfired; it was because of going to a public facility that Loving had a lead to us. If I'd driven right to our safe house, we'd be home free.

Just as I often pretend to be a lifter, to anticipate their moves, I wondered if Loving had stepped into *my* shoes, compiling names of hotels that'd make good halfway houses. Maybe he had the same list we did.

But so far, so good. We were in an armored SUV and my principals were unhurt. No sign of Loving. Most likely it had taken him longer than I'd thought to get here.

Rolling farther along the drive . . .

I could see the highway eighty yards away, then sixty, fifty.

Oh, how I wanted to be on that road. The Hillside Inn was a great place to be invisible and the suite we'd taken was good for defense. But here in front of the building were hedgerows and trees for cover and ponds to limit escape routes and a very serpentine drive—picturesque but hard to see in the dusk without headlights.

It was, in short, a great spot for an ambush.

Forty yards from the road.

I rolled fast over a speed bump.

Thirty yards.

Ahead, the driveway cut through a thick hedge, eight feet high, which separated the highway from the grounds. I saw a Nissan van waiting to make a left turn into the motel grounds from the far lane. The driver was a woman and I could see a child belted in beside her. Not a threat.

But then I hit the brakes.

"What?" Ryan asked.

"Why isn't she turning?" I asked no one.

The woman had been waiting too long for oncoming traffic to pass before she made her left turn into the inn's drive. I could see in her windshield the flash of an oncoming car's turn signal. That driver, making a right turn into the inn would have the right of way.

But he wasn't turning.

Then I saw the vague form of a man settling into the thick boxwood. Something in his hand. A weapon? That's why Loving was pausing on the road—somehow he'd spotted us leaving the back of the motel and he'd told his partner to climb out and flank us.

Did I have time to get away before he aimed and fired?

I jammed the accelerator to the floor. But as we leapt forward, Henry Loving's black Dodge Avenger skidded to a stop before us, blocking the drive.

I hit the brake pedal. We faced each other.

An endless moment, silence in the car, silence outside. Then the partner, hidden somewhere in the bushes, opened fire, as the tires on Loving's car squealed to smoke and he sped directly toward us.

Chapter 17

I slammed the shifter into reverse; a three-point turn would have taken too much time. I shoved the pedal to the floor.

I heard a jarring bang from the side of our vehicle as the partner continued to fire on us from the bushes. But I'd moved just as he was pulling the trigger and the slug hit the sheetmetal, not tires. Which was good; run-flats are impressive but they're not indestructible.

Another slam of a bullet on the body steel. The sound was very loud. Unlike in the movies, you never hear whining ricochets and you never see sparks. A bullet is a piece of lead that's moving about three thousand feet a second. You hear a big, big bang when it hits your car and it usually stays where it's sent and doesn't bounce around the neighborhood.

"Covering fire," I ordered. "Keep the partner down. But visible hostiles or neutral targets only. Do not shoot blind. Everybody else, stay down."

Ryan was in the far back—there were three rows of seats in the car—and Garcia and the women in the seats just behind me.

"Garcia, muzzle flash to your left!"

"Got it." He rolled down the window a few inches and began firing judiciously. Regulations prohibit us from discharging a weapon unless we have a clear target and there could possibly be bystanders nearby. Garcia shot toward where the partner had stationed himself in a thick stand of bush but was aiming only at a tree or the ground, to keep the partner down while making sure no innocents were hit.

Loving's car was pursuing us and, still driving in reverse, I called to Ahmad, next to me, to target him. But it was particularly difficult to do so because of the curvature of the driveway lined with trees. I had to swerve wildly, depriving my colleague of a clear shot.

Another slug from the partner's gun impacted the Yukon's side. Maree barked a brief scream, her hand to her mouth, eyes wide. Ryan was trying to open the rear window—which was sealed shut. His revolver was in his hand but at least his finger was outside the trigger guard.

In four-wheel drive, the Yukon bounded backward, churning up a nice cloud of dust.

My head spun around briefly, glancing behind us through the front windshield. I saw Loving's car coming after us fast, veering to avoid Ahmad's rounds. I turned back again to look out the rear window, in the direction we were speeding.

Ahmad called, "Loving's slowing." His voice was calm.

"Garcia, take your shot."

The FBI agent leaned over Joanne, who looked numb with fear, her purse clutched to her chest. He eased out the window. "The trees," Garcia called. "I don't have a clear shot."

"I'll do it!" Ryan muttered. "I'll get the fucker."

This brought Joanne to life. "No, honey, please! You've been drinking."

"Goddamnit, I'm a better shot drunk than all of them put together." He strained forward. But we were saved from a confrontation because we hit a speed bump and he was knocked to the side. Thank God his weapon didn't discharge.

Garcia leaned forward and fired in bursts of three with his handgun.

I couldn't tell if he'd hit anything. I couldn't be concerned with that now; I had the Yukon up to about forty in four-wheel reverse, the transmission screaming, and we were crashing over speed bumps and tearing the shrubbery apart.

A bullet thudded into the back of the Yukon, the fender or bumper. One glanced off the windshield. No glass broke; it was resistant but not bullet-proof, depending on the jackets of the rounds, so I was thankful there'd been no direct hit on the windows, though it made sense; Loving would not want to risk killing Ryan.

Then, about ten yards from the motel, a straight stretch loomed.

"Both of you," I called to Garcia and

Ahmad. "You'll have clear targets in about five seconds. Go for the grille of the Dodge. Take out the engine."

"No, the windshield!" Ryan shouted.

I said nothing else, not explaining that the rational move in a situation like this was to aim for a vital area of the car; you'd have to be very lucky to hit the driver.

But just as we leveled out, Loving ditched the lights and veered to the right. The Dodge skidded behind a bush beside a curve in the driveway and vanished over the lawn.

"No target," Ahmad called calmly.

But I didn't slow; I kept speeding backward, my sweating hands clutching the wheel so hard my wrists were cramping. "Garcia, call Fredericks. Let him know."

"Yessir."

He alerted Freddy of the situation, then disconnected and took up a defensive position again, basically sprawled over Joanne. Maree was huddled in the corner, sobbing.

"Hold on, watch your weapons." I hit the next speed bump at close to 50 miles per hour, still in reverse. We bounced into the inn's courtyard and I continued on, toward the back, with a fast glance into the lobby, where the panicked clerk was on the phone.

"Where?" I shouted. "Loving, where is he?"

"No sign!" Ahmad called.

The gears were screaming now and the floorboard seemed to be hot. Reverse was not made for these speeds.

"Coming to the end of the drive," I called. "Big bump! Fingers off triggers and hold on."

Without slowing we careened over the curb through the narrow gap we'd just taken on foot ten minutes earlier in our three teams, to get to the rear parking lot. I destroyed a low row of bushes and then bounded onto a concrete patio that jutted into the parking lot, sending the colorful lawn furniture sprawling over the asphalt. Glass from the tables shattered loudly. I skidded the vehicle to the left and braked to a stop, gasping for breath. My shoulders ached.

Running parallel to the motel on the other side of the parking lot was a six-foot stockade fence. To the left was a brick wall about four feet high. To the right was the driveway we'd just exited by and beyond that a small thicket of trees.

"No, no, no," Maree was wailing. "We're trapped. What're we going to do? Oh, Jesus."

"You'll be okay," Joanne said to her sister.

"I'm so fucking scared."

"Stay on the alley, the driveway and the trees," I said to Ahmad, nodding to what we'd just backed through and the small forest beyond.

"Garcia, the brick wall."

"Yessir. I'm on it!"

"Shadow in the alley," Ahmad said. "Somebody's coming. In a car, looks like."

"Now!" Ryan called. "Ram him! He'll be coming through there any second. He thinks you're still going. Hit the gas!"

I ignored him.

Ahmad had opened his window further and was aiming his weapon toward the alley.

"What are you going to do?" The urgent question came not from Ryan, as I might have thought, but from his wife.

I didn't answer her either.

Ahmad said, "Shadow's getting closer."

I glanced that way. A car was slowly following our route along the path we'd just torn along. Cautious.

"It's him," Ryan said. "The lights're out. Ram him! Ram him!"

"Garcia, the brick wall. Stay with it."

"Yessir."

"Forget the fucking wall. He's coming up the path between the buildings!" Ryan blurted. "You can see it!"

"No, he's not," I said. "Loving's forced somebody to drive their car up here slowly. Just like in Fairfax. He and the partner split up to flank us from the trees and from the brick wall. Ahmad, take out the tire of the car that comes through the gap. The driver'll get spooked and stop. Then watch the driveway and those trees beyond it. Garcia, the wall."

They acknowledged the orders.

The feint car hood edged slowly into view from the alley.

Ahmad shot out the tire and immediately lifted his weapon's muzzle, staring past the vehicle. "Can't see clearly but think there's somebody in the woods. Solo."

"Brick wall," Garcia called. "It's Loving's car. They're flanking us."

"Covering fire," I shouted. "Both directions. Mind innocents."

Both men fired, driving Loving back. The partner too vanished under cover in the woods.

"They're going to try again," Maree said, still crying. "We're trapped here!"

Now they knew we were ready for them. I dropped the transmission into four-wheel low gear and turned directly toward the stockade fence.

"What're you doing?" Maree gasped. "No! We'll get stuck!"

I nosed the Yukon against the wood and, a slight nudge, the panel of fencing broke free. I drove over it and into the farm field on the other side.

I ordered, "Target the gap in the fence. But don't fire unless you're sure it's them. There'll be spectators now." I was heading slowly down the hill toward a line of trees.

Surprisingly it was Joanne Kessler

who caught on. "You had that escape route planned. You cut mostly through the fence posts, so you could drive over it if you needed to. When?"

"A couple years ago."

I pick all my halfway houses for escape as well as defensibility and I do a lot of work on the properties late at night. The Hillside Inn people never knew I'd vandalized their fence.

"I don't see anything," Ryan said. "Not yet."

We rolled slowly down the hill, slick with dew, then through a series of soft dirt rows of recently harvested corn husks and stems. You could measure the progress in feet but we were moving steadily.

"Still nobody," Ahmad said.

I ordered them to keep targeting the opening in the fence we'd just eased through, though I knew that Loving would take one look at the ground we were traversing and know that his sedan couldn't possibly pursue us.

He'd make the only rational decision he could: to retreat as fast as possible.

Chapter 18

A half hour later we were on the highway again, heading for the safe house.

It was a little after 8:00 p.m. and I'd been driving a fast, complicated and unpredictable route generally north though Loudoun and Fairfax counties.

In the back Ryan Kessler sat brooding, looking through his canvas bag. For ammo? Or booze? Joanne was quiet, staring out the window. Maree, calm finally, fidgeted with a pacifier, her computer. She was coming out of her hysteria but hadn't yet returned to referring flippantly to me as a tour guide.

Principals get terrified, of course. Disoriented too, and a little bit crazy. I need the people in my organization to be 100 percent with me. My principals, though? If they can be 75 or 80, if they can do what I ask with a measure of promptness and intelligence, I'm content. A sizable portion of my task is fixing as many of their inevitable mistakes as I can and minimizing the principals' more destructive foibles and habits.

Which is not a bad philosophy of life, I'd decided.

In fact, this was a typical sampling of principals' behavior. From experience I found Joanne's numbness more worrisome than her husband's bluster and her sister's juvenile banter and hysteria. Principals like her could melt down suddenly and explosively, and usually it happened at exactly the wrong time.

I glanced back in the mirror and my eyes met hers, which were blank and unfocused, and we simultaneously looked away.

Now that I was comfortable that there were no tails—it would be purest coincidence that Loving would find us—I made the call.

"Hello?" the deep voice answered.

"Aaron."

My boss responded, "Corte, I heard from Fredericks, at the Hillside Inn. He said you were okay. I assumed you were on the run and I didn't want to call."

"Thanks." This was one of his best attributes: He might have no instinctive feel for shepherding but he understood how we operated and he accommodated his job to ours. I said, "I haven't talked to Freddy yet. Any casualties there?"

He answered, "No, but it's a mess. They picked up a lot of brass, must've been forty, fifty shots fired. Two slugs hit guest rooms with people inside. I can't keep the lid on this one."

"What'll it be?"

"Loving gave us an out with the press, believe it or not. We'll springboard on what he said in his fax—that there was talk of a kidnapping and some organized crime involvement. I'll trot out Bad Hector. I don't have much choice."

Hector Carranzo was a small-time Colombian drug figure who was named in a number of felony warrants both here and in various Latin American countries. The reports gave mixed descriptions and vague background but all included warnings of his dangerous nature and the admonition to be on the lookout for him anywhere in the country. He was known to pop up unexpectedly.

He was also a complete fiction. When we had a shootout like the one at the Hillside Inn, under circumstances where we wanted to keep the truth quiet, we blamed the incident on Señor Hector and "possible drug or other illegal activity we have yet to identify with specificity." After we collared the primary in the Ryan Kessler case, Ellis might come back in a few days with: Ooops, we were wrong; the real perp was actually so-and-so. But Bad Hector would keep the press busy for a time.

"We're on the way to the safe house now."

"Good. Get there and stay there." A pause. I knew what he'd say next. "We all want to get him, Corte. But I want you to sit tight in the safe house. No more attempts to engage Loving."

He'd be thinking of Rhode Island.

"Only the flytrap was offensive. What happened at the Hillside was pure defense. We were trying to get away."

"I understand that. . . . But there may

be some issue raised of why you used a halfway in this situation. Why you didn't go directly to the safe house."

Meaning, I supposed, was I subconsciously—or perhaps very consciously—trying to draw Loving to us? He wanted a reason. But, even though he was my boss, I wasn't going to answer.

He caught this and continued, "It was your call and I'm not questioning it. Just telling you that the question could come up."

I told him, "If I do anything at all, it'll just be to help Claire track down the primary."

"Fine," he muttered. Ellis was having a tough Saturday, so he wasn't treading softly any longer. "You didn't call Westerfield. You said you would."

"I will. It's been busy."

Which, though true, sounded lame.

We disconnected and I was scrolling through numbers to find Westerfield's. But then Freddy's name was recited on my audible caller ID.

I clicked ACCEPT and asked, "You get *anything* at the Hillside?"

Freddy said, "No trace. He vanished—

real fast. Like Houdini. Or the allowance I give my kids. Thin air."

"Aaron said no injuries."

"Right. People're shaken up. But so what? Life shakes you up. Nothing wrong with getting shook once in a while. Aaron's handling the press? There're more reporters than you can shake a stick at."

"He'll do what he can."

Freddy added that the hostage Loving had taken, to coerce her husband to drive his car after us as a diversion, was safe. "Not that it mattered but she said she couldn't identify her kidnapper. The husband got amnesia too."

I asked, "Any indication which way Loving went?"

"None."

"We take out their Dodge?"

"Yup. Fan and a tire. They left it fifty yards west, where they had switch wheels hidden. The abandoned one was clean. And the new one? No tire treads our boys and girls could find. And you know them. . . . If there's a pubic hair, they'll get it."

"So was there a fax with Ryan's picture on it?"

"Yep."

"Who was it supposed to be from? You guys?"

"Federal Department of Tax Investigation."

I nearly smiled. An outfit as phony as Artesian Computer Design. You had to hand it to Loving.

I told him, "It said the typical: Don't try to apprehend, just give a call if you see him? And an eight hundred number?"

"Prepaid mobile."

"Now deactivated," I said.

Freddy didn't need to confirm this.

"What was the incoming fax number?"

"Sent from a computer through a Swedish proxy."

Naturally.

Freddy wondered, "How'd he tip to the Hillside specifically and send the fax there?"

"I think he went fishing. Sent faxes to dozens of possible halfway houses. I'll bet they're sitting in front lobbies all over the area."

"Jesus," he exhaled, pronouncing the name with an initial *H.* Maybe he was worried about being sacrilegious. I knew he went to church at least once a week. "This guy's earning his fee. What the hell does Kessler know that's so friggin' important?"

Just what Claire duBois and I were going to find out in the next few hours, I hoped.

Then Freddy got my attention, asking, "You know somebody named Sandy Alberts?"

"He give you a call?"

"Came to the office. Works for that senator from Indiana or Ohio, Stevenson."

"I know who he is. Ohio. What'd Alberts want?"

"Just asking questions. About wiretaps, Patriot Act, so on and so forth. Got to say, Corte, your name came up. All happy, cheerful, good things. But, well, like I said, your name came up. Find that interesting."

Interesting, I reflected glumly. "And?"

"No 'and.' I told him I was busy. Had to go."

"Thanks," I muttered.

"For what?"

"I'm not sure."

We disconnected and I considered Albert's visit to Freddy.

Then I decided I could no longer delay the inevitable. I scrolled down and found Westerfield's number. Hit SEND.

The man answered on the second ring. My heart sank; I'd been hoping for voice mail. "Corte," he said and didn't slip into French. "Listen, we need to talk. But I'm in with the AG right now."

He was sitting in the U.S. attorney general's office on Saturday night . . . and he'd taken my call?

"I'll get back to you when we're through. This number?"

"Yes."

"You have an alternate?"

"No."

Click.

I pulled off onto a side road and stopped. Maree gasped and looked up, alarmed, her psychic pendulum still on the hysterical side. Joanne slipped from her coma long enough to say to her, "It's okay. It'll be okay."

"Why're we stopping?" the younger woman asked, her voice on edge.

I said, "Just checking the car. We took some hits."

Ryan began scanning the dark roadside like a sniper for prey.

Ahmad climbed out of the back and joined me and we inspected the Yukon carefully. It wasn't badly damaged from the shootout or the rough escape. The SUV was doing better than my back was.

As we checked the tires, I glanced up and saw Joanne, still in the back seat, look at her watch and place a call. It was to Amanda. From the conversation, which I could hear through the open door, it seemed everything was fine. She caught my eye again then lowered her head and continued the call. She was struggling to be animated as her stepdaughter apparently pelted her with a report of her day in the country.

Ryan took the phone and, his face softening, also had a conversation with the girl.

Parents and children.

For a moment some of those memories I'd had earlier surfaced, some children's faces among them, memories I didn't want. I put them away. Sometimes I was better at that than others. Tonight they vanished more slowly than usual.

I got back inside and when the door slammed Ryan spun around, startled, and gripped his gun. I tensed for a moment but he oriented himself and relaxed.

My Lord, did he want to shoot *everybody*?

As I started to drive, my phone buzzed and the caller ID voice announced a number I recognized as the Justice Department. My finger hovered over the ACCEPT button.

I didn't press it. The call went to voice mail and I steered the Yukon back to the main road.

Chapter 19

More dark, winding routes.

Nobody was behind us, unless he was driving without lights, which was possible, thanks to the new night vision systems. But the way I was driving—fast then slow, occasionally abrupt stops, sharp turns down roads that I knew well but I doubted Loving would—left me convinced that no one was following.

After forty minutes I hit Route 7 briefly then Georgetown Pike and took it to River Bend Road. Then, bypassing downtown Great Falls, I took a series of tangled roads and streets on which GPS was helpful but not definitive.

Finally, after a drive through dense woods, during which we passed no more than three houses—three very large houses—we arrived at the safe house compound, separated from the road by a seven-foot-high stockade and, farther along, six-foot chain-link fences.

The compound had a seven-bedroom main house, two outbuildings—one of them a panic facility—and two large garages, as well as a barn, complete with a hayloft. The grounds were nearly ten acres of rolling fields, bordering the Potomac River, the turbulent part, the narrows, where there is indeed a series of falls and rapids, though "Great Falls" is by anyone's estimation exaggerated; "Modest but Picturesque" would be a better name.

The property had been a bargain. You can't be in any government service nowadays without being aware of the bottom line. In the nineties, the compound had been the residence of Chinese diplomats, a retreat from the embassy downtown. It was also, the FBI had learned, where the People's Republic secret police regularly met their runners and agents, who'd been collecting information from contractors and low-level government workers and taking pictures of the NSA, the CIA and other unmentionable facilities in Langley, Tysons and

Centreville. Most of the work, it was learned, was commercial property theft rather than defense secrets. But it was politically naughty, not to mention illegal.

When the Chinese got busted, the delicate negotiations involved an agreement that the diplomats and fake businessmen would leave the country without prosecution and, in exchange, the government would get the house . . . and some other, nondisclosed, treats. The property was used by a number of agencies as a hideaway until Abe had grabbed it for us about eight years ago.

The large, brown-painted nineteenth-century house itself had been retrofitted with all the accoutrements of modern-day security that we could afford. Which wasn't as high-tech or sexy as people might expect. There were sensors on the fence, though they would deter only people who didn't know about sensors on fences. The grounds themselves weren't monitored everywhere, though at key approaches (not necessarily the obvious ones) there were weight sensors buried in the dirt. Of course, the whole place was amply covered by video cameras, some obvious, some not. I'd activated an employee, what we call spectators, or specs, that morning to begin monitoring the place. Ours sit in West Virginia, in a dim room, and watch TV screens all day long and—though they don't admit it—listen to really loud music, usually headbanging. They can do so because our cameras aren't miked. That takes too much bandwidth. Someday we'll be able to afford both, and the specs'll lose their sound tracks. But for now, it's silent movies of the compound and Def Leppard coming from the speakers.

I called the spec assigned to us and he answered immediately.

"We're here," I said, though he knew that since he'd been watching us for the past five minutes.

It was quiet, he reported. He'd seen nothing suspicious.

"Where're the deer?"

"Where the deer should be."

Because of this job and some other aspects of my life, I've learned a lot about wildlife—for instance, what intimidates deer and other animals and why. I've told my specs—and protégés—always to watch for patterns of animal behavior that might give away clues as to intrusion. I'd actually lectured on this at professional conferences. An uneasy badger saved the life of one of my principals a year ago, alerting us to a hitter's presence.

"No funny business with nearby traffic either," was the spec's twangy comment. I'd never met the man but I had some impressions. Given his residence in the mountains of West Virginia, his accent and his taste for heavy metal, how could I not?

I thanked him and punched in the code to the front gate, which swung open and a nearly invisible but impressive tire strip receded into the ground. We headed through the stockade fence and up the winding drive, which was about a hundred feet long. Garcia and Ahmad were looking around, carefully, as were Maree and the still alert Ryan Kessler, who I believed had snuck a drink or two. Joanne glanced out the window as if she were looking at a month-old magazine in a doctor's waiting room.

I parked and we got out. Beside the front door—looking like wood but reinforced steel—I opened a panel and typed on the keypad below a small LCD screen. The program confirmed via motion, sound and thermal sensors that the house was completely unoccupied (it can identify a beating human heart but won't bother me with the sound of a river rat nosing about for food or the water heater coming to life). I unlocked the door and stepped inside, then temporarily disabled the alarm; it would reactivate once we were inside and then would lock, though there was a panic button that would allow anyone inside to open it in the event of fire or intrusion. The same was true of most windows, which otherwise would open only six inches.

I got the lights on and the heat going—the temperature had dipped—and then I booted up our bank of security monitor screens, which mirrored the ones in West Virginia. Next the secure computer server. I checked to see that the shielded landlines were working. Finally, I verified that the generators were armed; they'd come on automatically if an intruder cut the main line.

I showed the principals briefly around the musty ground floor.

"Oh, neat!" Maree said, striding up to a number of old, sepia-tinted photographs on the wall, ignoring shelves of books and magazines and, yes, board games, though not ones I'd donated. Looking at the younger sister's giddy expression, I tried to recall when I'd had a principal who could so quickly forget that she'd been part of a shootout an hour earlier. Never, I decided.

I explained about food, beverages, the TV. Like a bellboy. I took the Kesslers to their room on this floor in the back, Maree to hers next to it. The young woman seemed impressed. "You're redeeming yourself, Mr. Tour Guide," she said. She offered me a dollar as a tip, a joke, I guessed. I didn't know how to respond and so I ignored the odd gesture. She offered another pout.

Ahmad, Garcia and I would sleep in shifts, with two guards always awake and on duty. The shepherd's bedroom was a small one on the ground floor, between the front door and the bedrooms for the principals.

I knew the layout of the compound and the safe house perfectly and Ahmad, who'd never been here, had studied the place. I'd tested him several times—most recently a month ago— and I knew that he was familiar with the layout. I had him brief Garcia and I explained to the FBI agent about the com system and the weapons locker. I gave him the combination to the lock. Inside there wasn't much; some H&Ks and M4 Bushmasters, tripped to fully auto, sidearms and flash-bang grenades, like the sort that we'd used against Loving at the flytrap.

With my principals now safely inside their fortress, I walked into the den, which I used as my office, sat at the ancient oak desk and booted up my laptop. I plugged it and my phone into the wall socket; in the personal security business there are many important rules, Abe had recited, but high on the list:

"Never miss a chance to recharge batteries or use the bathroom."

I'd done the former; I now did the latter, walking into the front bedroom. I washed my hands and face in the hottest water I could stand and checked the scrapes and bruises from the pursuit of Loving at the flytrap. Nothing serious, though my back ached like hell from the jarring escape in the Yukon at the Hillside Inn.

I walked through the house, checking sensors and making sure all the software and com systems were working. I felt like an engineer.

Personal security is a state-of-the-art profession; it has to be, since the bad guys know all the toys . . . and have seemingly unlimited budgets to buy them. Although, as you'd think with somebody who prefers board to computer games, I'm not inherently high tech, I nonetheless made sure we too had the latest gadgets: explosives sniffers as small as a computer mouse, which they resemble; high-density carbon-fiber detectors for nonmetallic firearms, audio sensors that can alert us to the sounds of an automatic weapon slide slamming a round into the chamber, or the click of a revolver cocking; microphones that will reassemble conversations from vibrations on the other side of the wall; communications jammers; GPS signal reorienters that will send the car following you right off the road.

I always carried in my breast or hip pocket a video camera disguised as a pen. It was linked to software whose algorithms alerted me that the body language of a person approaching was consistent with that of an impending attack. I also used it to record crowds in public when I was transporting principals, to see if faces of passersby in one locale turn up in another.

A second "pen" is actually a wireless signal detector to sweep for bugs.

There was even what we call a "mail box"; it's about a foot square and unfolded explosively outward when it heard a detonation of an IED, shooting a Kevlar and metal mesh—like knight's chain mail—upward, to intercept as much shrapnel and blast force as possible.

Sometimes these devices worked and

sometimes they didn't. But you do whatever you can to get an edge over your
opponent, Abe Fallow used to say. That
edge could be microscopic, but often
that was enough.

I returned to my computer and downloaded several emails that duBois had
sent. I was sending replies when I sensed
a presence. I looked up and saw the
Kesslers in the kitchen. I heard cabinets
opening, the refrigerator door. This facility does have a bar, which separated
the dining room and kitchen, but it's
stocked only with sodas. In the kitchen
our facilities person usually has some
wine and beer. Although we can't drink
on duty, of course, we try to keep our
principals as comfortable as possible—
and more important, try to give them
little to complain about.

Ryan limped to the bar and poured
some Coke into a glass that was already
half full of amber liquid. Joanne got a
Sierra Mist. "You want something in it?"
I heard him ask.

She shook her head.

His shrug said, *Suit yourself.*

He glanced into the den and saw me

looking at them. He turned and walked back to the bedroom.

I returned to my computer, reviewing the encrypted e-files duBois had sent me.

She was responding to several of my various requests that day and assured me that she expected to have more details about Ryan's two relevant cases. There was some more research I needed to do—by myself. I logged into a secure search engine we use—routing my requests through a proxy in Asia.

The information came back instantly; I wasn't looking for classified material but simply perusing the general media. For a half hour I read through hundreds of pages of news stories and op ed pieces mostly. Finally I had a portrait of the object of my search.

Senator Lionel Stevenson was a two-term senator, a Republican from Ohio. He'd been in Congress before that and a prosecutor in Cleveland before running for office. He was a moderate, and respected on both sides of the aisle, as well as in the White House. Judiciary

Committee for four years, now Intelligence. He was the one who'd hammered together a coalition to get just enough votes in the Senate for the Supreme Court nominee. One politician was quoted as saying of Stevenson's efforts, "That was tough work, building support—everybody seems to hate everybody else in Washington nowadays."

Too much screaming in Congress. Too much screaming everywhere. . . .

He made visits to Veterans Administration hospitals and schools back in Ohio and in and around D.C. He was part of the Washington social scene and was seen in the company of younger women—though, unlike some of his colleagues, that was not a problem, since he was unmarried. He was supported by political action committees, lobbyists and campaign fund-raising organizations that had never run afoul of the law. He was considered one of the icons in what was being called the New Republican movement, which because of its moderate stance was converting Democrats and independents and looked likely to win solid majorities in upcoming state and federal elections.

Maybe the most significant thing I found were his remarks delivered at a community college in Northern Virginia a few months ago. While in many ways a fervent law-and-order advocate, Stevenson nonetheless said, "Government is not above the law. It is not above the people. It is bound by the law and it serves the people. There are those in Washington—there are those in every state—who think that rules can be bent or broken in the name of security and attaining a greater good. But there is no greater good than the rule of law. And politicians, prosecutors and police who would turn a blind eye toward the will of our Founders are no better than common bank robbers or murderers."

The reporter stated that these remarks earned Stevenson a standing ovation from the hall full of future voters. Other articles observed that this philosophy had cost him votes at home from Republicans and occasional enmity from fellow GOPers in Congress. Which told me that his motive for the upcoming hearings on government surveillance was rooted in ideology, not winning votes.

I continued to scroll through the voluminous material, jotting a note or two.

I felt at sea doing this, and again I envied Claire duBois her research skills. This, however, was not an assignment I would give to her.

I glanced up to see Joanne stepping into the doorway between the kitchen and living room, leaning against the jamb, her stern handsome face a bit less numb than before. I saved the pages in an encrypted file and typed a command to bring up the password-protected screensaver.

I stared at the monitor for a moment, the images of chess pieces appearing and dissolving, as I reflected on what I'd just learned about Stevenson. Then I rose and walked to the doorway, nodding to Joanne.

The inside of the safe house was surprisingly cozy. Many women principals fell in love with it. A few men too. When a lifter or hitter is after you, the nesting instinct swells fast, like a helium balloon at Hallmark. I'd even come downstairs once to find my principals had rearranged the furniture. Another time, to my horror, a couple had swapped the drapes between two rooms, presumably standing in full view of naked windows to do so.

The comfort made this my favorite safe house—not for my personal ease, but professional; my principals felt less agitated and that made my life easier.

Joanne picked up the remote, asking me, "Okay?"

"Sure."

She turned on the TV, perhaps to see if we'd made the news. We had, albeit anonymously. "Possibly gang related," the announcer said, referring to the shootout at the Hillside Inn. Then the story was gone, replaced by snippets on the Orioles' chance in the playoffs, a suicide bombing in Jerusalem, a statement by the Supreme Court nominee, urging that the demonstrations in front of the Capitol, both for and against him, remain peaceful; there'd been some incidents of spitting and hurling bottles. I gave him my silent thanks for helping mask my transit to the flytrap.

Joanne sat staring at the screen, clasping her soda firmly. Her fingers separated as she tucked a strand of limp dark blond hair away. She still had her purse over her shoulder.

The comfort of the familiar . . .

Out of the blue, she looked at me and said, as if continuing a conversation we'd been having all along, "He's frustrated. Ryan. Very frustrated. He's guilty about bringing this on us. And when he gets guilty, he doesn't know how to handle it. He gets angry. Don't take it personally."

She might have been referring to his biting comment that he was a better shot than me and the others protecting him.

Or to his implication that we were cowards, afraid to engage Loving.

"I understand." I did.

"He's never quite recovered from the deli shooting. I don't mean the wound, the limp—he's okay with that, most of the time. I mean the psychology. How it affected him. He had to move to a desk. He loved working the street. That's what his father did, in Baltimore. After Ryan moved to Financial Crimes his father seemed to lose respect for him."

I remembered that both of his parents were dead and I wondered what the relationship between father and son had been toward the end. My own father had died young; it was always a regret that I had been too busy to make it to the birthday party that had turned out to be his last.

A regret too that, because of his death, he hadn't been at my son's first.

Joanne continued, "He does his job but his heart's not in it. Now they've saddled him with that administrative work." She paused. "They know about the drinking. He thinks he covers it up. He doesn't. You can't."

I reflected that I too would find it hard to give up what I do and not be able to play my games against people like Henry Loving, not to be with my principals.

But I didn't tell Joanne this, of course. I always have to be on guard against sharing things with the people in my care. It's not professional. They might spill something about you—if they were captured by a lifter or if they talked to the press. There's another reason too. Principals and their shepherds are going to part ways. That's as sure as the seasons. It's better not to form any connection; minimize the risk of emotional hurt. This is why Abe Fallow told us to refer to them as "my principals" only.

"Keep them anonymous, Corte. This is a two-dimensional business. You have to be a cardboard cutout of a person. That's how you have to look at them. Learn only what you need to learn to keep them alive. Don't use their names, don't look at their kids' pictures, don't ask 'em if they're all right, unless you've been dodging bullets and you need to call a medic."

But the irony is that principals love to talk to us shepherds. Oh, do they want to share. Partly it's the presence of mortality that puts them in a talkative mode. Confessional, often. They've done some things wrong in their lives—who hasn't, of course?—and they want to assuage the guilt by talking. More important, though, I'm no threat. I'm in their lives for twelve hours or forty-eight or at the most a few weeks. I go away at the end of that time and will never be in a position to repeat the secrets to their friends or loved ones.

So I listen and I nod, without being particularly encouraging, and I make no judgments whatsoever. Part of this is calculated, of course. The more they depend on and trust me, the more they'll do exactly what I tell them to—instantly and without question.

Joanne glanced at my computer, though I'd turned the screen so she couldn't see it. She asked, "Which of Ryan's cases do you think it is?"

"My associate's investigating them now."

"At ten o'clock Saturday night?"

I nodded.

"Ryan doesn't talk to me about his job much. You'd think it'd be pretty obvious who's the . . . what did you call it, the primary?"

"That's it, yes. You mean, to warrant hiring somebody like Henry Loving, there'd have to be a lot at stake?"

"Yes."

"True. But sometimes you never know. I've had plenty of assignments where the identity of the primary was a big surprise."

Maree appeared, poured herself a glass of wine and walked up to us.

I asked, "The room okay?"

"Very Martha Stewart, Mr. Tour Guide. Old paintings of horses. Tons of horses. They have skinny legs. Fat horses and skinny legs. I wonder if they really looked like that back then. You think they'd fall over a lot."

Joanne smiled at this—an observation worthy of Claire duBois.

Maree then asked, "How do I go on-line? I need to check email."

"I'm afraid you can't."

"Oh, not the spy stuff again? Please. Can I beg?" She said this with that teen-ager's coy glint in her eyes. Her lips, of course, pouted admirably.

"Sorry."

"Why not?"

"We have to assume Loving's found your account. If you read messages or send any, it's possible for him to corre-late time with router and server traffic in the area here."

"Corte, do you look *four* ways before crossing the street?"

"Mar," Joanne chided. "Really."

"Oh, puh-lease."

I said, "Just taking precautions." I regarded her serious expression and nodding head. "What's wrong?"

"If I can't get my masseur here, then somebody owes me a massage. . . . Say, Mr. Tour Guide, is that in your job description?" I must have been staring at her blankly. She said, "You don't joke much, do you?"

"Maree," her sister said sternly. "Give it a rest."

"Seriously," she said to me. "I'd just like to send a few emails. I've got to get some images to a gallery for a show."

"If it's really important, I can encrypt it, send it to our central communications department and we could route it through some proxies in Asia and Europe."

"Is *that* a joke?"

"No."

"So other people would read it?"

"Yes, three or four. And me."

"Then I think I'll just opt for the exciting alternative of . . . going to bed." She turned defiantly and vanished down the dim corridor.

Joanne watched her sister walk away, Maree's slim hips shifting under the wispy skirt as she took steady, almost flirtatious strides.

"What's she taking?" I asked.

Joanne hesitated. "Wellbutrin."

"Anything else?"

"Maybe an Ativan. Or two or three."

"And?"

"Nothing else she needs a prescription for. She never got insurance so I see her medical bills. Because I pay for them. . . . How'd you know?"

I told her, "Language, some of her behavior. I found out about her hospitalizations. There were two, right?"

Joanne barked a cautious laugh. "You know about those?"

"My associate looked into anything that might be relevant. Suicide attempts? That's what I deduced from the report."

Joanne nodded. "The doctor said more of a gesture than an attempt. She'd been dumped by her boyfriend. Well, not even a boyfriend. They'd only gone out for six months or so but she was ready to move in, have his babies. You know the drill, I imagine."

Her voice faded and she was looking me over, as if maybe I didn't know the drill. Ryan had probably told her I was a single man with no children.

She continued, "A note, a little overdose. The second time, same thing. A bit worse. Different man. I wish she'd get as obsessed about going to therapy as she gets about lovers."

I glanced up the hall and then asked softly, "Was it Andrew who hurt her?" I tapped my arm.

Joanne's eyelids fluttered. "You're good. . . ." She shook her head. "To be honest, I don't know. He *has* hurt her, in the past. He put her in the hospital once. She claimed it was an accident. They always do that, abuse victims. Or she says it was her fault. This time she was pretty convincing that some guy knocked into her. But I just don't know."

"And the forwarded mail? She broke it off with Andrew and moved in with you?"

Joanne caught her reflection in an old, scabby mirror and looked away. "That's

right. Andrew's got a lot going for him.
He's talented, he's handsome and he
thinks my sister's talented. Or at least
he tells her she is. But he's also jealous
and controlling. He convinced her to
quit her day job and move in with him.
That lasted a couple of months. He was
mad at her all the time but when she
moved out he got even madder. Thank
God we were in the area; she had someplace to go when she bailed."

Maree, who'd been born Marie and
never officially changed her name, du-
Bois had learned, also had been the
subject of some runaway reports, filed
with local police, when she was in her
teens, and a few drug and shoplifting
charges, which had been dropped; it
seemed the boys she was with had co-
erced her to join them. They'd tried to
set her up to take the fall.

None of this was relevant to my job or
to the conversation we were having,
though, and I said nothing about it.

"So you do your homework, do you?"

"For the job? Yes."

After a moment Joanne, who didn't
seem to joke anymore than I did, gave

me a brief smile. "What'd you find out about me?"

I wasn't sure how to answer. DuBois's research on Joanne had revealed a thoroughly unremarkable life. She'd been a responsible student, grad student, statistician and homemaker. She was on the PTO at Amanda's school. The only incidents that rose above, or descended below, the four decades of routine were in themselves not unusual: for instance, a backpacking trip abroad before grad school—the high point of her younger days, I imagined—and a serious auto accident years ago that required some months of physical therapy.

"I found out that you're the one I don't have to worry about."

The smile dissolved. Joanne held my eye. "You'd make a good politician, Corte. Good night."

Chapter 20

At 11:00 p.m., after making rounds inside the house, I stepped outside and settled into a nest of fallen leaves. I began scanning the property with a Xenonics SuperVision 100 night vision monocular. They're very expensive but the best on the market. We could afford only three in the department and I'd checked out the last one earlier today.

This was normally the work done by a clone but I believed that even we shepherds should get our hands dirty on the job regularly. Abe's philosophy, of course—a belief, you could say, that killed him.

I was concentrating on looking for anything that seemed out of the ordinary. I found my shoulders in a knot. I was breathing hard. I began reciting silently to myself: *rock, paper, scissors . . . rock, paper, scissors . . .*

Lulled by the flow of moon shadows from the slowly moving clouds, I began to relax. After forty minutes, my fingers numb and arm muscles shivering from the chill, I headed inside.

In the shepherd bedroom I unsnapped my Royal Guard holster and took a bottle of Draw-EZ from my gym bag. I massaged some of the gel into the natural-colored leather, now tanned as a beloved baseball glove. The smooth side fit against my skin, the rough facing outward. I didn't really need to work on the leather—I've timed my draws and they're acceptable—but I found it relaxing.

When I was through, I took care of business in the bathroom and then rolled into the lumpy old bed, blinds drawn, of course, though the odds of a shooter emerging from the glorious line of old oaks to pump a round into the room were pretty slim.

The window, though, was open a crack and I could hear the faint unfurling sound of the wind and the softer rustle of the water over the falls a half mile away.

I'm lucky because I can sleep almost anywhere, nearly on command. Which I've learned is particularly rare in my job. Not surprisingly, my principals suffer from insomnia. I knew I'd doze off soon but at the moment I was pleased to lie in bed, fully clothed, though minus shoes, and stare at the ceiling. I was thinking: Who'd lived in this house originally?

It had been built around 1850. I supposed it had been a farmhouse, with much of the land devoted to oats, corn, barley—staples, not the designer crops you see nowadays. I had an amusing image of a working-class nineteenth-century family kicking off supper with an arugula and spinach salad.

Though the property hosted ten thousand trees now, I knew the vista back then from Mathew Brady's and others' photographs. Much of what was now woods in Northern Virginia had been open agricultural land around the time of the Civil War.

Great Falls had been occupied early

by the Union Army. This area wasn't the scene of any major battles, though nearly four thousand troops met briefly at what was now Route 7 and Georgetown Pike, in December 1861, resulting in about fifty dead and two hundred wounded. It was considered a Union victory, though most likely because the Confederates saw no strategic point in occupying an area where they weren't greatly supported, and they simply walked away.

More than any other area in the Commonwealth of Virginia, Great Falls had been a place of mixed sympathies. Those favoring the Union and those the Confederacy were often neighbors. Here, "brother against brother" was not a cliché.

I knew this from reading history—another one of my degrees—though I've also learned a lot about world affairs and conflict from playing board games. I enjoy those games that re-create famous battles, which are almost exclusively of American design. The Europeans prefer economic and socially productive games, the Asians abstract.

But Americans love their combat. Among the games I have are Battle of the Bulge, Gettysburg, D-Day, the Battle of Britain, the Siege of Stalingrad, Rome.

Some people I've met through the gaming community shunned them, claiming they were disrespectful. But I believed the opposite was true: that we honor those who died in the service of their country by remembering them however we can.

Besides, who wouldn't admit that rewriting the past has a deep appeal? I once utterly defeated the Japanese military at a game based on Pearl Harbor. In my world, the Pacific campaign never happened.

My thoughts kept returning to the family who'd lived here when the house was new. It had been a large clan, I assumed; many children were the rule then. The seven bedrooms could easily have accommodated the offspring plus an older generation or two.

That always appealed to me: generations living together.

An image from the past: of Peggy and her mother and father.

I realized now that in appearance, and because of her quirky side, Maree reminded me of Peggy. None of Maree's darkness, of course, or the irritations and unsteady nature.

Mr. Tour Guide. . . .

Peggy had once called me a bad boy but it happened after I realized we'd been given a large order of fries at McDonald's instead of the regular and I said, "Let's sneak out without telling them."

More memories I didn't want.

I stretched, feeling the pain in my calves and joints from the pursuit of Henry Loving at the flytrap and in my back from the retreat at the hotel. I forced myself to play a few mental rounds of the Chinese game Wei-Chi against an invisible opponent I sometimes imagine to help me banish unwanted thought.

Then I decided it was time to sleep and rolled over on my side. In two minutes I was out.

SUNDAY

Players do not always take alternate turns to move their armies. Instead, a deck of Battle cards determines which player moves next, and which of his units can move and attack. No one knows whose turn will be next until the top Battle card on the deck is flipped over. In this way, the play sequence remains a mystery.

—FROM THE INSTRUCTIONS TO THE
BOARD GAME BATTLE MASTERS

Chapter 21

Doing nothing.

It's not such a problem for us shepherds; we're used to it. We're like airline pilots, whose life is routine 99 percent of the time. We expect this and—though we train for the rare moments of action to avoid calamity—we understand that most of our lives on the job will pass in a waiting state. Ideally so, at least.

But for our principals, time spent in a safe house often becomes a nightmare. They're plucked from their active lives and have to spend hour after hour in places like this, cozy though they may be, unable to work, unable to pursue projects around their houses, unable to see friends. Few phone calls, no email . . . Even TV is unsatisfying; the programs remind them of the world that exists outside their prison, fading reruns of our existence they may never see again, frivolous shows, both drama and comedy, that mock the tragedy they're living through.

Doing nothing . . .

One consequence of which is that they often opt for the oblivion of sleep; there's no reason for principals to wake early.

At 9:30 Sunday morning, I was sitting in the den at the desk, where I'd been since five, when I heard the snap of a door opening and creaks in the floorboards. I heard the voices of Ryan and Joanne, saying good morning to Lyle Ahmad, making small talk. He gave them details about coffee and breakfast.

I sent some more emails and then rose, stretching.

The night had passed in peace and a new spec in West Virginia told me in a deeper voice, though with a twang identical to that of his associate, that scans of the property had revealed nothing of concern. A car had driven by at midnight but it was taking a route that was logical for a local returning from dinner in Tysons Corner or the District. In any case, our GPS had measured his speed and he hadn't slowed as much as one mile per hour when he passed, which took him off the threat list, according to our algorithms.

I joined the Kesslers in the kitchen and we exchanged greetings.

"Sleep well?" I asked.

"Well enough, yeah." Ryan was bleary-eyed. He was moving slowly—because of the limp and, perhaps, a hangover. He wore jeans and an Izod shirt, purple, with his belly hanging over the belt buckle. He still wore his weapon. Joanne was in jeans too and a black T-shirt under a floral blouse. In a round compact mirror she inspected her lipstick—the only makeup she was wearing—then put it back in her purse.

Ryan said he'd talked to Amanda for a long time earlier and everything seemed okay at Carter's place. The girl had enjoyed fishing yesterday and they'd had dinner with neighbors last night, a barbecue.

I'd called Bill Carter too, that morning. I told the Kesslers this and added, "He said there hasn't been anything suspicious. Just that your daughter was still bothered about missing school tomorrow and her game and some volunteer job."

"A student counseling hotline," Ryan explained. "She practically runs the place."

Knowing what I did about the girl now, I wasn't surprised.

"Let's hope she won't have to miss anything," Joanne said.

It was still early on Sunday. If we got Loving and the primary soon, the Kesslers' lives could return to a semblance of normality by suppertime.

"What do we do today?" Ryan asked, looking outside. I'd seen golf clubs in the garage and I guessed he'd miss what might be a warm fall day on the links.

"You just relax," I said. I couldn't help but think of Claire duBois, who'd once commented to me as we were flying to Florida to collect a principal, "The pilots always say that, 'Now just sit back and relax and enjoy the flight.' What options are there? Do handstands in the aisles? Open a window and feed the birds?"

The Kesslers too had no options. I knew they weren't going to like my further instructions, which I now delivered, that they had to stay inside.

"Inside," Ryan muttered, peeking out through a slit in the curtain at a band of sun on leaves just beginning to color. He sighed and knifed butter onto an English muffin.

Doing nothing . . .

My phone rang and I glanced at caller ID. "Excuse me."

I headed back to the den, clicking AN-SWER. "Claire."

"I've got some information."

"Go ahead."

Her youthful voice offered enthusiastically, "The electronic trackers? This's interesting. They're made by Mansfield Industries. The small tracker has a range of six hundred yards, the big one a thousand. That sounds impressive but they're older models. The new trackers, like the ones we use, are GPS and satellite based, so you can sit in your office and track. The ones planted on you were cheap. That means they're used by police departments."

Yes, that *was* interesting. "And the model numbers—"

"—are the same used in the MPD." Ryan Kessler's employer.

"Serial numbers?" I asked.

But she said, "No serial numbers. So we don't know the specific source."

"Prints or trace evidence on them?"

"None."

I considered this information. A principal who was a detective and hardware that might have come from the same police department he worked for.

Another piece of the puzzle.

I asked, "Graham?" The Department of Defense employee whose checkbook was stolen. The man who'd surprisingly dropped the charges.

Her voice lost its lilt as she said, "Okay. About that."

Didn't sound good. "What?"

"I think I may need some help."

"Go on."

"A teeny problem . . ."

An adjective I never quite got.

She continued, "I was researching and making some headway. I found that the chief of detectives—"

"Lewis."

"Right. COD Lewis got a call from 'somebody powerful.' That's a quote, though I have no idea what 'somebody powerful' means. It sounds like what a scriptwriter would say when he's describing a bad guy, the nefarious character. Anyway, this power person had Lewis make sure the case wasn't being pursued."

"Somebody from the Pentagon?"

"I don't know. Then I got some numbers. Graham makes ninety-two thousand a year. His wife fifty-three. They have a six-hundred-thousand-dollar mortgage and two daughters in college, in addition to their son, Stuart. The girls're going to William and Mary, and Vassar. Their collective tuition is about sixty thousand a year. Room and board probably not too bad. I mean, with all respect to Williamsburg and Poughkeepsie. You ever been there, either of them?"

"No." I considered this. "So the stolen forty thousand is a bigger hit for him to swallow than we thought."

"Huge. I was thinking about when I

went to Duke. My folks saved every penny they could for my tuition. It'd take something disastrous for them to give up and doom me to a career of memorizing specials of the day."

"You mentioned a problem."

Teeny . . .

"Actually . . ."

"Claire?"

DuBois came in a quirky package— her dancing mind, her bizarre observations—but she was, in her way, as much a competitor as I was and it was hard for her to admit defeat, especially if she'd made a mistake, which was what I sensed had happened.

"I got this idea. Because of his clearance, Graham would have had to take a lie detector test."

All government employees with security clearances have to do this regularly. Some organizations have their own polygraphist; the DoD usually relies on the FBI.

"So I called up a friend at the Bureau to find out. Graham was scheduled to take one last week but he called the field office and said he was staying home. He had a bad cold. They don't let you take the exam if you're on medication. So it was postponed until next month."

"You checked log-in records at the Pentagon."

"Exactly. Graham *didn't* stay home when he said he had. And nobody got the impression he was sick. He lied to avoid the test."

"Good thinking. Go on."

"Apparently somebody in Records let him know I'd been looking into it. Graham got my name. He called. He wasn't happy."

It wasn't the best outcome, I agreed. I'd rather that Graham had been kept completely in the dark about our investigation. But I still wasn't sure why du-Bois seemed so upset. Then she explained. "I figured as long as I was blown, I may as well interview him, see what he had to say about withdrawing the complaint. He got, um, uncooperative. Actually pretty insulting. He called me 'young lady.' Which I don't really like."

I was sure not.

"He told me, kind of R-rated, where I could put my warrant."

"Warrant? How did a warrant come up?"

"That's sort of the problem. I threatened to serve him."

"For what?" I couldn't see any scenario in which a warrant made sense.

"I made it up. I just got mad, the way he was talking. I said if he wasn't going to answer my questions, I'd go to a magistrate, get paper and serve him to force him to talk."

I was silent for a moment. Lesson time. "Claire, there's a difference between bluffing and threatening. With a threat you have something to back it up. With a bluff you don't. We threaten. We don't bluff."

"I was sort of bluffing, I guess."

"Okay," I said. "Where is he now?"

"His caller ID put him at home. Fairfax. I'm sorry. He's stonewalling now."

Young lady . . .

"Tell you what. Meet me at the Hyatt in Tysons. A half hour."

"Okay."

After disconnecting, I joined Ryan

Kessler at a table in the living room, poring over documents. I told him about the trackers that Loving's partner had slipped into my wheel wells.

"They were from the department?" he asked, surprised.

"We couldn't source them. But they're the same model numbers the Metropolitan Police buys."

"Fact is, we never use them," Ryan said. "They're great in theory but that's not how most tails work. Reception gets screwed up, the signals get crossed. Mostly we put 'em in buy-money bags if there's a lot of cash and we're afraid of losing it. But you can also get them from almost any security gadget company."

"Anybody in the department you can think of who might be monitoring the Graham or Clarence Brown cases? Or one of your smaller ones?"

"Somebody inside working with Loving? Impossible. We don't do that, cops don't do that to each other."

I said nothing, though I thought: People will do anything to anybody—if the edge is right.

I returned to my computer and, not

wanting him to hear my request, wrote
an email to duBois, giving her another
item on her growing to-do list. She acknowledged it.

Garcia and Ahmad were making
rounds. I told them I was leaving for a
while to continue investigating who the
primary was. I stepped outside to the
detached garage and opened the door.
Inside was a Honda Accord, registered
to a fictional resident of Arlington, Virginia. Billy'd made some modifications
to it—run-flats, better horsepower and a
bit of armor—but it was still pretty much
off the shelf. I started the car and drove
out of the compound, cruising through
the tunnel of leaves and branches glowing in the sun.

I was about ten minutes from the safe
house when the phone buzzed. I recognized Westerfield's number. I'd forgotten
my promise to Aaron about keeping the
prosecutor up to speed.

So I answered.

I shouldn't have.

Chapter 22

"Corte, you're on speaker here with me and Chris Teasley."

"Okay."

"I've talked to the attorney general and he's agreed to move the Kesslers into a slammer in the District—Hansen Detention."

All because I hadn't returned his call? Seemed a little excessive. "I see. Why?"

Chris Teasley came on. She said, "Um, Agent Corte."

"Officer Corte," I corrected. My organization is an office, not a bureau or an agency. When Congress gave Abe the money that's what he created.

"Officer Corte," she continued. "I backgrounded you." She sounded uneasy; I was close to twice her age.

I concentrated on driving and looking for a tail, which shepherds do automati-

cally, all the time. Even when we go grocery shopping. But I didn't expect to be
followed and I saw nothing. "Go on."

"It's routine in cases like this," she
said quickly. So I wouldn't think I was
being persecuted. "One thing that came
up: an operation you ran in Newport,
Rhode Island. Two years ago."

Ah, so that was it.

"I have the whole report of the investigation here."

She kept pausing, as if giving me the
chance to confirm or deny. I remained
silent.

"The assignment involved you and
two associates from your organization
guarding several witnesses from the
same man involved in this case, Henry
Loving."

She paused again. I wondered if Westerfield was testing her the way I test
duBois and Ahmad and my other protégés. It's easy to do research. It's hard to
aim it at somebody and pull the trigger.

Apparently Teasley wasn't firing fast
enough. Her boss took over. "Corte, let
me read this: 'It was alleged that Agent
Corte—'"

The Justice Department's Internal Affairs Division had gotten the job title wrong too. Not many people know about our organization.

"'—had a conflict of interest in running the Kowalski protection assignment, endangering the two witnesses in his care. Although a half dozen personal security professionals within three government agencies stated that standard procedure would have been to secrete the two witnesses in protective custody in the Providence, Rhode Island, federal penitentiary, Agent Corte chose not to do so but to keep the witnesses first in a motel and then to transfer them to a safe house outside of Newport, Rhode Island.'"

"I'm familiar with the report," I told him, braking hard for a lazy deer.

But he continued to read, " 'The result was that Henry Jonathan Loving, who'd been hired to kidnap and extract information from the witnesses, injured a local police officer and a bystander. He came close to successfully kidnapping at least one of the witnesses in question.

"'During the investigation into the handling of said matter, it came to light that Loving was the same individual who had murdered Agent Corte's superior, Abraham Fallow, the director of . . . ' It's redacted. 'And a personal friend of Agent Corte's. The conclusion of the investigating panel was that Agent Corte, motivated by personal revenge, chose not to put the witnesses in question into the federal detention center but rather kept them in public, with full knowledge that Loving would attempt to kidnap them there.

"'He in effect used the witnesses as bait to capture or kill Loving. This is supported by the fact that the witnesses were convicted felons and, accordingly, Agent Corte would feel more at liberty to imperil them.'"

He concluded, "'It was only through good fortune that the witnesses were not lost and the trial proceeded on schedule.'"

"Good fortune," I repeated softly. Something I absolutely do not believe in.

"Well?"

The penitentiary in Providence was more dangerous than the worst parts of the city itself and that was saying something. My protégé at the time had learned that Henry Loving had done business with at least two people inside the slammer. As for the principals, yes, they were felons. But we shepherds never make moral judgments about the people we protect. The only quality in a principal that matters is a beating heart. Our job is to keep it that way.

But if I hadn't justified myself to my boss, I sure wasn't going to do so to Westerfield and his young assistant.

"It's the same thing here, Corte. The motel in Providence, the Hillside Inn. The safe house there, the safe house here. From what we can reconstruct, back at the Hillside, after Loving showed up and was in pursuit, you could have escaped right away but you paused in the back of the motel. You engaged him, with the Kesslers in the vehicle with you."

People who explain are weak, Corte. A shepherd can't be weak. He can be wrong but he can't be weak.

Abe's words, of course. I realized that Westerfield must be upset; he hadn't lapsed into French once during this conversation. I sped around a slow-moving Prius.

"So what happened is the trap in Rhode Island didn't work out after all, and your fox shows up still alive yesterday. So you set out to nail him all over again, using the Kesslers. And now, I understand from Aaron there's a terrorist component."

"A . . . what?"

"Ali Pamuk, aka Clarence Brown."

"We haven't found any terrorist connections. His father's Turkish, and he's contributed money to a mosque here in Virginia. He's also played with his identity. That's all we know at this point. We're investigating."

"But it's possible that a terror cell wants to kidnap Kessler and find out what he knows and who else might be involved in his investigation."

"Like I said, Jason, we don't know."

"Look, Corte, I appreciate you've saved the Kesslers from two tight situations. You're talented . . . and you were lucky. We can't risk that the third time Loving'll have more luck than you do."

Luck . . .

"Kessler may be the only key to a serious terror threat. We can't afford to have him jeopardized, like you've been doing. I have the attorney general's okay. I want the Kesslers and the woman's sister in a slammer now. The Hansen facility, we were talking about earlier. I've already contacted them."

I pictured him looking at Teasley with an expression that said, See, that's how it's done.

"I want to talk to my boss."

"This is coming from the attorney general."

Everybody's boss.

I found I was driving ten over the limit. I eased up on the gas.

Westerfield continued, speaking reasonably, "If this was some bullshit embezzlement or organized crime thing, I wouldn't care so much. But now there's a terror component, we can't fool around. We need to make sure we do everything we can to identify a threat. We also don't need any blowback."

Even spending so much time inside the Beltway I could never quite get used to the lexicon.

"I want them in Hansen as soon as possible. You want to keep after Loving, be my guest. You want to keep tracking down the primary, fine. You just aren't going to use my witness for cheese in your mousetrap."

His witness . . . The famous hero cop.

Westerfield continued, "I'm ordering an armored van now."

"No."

"I'll just call Aaron and find out where they are."

"He doesn't know."

"What?"

"I haven't told him."

Need-to-know . . .

"Well, that's . . ." Westerfield had trouble processing this, though I wasn't sure why. I doubted people in his organization shared everything with one another.

"I hope this isn't going to become a fight, Corte. *Mon Dieu . . .* that would not be good."

Ah, the French. At last.

Finally I said, "Here's what I'll agree to

do. I'll call Aaron. If he confirms that the AG's ordered them into a slammer"—I let that linger—"I'll arrange for one of *our* armored transports to get them to the Hansen facility. But I'll tell you . . . a District cop? Inside? Ryan's not going to be happy at all. I don't know how co-operative he'll be after we move them."

"You let me worry about that, Corte. This has to happen immediately. I can rely on you?"

Meaning he was going to call Aaron Ellis in about ten minutes to make sure I was doing what I'd said.

"Yes."

"Thanks. It's really for the best—for us, for them, for the country."

I didn't know if those words were di-rected toward me, toward Teasley or an invisible audience.

After I disconnected, I gave it a few minutes and, without bothering to call Aaron Ellis for the confirmation, dialed Billy to ask about an armored van.

Chapter 23

Hotels are good meeting places in our line of work. They never close and even if you aren't registered there, nobody pays much attention if you sit quietly in the lobby in a business suit and pretend to look over your computer, like you're waiting for a meeting.

Which was what I was doing now.

At 11:10 a.m. Claire duBois arrived at the Tysons Hyatt. She was wearing a black pantsuit but a different black one from yesterday. The pattern, I noticed. A thin burgundy sweater underneath. As she sat down I smelled jasmine. Her eyes were red. I supposed she hadn't gotten much sleep. Her face was troubled and for a moment I thought we had a security situation on our hands. But she simply said in a ragged whisper, "I heard Billy's signed out a secure transport for a run to a slammer in D.C. He was secret about it. I mean, I sensed he was. Inscrutable. I'm not sure exactly what that means but it seemed to apply. When I walked toward him he headed the other way."

That was duBois's very long way of asking a very simple question.

"First." I gestured across the lobby, picked up my laptop and we walked to the Starbucks stand. It wasn't my favorite coffee. But it had caffeine and that I did need. We got two cups and Claire duBois went for some food. A vegetable wrap. We returned to where we'd been sitting. I explained about Westerfield's call, though not the Rhode Island part or the inquiry. I supposed that duBois knew about the matter, which was there for public consumption, provided you were up for a little insidious digging, as Chris Teasley had done. It wasn't the sort of thing to bring up with your protégé and fellow workers unnecessarily.

When I told her the U.S. attorney had demanded the Kesslers and Maree go into a slammer, duBois blinked as if I'd said the District were seceding. "But he can't do that. You're in charge of the principals."

I told her, "But *he's* in charge of the sanctity of the nation. And of his career." I chose not to work the word "self-righteous" into my comments. I also chose to tell her nothing more. "In any case, that's not our priority at the moment. We need to find who's hired Loving. Tell me what you've got so far."

"I'm still checking on the email you sent, following up on the tracker situation, the police department."

Since I'd given her the assignment only a half hour ago I wasn't surprised or troubled there were no results yet.

"Here's the result of the phone call traces you asked me for." She handed me a folder. I read it fast but completely. The answer was pretty much what I'd expected.

DuBois then handed me a second file—dealing with the alleged Ponzi scam. This was filled with a lot of paperwork and documents. I glanced up and she summarized, "Clarence Brown, aka Ali Pamuk." She shuffled through them. "Detective Kessler hadn't gotten too far with the case."

"He told me. He was busy."

"And nobody in the Department or the SEC was that concerned."

"Poor, minority victims."

"Not much money involved. And no loudmouths to stand up for them. Like Al Sharpton. Pamuk has an office in South East but it's a short-term lease. All the furniture's rented. A secretary and two assistants. Neither of them've graduated from college. It just doesn't smell right. You'd think that if you were an investment advisor you'd have something that wasn't so cheesy. Now, I saw this movie. *All the President's Men.*"

"It was a book too."

"Was it? Well, in it—"

"I know the story."

"To track down what was going on, the reporters followed the money. I was thinking about it and that's what I did."

"Good."

She continued, "I know some people at Treasury and State. And this lawyer who's involved in international banking treaties." She seemed to know half of the under-thirty population in the District of Columbia. "Ever since the Swiss got scared, the UBS thing a few years ago, and started to chatter, it's not quite as hard to get information. But the trail's really complicated." She pulled a sheet of paper out of her file and showed me an elaborate diagram in her elegant handwriting. "I managed to find somebody at Interpol in Europe and MI6 in the U.K. They were working late or early or around the clock, I don't know. To summarize, the investors' money goes from D.C. to Georgetown—ha, that's funny, I just realized. The Georgetown in the Cayman Islands. Not the Georgetown where I go to Dean and DeLuca. From there the money goes to London and Marseille and Geneva and Athens. Then, guess where?"

Pamuk's dad was Turkish so I gambled on Istanbul or Ankara.

But the real answer was a lot more interesting. "Riyadh."

Saudi Arabia, the origin of most of the Nine-eleven hijackers. Westerfield's terrorist connection, which I'd thought was pretty speculative, was looking more and more possible.

"A British shell corporation. And from there, it goes to more companies throughout the Middle East but—how's this?—they're not Middle Eastern. They're registered in America, France, Austria, Switzerland, England, China, Japan and Singapore. They're all shell corporations. Every one of them. They get the money and from there it disappears."

I sipped the bitter coffee. I summarized, "So investors aren't getting their money out because it's being used to fund terror operations by Hezbollah, the Taliban, Hamas, al Qaeda."

"That's what I was thinking."

It was a clever idea, using a Ponzi scam to produce revenue for terrorists. And, if true, it was doubly effective. The money Pamuk raised would not only fund operations but would also have secondary consequences: destroying the lives of people in the West who'd invested their savings with Pamuk.

"Where are we now?"

"The Saudis aren't being cooperative.

No surprise there. State and Interpol
and local FBI're doing some digging,
trying to see who specifically is getting
the money."

I guessed that Pamuk could be a front
man, picked probably because he had
connections with the neighborhood—
and his sympathies to fundamentalism.
I wondered if he'd been the one who'd
hired Henry Loving or if that had been
someone in the Middle East.

"Any word about when they'll know
something?" I asked.

"By tomorrow, they hope."

They hope. . . .

"Now, about Graham," I said.

She grimaced. "Sorry."

We threaten. We don't bluff. . . .

I shrugged. She'd learned the lesson.
The question was what to do about the
situation.

I finished my coffee. I said in my mentor voice, "In this line of work?"

"Yes."

"Sometimes we've got to do things
that test us. Push us to the extreme."

She'd gone quiet. Unusual for her. But

she was looking me in the eye, nodding slightly.

"That's what we have to do now. . . . But it's really above and beyond the call of duty. I can't order you to do it."

DuBois touched the single button closing her jacket, subconsciously, I believed. Tucked in her waistband was a pistol similar to mine, the compact Glock. I'd seen her scores. She was a good shot and I remembered the image of her at our range, eyes focused and intense, beneath the yellow-lensed glasses, her short dark hair puffed out comically around the thick ear protectors. Always getting a tight grouping in the fifty-yard targets.

She'd be thinking, possible terrorist connection, possible New Jersey syndicate connection, even a Department of Defense conspiracy of some sort. Would there be a firefight?

She cleared her throat. "Whatever you need, Corte."

I sized her up. Her still blue eyes, taut lips, steady breathing. She was ready for what we were about to do, I decided.

"Let's go."

Chapter 24

"Mr. Graham?"

I was displaying my ID, which the man had glanced at as if he'd been expecting it all day, which he probably had been.

Trim-haired Eric Graham was about fifty, solidly built, though not overweight. He was in jeans and a sweater and he hadn't shaved since rising for work on Friday.

He looked at me without interest and at duBois with sheerly veiled contempt, once he learned her name.

"Agent Corte, there's nothing to talk about. The forgery case has been withdrawn. I really don't understand what the federal government is doing, involved in this."

"That's not what I'm here about,

sir. . . . You mind if we come in just for a minute or two? It's important."

"I don't see—"

"It won't be long." I was looking grim.

He shrugged and motioned us inside. He directed us to the den, whose walls were covered with photos, diplomas, certificates of achievement and memorabilia from his scholastic and athletic endeavors thirty years ago.

"As I explained to *her*," Graham said icily, "I'm in a very sensitive job. It's unfortunate that the money was stolen. But on the whole, in the interests of national security, I decided not to pursue a criminal case." He gave a tight, insincere smile. "Why burden the D.C. police department anyway? They've got more important things to do than deal with a careless computer jockey who left his checkbook where it shouldn't've been."

We sat down around a circular coffee table with a glass top and a recess in the middle. Inside were pictures of Graham's sports successes—college football and tennis. On the walls were some family photos: vacation, school pageants, holidays. I saw a few of his son, presumably the one whose future education had been derailed. I noted too photos of the daughters, also in college. They were twins. Many were of Graham with what looked like wealthy business associates and a politician or two.

There were no sights or sounds of family, though I saw two nearly empty coffee cups on the dining room table, around the remains of the Sunday *Washington Post*, and heard NPR talk radio on the stereo, the volume in the netherworld portion of the dial. I heard creaks coming from upstairs. A door closed. He'd sent the women and children off to the hills when the marauders arrived.

"I'm sorry about Detective Keller."

"Kessler."

"Who's had all this trouble. He seemed like a nice guy when he interviewed me. I know"—another nonglaring glare at duBois—"that some hit man or somebody was curious about him because of something."

Interesting way to phrase it.

"I'm sorry about that. But there's no way my situation could have anything to do with it. You're thinking that whoever stole my checkbook wants to kill him? That just doesn't make sense."

I held up my hands. "Like I said, we're not here about that. We're here . . ." My voice faded and I glanced at Claire du-Bois.

She took a deep breath. Her eyes down. "I'm here to apologize, Mr. Graham."

"To . . . what?"

"When my supervisor," she began, looking at me, "learned what I'd said and done in our conversation—"

"*Conversation*," Graham said sardonically.

"He advised me that I'd acted in an unprofessional manner."

"To put it mildly."

I merely observed; I said nothing but turned and studied the room.

Graham was smugly pleased I wasn't defending my aide. He looked to du-Bois. She explained, "See, we have profiling software. When I ran the situation through the computers, the scenario that was number one on our list was that Detective Kessler had been targeted because he'd learned something about your check fraud situation. What it laid out for us was that somebody, possibly a security threat, had stolen your checkbook and used the funds for something that might compromise you. They then blackmailed you into either handing over secrets or maybe sabotaging some of your designs for the DoD. It was a credible scenario."

He snapped, "Except it wasn't."

Nodding, duBois said, "I'm fairly new to this position. I don't know if you've worked in any place other than the federal government."

"I was in the private sector for a while."

She said, "I was too. I was a security consultant for a major software developer. I can't really mention which one but we had a huge piracy problem. Tens of millions, hundreds of millions of dollars were at stake. You're into computers, you know source codes."

"Of course." He gave a subtle eye roll.

I heard duBois say, "We had a situation where an employee was being blackmailed into giving important parts

of source codes to a competitor. I managed to track him down. There were
some similarities between that situation
and your case. I kind of leapt on that."

"I told you there wasn't a problem.
You kept pushing."

"Yes, I know. I got a little focused."

"Or blinded, you could say."

"Blinded," duBois agreed.

"So you had a taste of success at
your other company and you wanted to
relive it."

"I . . . that's about right."

"You're an ambitious little thing, aren't
you?"

She was silent.

"Ambition's fine. But you need the
goods, you need to deliver."

"Yessir. I didn't have the goods."

"If you don't have them, you can't deliver."

"Right."

"No delivery." He offered her a drippy,
condescending smile. "I'll give you two
pieces of advice. First, and this is from
somebody in the business: Computers
can only do so much. They point you in
a certain direction. You need to use that

pretty little brain of yours in deciding where to go from there. How do you learn that?"

"Well . . ."

"From life experience. The most important thing in the world. You can't bottle it, you can't buy it."

"Yessir. What's the second bit of advice?"

"Give people the respect they deserve. You're young, you're spunky. But you'll go further faster if you keep in mind where you fit in the scheme of things."

"That's true. I sometimes don't remember where I fit."

I glanced at Graham. "Anything else we can do?"

"Your little lady and I've come to an understanding. I don't think the matter needs to go any further."

"That's kind of you."

"You keep that attitude in check," he said to my protégée.

A fraction of a moment's silence, as duBois nodded slowly. Her skin turned ruddy. "My teacher in seventh grade said the same thing once. Of course, he—"

"Thank you for your time, Mr. Graham," I interrupted quickly. "And your generosity. We'll leave you alone now."

We walked out the door, then climbed into the Honda. As we pulled out, watching a smug Eric Graham close the door, I said to duBois, "That was helpful."

My highest compliment. It didn't seem to wash today, however.

She nodded, glum.

"I know it was tough."

"Yeah."

The clipped one-word response meant duBois was very upset. I couldn't blame her. I supposed she would have preferred a rolling, four-person tactical entry against an armed hostile to the humiliation she'd just suffered.

But I'd had to ask her to do it. There was absolutely no logical explanation for Graham's dropping the case, and the fact that "somebody powerful" had gone to the MPD to make sure the investigation died suggested all the more that this was a likely motive for Ryan Kessler being targeted. I needed to do

whatever I could to find out what was
going on with Graham, even if it meant
my protégée had to suffer.

Pretty little brain . . .

Claire duBois's prostrating herself to
an arrogant chauvinist like Graham was
bitterly hard for her, especially since
her star shone a thousand times brighter
than his. But I'd remembered what Abe
Fallow had told me.

*Keeping people safe is a business,
like any other. You ask yourself, What's
my goal and what's the most efficient
way to go about achieving it? If that
means you beg, you beg. Grovel, you
grovel. If that means you bust heads,
get out the brass knuckles. Cry if you
need to. A shepherd doesn't exist outside the context of his mission.*

So I'd had to put duBois in play—to
beg forgiveness—while I had become
invisible and studied Graham's reaction
when duBois told him again about our
theory that he was being blackmailed.
I'd noted his mannerisms, his eyes, his
verbal and body language. I'd also gazed
around his study for anything helpful.

Which I believed I might have found.

I plucked the video camera pen from my breast pocket and handed it to her. "I captured about a dozen pictures of people on Graham's wall. Upload them to our server. I want facial recognition on everybody. Run all the data you get, along with the facts of the case, through ORC."

This was the computer that duBois had alluded to in her mea culpa performance with Graham. The official name of the impressive program, residing on our tech wizard Hermes's massive servers, is the Obscure Relationship Pattern and Connection Determiner. But we shorthand it to Obscure Relationship Connector and tighten it even more to the evil creatures in Tolkien's fantasy novels, a thought of mine after a marathon bout of playing Lord of the Rings, which is a very good board game.

The algorithm at ORC's heart was elegant—the mathematician in me was truly impressed with how it worked—and if there was any relevance to be found in the evidence I'd gathered, ORC could do so. "And run a facial and kinesics profile on him. A lie-detector scan."

DuBois took the pen, hooked up a USB cable and sent the video into the stratosphere. She stared out the window. I wondered for how long I'd lost her.

I wondered too if this had changed something permanently between us.

As we drove back to the Hyatt in silence to collect her car, I heard my phone buzz. It was still in her hand. She started to hand it back, saying, "You've got a text."

"Read it."

"It's from Transport. A copy of a message to Westerfield."

"Go on."

She sighed. "The armored van you'd ordered left the safe house fifteen minutes ago. It's headed for the prison now."

Chapter 25

As the sky grew more and more overcast, I pulled into the safe house compound in Great Falls.

I climbed out and stretched, as leaves tumbled past in the fitful wind.

The rustic setting made me feel very much at home—the trees, brush, sloping fields of renegade grass. My early adult life was rooted in classrooms and lecture halls, and my recent professions and personal life have found me in offices and safe houses, but I have always found a way to get outside, sometimes for hours or days at a time.

I glanced enviously at the paths that led to the Potomac or farther into the dense woods, then I turned away, looking down at another text from Billy about the progress of the armored van to the slammer in D.C. I wondered if Jason

Westerfield and his associate would be there to greet it. Then I realized: Of course they would.

Climbing the stairs, punching in the code. The door of the safe house eased open.

And I nodded a greeting toward Maree and Joanne, who sat across a wobbly card table from each other, with tea and cookies at hand.

Yes, and armored van *was* en route— a lengthy, complicated route—but it was empty.

Inscrutable . . .

There was no way I was going to send the Kesslers to a slammer, especially a medium-security facility in the District. Nothing had changed from earlier, when I'd refused to incarcerate them, and if Westerfield was convinced I was using my principals as bait, that was a problem of his, not mine.

I knew that if the stink got big enough, Aaron Ellis might fire me. But he wouldn't fire me until the job was concluded. For one thing, he didn't know where I was and it would take some effort to find out. Nor could he do so without risking that somebody on the outside would learn of the Kesslers' whereabouts. Which he wouldn't do.

I was amused to see that the sisters were playing a board game plucked from the shelves in the living room. Backgammon. The game, where you roll dice and move markers in an attempt to remove all yours from the board first, goes back nearly five thousand years. A variation was played in Mesopotamia, and the Romans' Game of Twelve Lines was virtually the same as the backgammon people play now.

I left the sisters to their competition and greeted Ahmad, who stood at the back door, looking out. He assured me everything had been quiet. I made a call to the spec in West Virginia, who reported that there'd been no hint of surveillance from the outside.

Nor had the deer, badgers or other animals been behaving oddly.

Ahmad was standing in a way I could only describe as anticipatory, shoulders at one angle, hips at another. Eyes were scanning the windows, his job, but also avoiding mine. He said, "I heard you or-

dered a transport to the Hansen Detention Center."

"That's right."

He was nodding, understandably confused; the people supposedly inside the
van were no more than thirty feet away
from him.

I asked, "Anybody call you about it?"

"It went out over the wire."

I told him of my ploy. "You won't be in
trouble. You can plead ignorance."

The young officer nodded, curious,
but I said nothing more. Like Abe Fallow, I'm always aware of my responsibility to teach protégés what I can about
our business—there is so much to learn.
But this was a situation I decided not to
elaborate on, since I hoped he'd never
find himself in one like it.

All he said was, "It was a good call,
sir. A slammer'd be wrong for this situation."

"Where's Ryan?"

"Working in his room. That accounting project of his, I think."

I realized the downstairs was filled
with a new smell, spice, which I took to
be from shampoo or perfume.

I was struck by the domesticity, re-played hundreds of times in the safe houses where I've stashed my princi-pals, and it's always jarring to me, the contrast: the homey, even mundane rou-tine that's the antithesis of the reason these men and women are here.

As it did occasionally, the comforting imagery made me feel somewhat senti-mental. Certain memories again arose but I didn't shoo them away quite so quickly this time. I recalled last Friday night after work, alone in the town house, eating a sandwich for dinner before I went to my gaming club up the street. I'd found the list for the party that Peggy and I had thrown years ago. I'd stared at it, my appetite gone. I'd become aware of the smell of the place, bitter from the cardboard, paper and ink of the many boxed games lining the walls. The town house had seemed unbear-ably sterile. I thought I should get some incense or do what people did when they were selling their houses, boil cin-namon on the stove.

Or bake cookies. Something domes-tic.

As if that would ever happen.

The game between the sisters now ended and Joanne returned to her room. Maree gave me a smile and booted up her computer.

I asked, "Who won?"

"Jo did. You can't beat her. At anything. It's impossible."

As a statistician, Joanne would have had a talent for math and that meant a talent for games—certain types, in any event. I knew my skill at numbers, and my analytical mind, helped me play.

In backgammon, which I happen to be good at, I knew the general strategy was to play a "running game," moving quickly around the board, offensively. If that didn't work, players had to fall back on a holding action, trying to create an anchor on the opponent's side. While not as complicated as chess, it's a sophisticated game. I would have liked to see how Joanne played. But the interest was purely theoretical. In all my years as a shepherd, I'd never played a game with a principal, though on occasion I'd been tempted.

Maree gestured toward her computer. "Tell me what you think?"

"What?" I asked.

"Come 'ere, Mr. Tour Guide. Take a look."

She motioned me over and typed some commands into her computer. A logo came up, *GSI, Global Sofware Innovations*. I'd heard of them but couldn't recall where. After a moment the program loaded. It was apparently a picture editing and archiving program; folders of Maree's photos appeared.

Maree's fingers paused, hovering over keys. I thought at first she was unfamiliar with the software, but it turned out the hesitation was due to another reason. With a wistfulness in her eyes, she said, "It's Amanda's program. We had a lot of fun installing it together. . . . I feel bad for her. She's got to be terrified about this whole thing."

I glanced into the woman's eyes, focused blankly on the logo. "She's stronger than a lot of my adult principals. She'll be fine." This was not just for reassurance; it was the truth.

Maree exhaled softly. "Jo thinks she's

stronger than I am." A look up at my face. "As a rule I never agree with my sister but she's right about that."

Then she seemed to toss aside the serious thoughts—as I'd been doing all day—and concentrated on the photo software.

She typed quickly and two pictures flashed onto the screen side by side.

"I can't decide which of these two are the best." She laughed, looking up, and patted the chair beside her. "It's okay, I don't bite."

I hesitated then sat down. I noted that, unsurprisingly, she was the source of the pleasant spice, not Joanne. And, as I'd observed yesterday, she was wearing makeup, skillfully applied. She had ironed and donned a new outfit—a sheer skirt and silk maroon blouse. This was curious. Not only do principals tend to ignore fashion like this when their lives are in danger but if Maree was as flighty as she seemed and the artist she claimed to be, I would have thought she'd have been inattentive to personal details. Or been more of a jeans-and-sweats woman.

She leaned close. I felt her arm against

mine and the sweet aroma wafted around me. I must have eased away slightly because she laughed again.

I felt a ping of impatience. But I did as she'd asked and I looked at the computer screen. "The gallery show I was telling you about? I'm submitting one of these. I've got to send it in by Tuesday to meet the deadline. What do you think?"

"I . . . what're you asking? Which one I like better?"

To me they were almost identical although one was more tightly cropped than the other. They depicted two somber men in suits, businessmen or politicians, having an intense discussion in the shadow of the government building in downtown D.C.

"Who are they?"

"I don't know. It doesn't matter. I was just walking down the street last week, near the Treasury Building, and saw them standing there. They look powerful, they look rich. But don't they seem like little boys in a way? On the school yard? Forty years younger, they would've started a shoving match."

At first, I didn't get that but then I saw, yes, she was right.

"The theme is about conflict," she explained.

"I don't see much difference."

"The one on the left? It's tighter. The emphasis is on the men. But there're no angles, no sense of composition. The one on the right is better stylistically. You see more of the Treasury Building. You see the sunlight, that band of light there, cutting into the stairs near them? It's aesthetically better . . . So?" she asked.

"Which one I like better?"

"That's the question, Mr. Tour Guide."

I felt suddenly awkward, like I was being tested on something I hadn't studied for. I didn't really know which one I liked more. The only photos I looked at regularly were surveillance and crime scene shots. Aesthetics didn't count.

Finally, I pointed to the picture on the left. "That one."

"Why?"

I hadn't known I had to show my work. "I don't know; I just do."

"Uh-uh, commit."

"I really don't know. They're both nice."
I glanced up the hall. "I've got to talk to
your brother-in-law."

"Come on, Corte. Humor me. You've
screwed up my weekend pretty bad.
You won't even be my masseur. You
owe me."

I banked my irritation again and looked
at the pictures. Suddenly I had a thought.
"I like it because you have to ask yourself, what's your goal? You said it was
to show conflict. The one on the left
does that better. It's more focused."

"Even though it's less artistic."

"I'm not sure what artistic means, but
yes."

She lifted her hand to give me a high
five. Reluctantly I lifted mine and she
slapped it. "That's just what I was thinking."

Maree then touched the pad. The GSI
software instantly shrank the pictures to
thumbnails and she directed them back
to a folder. She then started a slideshow
and the pictures faded up to fill the
screen, remained for a few moments
then went to black and a new one was
displayed.

I have no artistic ability whatsoever but I can appreciate something that's technically well executed. Her pictures were all in focus and seemed well composed. But it was the subjects that appealed to me. Had they been still lifes or abstracts I wouldn't have been interested but Maree specialized in portraits and she seemed to be able to capture the spirit of her subjects perfectly, though I supposed since she used a fancy digital camera there were a hundred outtakes for every keeper. As the show continued I noted the controls and paused several of them. Maree was leaning close.

Workers, mothers and children, businessmen, parents, policemen, athletes . . . There was no theme, but whoever they were, Maree had caught them in a moment of emotion. Anger, love, frustration, pride.

"They're good. You're talented."

"You do something enough times, you're going to get a few chops down. Hey, you want to see who you're guarding?"

I frowned.

She typed and another folder appeared. It took me a moment to realize what she meant—and what I was looking at. Family albums of Maree, Joanne and who I guessed were their parents and other relatives. Maree was calling out names and information.

I heard Abe's voice.

Learn only what you need to learn to keep them alive. Don't use their names, don't look at their kids' pictures, don't ask 'em if they're all right, unless you've been dodging bullets and you need to call a medic. . . .

I said, "I really have to talk to Ryan."

"Don't be scared of a few family pictures, Corte. They're not even your family. *I'm* the one who should be scared."

A picture of a trim, crew-cut man in khaki slacks and a short-sleeved shirt faded in. Maree hit PAUSE. "The Colonel. Our father . . . and, yeah, people called him 'the Colonel,' capital *C.* Lieutenant colonel, a little bird, not a big bird."

Still, the man was imposing, no question.

Maree's voice dropped. "Don't tell Freud but Jo thought she was marrying

him. She got Ryan instead. Dad was career military, strong, quiet, distant, didn't
laugh. . . . Ha, like you, Corte. . . . Hey,
you know I'm messing with you."

I ignored her comment and continued
to look at her pictures. Many of them
showed Maree by herself and Joanne
with their father.

"She was his darling, Jo was. The
perfect athlete, the perfect student in
school. Not a lot of fun, I have to say . . .
Dad'd take her to her soccer matches
and track events. He tried with me, I'm
not saying he didn't. But I sucked at
sports and activities. I was a total
klutz . . . Dad never rubbed it in my face,
you know. 'Oh, your sister's perfect,'
none of that. But that's what it smelled
like. So I went the other way. I was the
wild one. The big I—Irresponsible.
Dropped out. I had a DUI, well, a couple, when I was seventeen or eighteen.
Drugs, a little shoplifting."

Thanks to the boyfriends, I recalled.
But said nothing.

"I just didn't fucking care. Squeaked
by in a community college . . . Jo graduated second or third in her class. She

majored in political science, nearly went into the army, like Dad, but he talked her out of that. I think she would've been good, actually. Drill instructor. You have brothers or sisters, Corte?"

"No."

"And no kids. Lucky man."

One picture of Jo revealed that she'd lost a lot of weight and looked gaunt. "Was she sick there?"

"Car crash."

I remembered that from duBois's bio.

She looked around. "Pretty bad. She lost control on some ice. Needed a lot of surgery. It's why she can't have kids but we don't talk about that."

So the child question was answered. I realized one of the other attractions of the hero cop—he not only saved her life; he offered her a built-in family.

The pictures slipped past again and I kept looking at them. Some of the scans were sepia pictures, going back a hundred years; some were black-and-white; some were oversaturated, from the sixties and seventies. Many were recent, direct digital.

Finally, I'd had enough.

"I really better get some things done,"
I told her.

"Sure."

"Those are good pictures."

"Thank you," she said formally, maybe
mocking my tone.

Mr. Tour Guide . . .

As I was walking up the hallway to
find Ryan and tell him what duBois had
found about his cases, my phone
buzzed with a text message. I figured it
would be from Westerfield or Ellis—not
risking a voice call that would end in a
coward's voice mail. But I glanced
down and saw it was from duBois. I
was pleased, thinking maybe she'd finished her investigation from my espionage at Graham's house. Or perhaps
she'd returned to her chatty self and
forgiven me for the trial she'd had to
endure there.

But the message was brief and about
something else altogether.

*Problem . . . Hermes has a bot
roaming websites, etc and he
had a hit. This was posted fifteen
minutes ago. Here's the URL.*

I hurried into the den, unlocked my computer and typed the Web address she'd sent.

The site was a blog, written by someone with the screen name SassyCat222. I was expecting something about Clarence Brown—well, Ali Pamuk—or Eric Graham or even Ryan Kessler himself: information that Loving might use. I skimmed quickly. The postings were typical of all blogs, containing more information about daily life than anybody cared to read. Some were humorous—a boring Saturday night at the mall when a date fell through and a music review of a really bad rock concert—and some sobering: a report about overcrowded classrooms, a call for an AIDS awareness campaign and the start of a series about the suicide of a teenager the blogger knew through her volunteer work for a self-harm prevention program at her school.

I froze when I noticed that last entry. With a sinking heart, I grabbed my phone and dialed.

"DuBois."

I asked, "SassyCat . . . she's Amanda

Kessler, right?" I remembered that she'd volunteered for a counseling program at her school.

"That's right. It's her."

The girl must've thought it was safe to post under her screen name and from a friend's computer.

"Hermes says it was posted about an hour ago, with a naked IP address. It took him two minutes to find it was a private residence in Loudoun County. Near White's Ferry."

"Bill Carter's house?"

"Next door."

If we had a bot, Loving would too. He'd check the property records of everybody in the area and find Carter's name. He'd learn that Carter's main residence was five minutes from the Kesslers' in Fairfax. He'd know we'd stashed the girl there.

Caller ID sounded on call waiting. It was Westerfield's number. He'd just learned that the armored van was empty, I guessed. Then it buzzed again—I can juggle four calls on this phone. My boss's number.

I ignored them both. I told duBois,

"I'm going to Carter's myself. It's less than a half hour from here. Call Freddy and have him get some tactical troops there. You have the location, right?"

"Yes."

I disconnected all the calls and slipped the phone away. I briefed Ahmad and then threw my laptop, along with extra ammunition, into my shoulder bag and headed out the side door, hitting the speed dial for Bill Carter's phone. As I leapt into the front seat of the Honda and sped down the drive, it rang three times and went to voice mail.

Chapter 26

Answer . . . Please answer.

Was Carter dead and the girl in Loving's hands already?

The next occurrence would be a call from Loving via a cold phone to the FBI asking to be connected to Ryan Kessler, to inform him that his daughter was captive and requesting the information that the lifter had been hired to extract.

When that call came through, it would fall to me to make the decision to put Loving in touch with Kessler and try to negotiate the girl's release.

Or not. And write Amanda's death warrant.

I hit REDIAL.

Click. The electronic voice of the phone urged, "Please leave a message."

No . . .

I disconnected and nudged up the

RPMs on the hissing engine, hitting seventy, about the fastest I could do along Route 7 and the country roads that roughly paralleled the Potomac River. It was 3:00 p.m. on a pleasant Sunday and there were brunchers and golfers and sightseers out, which made the going slow. I'd called in a clear-transit request to Loudoun and Fairfax County Police, which I didn't want to do, because it would identify my Honda to anyone who thought to check, or to hack, the system but I couldn't afford to get stopped now.

I tried the phone once more.

One tone, another . . .

Then finally: "'Lo," Bill Carter answered.

I exhaled in relief. "It's Corte. Loving's on his way there."

"Okay." Instantly alert. "What should I do?"

"First, you have your weapon on you?"

"My old sidearm. Smittie thirty-eight. Yessir. And a twelve-gauge on the mantel."

"Get it now. Double, pump, auto?"

"Over-under."

It'd have to do. "Load it, extra ammo in your pockets."

"Need my hands. I'm putting you down for a minute." A faint hollow clink of metal. I heard, "Okay."

"Where's Amanda?"

"Getting the tackle together. We were going fishing in about a half hour."

"I need you out of the house."

"She'll get upset," Carter said.

"Then she'll be upset."

"How'd it happen?"

"She posted something from her friend's computer."

"Goddamn. We were over there for brunch. The girls disappeared for a time. I should've thought."

I heard footsteps, then his voice telling Amanda that there was a problem and they were leaving immediately. She said, "That's your gun. Why do you have that, Uncle Bill? . . ." Her voice trailed off. He sounded reassuring as he talked to her; there was no recrimination. Good. No time for that now.

"Okay, Corte. What next?"

Glancing down to my computer screen, then back to the road, I explained, "I've got a satellite picture of your property from Earthwatch. It's not real clear but I see a road your drive connects to. That's the only access, right?"

"Aside from the lake."

"Have you seen any cars on the road?"

"Mandy, it's okay. Everything's going to be okay. . . . All right, cars? I was just raccoon-proofing the trash and I saw one go past."

"That unusual?"

"It's pretty deserted around here but we get drivers some. He didn't slow up and I didn't think any more of it."

"Description?"

"Truth is, I heard it more'n saw it. Where do you want us?"

"Don't drive. Don't go near the car. Go to some place on the property where you can see somebody coming and you've got good cover." I risked a glance at the satellite image. "I think I can see a little clearing in the . . . I guess it's the northeast section of your property, near the road."

"Yeah, it's a little meadow. There're

some trees on the other side. We can get there. It's high ground."

"Good. You have any camouflage?"

"Fishing jackets. Dark green."

"That'll do. Put the phone on vibrate."

There was the sound of clanks and zippers. "How's this, Uncle Bill?"

"Good."

It seemed that the girl wasn't panicking. I was pleased. I continued, "Loving's armed and he's got a partner who's armed too. Has sandy-colored hair, maybe a green jacket. Slim. But don't trust anybody. All right, get moving. I'll be there in fifteen. The Bureau's on their way too."

"What about the neighbors?"

"Loving knows where you live now. He won't bother with them. Get to the meadow. We're going to hang up. I need you to concentrate."

I needed to as well, focusing on my driving. I was reflecting that if Loving had in fact tipped to Amanda's blog, I knew he'd be pleased to learn her whereabouts. When it comes to edge, snatching a principal's child is as good as it gets.

Chapter 27

Thirty-three minutes after leaving the compound, I eased the Honda to a stop in a stand of bushes in front of Carter's lakefront property and climbed out. I activated the silent alarm.

I pulled a forest green jumpsuit out of my gear bag—one of two; the other was black—and tugged it on. I slung the bag over my shoulder and walked quickly along the road, examining the ground. I could see evidence that a car had pulled over here recently, paused and then started up again. Footsteps in the soft earth headed toward where I knew the house would be—about three hundred yards into the woods.

I'd have to assume Loving was here.

Surveying the ground, I decided the logical route he'd have taken. I hopped a low stone wall meant to deter only the most stupid or nervous of animals and moved quickly along Loving's path, which would be invisible to many people but was evident to me—because of an interest I've pursued for years.

In my twenties I was in Austin, Texas, finishing up yet another degree. I'd always loved hiking and, sick of the sedentary life of academia, I'd joined the orienteering club at the university. The sport, which originated in Sweden, is a competition in which you use a special map and a compass to navigate through wilderness you've never seen before, stopping at checkpoints to have a control card physically or electronically stamped. The first competitor to hit the "double circle"—the end of the route on the orienteering map—is the winner.

I fell in love with the sport—I still compete—and found it a welcome relief from the static hours in the classroom or in front of computers or poring through obscure texts.

During one meet in Austin I became friends with a fellow competitor, a Drug Enforcement Administration agent. He was a sign cutter—an expert at tracking people, mostly illegal immigrants and drug runners—and he got me interested in the subject. There're no competitions in sign cutting, as with orienteering, but Border Patrol and DEA hold regular training sessions and he arranged for me to attend some.

Sign cutting was to me like some huge board game that you played outside, with yourself as a game piece. I fell instantly in love with it and when I wasn't at orienteering competitions I would head outside and practice, tracking animals and hikers, who never knew they were being pursued. I even made a little extra money from the DEA on weekends, during their training sessions—I pretended to be a drug mule and tried to escape from sign cutting agents. I was pretty good, since I'd studied the techniques and knew how to cover a trail as well as find one.

The art had come in handy to me as a shepherd on a number of occasions.

I was using the techniques now, carefully scanning the ground and branches for indications of where Loving had passed. The signs were subtle: a sun-bleached branch upside down, pebbles or deer shit out of place, leaves where leaves shouldn't normally be.

Sign cutting taught me that terrain determines the route the prey follows 90 percent of the time: you generally have only to follow the path of least resistance to be pretty sure of remaining on the trail of your target. Henry Loving was different. His route took him in directions that didn't seem to make sense, less direct and more difficult.

But his strategy became logical when I realized that he was pausing repeatedly and turning to his left and right, presumably to look for pursuers.

Rational irrationality . . .

Now that I knew his strategy of taking the high, difficult ground and pausing, prepared to engage, I moved more quickly, since he wouldn't expect someone to follow his exact route through the dense foliage. His path wove through patches of forsythia, dense blankets of kudzu and ivy, vines, brambles and brush whose pedigree I was unfamiliar with.

I paused to listen too. Dogs track by

smell first, then sound and then sight. Humans are different but hearing comes second with them as well. Always listen and listen carefully. Your prey makes noise escaping and those preying upon you make noise moving in for the kill (humans tend to be the loudest approaching that climactic moment; other animals, the opposite). You'd think that snaps and rustling would seem to come from everywhere. But it doesn't take long to learn to compensate for echoes, judge distances and know with more or less certainty where the source is located.

After a few moments I detected some faint snaps ahead of me. Maybe they were from branches clicking together in the increasing breeze, maybe a deer, maybe they were the footfalls of a man intent on kidnapping a sixteen-year-old girl.

Then, about a hundred yards away, near a body of water, I saw the outline of Carter's house. I scanned carefully. No movement other than leaves stirred by taut wind.

Moving closer.

Pausing and scanning again.

I was two hundred feet or so from the house when I spotted Loving.

Yes, it was definitely the lifter. I caught a glimpse of his face. He was wearing the same clothes, or similar ones, as yesterday when we'd had our meeting at the flytrap. He wasn't carrying his weapon; he was using his hands to move aside brush and branches as silently as he could. I'd hope to catch him on the path; he'd be less cautious there than at the house, where he would anticipate danger; he would have done his homework and learned that Bill Carter was a retired cop and surely armed.

Loving now drew his weapon and pulled back the slide slightly to make sure a round was chambered.

I drew mine as well and started after him.

I couldn't help but think: What would Westerfield, or anybody, say if he were observing this? Wasn't my job to get my principal, now hiding three hundred yards away, to safety as fast as I could?

Then why was I stalking the lifter?

There are herding dogs that move

*sheep around in a field and then there
are herding dogs that both guard the
flock and attack predators, however big
and however numerous. . . .*

Sorry, Abe. I'm the second type. I
can't help it.

I narrowed the distance, debating my
next strategy. I'd called Freddy from the
road and knew there were officers and
agents en route, running silent. Already
local officers would be setting up roadblocks. Freddy's ETA was probably
twenty minutes.

This was a poor area to stage a one-
on-one tactical assault and, though the
ID was certain, I had no clear target presenting. Loving was in and out of shadows. A missed shot would be far too
dangerous and not worth the risk.

And where was his partner?

I continued on. Once he was in the
house, it would take him ten minutes to
search all the rooms and realize that his
edge had left and was not hiding in the
obvious places.

I was moving closer, still under good
cover and largely silent.

He approached the garage and looked

in. He'd see Carter's SUV inside. He eased into the bushes separating the building from the house itself. He crouched and moved along a low gray fence connecting the two structures. The foliage was high there and dense. It was hard to see his form but I could just make it out. Then I stopped, a twitching in my belly. If Loving continued another fifteen feet or so in the direction he was headed, he'd be in a clearing. And would present a perfectly backlit target.

I lifted my weapon and aimed where he'd appear. I was about eighty feet away. Not a particularly long distance for a powerful handgun like this—a .40 caliber. Even with the short barrel, a cluster would likely kill him. I remembered the training. Three shots high, three low. Move aside from where your muzzle flash would've registered and prepare to fire again. Count rounds expended.

He kept going. Ten feet to the break in the plants.

Then eight, then six. . . .

I suddenly felt my heart rate increasing, my palms cooling from sweat.

Here was Henry Loving in front of me, nearly in my sights. . . .

Two thoughts came into my mind: We have specific rules of engagement that require us to make a surrender demand unless we or someone else is in imminent danger. That rule applies to every hostile, even those who are armed and who are willing to use a sixteen-year-old girl's screams to force her sobbing father to tell what he knows.

Even those who'd tortured and killed a good man like Abe Fallow.

But my second thought was: three high, three low, step aside, prepare to shoot again.

I curled my left hand under my right, aimed steadily, evened my breathing.

Four feet until the shadow that was Henry Loving would break from the brush and I'd have a perfect shot. He now approached the clearing but, instead of standing, he dropped to a crouch, still obscured by the thick brush.

Stand up, I thought. Stand up, goddamn it! I felt a flush of anger, unusual for me, as I squinted at the darkness of his form on the other side of the brush.

Hell, just go for it, I told myself suddenly. Empty your entire mag and reload. . . . A slow breath. Now! I went into a shooting stance and leaned forward, started applying pressure.

I felt as if I could will the bullets to strike their target.

I probably got to four pounds of pressure on a trigger with a pull of five and a half, then gave an inaudible sigh and lowered the gun.

I reflected on what I'd just thought: *willing the bullets.*

Shooting is physics and chemistry, vision and steady muscles, choosing the right strategy of firing position, having a clear target. There is no will involved. There's no luck involved.

I was a shepherd. I couldn't afford to be emotional.

If I'd shot and merely wounded him or missed, he would have had my position. For all I knew the partner was fifty yards behind me, waiting for *me* to present. Or, hearing the shot, Bill Carter and Amanda might leave cover to come see what had happened.

Unnerved that I'd nearly given in to

emotion, I checked the ground in front of me to make sure I could move silently and I started forward again.

Still using the plants for cover, Loving slipped up to the gate and tried it gently, testing for squeaking. I saw him extract something from his pocket and he appeared to oil the hinges. Then, still halfway out of sight, he slipped through and made his way toward the house, under good cover.

Debating, I finally picked my strategy.

I turned away and headed for the clearing where Bill Carter and Amanda waited.

It was one of the hardest decisions I'd ever made.

But my goal was clear. For me, solo, to try to take Loving in the house was inefficient. A tactical move would have required at least two and ideally four others. My best strategy was to find my principals and get them out. Loving's going inside would buy us ten minutes. I'd let Freddy and his crew run the takedown.

I oriented myself and backed up the way I'd come, then turned left, toward where I knew the girl and Carter were hiding. It was some distance, maybe three hundred yards, across the length of the property. But I had a sense of the forest now and I noted the area ahead of me was largely coniferous—with plenty of pine needles dampening the ground, leaving resinous branches that didn't snap when you stepped on them. One could move quickly and in virtual silence here.

Which was why, as I took my first step forward, Loving's partner got me from behind; I never heard his approach.

A grunt of a whisper: "Drop that weapon. Hands out to your side." I felt the muzzle of a gun kiss my back.

Chapter 28

As the partner pressed his gun harder into my spine, I thought: Is this what Abe Fallow had heard not long before Loving had gone to work on him?

Hands out to the side. . . .

I was about to die too.

But not right away.

Because like my mentor, I was valuable. I wondered if Loving had created a flytrap of his own. Maybe he'd used the girl not as an edge on her father but to get me to give up the detective, speculating that it might be logistically difficult to let Ryan know they had his daughter.

I'd been the bait in our flytrap; Amanda was the bait here.

"I told you. Gun. Drop it."

I did. You can't spin around faster than a bullet.

How long could I hold out? I wondered.

Sandpaper and alcohol . . .

Memories of Peggy and the boys, Jeremy and Sam, surfaced.

Then the voice behind me whispered, "Wait."

Curious. It seemed that he was speaking to himself.

Then I heard pleasantly, "Oh, that's you, isn't it, Corte?"

My hands started shaking and I turned around slowly to see Bill Carter, holding a twelve-gauge over-under shotgun pointed directly at my chest. His finger wasn't outside the guard. Amanda was behind him, eyes wide.

Breathing hard now. So hard my chest hurt.

He lowered the scattergun.

"You didn't go to the clearing," I whispered.

"No. Seemed too far. And looks like you weren't in any big hurry to come visit either."

True, I reflected.

Amanda gazed at me with cautious but steady eyes. Definitely her father's eyes. She still had around her shoulder her plush bear purse.

I studied the area around us. It wasn't defensible—we were in a low point. I wanted to get back to the car and leave as fast as we could.

We crouched. "He's in the house. He'll know you're not there any minute now."

I gestured toward the road and to the right. "My car's past the rock fence in front. About two hundred yards. Let's go now. Come on, Amanda. It's going to be fine."

She didn't look like she needed reassurance. I got the feeling she wanted to go after Loving herself.

Grit . . .

I guided us up the incline of the ravine and toward the road. We moved slowly and I was getting dizzy from looking from side to side and behind us so often. There were a thousand configurations of shadow and shapes of green that took on the dimensions and postures of a hostile.

Still, none broke away from the backdrop and became an armed human.

Twenty yards, then thirty, then fifty.

Suddenly Amanda gasped. Our weapons up, Carter and I dropped to our knees and I pulled the girl down, looking in the direction she was.

The deer emerged from the bushes he was grazing on and stared at us with a face both blank and cautious. Two others joined him. Carter picked up a rock and was going to toss it to scare them off, presumably to make Loving think that any noise he might've heard was from this fauna. But I shook my head, opting for quiet.

Sometimes you can outsmart yourself.

Looking down and verifying that there were no signs the partner had come along the path I'd chosen to follow, we continued on silently. The deer went back to destroying a bush for lunch.

More noises near us.

Animals? Or Loving? The partner?

We came to a bald strip of the property, about fifty feet across. To keep to cover, going around, would have taken too long. I motioned us across the open space.

Just as we reached the other side, I

looked back. About a football field's distance, I caught a glimpse of the house.

And I saw Henry Loving stepping into the front yard. He looked our way and froze.

Then dug into his pocket for a radio or mobile.

"He spotted us. Move fast!"

I indicated the asphalt and we started to run.

"Bill, watch the rear. If you see him, aim low. He'll be crouching."

Better a minor wound on the feet and ankles than a miss over the head, Abe used to say.

"Got it."

I whispered, "Come on, Amanda. We're doing fine."

Keeping low, gasping, we ran through the thinning undergrowth, not caring about noise. I expected to hear at any moment the near simultaneous snap of the bullet and the boom of the weapon from behind us. But neither Loving nor his partner fired. Amanda was no good to them dead. You need your edge relatively healthy.

Finally, all of us breathing hard, we

approached the road. About fifty yards away was my car, on the other side of the stone fence. We sprinted through the low brush.

Carter glanced back. "I think I see him. Go on, get in the car. I'll cover you."

"No." We ran a bit farther then I pulled the others down beside me, under the cover of a fallen tree, old enough that as a youngster it might have given similar protection and comfort to Union or Confederate soldiers making their way south after the carnage of the most deadly battle of the Civil War, Antietam.

I was sure I saw Loving behind us, not far away, maybe sixty, seventy yards or so. He too had ducked behind a tree next to the wall.

I said to Carter, "We're going to move up close to the car. I'll be in the rear. I'll start it remotely. When it starts, fire both barrels into the woods across the road. This time I want you to aim high. Reload and fire two more. Fast. Then, you both go over the wall. Amanda, get in the backseat and get down. Bill, drive maybe twenty feet or so forward, then stop, cover the forest across the road with your sidearm. I'll join you in a minute."

"The partner's over there?"

"That's right."

He didn't ask how I knew and I wasn't inclined to explain that it was simply rational.

A glance at both faces, sweaty and flecked with leaf debris. "Ready?"

Nods.

I pressed the ignition button and the engine came to life. Our cars have special mufflers to deaden the exhaust sound but there's nothing you can do about a starter.

Carter didn't hesitate. The instant the car started, he did as I'd asked: rising over the fence and firing two hugely loud rounds. He reloaded, fired two more and reloaded again, as I fired a burst of six in the direction where Loving was hiding. Carter grabbed Amanda by the hand. They ran to the car.

It squealed away, while I rolled over the stone fence and lay in tall grass on the shoulder of the road, prone, aiming back toward Loving.

I felt a tickle on my spine. Loving

would think I was in the car but the partner might have seen the ruse and gone for a shot at me in the shallow weeds.

Come on . . . come on . . .

Then Loving presented.

He jumped over the wall and started to aim at the car.

I didn't have much of a shot, with the brush and the wall partially blocking my view, yet it was something. But just as I started to fire, Carter slammed on the brakes—as I'd asked him—and Loving realized my strategy. He didn't see me but he knew what had happened. He spun around and started back over the wall. I emptied my magazine at him. Chunks of rock flew from the wall and dirt from the ground. Loving vanished over the rock. I couldn't tell if I'd hit him.

Reloading, I saw motion in the leaves across the road—it would be the partner—and I sprinted to the car. I leapt into the driver's seat as Carter scrabbled over to the passenger's.

I floored the accelerator and we sped away.

Carter was looking behind us. "Yeah, there's the partner, climbing out of the woods. And Loving's joining him, they're in the road. Loving's hurt, I think. Doesn't look too steady."

A few minutes later I skidded around a bend in the road and slowed from eighty-five.

Carter laughed, pointing up. "Your boys're here."

A chopper swooped in fast, descending as it sped directly for Carter's house. A moment later a stream of black SUVs, in the oncoming lane, braked to a stop, blocking me. They approached with weapons drawn, cautious, and I held my ID out the window.

A young agent, covered by two others, looked into the car and then motioned the vehicles containing his fellow agents around him, to continue on to the house.

"You all right, sir? Everybody's fine?" The agent looked us over.

"Yes, we are. Is Agent Fredericks here?"

"He's about five minutes behind us."

"All right, tell your agents there're two of them. Loving and his partner, both armed. Loving may be wounded. I don't know where they stashed their vehicle."

"We'll check it out, sir."

"I was looking over a map earlier and saw across the lake there're a dozen houses and some easy routes to the interstate. I'm thinking they may try to row over, hijack a car."

"I'll get some of the team over there," the agent said.

I told him, "Can you patch me through to the chopper pilot? I'll give him a description of the property."

"Chopper?"

"Your tactical air unit." I gestured toward the sky.

He looked confused. "Well, sir, we don't have a helicopter involved in the operation."

Chapter 29

Bill Carter sat silently beside me and a glance in the rearview mirror revealed Amanda in the backseat, staring out the window at the overcast fall afternoon. We were ten miles from Carter's lake house.

I was not thinking of what had just happened at Carter's property but was wrestling with a difficult memory. Peggy, the boys and I were driving in the country and I spotted a bad roadside accident ahead. I'd stopped to see if I could help the stoic but young and shaken county troopers. They say that mothers are better than fathers at remaining detached around accidents and blood and trauma. Not Peggy. She'd climbed into the back with the boys and clutched them to her. The ostensible purpose was to make sure they looked away from the

overturned cars and the mangled bodies, as yet uncovered, but in fact she
was hiding her face, as well as the boys'.
(Thinking again about another similarity
between Maree and my wife: the whip-
sawing between carefree optimism and
edgy distress.)

Back then, at the site of the accident,
Sammy and Jeremy had managed to
peek, despite their mother's huddle. Jer,
the oldest, was horrified at what he saw
and began sobbing uncontrollably. Sam,
though, said, "Daddy, that man lying
there. He doesn't have a hand. How can
he eat ice cream?" Not a tragedy to him;
a mystery.

You just didn't know how young people would respond to trauma.

I saw Sam's face, unperturbed and
curious, reflected in Amanda's.

"You all right, honey?" I asked, surprised I'd used the endearment.

She looked toward me, nodded and
then studied Carter's Beretta shotgun,
open and sitting on the seat beside her.

Hitting a speed dial button, I called
Freddy.

"Hey," he said.

"You there?"

"Nice place. I may retire here."

I hadn't really appreciated the comforts of Carter's summer home.

"Anything?"

"They're gone."

"The chopper?"

"Had to be."

"No," I said. "I know that's how they were extracted. I mean do you have any details on it?"

"Negative. So far. We're still canvassing. Some wits reported hearing a helicopter low and nearby. They thought it was going down, you know, crashing. A couple nine-one-one calls. Nobody—"

"Saw anything?"

"Interesting question, son. They looked but they heard only a ruckus and saw leaves and dust. Landed between two stands of trees thirty feet apart. That takes some skill."

"More, it takes some equipment. Expensive . . . Find the car?"

"Stolen months ago. Somebody else's tags. We were hoping to get the partner's prints but didn't find a single, solitary swirl."

"The neighbors?"

"They're fine."

I told Carter and Amanda about their friends, then turned my attention back to Freddy. I told him, "I'll get Claire tracking down the chopper." Our organization is always flying our principals around the country, sometimes internationally, so we had good contacts with the FAA and private charter companies. The fact that the craft seemed small, which meant it had a short range and would have to be based somewhere near here, would give duBois some guidance in finding the lessee.

Freddy continued, "Somebody's hurt. We found blood."

"Where?"

"Roadside. The wall and some bushes. A path too."

"It's Loving. I got him. He was on his feet afterward. How much blood?"

"Not a lot. Found his footprints and the partner's."

"I'll have Claire look into medical treatment."

"Who is this gal of yours, Corte? She Claire-voyant?"

Jokes again.

"Listen, Corte . . ."

"Westerfield," I said.

"My voice give that away, son?" Freddy asked.

"What about him?"

"For one he keeps calling. He's calling me. He's calling everybody. What'd you do?"

I said, "He wants my principals in a slammer. He's wrong but I couldn't reason with him. So I basically . . ." I tried to think of a good euphemism.

"Put your job on the line by scamming the attorney general of the United States of America. And pissing off half the federal government."

I said, "Loving's got too many contacts in D.C. I couldn't risk it."

"I don't care. That's your business, Corte. It's no skin off my nose."

"Call me if you find any forensics. Loving went through Carter's house too."

"Will do."

We disconnected. As soon as I did, my boss's number came up on caller ID. So did Westerfield's. I rejected both calls and dialed duBois. I explained to her what happened and then told her about the helicopter. "Find it, if there's any way."

"Okay." She took down the details.

Then I said, "And Loving's wounded."

The demure young woman said, "You got a piece of him. That's good."

"I want you to try to find where he'll go for treatment."

There's a legal requirement that medical personnel must report gunshot wounds to law enforcement. Gangs and organized crime have doctors or nurses or even vets on call who treat wounds and conveniently forget to dial 911. We knew some of these medicos and routinely monitored them (we didn't arrest them since they were invaluable as sources to find and track wounded lifters and hitters).

Loving, though, would avoid any of these, of course. I told duBois this and said, "He's going to find somebody private, somebody we don't know about. Look through all the files we have on him, checking addresses he's been seen

at, phone calls, everything. Public records too."

She'd use ORC and other data-mining
programs.

"I'll see what I can find," she said.
"And, Corte?"

My name again. "Yes?"

"Those images you got at Graham's
house? I'm still running the analysis."

"Good."

She was pausing. "I thought about it
and there wasn't any other way to get
the information from him. What you
asked me to do. I didn't like it then, I
didn't like it later. But it was pretty smart.
I'll remember that."

"There wasn't any other way," I repeated.

We disconnected and we drove in silence for a half hour. Carter asked to put
the radio on and I said, "You don't mind,
I'd rather keep it off. Better to concentrate."

"Oh. Sure."

I saw that Amanda was looking at me
in the mirror.

"Was that all because of me, back
there?" she asked. "Because of my blog?"

"Yes. He'd linked your screen name to your real name through a social networking site. He tracked the post to Bill's neighbors and then to his house."

She closed her eyes. "I'm sorry. I . . . I thought you meant I couldn't use *my* computer. I didn't know he could track us. I used my nic."

But she was a smart girl. She'd have had an inkling of the risk but in the oblivion and zeal of adolescence she hadn't thought it through or hadn't cared. Most likely, a little of both.

Amanda then added, "It's just I felt really bad about Susan—this sophomore at school."

"The one who killed herself?" I asked.

"That's the thing. It was a car crash but she was driving real fast and stupid, like she didn't care if she lived or not. That's a kind of suicide, our counselors tell everybody. I wanted to blog about that, make sure people know that being reckless can be just like taking pills or hanging yourself."

A curious thought struck me: Here was this young girl devoted to looking out for people. She was, in her own way, a shepherd. I wondered, if I had had a daughter, would she have turned out like Amanda? I would've been proud of her, I knew that.

But that thought, like so many others today, got carted off to the dust bin.

She asked, "He wanted to kill me?" in the monotone of somebody who doesn't really believe they could ever die.

Carter stirred and was about to reassure the girl. I now knew, though, that she required little coddling. "No, he wanted to kidnap you and get your father to tell him something."

"Tell him what?"

"We don't know."

She fell silent and stared out the window.

Some lifters have standards. Some won't hurt women or children. Some rely on mental or professional pressure or risk of embarrassment or financial loss. There are some cases they won't take on and some limits to what they'll do to coerce information out of people. They assess the principals and use the minimum edge necessary to get the information they've been hired to get. At the other extreme are the ones like Henry Loving. They'll take whatever steps they decide are appropriate.

Curiously, I respect these hitters and lifters more than the others. They're as true to their standards as I am to mine. They determine their goal and achieve it in the most efficient way possible. This makes them more predictable.

Amanda asked, "Is Jo totally freaked?"

"Not really," I told her.

"Are you sure?" The question was wry.

"Okay, she's freaked. But she's safe, with your father and aunt."

"Good. . . . I'm sorry, Uncle Bill. I kind of messed things up."

She didn't hesitate to accept responsibility for what had just happened.

"Everything's going to be fine."

I slowed, then signaled and turned. Amanda frowned, looking at the low stone building we were now approaching. She said quickly, "I . . . Are you taking me here because of what I did? I mean . . ."

I couldn't help but smile. "No, no, it's

just a safe place for you and Bill to spend the night."

I pulled up to the entrance gate of Northern Virginia Maximum Security Federal Detention Center.

Chapter 30

"What's going on? Where have you been?"

My boss's voice clattered urgently through my earbud. Irritation and anger—any emotion—always seemed muted when filtered through Chinese plastic and metal but there was no mistaking his mood.

"Loving got a lead to the Kesslers' daughter. She's safe. Loving's wounded."

Ellis asked, "How bad?"

"We don't know. Didn't lose a lot of blood . . . Aaron, he had a helicopter extraction."

"He *what*?"

"Claire's tracking it down, if she can. You ever hear of a lifter having a chopper on call?"

A thoughtful moment. "No, I never have."

"Means his primary's rich or got professional access to choppers you don't need paperwork on."

"What's your next step?"

"I just stashed the daughter in a slammer. It's safe. She's under a Jane Doe, a material witness to a drug hit. If Loving's got anybody inside, I doubt he'll pay attention and I've had the warden cut all outgoing communication for the day. We're still looking into Kessler's two main cases to find the primary. Claire's tracking down doctors off the grid Loving might use to get stitched up."

Ellis said, "Listen, Corte, I'm doing the best I can—"

"About Westerfield."

Hence, my boss's mood, of course.

"About Westerfield. Why didn't you just ignore him? Why'd you lie about the slammer in D.C.?"

"To buy time. If I'd ignored him, Aaron, he might've tried to find me. I was in the field. I can't afford to be detained when I've got principals. Not in a case involving Henry Loving."

Ellis said, "He could still get you fired."

"I thought we'd have an answer by now. The primary."

Or Loving in a body bag. Had he stood up when I'd hoped at the lake house in Loudoun County, the case might well be over.

"But we don't."

"No. Please, just keep him off my back for the night, Aaron. Tell him we've got a delicate operation going."

"To find Loving?"

"No. That's gas on the bonfire. Tell him I've got some leads to the primary. Tell him the terrorist connection is panning out."

"For real?"

A legitimate question, considering how deceptively I'd been running the job so far.

"Yes. There's money going into the Middle East. Some of it's ending up in Saudi Arabia, a dozen shell companies."

"Now that's interesting."

"Westerfield'll love it. A good federal case for his cap."

"Cap?"

"Feather in his cap. Claire's checking out some reconnaissance I did at Graham's place—the Department of Defense guy with the forged check. We're moving ahead. But I'm keeping the Kesslers. Make me out the heavy. I'm fine with that. But I can't let them go."

A sigh. "I'll do what I can."

We disconnected and I made the turn to head back to the Great Falls safe house. I'd called Ahmad, briefed him and learned everything was quiet there, though apparently Joanne and her husband had been squabbling. It was over something petty. The fights among principals invariably were, I'd noticed. I spoke to Ryan, who sounded sober, and told him that there'd been an incident at Bill Carter's but everybody was all right. Amanda and he were in federal protection. I ended the call before an alarmed Joanne could get on the line.

The time was nearly 6:00 p.m. and fatigue was seeping in.

My caller ID announced duBois.

"Me. Go ahead."

"I've got a couple of things. First, the helicopter . . . One thing I noticed. Women don't say 'choppers.' I've talked to six people, three men and three women. The men all say 'chopper.' The women say 'helicopter.'"

DuBois's observations were back. She'd largely recovered from the Graham ignominy.

"There was no flight plan filed. I was thinking about what that would mean. I assume it wouldn't be a government helicopter, like fire or police—"

"Not likely."

"Which means it's not a charter. Leasing companies're very buttoned up about flight plans. They could lose their tickets if one doesn't get filed. So the bird's privately owned."

"Bird."

"Nobody called it a bird. I made that up."

I said, "Somebody like Pamuk, an investment banker, could have one. Or maybe he's working with a rich client."

"And on the Graham situation, I've got some results from the ORC analysis."

"Well, that was fast."

"You said you wanted it fast. I have addresses."

"Any in the area?"

"As a matter of fact, yes. DuPont Circle."

That had been one possibility, I'd speculated. Greenwich Village or Fells

Point in Baltimore were others but they would have been more problematic since I'd prefer to go there in person.

"Email them to me. Good job."

"I'm still looking into doctors. I'm cross-referencing specialties. Where do you think you hit Loving?"

"I couldn't say."

"If you hit a bone, that might make a difference."

"How so?"

"He'd probably try to find somebody with orthopedic training. Narrow the search down, I mean. You can't remember?"

"No."

"Oh." She sounded frustrated. "I wished it was a specialty. I was trying to think of others. Ear, nose and throat."

"Well, I don't know where I hit him."

"Okay. I'll track it down. I'm texting now."

We disconnected.

A moment later the information from the Graham case slipped into my mobile. I read through it quickly, then pulled off the road. I cut and pasted one of the addresses into my GPS, hit START ROUTE and obediently followed the synthetic woman's commands.

Chapter 31

I drove to DuPont Circle, once the home of cottage industries, a pungent waterway and a famous slaughterhouse. Now the hood was among the more trendy parts of the nation's capital.

GPS—whose voice I had decided sounded unnervingly like Chris Teasley's, Westerfield's assistant—took me to a storefront off Connecticut Avenue. It was a used-CD store, manned by a few slow-moving clerks. The customers were mostly in their twenties, along with a few smudged, bearded music lovers about my age. I walked up to one young man behind the register, flashed my ID along with a security picture of the Asian man who'd collected the gold coins in New Jersey, a perp in the Graham forgery case.

He claimed he knew nothing. I asked

four or five other people. Nobody seemed to know anything about funny checks or the Asian.

Finally, with a last glance around the store, I pushed out the door, which had a quaint old-time bell on an armature. I looked around and headed into a coffee shop nearby. DuPont Circle survives on chic and Café Cafe had that aplenty. The accent mark was a clue, as was the $25/LB. sign in one bin of dark beans. I ordered a black filtered Colombian, the cheapest thing on a menu full of exotic concoctions, none of which were to my mind coffee, tasty though they might be.

I recalled an image from years ago, another one I didn't particularly want. Peggy ordering her favorite, a mochaccino. I was never sure what that was exactly. But I remembered her heart-shaped face turning toward the drink with effervescent anticipation. She'd once commented that she loved grocery shopping because she felt comfort in watching people buy their special treats.

"It's a tough life," she'd said. "It's the little things that get us through the day."

How true, I'd thought at the time. How true I knew now.

I sipped the coffee, set down the steaming cup and began to compose a text message about my progress on the Graham case, when I heard a squeak—the front door. I was gazing down at the screen of my phone when I felt a shadow over me. I looked up and behind into the face of a man in his early twenties. He was white, good-looking, slim, wearing jeans and a seriously wrinkled striped shirt.

"Yes?"

"I work in the CD store you were just in?"

When I didn't say anything he repeated, "I work there."

"What's your name?"

"Stu." He eyed me carefully. "You were asking some things? In the store?"

His statements were inflected as questions.

I stared at him. He looked down fast.

"What do you want?" I finally asked.

"You were asking about Jimmy Sun? I know him."

"You know where he is now? I need to find him."

"You're like an FBI agent?"

"Where's Jimmy? Do you know?"

A hesitation. "I don't, no."

"Sit down." I gestured at the table.

He sat and clasped his hands together in front of him. People I deal with occasionally sit in exactly this position, except that they do so because their wrists are in cuffs.

"How do you know Jimmy?" I asked sternly.

"He comes into the store sometimes. He likes music. Why were you looking for him there? At the store?"

"Traced him through credit card receipts. He shops there."

"Oh. Sure."

"He's in a lot of trouble. It'd be a big help if we could find him."

"I thought . . . I mean, I heard there was some problem. Something about a check."

"A forgery case."

Stu said, "But, the thing is, the case was dropped. I heard it was dropped. So he's not in any trouble anymore." He lifted his hands and offered a shallow smile.

I didn't smile. "It was dropped by the police department in D.C."

"Um . . ."

I went on to explain, "But you see, there are different jurisdictions for a single crime. Jurisdiction can be geographic. Like if you commit mail fraud, you can be guilty of a crime in all the states you scammed people in, all fifty of them, maybe. Separate crimes in each one. Or jurisdiction can be the power of a governmental body. Murdering a federal agent, for instance, is both a federal crime and a state crime."

"Oh."

"This Jimmy Sun, he stole the victim's checkbook in the District. The D.C. police can decide to drop that case. But he used the Internet to launder money."

"Launder money?"

"He bought gold coins and presumably he sold them to get cash. That's money laundering."

"It is?"

"Yes. That's *my* jurisdiction. It's a federal offense and a serious one. Now, Stu, if you have any information about this Jimmy Sun, I advise you to tell me.

Lying to a federal officer's a crime too. And harboring a suspect could result in an obstruction charge. Those are very serious."

"But if no one was hurt and the victim didn't want to pursue it . . . I mean, what's the problem?"

"The victim's feelings are irrelevant."

"That doesn't make sense."

"Well, Stu, let's say I murder you." He blinked. "You're dead. You don't have any feelings one way or the other. Right?"

"I guess not. I mean, no."

"But that's still a crime. Or say I'm a thug, okay? I steal your car but you're afraid of me and don't want to report it. But there are lots of witnesses who saw me. The police can still arrest me. You don't testify but other people can. I go to jail."

"I didn't know that."

"I've got an arrest warrant for Sun." I tapped my jacket pocket.

"You do?"

"There were videos in the Post Boxes Plus store where he picked up the coins he'd bought. With the money from the forged check."

"But—"

"How exactly do you know Jimmy? Be honest, Stu."

The young man's head was down again. "He's my partner. My lover."

"I see. He lives with you?"

"No. His parents are real traditional. They suspect but they don't know."

"You'd be doing him a favor to have him turn himself in. Homeland Security's already started a file."

"Homeland Security?"

"The terrorist issue."

"Terrorist?" Stu appeared horrified.

"It's looking like Sun stole the checkbook as part of an operation by the North Korean government to blackmail the victim—Eric Graham. He works for the Pentagon."

"Oh, Jesus. No, no . . ."

"Is there anything that you've seen about Jimmy that would support that?"

"Of course not. He's a great guy. He's sweet. His family's from *South* Korea!"

I smiled. "Well, terrorists can be very charming. There are a lot of operatives from the north in and around Seoul."

"He's *not* a terrorist," Stu whispered.

"Well, that's for the prosecutor and the courts to decide. It's just my job to bring him in. Without hurting him, I hope. But . . ."

"Oh, Jesus."

I leaned forward. "The profile of people like him is that he's probably very dangerous. We have an assault team active in the area. They were ready to move into the store, if he'd been there. They're pursuing other leads now." I glanced at my watch, frowning. "I heard from one team twenty minutes ago. They think they might know where he is. The FBI's authorized a lethal takedown if he doesn't surrender immediately."

The young man gasped.

I regarded the sallow face before me. "If you care about him, you should help us out. If it comes down to a fight, he could lose his life. Our tactical teams are trained to expect suicide bombings and other life-threatening behaviors."

Stu began to cry, big drops of tears. His voice cracked. "It was all my idea, not Jimmy's. He was just helping me out. . . . Jesus, call them—those FBI people you were telling me about. Tell them he's *not* dangerous."

I frowned. "You need to explain yourself."

"*I* stole the checkbook, *I* opened the online pay account. It was me, not Jimmy. All he did was pick up the coins at the mailbox store."

"I'm not following, I'm afraid."

Stu wiped his face. "The man whose checkbook was stolen?"

"Eric Graham."

"He's . . . he's my father."

"So, you're Stu *Graham*."

He nodded. "Oh, I can't believe how stupid I was. I . . . Oh, man, have I fucked this up. Please, call them!"

"Not until you explain everything."

"It's so stupid!"

"Tell me, Stu. The sooner we know the truth, the better it'll be for Jimmy."

He dabbed at his eyes. "Father's kind of . . . he's pretty tough. He always wanted me to go to his school, Princeton. He was a BMOC. Big Man on Campus, you know? He wanted me to be one too. But I hated it. I fit in here." His hand lifted outward, meaning presumably DuPont Circle. "This is where I belong. I love Jimmy, our friends. I'm not the rah-rah Ivy League sort. But Father wouldn't listen."

"What's this have to do with the forgery?"

"Because I'm a fucking coward." He grabbed another napkin and wiped his nose. "I couldn't tell Father I didn't want to go back to college this fall. I'm afraid of him, Mom's afraid of him. Everybody's afraid of him. He was always saying things like, 'You're not going to be my third daughter, are you?' I had to try out for the football team. I weigh a hundred and fifty-two pounds. Me on the football team? But he kept on me all the time. 'Be a man. Do me proud. Follow in my footsteps.' I couldn't say no."

"So you forged the check so he couldn't pay tuition?"

"How pathetic is that?"

"You had Jimmy pick up the gold coins you bought."

Stu nodded. "He didn't do anything bad. Swear to God. He just helped me out. He's got family in New Jersey. He's there a lot. So we figured we'd have the coins shipped there, not to D.C."

"And your father found out and withdrew the complaint."

He nodded. "Oh, man, yeah, he found out."

I imagined that had been one pyrotechnic confrontation.

"What'd you do with the money?"

"It wasn't about the money."

"I understand but I want to know what you did with it."

"We kept a little, the rest we gave to an AIDS research fund and to Amnesty International. I hate it that my father makes weapons for a living. That's what he does for the Pentagon. He's so proud of it. So smug. I wanted his money to do something good."

I said, "Give me the name of somebody at Amnesty who can confirm it."

Stu looked through his BlackBerry and recited a name and number.

"Got that?" I asked.

He blinked again, frowning.

I said, "I'm not talking to you."

In my earpiece Claire duBois said, "I'm calling now."

I said to Stu, "We wait a minute."

The man slumped, blew his nose again. He looked around the coffee shop and gave a faint laugh. "We come here all the time? Jimmy and me?"

I said nothing.

"You know what he was telling me just the other day?"

"What?"

"Korea, right, you'd think it was tea, tea, tea. Like China and Japan. But the last emperor of Korea, his name was Sunjong, the nineteen twenties, he loved the West and always had coffee at the palace. He and his father would sit around drinking coffee and talking about world affairs. Word got around and the citizens began to drink coffee. They liked to do what their emperor does. There're more coffee drinkers in Korea than any other Asian country. They even have coffee shop hookers. Dabang girls, they're called."

He fell silent. I'd rarely seen anyone looking more miserable.

Tears running again. "Please," he begged. "Call the FBI. Tell them Jimmy's not dangerous!"

Then I heard duBois's voice: "Corte. It checks out. They gave Amnesty International thirty-one thousand."

"Okay." Then I said to her, "Tell the troops to stand down."

"What?" she asked, confused.

"I'll call you in a minute." I cut off the com device.

Under other circumstances I might have let Stu spin in the wind a little but I couldn't forget Graham's arrogance and his insulting duBois. I said, "I don't think we need to pursue this any further. I'll hold off the investigation for now, provided there's no recurrence."

"No, sir. No! I promise."

I rose and started for the door. I turned back. "Next year, your dad could get more money. Or he could get a loan for your tuition. I'm just curious. What're you going to do then?"

The young man turned his red eyes toward me. His jaw was set. "I'm going to tell him to go to hell."

I believed him. I couldn't help but respond, "Good."

I left the coffee shop.

Well, I had the answer about one of Ryan Kessler's cases. I called duBois.

"You were right," she said.

The theory had presented itself in Eric Graham's den, when I'd looked over the decor and photographs and had studied his reaction when duBois had laid out our theory as to why Loving had been hired. I'd decided he was telling the partial truth—nobody was blackmailing him. DuBois's computer analysis of his expressions and body language bore this out. On the wall were pictures of the young man I'd deduced was his son, along with a man about the same age of Asian extraction, who closely resembled the suspect on the security video, involved in the forgery scam. Backed up by the ORC computer analysis, she'd run credit cards, DMV information, face recognition analysis, blog and social networking site postings, school records, insurance claims, phone records, dozens of other databases.

The slim Caucasian was in fact Stuart Graham. The Asian was James Sun. No record, active in gay rights, a grad student at George Washington, a resident of DuPont Circle.

I'd learned that Stu had a part-time job at the Music Gallery, also in DuPont Circle.

When I saw that the arrogant Eric Graham had turned his den into a shrine to Princeton University, I figured there could be a major gulf between father and son, and that the young man might be behind the theft. But I needed to confirm my theory, which my visit here had.

"So, can I ask?" DuBois's voice had an inquisitive lilt to it. "You were *threatening* with your warrant but I was *bluffing* with mine."

Good, I thought. My protégée was feeling her oats.

I explained. "My fake warrant was supposedly in *Jimmy's* name. He wasn't at the coffee shop to call my bluff. Yours would have been in *Graham's*. If he'd asked for it, what would you have done?"

"Oh. . . . Paper covers rock."

Though I keep much of my private life secret, even from her, duBois has heard about my fondness for games. "That was clever," I told her and I meant it.

"So we're back to the Pamuk case being the likely reason Ryan was targeted."

"That's right."

"I was—wait." Her voice had taken on urgency. "I've just got an email . . . a lead to somebody who could treat Loving."

"Go on."

"I'm reading. . . . It's his cousin."

After Loving killed Abe Fallow, we'd fleshed out his bio and tried to track down family. He'd been born in Virginia, we knew, but had no relatives within a few hundred miles of the capital. His parents were dead. Of siblings he had one sister and he'd kept up some contact with her but she'd died in an accident a few years ago.

I knew of the cousin. "He was the one who went to medical school in New York, right?"

"Right. But he got his ticket here and moved to Falls Church about two years ago. He's a doctor at Arlington Hospital." DuBois continued, "I'm looking at phone records now. . . . About a half hour after Loving was wounded at Bill

Carter's place, the cousin got a call on his landline from a blocked number. It lasted three minutes."

"What's the story on him?"

"Single, thirty-two. No record, other than a few traffic stops. Name's Frank Loving. ER background and now he does internal medicine. He had good grades in medical school—he went to SUNY."

She gave me the address.

I thanked her and fired up the Honda and punched the address into GPS, then pulled into traffic. I called Freddy and told him that I'd eliminated Graham's forgery as a lead to the primary. But more important I had a lead to where Loving might've gotten medical treatment.

"He still there, you think?"

"He'd get in and out as fast as he could. But let's assume he is. Move in slow and quiet, with a couple of small tactical teams."

"I'll put it together."

"And Freddy . . ."

The agent filled in, "Don't tell Westerfield."

I said, "Exactly."

"No problemo. Man can be a dick, I'll give you that. On the other hand, that assistant of his is hot."

"If you like pearls," I said.

"That was good, son." Freddy gave one of his chuckles. "This job's bringing out a whole 'nother side of you."

Chapter 32

Frank Loving looked younger than the age duBois had recited. He was crew-cut, tall and in the fit shape that most medicos of his age seem to be.

He was also very nervous. Understandable, considering his murderous cousin had just paid him a visit—and a half dozen armed FBI agents had just searched every nook of his residence.

He lived in a luxury town house in Arlington, one of those four-thousand-square-foot places with columns and arches and rococo trim, all of it prefabricated and bolted into place efficiently over the course of a busy few weeks. The walls, where you'd expect prints-on-canvas of shot pheasants or Venice or medieval still lifes, were incongruously covered with sports posters. The Redskins mostly; what else?

Glancing into the kitchen, I could see bloody towels and discarded white and orange sterile packets from dressings or disposable instruments and syringes. A bottle of Betadine sat on the counter, an orange ring from the disinfectant staining the pale marble. Frank had been trying to scrub it away.

"I don't know where he is, really," Frank said. "Honestly."

Freddy's tactical team had cleared the house and was outside, talking to neighbors who might have seen Loving or his car.

I asked the doctor to join me in the sparse den and held his eye as I said, "Let me tell you something, Doctor, an hour or so ago, your cousin was about ten minutes away from kidnapping and torturing a sixteen-year-old girl to force her father to give him some information."

Eyes widening, he seemed genuinely horrified at this. He whispered, "We knew he was a fugitive. I mean, I was mostly shocked to see him alive. I should have called somebody as soon as he left but . . . I didn't."

"Why not?"

"He scares me."

I said, "Doctor . . ." Respecting the title goes a long way if it's an M.D. you're talking to, I'd learned from protecting a few of them. "Doctor, we really need some help here."

The man grimaced and played with his watch. "Honestly, I don't know where he is. Please. You have to believe me."

"A sixteen-year-old girl," I said slowly. And stared into his evasive eyes.

He slumped. "What can I tell you?"

"First, how badly was he hurt?"

"Bullet wound to his abdomen, six inches above the left hip bone. In and out. I cauterized some small veins, cleaned and stitched. Oh, also a small splinter of rock was lodged in his thigh. I removed it, cauterized the vessels and stitched that too. Did *you* shoot him?"

"Yes."

"To save the girl."

I nodded.

"She's okay?"

"Physically." I let that sit for a moment. "I need to find him. Can you tell us any-thing that'll help? Car?"

"He didn't park in front, I know that.

He'd walked from someplace else. Look, Officer, I saw the news about the shoot-outs. I didn't know it was him. He said he'd been robbed and this guy from South East shot him. If I'd known . . ."

He was lying, I could see, but it sounded like typical improvised back-pedalling when speaking to law enforce-ment, not co-conspirator deception. All I wanted was for him to focus on the visit. "What else did he say? Think back. Anything at all."

The doctor frowned. "Well, you know, there was one thing. He wanted nitrous oxide for the procedure—he didn't want to be out. But I didn't have any gas. I had some Propofol. Very short-acting—the sort of thing they use for colonosco-pies. He didn't go out completely but he went into that zone, you know? I was doing what I always do with patients, just chatting away, distracting them. He said something I didn't think about at the time. He said he wasn't happy that they were doing all that development out in Loudoun County. That made me think he'd been to his parents' house. Near Ashburn. Maybe he's staying there."

I knew of the place. When Loving killed Abe, we'd learned about the house where he'd grown up. But it had been sold years ago. We never followed up on it. I told the doctor this but he said, "Well, it wasn't exactly sold."

I frowned and told him to go on.

"Technically, yes. The deal was that Henry and his sister—the heirs—sold it on the cheap to the man who owns it now. But he agreed to lease it back to them for . . . I think it was twenty years or something. Henry's sister was sick— it was terminal—and I assumed he wanted to get the property out of his name but make sure Marjorie had some place to live until she passed."

Henry Loving's only close family connection was this sister, a few years older. She'd suffered from cancer but her death a few years ago had been in a boating accident. Her boyfriend, the one driving the powerboat drunk in the Occoquan River, had died not long after. I'd assumed Loving had been behind the death; the young man had also drowned, but in his bathtub—exhibiting the same symptoms of someone who had been water boarded for two to three hours.

I couldn't recall where the family house was. Frank Loving found the address and I wrote it down.

I then asked, "Is he on painkillers now?"

"He wouldn't take any Demerol or Vicodin with him."

No, Loving would endure agony to keep a clear head.

"I gave him some preloaded lidocaine syringes for the pain. Topical." Frank looked down at his large hands. "I remember him from when we were kids. It wasn't like he was beating people up or getting into fights. Just the opposite. He was quiet, polite. I remember he was always watching."

"Watching what?"

"Everything. Not saying anything, just looking. He was smart. Really smart. His best subject was history."

One of my degrees. I hadn't known that about Loving.

I called, "Freddy?"

The agent appeared in the doorway.

"Got a lead. Let's get the teams to

Ashburn." From my notebook I tore a slip of paper containing the address Frank had given me. I handed it to the FBI agent. I'd already memorized it.

Chapter 33

People want to avoid the past.

I suppose that's natural. When we tally up all we've said and done over the years, despite the wonderful memories, the regrets may be fewer but stand out more prominently, glowing coals that we can never quite extinguish, try though we might.

Yet without the past my job wouldn't exist. Whether it's because of the good things that people like Ryan Kessler have selflessly done that land them in a lifter's sights or the bloody histories of professional killers, they're in my care as a consequence of what they did months or years earlier.

At the moment, though, driving as quickly as I could over the dusk-filled, slippery roads that would take me back to Loudoun County, I was thinking of the past for a different reason. Twenty minutes ahead lay the past of the man who was a threat to my principals, a past that could be very helpful in finding evidence of his present.

The past of a man who had tortured and murdered my mentor.

And I wanted so badly to flip back through the years and learn what I could about him.

From what his cousin had told me— that the family house sale was a scam, in effect—it was possible that inside were decades' worth of family artifacts. Would I find pictures of Loving as a child? Would I find toys he once played with?

I thought again of one of duBois's first assignments for me, before the run-in with Loving in Rhode Island. My proté-gée's job had been to learn all she could about Marjorie, Loving's sister. DuBois had leapt into the task with typical ex-hausting energy and had written a bio of the woman, who'd spent much time with her brother in their teen years, before he turned to crime and fled the family. I was convinced—incorrectly, it turned out—

that details about his sister could somehow lead us to him. DuBois learned of
her bouts with cancer, the remission, the
onset once again . . . and then the tragic
death in the Occoquan, the river feeding
into the Chesapeake.

Nothing helpful in the pursuit, but I'd
grown fascinated reading duBois's notes
about the one person with whom Loving had had some authentic and recur-
ring connection.

I wanted to know more and hoped the
old house would deliver.

Of course, when his parents found
out about their son's crimes, they might
have eradicated any trace of him and
the house would be as vacant as air. If I
had a child as troubled as Loving, would
I do so?

Claire duBois called. She'd run a title
search and collected what information
she could about the house. The single-
family, eighty-year-old structure was on
about two acres outside Ashburn, a
large area of scattered town houses and
single-family homes halfway between
Dulles Airport and Leesburg, growing

rapidly, as commuters moved farther and farther from D.C.

The Loving house had been unoccupied for nearly a year and a half, though the owner who'd been deeded the property sent a handyman occasionally to fix and prune. The owner reported that Loving hadn't contacted him for years but had prepaid more than ten years' rent.

"You didn't find all that on Google," I complimented duBois.

"It's interesting, I could tell the owner was sort of guilty, even though he hadn't done anything illegal. When you're sort of guilty you sort of want to talk."

Ten minutes later I slowed on the winding asphalt road, no streetlights, and checked numbers. I braked and pulled into a thick stand of bushes, about fifty yards from the house. There were six or seven houses in the vicinity, all of them set back some distance from the road. Trash littered the ground around me and a fragment of red brake light plastic attested to the treacherous curves and bad visibility.

I pulled out my mobile and placed a call to Freddy.

"You get the warrant?" I asked. There was an argument that we wouldn't need one but in legal proceedings it's best to avoid arguments in the first place and, in case we found helpful evidence inside, I wanted to make sure a good defense lawyer didn't get it excluded.

"Yep."

"Where are you?"

"About fifteen minutes away, probably less. You?"

"Just got here."

"Jesus, Corte, your outfit doesn't have those cars with flashing lights on the top. You're gonna kill yourself driving like that."

"I wanted to move fast. I thought there was a chance I might find him here."

"But you didn't."

"I didn't. I'm looking at the house now," I told him. "No lights, no movement. But there're about fifty good shooting positions in the woods all the way around the place. You guys have thermals with you?"

"Sure, but mostly, if you're talking for-

est, the deer'll light up the equipment.
And Bambi doesn't do much sniping."

Eyes on the house, I told him, "I'm going quiet."

We disconnected and I climbed from
the car. I removed my body armor vest
from the trunk, strapped it on and
donned a jumpsuit, the black one. I
moved through the cool autumn air,
stopping between two broad oak trees.
Mist floated around the house, which
was about two hundred feet off the road.
I could hear the creak and groan of insects that had survived the end of summer. Frogs too. I sensed the faint flutter
from invisible motion above me, bats.

I have no superstition within me whatsoever and I don't believe that we can
feel the spirits of the dead. But I don't
deny that there sometimes occurs a ripening of impressions, clues and the
memories of experience that trigger an
understanding within us that seems like
a sixth sense. I had no sense of dread
or foreboding but I suddenly knew that
I had to draw my weapon immediately,
kick my mind into a defensive mode and
keep it there. I nearly got a crick in my

neck as I spun behind me and saw the shape of a man. Finger on the trigger of my Glock, I drew a target. Breathing hard, I eased against the solid, rough tree trunk. Only a moment later the saplings that had configured themselves into the lifter separated in the breeze and then gently drifted back.

The shape of a man but not a man.

Which didn't mean that my concern was unwarranted. Loving could easily be nearby.

I turned back to the house. The two-story country manse, gabled, was painted dark brown. The handyman the owner had hired was long on landscaping and short on woodwork and painting. The railing was sagging, the stairs dipped and three of the beige shutters hung from their last hinge. Scales of dull paint rolled from the siding. On the front porch, which extended across the front of the entire house, a swing was attached to the beams above by only a single chain.

Another look around me. No sign of human life. Gazing at the porch again, I wondered if Loving the boy had spent any time in the swing on summer or fall evenings. And with whom? I noted farmland behind the broken-down picket fence in the back. Would he have gone hunting small game there? I'd heard rumors that he'd tortured animals when he was young. But I didn't believe that. There was no evidence suggesting that Loving was a sadist and enjoyed the physical pain he inflicted; when he set the sandpaper and alcohol bottle in front of the person he needed to extract information from, I knew that the main thought in his mind was my own: What's your goal and what's the most efficient way to achieve it?

I stared at the dark windows, two of which were broken from BB gunshots or maybe a .22. Unoccupied places like this would be, as the law said, attractive nuisances to local kids. I knew this from the house in Woodbridge that Peggy and I had owned. Two doors down from it was an abandoned Victorian and every neighborhood kid at some point tried to sneak inside the dangerous place. I'd gone to town hall to have the city put up better fences, which they ultimately did.

Once more I wondered if it was the Kesslers or Henry Loving conjuring these memories within me. I pushed them away. No more distractions, I resolved.

I heard cars approaching, though I spotted no lights. I gave Freddy a call to tell him where I was. A few minutes later he and the tactical officers joined me.

"Anything on a car at his cousin's?" I asked Freddy.

The senior agent was looking over the lay of the land, as were the tactical officers, each covering a different quadrant. "We found a few drops of blood in a parking space about fifty feet away. Nothing else helpful. No tread marks. No trace. But what do you expect?"

True, with Loving, you weren't going to find the quality of evidence that led you back to his hidey-hole.

"I want to get moving," I said, gesturing at the house. I was uncharacteristically impatient. I glanced at the tactical agents and whispered, "I haven't seen any sign of anyone since I've been here.

Loving might not remember what he told his cousin—he was doped up—and he might've come back to go to ground or at least to pick up his things." I regarded them gravely. "And it's possible he said what he did to the cousin to make sure it was relayed to us. This could be a trap. And remember, he's got a partner."

They scanned the grounds, the trees, the black windows of the house with keen eyes.

We divided into three groups and, Freddy and I leading, moved forward.

Chapter 34

Aware of the fine shooting that the partner was capable of, we didn't expose ourselves by surveying any vantage points for more than a second or two before dropping to the ground or crouching behind trees.

In five minutes we arrived at the house and made arrangements for the tactical entry. This is not my area of expertise, nor was I as heavily armed as everyone else in the group. I would remain outside on the front porch and keep an eye out for any flanking movement until the house was cleared. Another tactical officer would do the same at the back door.

Freddy gestured to one of his tac officers. The large man examined the door and with a single kick sent it flying inward, simultaneously blurting the requisite, "FBI, serving a warrant!" Agents streamed inside through the front and back doors. Flashlights clicked on but I ignored the search and continued surveying the front and side yards, crouching and presenting as little target as I could to a sniper in the surrounding woods. Using my night vision monocular, I scanned but spotted no evidence of shooters.

Finally Freddy stuck his head out the front door. "We're clear."

"Any sign of inhabitants recently?"

"Yep. Food and drinks with pretty far-off expiration dates. A set alarm clock. Five a.m. Boy's an early riser. Fresh linens. Some clothes that don't seem too old. Loving's size."

So he had been staying here.

I walked inside and drew closed any open shades and curtains, then clicked on the lights. The air was musty and tinged with cedar and rot. An agent appeared in the doorway; he'd checked for evidence of the vehicles but reported that the driveway and apron were gravel and he'd found no tire prints.

"What are we looking for?" another

agent called. Freddy tipped his head to me.

"Credit card receipts, correspondence, computers or hard drives, bills . . . anything with or without Henry Loving's name on it. He uses fake identities a lot."

I doubted we'd find much about his immediate plans; he was too smart to leave obvious evidence but even a player as conscientious as he made mistakes sometimes.

Game theory takes this into account. In a "trembling hand equilibrium," a player can accidentally pick an unintended strategy—say, when you reach for a queen's bishop's pawn and accidentally move the knight's in error. If you release the piece, you've made the move, even if the consequences are the opposite of what you'd intended and are disastrous.

Still, we found little or nothing that was helpful.

But one thing I did indeed find was Henry Loving's past.

Virtually all of it. Neither he nor his family had eradicated his history.

Everywhere throughout the house were photographs, framed postcards, ribbons from awards won at state fairs and carnivals, pictures of Loving family vacations. On the mantelpiece and on the shelves in place of books were souvenirs and memorabilia like ceramic animals, ashtrays, hats, candleholders.

And, in the den, scrapbooks. Probably thirty or forty of them. I checked quickly but none was more recent than about five years ago. The most current one contained only a single item about Loving himself. It was a clipping from the *Washington Post,* the same clipping I had in my office, as a matter of fact. About Loving's murder of Abe Fallow and the woman he'd been guarding. Had he clipped it? And if he had, why? I guessed it was a matter of craft: to see how the authorities were handling the investigation.

I flipped through the memorabilia and examined the many pictures of a younger Henry, his sister and their parents. I was struck by the fact that in most of them he seemed somber and preoccupied, rarely smiling and seemingly distracted.

But there were also a number of images of the young Henry laughing. One or two showed him with a girl, presumably on a date, though there was little physical contact between them.

Young Henry's sports were track and archery. There were no pictures of him with teammates. He seemed to enjoy solitary pursuits.

I went back even earlier. I opened one page and stared down at it. Beneath a piece of yellowed Scotch tape was a tuft of clipped brown hair. I read the careful script below. The hair was Henry's, at one year of age. I started to reach out and touch it. Then withdrew my hand when Freddy walked into the room.

"Whatcha think, son?" Freddy asked. "Anything helpful here? You're looking like you found Bernie Madoff's stash."

I shook my head. "Nothing pointing to his next move. But everything pointing to *him*."

"That helpful?"

"Not immediately. But ultimately, I hope so. Only there's a lot here to go through. We'll collect it all, take it in. You folks have evidence bags?"

"In the cars."

I then noticed something against the opposite wall: another shelf on which a dozen shoe boxes sat. I picked one up. Inside were stacks of photographs. I supposed the family had stored them here temporarily until somebody got around to pasting them into a scrapbook. I realized, to my surprise, that there was a dust-free rectangle at the end. The last shoe box had been removed—today, if not within the last hour or so.

Had he sped back here from his cousin's for the purpose of grabbing this one box?

What was there about it that Loving wanted?

Did it reveal something about his past that he wished to keep secret?

Or was there something sentimental connected to it?

I mentioned this to Freddy, who noted it without much interest. I flipped through the others. Like the scrapbooks, they revealed nothing immediately helpful,

though we'd have forensic teams prowl
through them for clues to summer
houses or family members we hadn't
been able to locate earlier.

"Corte?" Freddy asked. He was getting impatient, I supposed.

"Okay," I told him.

"Got something here," a tactical officer called from the hallway that led to
the kitchen in the back of the house.
Freddy and I joined him.

"Looks like bills, sir."

Sitting on the floor beside the kitchen
table was a stack of envelopes, bound
with a rubber band.

"He must've dropped them and not
noticed."

Trembling hand . . .

The agent picked them up but then
froze. They only came halfway and
tugged to a stop.

"Fuck," he muttered and we all stared
at the thin strand of fishing line that vanished through the hole in the floor.

Freddy grabbed his radio. "Clear the
house, IED, IED!"

From the basement I heard the bang
of the booby trap—softer than I ex-

pected—and saw on the foliage and trees a brief flare as the flash radiated through the basement windows.

The room was eerily silent. For a moment I thought the device might be a dud and I'd have ample time to collect the scrapbooks and shoe boxes.

But I'd taken only one step toward the repository of Henry Loving's history when the nearby basement door blew outward and a vortex of orange and yellow flame shot into the hall, while simultaneously the fire raging in the basement erupted from every floorboard vent and crevice on the first floor.

Chapter 35

The device must have been made up of a grenade or small plastic explosive charge attached to a large container of gasoline. I could smell the distinct, astringent odor of burning fuel. In seconds, the fire was racing up the walls and consuming the rugs. I kicked the basement door closed but the flames and heat muscled it back open, as the fire spiraled outward and up.

"Freddy, anybody down there?" I shouted.

He called, "No. After they cleared it they came upstairs."

I started forward again toward the den. Yet every time I edged a few feet through the smoke, there'd be another flare-up and I'd have to spin backward to keep from losing eyebrows and skin. I looked around for water or a fire extinguisher or even a blanket I could use to protect myself to get to the scrapbooks and shoe boxes and save as many as I could.

I supposed that Freddy wasn't as convinced of the importance of the memorabilia as I was but he knew that this was my expertise—dealing with lifters and hitters from a strategic, rather than tactical, position—and he helped me push furniture against the vents and fling rugs over the flames that sprouted from the floorboards. I didn't think we could control the fire—it was going to win—but at least we might contain the flames long enough to get to the books.

We tried for three or four minutes but finally the heat was too intense, the smoke blinding. I was close to vomiting from the fumes and ash. I grew light-headed and knew that to faint here would mean death. Choking, our eyes streaming, we had to retreat. The living room was now a mass of flame and so was the kitchen. We kicked out a side window and rolled onto the ground. The rest of the agents were nearby and, thinking that the fire could be a diversion, they were covering the trees, the logical position for a sniper to take out those fleeing the house.

But there were no shots. I wasn't surprised. Loving, I knew, would be gone.

"Report!" Freddy shouted. His fellow agents called back about their condition. They were all accounted for. One had a slight burn and another had been cut, breaking through a window to flood the basement with water from a garden hose—a futile effort, of course. There were no serious injuries, however.

No, the only victim here was Henry Loving's past.

I rubbed my stinging eyes, wondering if, as I'd speculated, this had in fact been a trap all along.

I was alive but this round of our game was a decided loss for me.

Scissors cut paper . . .

The roar of the flames was so loud that the fire trucks were almost to the property by the time we heard the sirens.

Freddy said, "A shoe box with pictures in it. He destroyed everything else. Why'd he save that? What's inside?"

A good question and one that I knew I'd ponder into the early hours. Did it contain photos of his sister? Of himself and her? Some place he liked to go? Pictures of a cabin in the woods or a lake somewhere he planned to retire to? I said nothing but stared at the fiery tornado that had been the family house. I walked back to my car to call the safe house in Great Falls and check on my principals.

I didn't, however, get very far.

Two black vans, with flashing red and blue lights on top, skidded to a stop not far away and a small entourage got out, making right for me.

My eyes closed momentarily as I realized who was leading them: Jason Westerfield and Chris Teasley, his assistant, possibly sans pearls. She wore a zipped-high jacket; I couldn't see any necklaces.

I shouldn't have been surprised to see these two. I now realized that, of course, Westerfield would have learned about the house and that I'd probably be here, because we were on record: We'd gone to a federal magistrate to request a warrant to search Loving's family's house.

The U.S. attorney had sped directly here to find the man who'd lied to him and sent him an empty armored van.

I'd hoped that he'd be satisfied with a dressing-down in front of the troops and I could get back to work, but he had a different agenda. He glanced toward Freddy, standing nearby, and announced, in a voice louder than I thought necessary under the circumstances, "Arrest him. Now."

Chapter 36

The FBI agent made no move to put me in cuffs and I thought that on one level the U.S. attorney was going more for effect than to see me in chains. But I was hardly sure.

I looked at the occupants who'd been in the second vehicle. They had FBI jackets on too and could have arrested me themselves but they were deferring to Freddy, who was senior and technically their boss.

Freddy stepped between us, like a referee. "Jason." He nodded to the other agents who'd accompanied Westerfield here.

"I want him arrested. I want somebody else to take over baby-sitting."

I wasn't sure what the actual charge would be. Using an armored van to not deliver something you said you would isn't a federal crime.

"He lied to an officer of the federal court. That's the charge."

On reflection I wasn't even sure I'd done that. I couldn't remember my exact words. Which wasn't to say I couldn't be arrested in the first place, even if the charges were ultimately dismissed. That had happened to me before.

Westerfield glanced my way. "I want the Kesslers downtown, near me. I want to interview Ryan personally. That is going to happen immediately."

"I can't do that," I said.

"Release them to me or somebody Aaron Ellis recommends. You do that and give me access to interview Kessler, I won't pursue the charges."

"I can't do that," I repeated.

Freddy, at a tennis match.

"Agent Corte, I think we've been in this business too long to play games," Westerfield said.

"A slammer was not the right strategy, Jason. You kept pushing. I had no choice. My first job's to keep my principals safe."

"Interesting to hear that. My impression would be that you felt your first job was to harpoon your white whale. Agent Fredericks? Could I see some handcuffs, *s'il vous plaît*?"

Freddy, who worked more for Westerfield than he did for me, seemed nonetheless marginally on my side. He said, "Whatever he's doing is working, Jason. The family's safe."

"But I can't help but notice he's here, not with them. . . . And, on top of it all, Loving got away." He waved to the burning house.

That was true, though I hadn't expected to find him here. I was more interested in clues to his life—now, of course, dissolving into ash and embers.

Westerfield glanced toward the senior FBI agent. "Are you going to arrest him?"

"Probably not."

A disgusted sigh. The U.S. attorney looked my way, "Corte, you've even missed the boat on the primary."

I looked away from the house to him. "What do you mean? We've eliminated Graham. Now we're concentrating on Ali Pamuk."

"Pamuk's not the one either. You said he was a terrorist."

"I said that was a possibility since most of the fund's money was showing up in the Middle East. My associate is still investigating his involvement."

"Ms. duBois."

"That's right." I wondered how he knew about her. And—more interesting yet—how he knew the name was pronounced the non-French way. "You got it wrong, Corte. You've been spinning your wheels with Pamuk. We've been doing some work on our own. I've found the primary."

"Who?" Freddy asked.

I was frowning and I said nothing.

He turned to Teasley. "Chris, could you tell Officer Corte and Agent Fredericks what we've learned?"

She said, "Detective Kessler has been involved in some internal administrative work for the Metropolitan Police."

I said, "Something about the budget, accounts."

"So you know about that?" Westerfield said with some satisfaction.

"He mentioned it, yes."

"You didn't think it was relevant?"

"To Loving and the primary? No."

Westerfield glanced toward Teasley again.

She continued, "A year ago, there were some mix-ups with expenses in the police department. Overtime charges. Nothing big, it seemed. But the head of budgeting told the chief of police, who thought it'd make sense to have somebody—somebody in their financial crimes division—look over the books and see what was going on."

"It *seemed* to be nickel-and-dime stuff," Westerfield filled in. "But bottom line . . . tell him the bottom line."

Teasley continued, "Expense checks were issued for tens of thousands of dollars but the money ended up in different department accounts. Been going on for years."

I said, frowning, "You're saying that it was intentional? Some kind of a plan to skim money out of the police budget?"

"Exactly," Westerfield said.

Catching on, Freddy said, "And whoever was behind it—somebody senior in the police or city government—got scared because Kessler had a background in investigating money crimes. He was getting close to figuring out who."

I looked absently at the burning house and mused, "High up in the city government—somebody high enough to have access to an MPD helicopter. Claire couldn't find a flight plan or charter." I grimaced and shook my head. "She even wondered if it was a government chopper that'd been used to extract Loving and the partner but I said, no, it was probably private. I didn't have her check police department logs. My fault."

Westerfield wasn't gloating but he liked my last sentence.

I said to Freddy, "And somebody within the department would have access to police equipment too."

"What equipment?" Westerfield asked.

The senior agent answered, "Loving's partner tried to plant trackers on Corte's car earlier. They were the same model that's used by the District of Columbia police."

Westerfield liked this addition too and he shot a look toward Teasley, questioning why this helpful piece of the puzzle had eluded her.

I cocked my head, frowning in thought.

"What?" Westerfield asked.

"Just that Kessler's mentioned Chief of Detectives Lewis a few times. The chief's shown an interest in what he's doing. A lot of interest. I didn't think about it at the time but why would the man in charge of *detectives* be interested in some accounting issue that involves *all* the departments? Transport, Com, Patrol, Crime Scene? Everything."

It seemed I'd made a good contribution to Westerfield's new case. "Good question."

"Lewis . . ." Freddy mused. "Always wondered about him. Think there were some whispers in his past."

"About what?" Westerfield asked quickly.

"I don't know. They were whispers."

The government attorney now said, "Corte, look, you've been so busy trying to tree Loving that you dropped the ball on the primary completely."

Treeing prey and dropping balls. I supposed in court, before a jury, he didn't mix metaphors so relentlessly.

"And Lewis, or whoever's behind this, has had a chance to destroy evidence and get to other witnesses, thanks to you. I really think it's time to hand the case over to somebody else."

We fell silent for a moment; the sound track to our thoughts was the crackle and crash of the house dying, the shouts of the firemen. Flashing lights rippled on every nearby leaf.

Finally I asked, "Jason? Can I talk to you?"

We stepped aside, walking with heads down, away from the others, about ten feet or so.

Westerfield glanced at the embers and sparks. "You get any clues there?"

"Nothing helpful. We weren't in time."

"Anybody hurt?"

"No." I noted it was his first inquiry about casualties. Then, staring at the sparks being sucked upward into the vague cloud of smoke, I said, "You mentioned evidence that Lewis might destroy."

A nod.

"What if I told you that Kessler has it

all with him. All the spreadsheets, the memos, the accounting books."

"In the safe house?"

"That's right."

A sparkle of enthusiasm lit his eyes.

I lowered my voice further. "All right, Jason, how's this? I'll admit I've been a little focused on getting Loving and I *haven't* focused on his primary as much as I should've. . . . A city-wide financial scandal? That's just the sort of thing a primary'd bring Loving in for. It could go way to the top."

"Go on." Meaning, Let's hear your offer.

"What do you say to this: I'll get you copies of everything Kessler has. To-night, as soon as I get back to the safe house. But I keep the protection detail. I control the Kesslers and their where-abouts."

"I'll want to interview him."

I debated. "By secure phone. Not in person."

The U.S. attorney chewed on a lip. "There'll be some fallout," he said. "You outright lied to me."

"We'll deal with that afterward. After Loving's collared and Lewis's in jail. Or

whoever at police HQ or city hall's behind it."

A nod. It amounted to a handshake.

He, Teasley and the other agents returned to the black SUVs and headed
off and I was treated to one of Freddy's
particular looks.

"The hell are you doing, son?"

I said nothing but called the safe
house and asked Rudy Garcia for an
update.

"Everything's fine, sir," the agent told
me. "Just checked with West Virginia
and the grounds're secure. The fellow
there said, if you call in, to tell you the
deer're where they're supposed to be.
He said you'd know what that means."

"Good. How're the principals holding
up?"

His voice lowered. "Kind of a soap
opera."

The nature of our work.

"The husband and wife got into it
again. Over something crazy. Didn't
amount to squat. Maree wanted to take
pictures of me, portraits. I had to tell her
no and she started to, well, pout. That
woman's a handful." That last sentence

was delivered in a whisper. He continued, "At least the game was on. Baltimore. That gave Ryan something to do. At home we're an Orioles family. How 'bout you, sir?"

"Sorry. I go for Atlanta." Sports don't appeal to me much but spending so much time in hotel rooms and safe houses with male principals, I've watched plenty of games and over the years have developed an interest in baseball. I like the strategies involved. Football, not so much.

Garcia continued, "My son's only six but my wife told me he said Brigham blew the game when he tried to bunt. The man just doesn't know his way around a bat. Funny, but Ryan and I had just been saying the same thing."

"And your boy's just six? That going to be his sport?" I asked.

"Soccer probably."

I could have mentioned that once I had coached a children's soccer team but, of course, I didn't. I told him I'd be back to the safe house as soon as I could, then disconnected and called Claire duBois.

Chapter 37

The house was small but well kept up.

The garden was nice. I didn't know the names of the plants but, in the low-voltage landscaping lights, they seemed plentiful and trimmed and subtly colorful, burgundies and blues, probably varieties of perennials that Joanne Kessler would have appreciated.

When we lived in Woodbridge, Peggy had tried gardening for a season. It didn't last.

I parked on the street and climbed out, felt a bone in my back pop. The smell of smoke followed me. In the car I'd changed into a fresh pair of jeans and a sweatshirt but hadn't had a shower, of course, and the acrid scent from the fire at Loving's rose from my skin.

I went to the door and knocked. A

pretty blonde, around thirty, opened it partway and peered at me cautiously from behind a thick chain. I recognized her from Claire's research.

She examined my ID and then, still cautious, asked how she could help me.

"Can I come in?"

"What's wrong? Is anything wrong?"

"Please."

She let me inside. This was a house of children—toys, cups, crafts and clothes—and she was about five or six months' pregnant.

"Cheryl, right?"

Her head bobbed.

"We don't think there's anything to be concerned about." Words that of course made her instantly concerned. Her eyes widened.

"I'm afraid we're having some trouble getting in touch with your husband."

"Oh, my God, no! Is he hurt?"

I told her reassuringly, "We have no reason to believe that he is. But we can't get through on his radio."

Tears running down her face, Cheryl was breathing hard as she compulsively bent down and gathered children's pajamas and other clothes stacked on the floor. I'd interrupted a laundry session.

I said, "We know he was running a drug surveillance operation but the dispatcher at headquarters didn't know where. Do you have *any* idea where he is? Did he say anything to you?"

"Yes, yes."

"Where?"

She gave me the location. Then added, "But why can't you get through? What's happened?"

"I don't know," I said gravely. "But there's a mobile command post not far from there. Hold on. I'll text them."

I looked down at my phone and typed on the keypad, hit SEND. I could feel the electric tension as she rocked back and forth, staring at the phone.

"Please . . ."

Then I looked up and smiled. "He's there. He's fine. The radio broke is all. Our supply division's bringing a new one now."

"Oh, thank you, God." The tears continued for a moment.

"I'm sorry to have bothered you."

"No, no. And he's okay?"

"Yes, he's fine," I repeated. "Sorry for the scare. Oh, but do me a favor."

"Yeah, sure, anything."

"He's in the middle of the surveillance operation now. It'd be better if you don't call him until the morning."

"Of course. I'm so relieved. I can't tell you. I'm so relieved," she repeated manically, wiping tears.

I stepped outside and walked back to my car, the gravel crunching beneath my feet and the smell of smoke wafting around me.

One aspect of board games that I happen to like is that you can play the part of somebody else. For instance, in the classic German-style game The Settlers of Catan, designed by the famous Klaus Teuber, you are just that—a settler on a mythical island. To win you need to develop the resources more successfully and more quickly than your opponents. In Agricola, another German-style game, you have fourteen turns to become the most successful farmer among your fellow players. American-style games, which tend to involve more combat than European games, might give you the chance to be a general or admiral.

In my job as shepherd too, I have to engage in fictions from time to time. Usually I enjoy the acting, especially if it has positive results that are helpful in guarding my principals, as in my performance with Stu Graham earlier today.

But there are some times when the role-playing leaves me feeling cheap, dirty.

The performance I'd just given was of this sort.

That it was necessary didn't lessen the probability that the woman's tearful face, filled with horror at the news I'd delivered at first, would stay with me for a long time.

Chapter 38

At a little after 10:00 p.m. I arrived back at the safe house in Great Falls and did the code ritual to lower the drawbridge.

Once inside the compound, I noted another car, the engine idling. It was being driven by a young associate from our organization.

He spotted me, shut the engine off and climbed out. The trim African American, about thirty, gave a nod and joined me at the steps to the porch. I could see his nose twitch as he got close and realized that I'd grown accustomed to the smell of scorch. I couldn't sense it any longer.

"Hello, Geoff."

"Corte. You okay?"

"Fine." I glanced into his car, in whose front seat was another young man, with a round crew-cut head and eyes that took me in briefly and then returned to scanning the property.

"We waited out here, like you said."

Geoff had picked up an FBI special agent, named Tony Barr, at a rendez-vous point halfway between here and his house, a place that Freddy and I had agreed on. Since the truce with Wester-field was pretty tenuous, I'd decided I wasn't going to give anybody outside my organization the location of the safe house directly. I was afraid the U.S. at-torney might find out and descend in person to interview his new star witness in the MPD financial scam case.

There's also my general reluctance to give away information of any kind.

"ID?" I asked. With Loving involved you could never be too cautious. But Geoff said that Freddy's office had sent our office a picture of Barr and that facial recognition confirmed he was the agent.

"Impression?" Nodding toward the front seat.

"Military, focused, tactical time under his belt. Didn't talk much."

Freddy had given Barr high marks.

"Hang tight for a minute. Both of you."

"Sure, Corte."

I walked to the front door, hit the key-pad and opened it.

I was pleased the Kesslers were not within earshot. Maree either. Ahmad and Garcia were; they'd known that the car was from headquarters but didn't know why it was here.

I said to Rudy Garcia, "Talk to you for a minute?"

"Sure, sir."

I told Ahmad to do a perimeter check and he headed out immediately.

"I talked to Agent Fredericks on the way over here," I said to Garcia.

"Yessir. I mean, Corte."

"He's relieving you of duty."

The man was silent; the stillness in his face was the equivalent to a gasp of shock.

"I'm sorry, sir. I don't understand."

"I went to see your wife, Cheryl, about a half hour ago. At your house."

His jaw drooped a bit. "You . . . ?"

"When I called earlier, you told me you'd talked to her. About your son and the game—that's how I knew. So I went to see her."

He realized where this was going. I'd said no personal communications from the safe house. None. "I . . . It's just she's pregnant. I like to check on her. It was, like, for three minutes. I used a cold phone."

"I told her I needed to find you, something was wrong. She told me you were in Great Falls off Harper Road." I didn't mention the shock and dismay the woman had felt when I'd flashed the ID and told her that her husband had gone missing.

His round face grew puffier, it seemed, and ruddy. His eyes scanned the floor. "I . . . I didn't even think about it. . . . Oh, shit. She just asked whether I was in South East or some dangerous place. I just said it was like a bed-and-breakfast in Great Falls. . . . Christ, do you think Loving picked it up?"

"No." On the way here, I'd had Hermes run a signal scan around the Garcia house. If Loving had been eavesdropping the receiver would still be there, to collect any new information. There was no evidence that he'd planted anything nearby. Realistically Loving probably had no idea who Garcia was or what job he was assigned to, nor could he track down his wife. But that was beside the point.

"Is she . . . ?"

"Agent Fredericks had her picked up and moved to a safe location with your children. I'm going to move you there too, to be with her. We'll keep you both incommunicado until the job's concluded."

Nodding, miserable. "I'm sorry, sir. . . . I don't know what to say. This is all new to me. This protection work."

It was, of course. But his offense had nothing to do with the job of being a shepherd or clone; it was that he hadn't obeyed the orders I'd given him. Which were about as simple as they come.

"I don't want to get fired, sir. I can't. I love my job."

"I understand, Rudy. We're simply relieving you of this detail. I'm not going to write you up. What happens to your career is between you and Agent Fredericks. Now get your things together. My associate outside'll take you to your wife and kids."

"Yessir. Thanks for not being a hard-ass, sir."

He didn't know that my generosity was rooted in simple self-interest. I couldn't afford to have a disgruntled former employee—one who knew the location of my principals, even if he was in lockdown. Not until the job was over. After that, I didn't care if he got booted or not. I'd recommend to Freddy that he should be fired.

Efficiency. Rational strategies.

A moment later Joanne burst into the hallway. She walked up to me, blinking at the smell and what I supposed was the soot on my skin. She blurted, "My stepdaughter. How is she?" Ryan joined us too, eyebrows raised.

I'd called them from the car, of course, to tell them about the successful escape from Carter's and that both he and Amanda were now safe. But the parents would want more details and reassurance. I told them what I'd done, putting Amanda in detention.

Joanne was saying, "I wanted to talk to her. I tried the phone but it wasn't working."

"For the time being I don't want any-body in communication with her. I want to keep her location completely secret."

"What's the problem with me talking to her?"

"She might mention where she is."

"Why can't we know?" Ryan asked.

"Loving recognizes her value as an edge over you. I don't even want a hint of it on the airwaves. We know she's completely safe. Carter's with her and they're in lockdown."

"I thought you didn't want to use a slammer," Joanne said.

I noted how quickly she'd caught on to the terms of our art.

"Normally, I wouldn't. But circum-stances changed." To reassure them I added, "She seemed to be doing better than Carter. What he said about her, having grit, that's true."

Ryan was drinking coffee. I couldn't smell liquor. I said to both him and his wife, "We can eliminate the Graham case."

"What'd you find?"

I explained about Graham's son forging the check, adding, "Because he didn't want to go back to college."

Joanne shook her head, dismayed, perhaps, at the dysfunction of a family that required the children to engage in such tactics.

Massaging his game leg, Ryan said, "Most kids just drop out. They don't commit felonies across state lines. It's still a crime, even if he withdraws. I could go after the kid anyway."

I hesitated for a moment. Then asked, "You met Graham. What did you think of him?"

"A prick." Kessler seemed to get what I was saying. He nodded. "I don't blame the boy for doing his own thing. I think I'll just let it go."

Joanne wondered aloud, "Who called to pressure Ryan's department not to pursue the case?"

Somebody powerful . . .

"Probably one of Graham's bosses at the Department of Defense. Doesn't matter at this point. It's a nonissue."

Without a glance my way, Rudy Garcia left. I walked to the door and watched him get into the car and gestured Tony

Barr inside. I introduced the quiet, unsmiling FBI agent to my principals and
Lyle Ahmad, who—with a nod from
me—gestured him aside to give him the
details of the procedures we followed in
the safe house. He caught on right away
and I was pleased Freddy had recom-
mended him.

I then said, "Ryan, I need you to do
me a favor."

"Sure, what?"

"All the files on that administrative
matter you're handling?"

"The . . . you mean that accounting
crap?" He waved his hand toward the
dining room table, covered with police
department files.

"Exactly. I need copies sent to a U.S.
attorney."

Joanne said, "You mean you think
that's the reason somebody wants
Ryan? He's uncovered something illegal, something within the department?"

"No," I said.

"Then . . . ?" Joanne asked.

I thought how best to describe my
strategy with Westerfield. I came up
with, "I need to toss a dog a bone."

Chapter 39

Though neither was aware of it, Joanne and her husband frowned in identical ways.

Normally I don't share much of my strategy with my principals. But now I thought it was prudent to let them know what was going on.

I explained to them that when I'd been talking to Claire duBois about the trackers, just before we met at the Hyatt, it had indeed occurred to me that Ryan's accounting assignment might be the reason he'd been targeted. "I had my associate look into that, checking out Chief of Detectives Lewis, the police chief himself, people on the commission. Even a few people in city hall."

But, I added, duBois had found no evidence of any malfeasance. She'd spoken to dozens of officers and administrators within the department, armed with her pen and calculator. What Westerfield and Teasley had found, the money shifting from one account to another, seemed to duBois to be innocent.

"It was," Ryan confirmed, frowning. "Yeah, some money went to the wrong accounts but it just sat there until somebody found it and then got transferred back. That's why I was involved—not investigating, just coming up with better procedures to move cash between the various departments."

"Well, the U.S. attorney thought it was a chance for a great political corruption prosecution. I didn't let on that it was a dead end. I kind of egged him on when he started down that path." I didn't mention to the Kesslers that Freddy had caught on and helped.

I don't know. They were whispers. . . .

Joanne said, "Don't you people work together?"

A good question and the answer was: not always.

Ryan shrugged. "I'll send him whatever you need, sure."

"Everything. Only, the most impene-trable first."

He gave a smile.

"Westerfield's going to want to talk to you too. Just tell him the truth, let him sort it out."

"But be a little mysterious," Ryan offered.

"That'd be great. Think back to any conspiracy theory books you've read."

Joanne remained for a moment, standing awkwardly, shoulders forward. I knew she wanted to call Amanda. But I couldn't let her. I didn't want anybody other than my contacts at the slammer in Loudoun to know the girl and Carter were there. She didn't ask again, though, just said good night, then headed down the hall.

I noted Maree's computer, sitting on the couch. She'd probably gone to bed too; I was suddenly aware that with the young woman absent, the safe house was oddly sedate. Whatever else you could say about her, Maree livened up the assignment like no other principal I'd ever had.

Mr. Tour Guide . . .

Ryan brought all the files into the den, where I was sitting and checking emails. He began to organize them and set them in neat stacks on the desk.

"Here's the first batch," he said. He dove back in.

The defensiveness and hostility from when we'd met were gone completely. "Ask you a personal question, Corte?"

Normally that sets off klaxons but for some reason I said, "Sure."

"How'd you get into this baby-sitting job? Wait, is that an insult?"

"Not to me."

"Right." He laughed. "How'd you get into it? Were you like somebody's personal bodyguard or anything?"

"The short answer is I got arrested."

An amused glance. "Now that deserves an explanation." Ryan limped to the kitchen, called, "Coffee?"

"Sure," I replied.

He brought me a large mug, remembering I liked it black.

"So?" Ryan continued to leaf through his documents.

I explained how I'd started orienteering at the University of Texas in Austin and had gotten interested in sign cutting.

He frowned at that and I explained.

"Tracking, like Indians?" he asked.

"Exactly. Well, one weekend I drove down to San Antonio for an orienteering competition. It was a long one, all day. I'd hit the halfway control point and I'd decided to take a different route to the next point, not the straightest one. Sometimes the straightest take a lot longer.

"Well, I was moving through some brush and heard what I thought was somebody crying. I went to see and I found a family. They were obviously illegals who'd come over the Rio Grande sometime in the past day. I thought maybe one of them was hurt, so I went up to them."

"You speak Spanish?"

"It helps in Texas." And in my present line of work.

"Guess it would."

"I was in competition gear—like a tracksuit—so they didn't think I was police. I asked what was wrong. They said some men were after them. They'd sto-

len the father's wallet—all his savings—
and tried to rape the couple's teenage
daughter. The father grabbed one of the
men's guns and they fled but the men
were after them. I had my mobile and I
said I'd call for help. They panicked at
that and begged me not to."

"Because they were illegals."

"And because the attackers were our
guys, Border Patrol."

"Ah."

"The family'd managed to lose them
but they were getting close. I could see
four or five of them following the trail.
There's sign cutting but there's also sign
pushing. Cutting is looking for sign.
Pushing is *catching* the person who left
the sign. That's what the officers were
doing—they were coming to get the
family. I knew what'd happen if they
found them. We could see them about
a half mile from where we were hiding."

"'We.' That sort of tells me where this
is going."

"I couldn't leave them. They'd be killed
for sure. So I led them away, covering
up the signs as best I could. It was kind
of a cat-and-mouse chase but we es-

caped. About three hours later I got them to San Antonio and a refuge at a church."

I was twenty-three then and most of my life had been in academia. That afternoon had been, hands down, the most exhilarating experience I'd ever had.

"You said you got arrested. I'm not sure you really did anything wrong. You could have just said you didn't know they were illegal, technically. You were just helping out some people get away from some attackers."

"I didn't mention that we found one of the agents had driven ahead through an arroyo. The only way we could get out of there was with wheels. I was afraid the father would shoot the agent so I took the gun, snuck up behind the agent and stole his jeep and weapon."

"Okay. That's arrestable," Ryan said.

"After I dropped the family off at the church I threw the gun in a lake and left the jeep in a grocery store lot. Caught a cab back to the orienteering course."

"How'd they catch you?"

"Stub check." I explained, "It's a safety

procedure in orienteering. Officials compare the starting stubs with the control cards at the finish. If somebody doesn't make it to the end, they send out searchers to look for you. The Border Patrol agents had seen the checkpoint flags— they're orange and white, hard to miss— and found out about the competition. They tracked me down at school the next day. Arrested me and the case went to an FBI agent who was in town from D.C., Agent Fredericks. The one I'm working with now."

"But if you're a federal officer now you couldn't've been convicted of a felony."

"Turned out that Freddy was in Texas to investigate cases of Border Patrol officers robbing and assaulting illegals. So, instead of a defendant I became a witness. Helped get four convictions."

"And the illegals?"

I gave him a smile. "Somehow I forgot where I'd taken them."

"Good for you."

"I finished up a degree or two and started teaching. But I couldn't quite get that weekend out of my head. A few years later I called Agent Fredericks and he put me in touch with some folks at Diplomatic Security in Washington— State Department—and I signed on and spent a few years with them, protecting our people at embassies and foreigners in the U.S. Eventually I didn't want to travel so much. I'd heard about the out- fit I work for now. Joined them and I've been there ever since."

Ryan finished assembling the material to send to Westerfield. It looked to be about two hundred sheets cluttered with numbers and charts that were incom- prehensible to me.

"Perfect," I told him.

"Ask you a question, Corte?"

"Sure."

"How many of your principals you told that story to?"

I answered honestly. "None."

He grinned. "How much of it's true?"

"The whole shebang," I said.

MONDAY

Remember that this is a game of defense as well as offense and be prepared to protect the areas which you occupy.

—FROM THE INSTRUCTIONS TO THE
BOARD GAME RISK

Chapter 40

Claire duBois called just before 9:00 a.m.

What she had to tell me was illuminating.

And discouraging.

I took down the information and went into the kitchen, where the table, covered with a yellow gingham cloth, was littered with breakfast: bagels, cream cheese, jam. Both of my principals were drinking mugs of coffee. Joanne was sitting at a laptop, staring intently at the screen. She gave me a quick look of greeting but returned immediately to the computer.

"Where's Maree?" I asked.

"Still asleep," Ryan said.

"I've just heard from Claire," I told them grimly. "It's not your other case."

The detective asked, "The Clarence Brown scam . . . I mean, Pamuk?"

"He's not the primary."

"But he has to be," Ryan said, dismayed.

"I thought so too," I said. "But it's not a Ponzi scheme. Pamuk's business is legitimate."

"But the fake companies, the fake name . . . how can it be legitimate?"

"His name was legally changed. And all the doing-business-as certificates have been duly filed. It's true the investments were made through shell companies but it seems that's not a crime. Pamuk's outfit is financially solid. The books are solid. It all checks out."

Ryan asked, "What about the people who wanted their money back? Pamuk kept stalling."

"Some of them have been paid. The others will be in the next few days. We got information from Interpol Economic Crimes. They were in contact with forensic accountants and securities people in London, New York, Paris and the Grand Caymans. They put the company through an X ray."

Ryan laughed sourly. "I tried for weeks to get the international boys to talk to me. The French never even returned my calls. Neither did anybody in Georgetown. You carry more weight than us D.C. gumshoes, it looks like."

I remembered the cop's sour characterization of his status in the department.

Small potatoes . . .

Joanne lifted her head, showing modest interest, but returned to the computer. I wondered what held her attention so raptly. She couldn't go online so it had to be files stored on the hard drive.

I continued, "Here's what happened. Pamuk sends his investors' money to the Middle East, through dozens of shell corporations registered in America, Europe and Asia."

"Right. To fund terror operations, you were thinking."

"No. It's all real equity and debt investing. He did it that way because he honestly feels that Arab companies are solid ways to make money but he knows that Americans might be reluctant to invest in them. Patriotism. And some of the stockholders over there wouldn't be too crazy about knowing that their fellow investors have beer and pulled pork for dinner and go to church on Sunday.

So he set up layers of shell companies. If you dig deep enough, you'll find the details."

Ryan sighed.

I continued, "If somebody wants their money out early, it takes longer than with a U.S. fund because of the layers of corporations and the laws overseas. It's time-consuming but completely legal. Nobody's been robbed. In fact, the return on investment beat the Standard and Poor's Index by four percent this year."

"No crime, no reason to hire a lifter."

"Right."

"Goddamn it," he muttered. "Dead end."

So there we were. One of the best lifters in the business was after Ryan Kessler. It wasn't because of his two major active cases. And it wasn't the administrative work he was doing.

Game theory accounts for both unknowns and knowns in the equation. You don't know how the dice will fall, what card will be the next you pick up or are dealt; you don't know what strategy your opponent will select for the next move.

Your trembling hand sometimes makes you move in error.

But one thing you always know is who your opponent is, what goal he seeks.

This game, though, was different. I didn't know the opponent—only the playing piece, the knight or rook: Henry Loving.

And I didn't know the object of the game.

Were we playing bridge, Arimaa, backgammon, Go? The Game of Life? Poker?

Unknowns, complete unknowns.

Ryan Kessler massaged his bad leg and stared at the painting above the fireplace, more fat horses with skinny legs. "Maybe it *is* one of the smaller cases. I didn't think so but that could be it. The identity theft or the credit cards."

Then a voice behind us, Joanne's, said firmly, "No, it's none of those."

Ryan and I both turned to her.

"I've got the answer," she whispered, looking up from the computer and waving at it contemptuously. "It's not Ryan that Loving's after. . . . It's my sister. He's after my goddamn sister."

Chapter 41

Ryan was frowning. "Maree? It can't be her. Her last name isn't even Kessler."

Joanne looked my way. "Did anybody actually see the phrase, 'Get Ryan Kessler'? In that email you were talking about?"

I asked, "The go-ahead order? No. But it said 'Kessler' and gave your address."

Joanne countered, "Which is how you'd describe where Maree's been living."

I considered this. "True. But why do you think it's her?"

She nodded at the computer, her sister's. "Mar left it out here last night."

I remembered seeing it when I'd come back from Garcia's house.

Joanne said, "I wondered if Andrew was behind this. I wanted to see if there was anything in her saved emails that suggested that."

Her husband glanced my way. "Andrew. Is that possible?"

I said, "No, we checked him out. I had my associate look into him as soon as I heard his name mentioned. In the car, on Saturday? Remember, I told Maree she should call him? I did that to capture his phone number. Claire checked him out. He's clean—from our perspective. He's got some assault charges, two battery domestic abuse counts a few years ago. Some restraining orders. But he has no connection to Henry Loving."

Joanne said, "I'm not talking about Andrew. I found something else. Look." She spun the computer toward us. I saw the Global Software Innovations logo on the screen, as Joanne opened folders with the editing and archiving software. She called up some of her sister's recent photographs—the series in downtown D.C., which included the pictures I had helped her choose from. She paused at another image, one I'd looked at but had paid no attention to. It was also of two men, engaged in a serious conversation, as they sat at an outdoor café somewhere near the Mall. One appeared to be in his late fifties, the other about twenty years younger. The background was blurred—intentionally out of focus, I judged—and the intense faces of the men took the viewer's attention.

"You see anything unusual?" Joanne asked.

I studied the picture carefully. Then I noticed that the older man was dropping something into the hand of the younger one. It was impossible to see for certain what it might be. But it looked like a thumb drive for a computer. I asked her if that's what she meant.

"Yes."

"So?" Ryan asked.

His wife continued, "Don't you recognize the older man?"

"No," I said. "Should I?"

Ryan shook his head.

"Martin Allende. He was on the news last week." Joanne explained that he was a Colombian diplomat suspected of laundering al Qaeda money through banks in his country.

I took her word for it. I had only a vague memory of a passing news report.

Joanne added that the story reported

no charges could be brought because authorities couldn't find a trail to the terrorists or offshore banks. "Maree got a picture of him with his contact—the younger man," she raged. I saw her hands were shaking in anger. *"That's why they're after her. To get her camera, computer, find out if she made any copies, see if she took any more pictures. The terrorist cell is worried that somebody in national security—the CIA, the FBI, Intelligence Assessment—could identify who Allende's with. Remember the man who bumped into Maree, knocked her down? I bet it was to grab something from her purse, find out her address."*

I looked closely at the picture. I leaned over, plugged a cable into her computer and downloaded the picture to my phone, wrote out instructions to duBois and uploaded the email with the phone.

Joanne was sitting forward. The numbness masking her face all weekend was now gone. She was furious, her face flushed, eyes flaring. "My little innocent sister poking her nose where it doesn't belong. . . . Does she ever use her fucking brain? What did she think would happen when she started taking pictures of people in public? Did she ever think that might be a stupid idea?"

I wondered if she was heading for the predicted breakdown. She'd bottled her feelings up since Saturday morning. The explosion loomed. I'd seen it happen dozens of times.

"We'll find out," I said, nodding at the phone.

"She never thinks there could be consequences. . . . And who's taking the shit? Us. Our daughter was almost killed because of her! Because I took her in. No good deed goes unpunished, right? I didn't even want her in my house. It's been the worst month of my life. She lectures about the sanctity of art but she can't even afford to pay for the food she eats. Ever since she moved in, Ryan and I've been at each other's throats. It's been a fucking nightmare."

"Jo," her husband said.

She snapped, "I *should* let her go back to Andrew. They fucking deserve each other. Let him beat some sense into her."

A piercing alarm made us all start. Ryan reached for his weapon and I went for mine. Though I recognized the tone; it wasn't a break-in but the emergency door release. Somebody inside had hit it, to get out.

Ahmad appeared immediately, holding a black M4 Bushmaster, the stock racked short, his finger outside the trigger guard. Tony Barr, pistol in hand, was behind him.

I held up a hand.

"Oh, no," Joanne whispered, eyes wide. She was looking out the window to the side porch, where Maree stood, staring back through the glass. The younger sister had heard every hard word uttered about her. Her face, twisted in pain, continued to stare for a moment. Then she turned away and fled down the porch and over the lawn toward the woods.

"No, please! Maree! No!" Joanne leapt up.

"Stay here," I said firmly. I told Ahmad and Barr to secure the principals and sprinted outside, tucking my gun away.

Chapter 42

The DEA agent I became friendly with in Texas told me that when sign cutting and tracking, it helps to know the goal of the person you're pursuing.

Some of the people you're after have in mind nothing more than being anywhere that you're not. They'll escape wherever they can, however they can.

Those are the hardest to track.

The easiest to find are those who have a destination that you know or can deduce.

I believed Maree had such a place in mind. I needed to find her path, though, because there were a number of specific places she might head for. I absolutely had to get there before she did. I paused at the edge of the forest and looked around me, at the puzzle of tree trunks and branches and foliage. Much of the greenery had been cut away to provide a clear view around the house, a perimeter for security purposes. But beyond that, a lot of the area was impenetrable.

I spotted overturned branches, leaves disturbed, pebbles slightly out of place and then a few good prints from stylish shoes. I began to sprint.

A hundred yards into the trees, I gave up on looking for sign. I no longer needed to, since I heard Maree pushing relentlessly through the brush. That wasn't all I heard. Growing in my ears was a roar—bearing out my deduction about where she was headed.

A few moments later I broke from the woods into a clearing and saw the young woman ahead of me—knowing how to move quickly through the foliage, I'd closed the distance but she was still a hundred feet away.

Looking back she saw me and stopped.

As a shepherd I've pursued many people until they cease running. Usually it's because they've run out of feasible routes or out of gasoline or physical stamina.

On occasion they stopped simply because they'd reached their destination.

Maree was on the edge of a rock cliff overlooking the source of the noise: the Potomac River. The woman who had twice tried to kill herself was looking down at the water cascading over the stones below. It was only thirty or forty feet to the surface but the river here was strewn with rocks and the current was swift and deep.

This seemed the perfect setting for somebody who wished to take her life. I moved in closer, slowly. I didn't want her to spook.

She sat down, looked back at me with a hollow, red face. And slipped over the edge.

I gasped and ran forward.

But then her head emerged and I realized she'd slid down to a rocky outcropping below the side of the cliff. She was just sitting there, on a shelf jutting over the boulders and speedy water.

I continued forward slowly, noticing some people on the distant shore of the river, tourists strolling along the path there, which bordered the Chesapeake and Ohio Canal, which travels all the way from Georgetown to Cumberland, Maryland.

I got to the edge and looked down at the turbulent brown and gray water, the froth, the shiny rocks. To my right, Maree was huddled on the ledge, legs crossed like a yoga practitioner's.

"Maree," I said.

She was fiddling with her camera. I moved in closer and made sure she saw my slow, unthreatening transit toward her. I stopped when I was about twenty feet away, at the top of the cliff, and also sat—partly so that I wouldn't be seen as a threat and partly because I myself am not a great fan of heights. She glanced toward me and turned her attention back to the Canon. She lifted it and took some panoramic pictures of the view, then aimed down at the rocks below her. Then, curiously, she turned the lens to her face, which was puffy and damp with tears. Hopeless.

Even over the roar of the water I could hear the click of the camera.

"Maree?"

She said nothing but continued to shoot. She then turned toward me and took a picture. I gave no reaction and she leaned back against the rock.

I looked at her haunted eyes. Was she about to take her own life?

"Maree. I'd like you back inside now."

Finally she called, "It's beautiful here. . . . You gave me my money's worth for the tour."

"Please."

"How would this be for a photo series?" Eerily, the sisters had swapped roles. Joanne was the emotional one now, whipped into a frenzy. Maree was the opposite, numb, calm.

Too calm.

"What do you think?" she continued. "A series of images of someone falling into the water. I wonder how long the camera would keep shooting. I could put it on automatic. But I suppose the battery would short out pretty soon. How long do you think it would last?"

"Maree. Come on back."

"Not very long. But the pictures'd be stored on the chip. . . . It's hard to get a gallery show. Hard to sell your images. But I'll bet that series'd be a winner. Put me on the map."

My job is to keep my principals safe from everything, even their own self-destructive behaviors. Which was often the hardest part. In the extreme circumstances of the world I operate in, it's not unusual for people to consider suicide. None of my principals has ever gone forward with the act but I've known shepherds who have lost people to their own hand. Usually it's on longer assignments, when the days of seclusion amble slowly into months and the principals begin to hear more and more frequently sounds that are innocent enough but that they take to be lifters or hitters getting close for the kill.

More insidious is their own reasoning, convincing themselves that the life they've lived is over with, that family and friends will fade away, that they have nothing to look forward to. And for the rest of their days they'll be pursued. Death is a peaceful alternative.

In Maree's case, she was starting from a disadvantage: her self-destructive nature. Falling for abusive boyfriends, neglecting to provide for the basics in her life, jumping from caretaker to caretaker, who in fact only took advantage of her and then got tired when the appeal of the flirt, the cuteness, the artiness, wore off.

She looked down at the water.

I rose carefully and walked a little closer, then sat down again. "Don't worry, I'm not trained to tackle people and save them from ledges. The fact is, I'm fucking scared to be up here."

Her look said, Spare the jokes, Mr. Tour Guide.

Then she regarded the distance between us and judged, it seemed, that she could still leap into the water if I did rush her, and continued to aim her camera and press the shutter. Neither of us said anything for a moment. I broke the embargo. "Whatever your sister was saying, we don't know for sure that it was your pictures."

"Images. We call them images."

"I'm getting more information."

"But it does make sense, doesn't it? Taking pictures of people who wanted to stay anonymous. Sticking my nose into other people's business?" she added bitterly.

"It's a possibility." I wasn't going to coddle her.

"I'm surprised you didn't think of that, Corte. You think of everything else."

"I'm surprised I didn't think of it either." I was being honest. My investigation into Maree had ended when we cleared Andrew as the possible primary.

She took more pictures.

"I want to say something," I told her. "It's important."

"Under these circumstances," she said, with a dark grin, "one wouldn't really expect unimportant, now, would one?"

"One of the hardest things I have to teach my principals is that it doesn't matter if they're at fault for being targeted or not. A lot of times they are—it's *because* they did something wrong that I'm looking after them. But, yes or no, that's irrelevant to me. Every principal has the right to stay safe and alive. If you committed a crime, you can pay for that in court. If you did something that was morally wrong, you'll answer one way or another. None of that's my business. All I care about is keeping you alive so that you can go forward with your life—whether that's prison or a happy retirement."

"But what about what *I* want, Corte?"

I lifted an eyebrow.

"What if I don't want to stay safe? What's in it for me? What's back there that I could possibly want?" A nod toward the safe house.

"Your family."

"Two people who don't care whether I live or die."

"Of course they do. Maree, if I'm involved, that means this is the worst time people've ever gone through and ever will. They say terrible things when they're under protection. But they don't mean it. It's the fear talking. The frustration."

A few minutes passed and I studied the river. I've had principals at this safe house maybe three dozen times and I've walked the entire perimeter, looking it over for offensive and defensive positions, ordered trees taken down or plantings put in. But I must say that for all my love of orienteering and sign cutting and hiking, I've never actually taken time to enjoy the place.

I turned back and noticed she was rubbing her arm.

"Why did Andrew hurt you?"

Her head dipped. "Didn't buy the rude businessman thing, hm?"

"No."

"How'd you guess?"

"I've been doing this a long time."

I suspected she'd stonewall but I was surprised. She answered almost immediately, "The question is what *didn't* I do." An odd laugh. Humorless and stone calm. "And you know, Corte, the scary thing is, I can't remember. I probably didn't cook the right dinner or I cooked the right dinner but the wrong way. Or I drank too much wine when his friends were over. I don't know. All I know is he grabbed me . . . grabbed and twisted. A tendon popped." She was gripping the joint. "I cried that night, most of the night. Not because it hurt. But because I was thinking I knew some people's elbows get hurt doing things like skiing or windsurfing with the people they love.

But not me. No, no. I got hurt because somebody I loved wanted to hurt me."

Staring down at her camera. "But life's all about trade-offs, isn't it? I mean, who ever gets a hundred percent? I get excitement, energy, passion. Some women get boredom and drunks." She didn't look back to the safe house. "I'd rather have the thrill and a bruise now and then." A breathy laugh escaped her narrow pink lips. "How politically incorrect is that? But there it is. I'm honest, at least."

I debated a moment. A long moment and an intense debate. I eased down to the ledge and sat beside her. She made no effort to move away. It was a very small space and our legs touched firmly. I hated being up here and I had to admit I liked the comfort of the proximity.

I considered how much to tell her. I decided on a quantity and said, "I got married just after I graduated."

"Jo said you're single now. I wondered if you'd ever been married. The way you looked at Amanda, it was the way a father or uncle looks at a child. You had children?"

I again hesitated and finally nodded but it was clear from my expression that I wasn't going to talk about that. Maree sensed she'd stepped over a line. She started to say something but didn't. I continued quickly, "After we'd been married a few years we had a situation. There was a man from my wife's past who became a problem."

Maree may have noted that I said "wife" and not "ex," which imparted some information to her. She was smarter than the package suggested. She frowned her sympathy, which I didn't respond to.

"They'd worked together." I hesitated. "They were both single. They went out a few times . . . they spent the night once or twice." Maree seemed almost amused at my delicate euphemism. "This was a few years before Peggy and I met."

"Temper problem too, this guy? Like Andrew?"

"No. Nicest guy in the world. I met him."

"You met him?"

"They were in the same profession. Saw each other occasionally."

Peggy and he had done their residencies at the same hospital. I didn't give Maree these details, though. "They broke up and she met me. After a couple of years, he showed up again. Just called to say hi, see if they could have coffee, a drink, for old times' sake. But little by little it got to be strange. He began calling more frequently. Leaving messages. Innocent at first. Then getting slightly more aggressive when she didn't call back. Then he started calling *me.* And showing up at the house. He even called . . ." I stopped speaking for a moment. I said, "Then the serious stalking began."

I was silent, recalling those days, seeing Peggy's face, the faces of the boys too, very young but prescient and intuitive the way children are. They'd been scared.

"I realized finally what the problem was," I told Maree. "It wasn't him. It was my wife. She was treating him like a normal human being. Polite, giving him the benefit of the doubt, humoring him. She was a good person, just thinking about who he'd been when they'd been going out, charming and funny. But that was the past. When all this happened he wasn't a normal human being. He was something else. You can't be friends with a shark or a rabid dog, Maree. That's where you get into trouble. Andrew's a different kind of danger but that doesn't matter. Anyone who isn't good for you is as dangerous as Henry Loving."

I felt her hand take mine. For such delicate appendages, her fingers were surprisingly warm on this chill morning.

"Can I ask what happened?"

I shrugged, looking over the water. "It finally ended." I added, "It became a police matter."

Neither of us moved for a long moment. Maree turned and her arms snaked around me and we were gripping each other hard. She kissed me gently at first and then with more passion and desperation. Then, with a smile, she eased back slightly and slipped my hands inside her jacket, against her breasts. I felt a complicated bra. She pressed closer and kissed me again, more playfully this time, her tongue flavored with cloves or cinnamon.

Then she sat back and took my hand in both of hers. "Jo says I like bad boys. That's one of my problems. Andrew's a bad boy." She looked at me and I believed the sparkle in her eyes came from something other than the transit of cloud beneath the hazy sun. "You're one too, Corte. You're a bad boy. But I think you're a good bad boy."

I recalled that I'd recently been remembering that Peggy had said much the same about me.

"Let's go back in."

"You don't want to stay out here and enjoy the view?"

I smiled. "Duty first." I rose and pulled her to her feet and we headed back to the house.

"You ever take time off, Corte?"

"Sometimes."

"What do you do?"

"I like to play games."

Which she seemed to think was very funny.

Chapter 43

When we returned to the house, I punched in the code and the door unlocked.

Inside we were greeted by two solemn faces staring our way. Her face white, mouth open, Joanne looked at her sister and walked forward.

"I'm so sorry," Joanne whispered. She tentatively touched Maree's arms and then stepped back. Maree's face was neutral. Neither accepting nor rejecting the apology.

"Mar, look, I was possessed. . . . I was so upset. . . . Amanda."

The young woman shrugged, walked to her computer, picked it up. She flopped down on the couch and scanned through it. This was something else I'd noticed that my principals had done more and more recently, in the safe

house and halfway motels: withdrawn
into their cyberwombs.

Joanne continued, "Please . . . say
something."

"I'll be moving out when we get out of
prison." Her voice was eerily soft. She
continued to look through the files of
pictures.

Images. We call them images. . . .

Joanne lowered her head, about to
say something more, but couldn't con-
jure the words.

It was then that my own computer
pinged. I stepped into the den. It was
an email from Claire duBois, with, I
hoped, an answer to what I'd had her
research when Joanne had told us
about the Colombian diplomat.

I was prepared for some of the contents. The rest was a bit of a shock.

I stared at the screen for some moments then printed out the documents
and returned to the living room. As I did,
my face must have revealed something
because I found the mood in the room
had changed from recrimination and
contrition—in varying degrees of sincer-

ity—to intense anticipation as they gazed at me.

I read through the four or five pages carefully once more. Then I glanced toward my principals. "It's not Maree. She has nothing to do with Loving."

Joanne sighed. "I just thought, because of Allende . . ."

I continued, "My associate just talked to some people involved in the investigation. They know the man in the picture. He's Allende's mistress's son. Has nothing to do with any illegal operations. He was sharing music downloads on the thumb drive. Even if they saw Maree was taking pictures, they wouldn't have an interest in hiring Loving to get any information from her. And his phones and travel records are clean."

Joanne shook her head. She may have continued to speak. I didn't know. I was reading the rest of the documents duBois had sent, a third time now, just to make sure.

They drooped in my hand.

"My associate found something else," I told them.

"What?" Ryan wanted to know. He was absently massaging his game leg.

"The answer—why Henry Loving's been hired." I looked up, toward Joanne.

She froze. Her eyes regarded the sheets in my hand as if she were identifying the body of a loved one.

In a low, grim voice, very different from her tone throughout the past few days, Joanne said to me, "It's not a problem, Corte. It's been looked into."

Maree stared at her sister. Ryan took in Joanne's face, flushed, lips taut.

He asked her, "What are you talking about?"

I was the person who answered. "Henry Loving's after your wife, not you."

Chapter 44

"What?" He laughed.

An endless moment followed, during which no one spoke, no one moved. The only sound was the wind and the clatter of the automatic ice maker in the refrigerator.

Shaking her head, Joanne walked to the window. I studied her cool eyes as a number of mysteries fell into place.

Maree asked, "What do you mean, Corte? What does Jo have to do with this?"

I didn't answer.

"Jo," Maree snapped. "Jo! Say something. What's he talking about?"

"Well?" I asked her firmly. I needed answers and I needed them now.

Again her voice steady and chill, she said, "I told you, Corte. It's been looked into. There's no problem. Forget it."

Ryan muttered, "Looked into?"

She ignored him and spoke to me. "Don't you think it was the first thing that occurred to me? As soon as I heard there was a possibility of a lifter, the *minute* I heard, I made the call. There've been a dozen people looking into it. They've found nothing. Not a thing."

"Henry Loving only works for people who make it very, very difficult to find out anything about them."

She answered calmly, "And the people I'm talking about are very, very good too."

"Jo, what is this?" her husband said, mystified.

"Why didn't you tell me?" I asked her.

Her face was a mask of disgust.

"Why?" I repeated.

"I am not allowed to tell you," she said in a raw tone.

"Somebody answer my fucking question," Ryan snapped. His perplexed humor had evaporated.

"Honey . . . Ry, I'm so sorry. I just can't. It's very complicated."

"Uncomplicate it. No bullshit. Tell me."

Joanne asked, "Can I see what you have?"

I handed the pages to her. Her first reaction was professional. Squinting, she skimmed through the printouts, the header on each, "Top Secret," a cliché, yet in fact the highest document security classification that the U.S. government uses.

A nod. "How did you get into these servers?" She shook her head. "Never mind, never mind . . ." A sigh. "I suppose I knew from the beginning that it would come to this."

I said to her sister and husband, "It looks like someone from Joanne's past is responsible for hiring Henry Loving."

Maree said, "You mean, like a boyfriend or something?" Thinking of our prior conversation, on the ledge, I imagined.

I glanced toward Joanne, giving her the option to talk. I sensed she was ready to surrender. No tears—that in fact had been another clue to the truth I'd missed. I can count on my principals to cry at least a few times, especially after an assault. But not Joanne. I realized now that her expressions and demeanor of the past few days—the numbness, the blank gaze—weren't because the sheltered housewife with an abhorrence of violence had fallen into this horrific, incomprehensible situation.

She was simply unemotional because of her training or her nature. Probably both.

Joanne said evenly to her husband and sister, "He's talking about my job."

Maree said, "Your job? You crunched numbers for the Department of Transportation."

"No. I did work for the government. But it was with a different group." She looked at me, grimacing. "I know how you figured it out. I mentioned Intelligence Assessment, right? I couldn't believe I said it out loud. I was mad. I was emotional. I didn't think you'd notice."

"That's it."

They're worried that somebody in national security—the CIA, the FBI, Intelligence Assessment—could identify who Allende's with. . . .

The government's Intelligence Assessment Department is a very small

federal agency with very large computers, located in Sterling, Virginia. The
IAD's purpose is to maintain files of
names, faces, physical attributes and
personal preferences of national security threats and to analyze data about all
of the above. If anybody's ever wondered why the CIA or the military can
be so certain that one bearded thirty-
year-old on the streets of Kabul is an
innocent businessman and, to our Western eyes, an identical one a block away
is an al Qaeda operative, IAD is the reason.

However, nobody outside the highest
levels of government security knows it
exists. No news story would have reported about it. There was no way
Joanne could even have heard of IAD,
let alone know that it could identify the
man in the pictures with Allende . . . unless she had some clandestine connection with high-level national security operations.

It had raised my suspicions. My encrypted message to duBois after Joanne
had found the picture on her sister's
computer had been not only to have

ORC analyze the photos but to see if anybody had made an IAD request about Allende and his associate in the past twelve hours. And, if so, could that request somehow be linked to Joanne Kessler?

DuBois had earlier, of course, run the basic profile of the woman—learning about her scholastic and professional histories, as well as things like her car accident. But if Joanne knew about IAD, that suggested to me the public information could be a cover and that her real job history and profile would be in classified archives and records.

So you do your homework, do you? . . . What'd you find out about me?

No wonder she'd asked the question.

DuBois reported that, yes, this morning somebody with a high clearance had submitted an IAD request to identify two people in a photograph that had been uploaded from an unknown location. The analysis was pending.

Regarding Joanne Kessler's real résumé, well, that had taken some true finesse to find. Aaron Ellis had helped, duBois explained in her email, and he'd pulled in some markers from Langley and Fort Meade.

Ryan blurted, "But your job . . . I went to see you. We had lunch. A half dozen times. We went to Air and Space, we went to the National Gallery. I walked you back to the office. The Highways Analysis Bureau. On Twenty-second Street. I was there!"

"Honey . . ." The endearment seemed to jar. "It . . . it was a cover."

He asked, "You were with the CIA? Something like that?"

"Like that."

Maree was getting worked up now. Nothing flighty or youthful about the woman any longer. "You're still not giving us any details, Jo."

Stoic now, as if she were speaking before a congressional committee, she said, "My organization was involved in domestic national security projects."

"What does that mean?" Ryan was trying desperately to reconcile this information with accounts of her life she'd told him earlier. What was true and what wasn't? How deep did the lies go? He'd be thinking of places she said she'd been, people she said she'd known. Was there some honesty in the stories that could legitimize their marriage and family? Because that's what was at risk now, of course.

For her part, Joanne would be considering exactly what and how much she could tell him—which, in theory, was nothing. The British have their Official Secrets Act, which forbids government employees from talking about their activities while they were in the employ of certain agencies. We don't have quite such a grandly named law but similar regulations are in effect. She'd already committed federal offenses by her disclosures here in this rustic, cozy living room. If she went further, the crimes would be compounded significantly, I understood.

But Ryan Kessler was no fool. He investigated crimes and he put people in jail for a living. The pieces were coming together—yes, slowly and in a patchwork way, but he had a clue as to where this was going. In a whisper he asked, "There was something going on when we met. You talked about a boyfriend you were breaking up with. You'd call him occasionally. Late at night. But he wasn't your lover, was he? You *worked* with him, right?"

"Yes. I called him my former boyfriend but that was part of the cover." Joanne was slumped forward, shoulders drooping. It was a confessional pose. "We were supposed to talk about each other like ex-lovers. Those were operational rules."

Her sister broke in. "I don't understand any of this, Jo. You're talking like you were in the army. Like Dad used to talk."

Joanne surprised me, at least, by laughing. "Dad . . . funny you should mention him. He's the one who helped me get into my organization. Right after college."

"But you backpacked through Europe."

"No, Mar. The post cards were fake. I went to a training center in the States. I can't say anything more about it."

As often happened in this line of work, I realized that one of my principals was speaking to someone else in the room through a third party. Doing this seems easier. It was safer for Joanne to confess to her sister than to her husband—the person she was really communicating with. I'd learned that when it comes to deception, we believe that the gravity of the sin depends not on the nature of the lie but on the person lied to.

But Ryan asked directly, "Projects, Jo? National security projects?"

She finally turned to face him, held his eyes. "We did risk assessment." Then she took a deep breath and I knew that the complete truth was about to come out. She added in a voice that was barely audible, "And we did risk elimination."

"You and your partner?"

"Partners," she corrected. "I was active for eight years. I had a number of partners."

Maree said, "For God's sake, Jo, tell me in English what you mean. Risk assessment, risk elimination?"

Ryan Kessler said evenly, "Maree, your sister killed people."

Chapter 45

"Ryan, don't be crazy. That's bullshit. Of course she didn't. Jo, tell us. What were you really doing?"

But it was the truth, I understood.

Joanne's federal government employment history had been hidden very efficiently, of course. DuBois hadn't found anything specific about what the woman or her coworkers did. But you could deduce their mission from what my protégée did uncover: the group's funding (lavish and murkily channeled through nonexistent government agencies) and jurisdiction—in the U.S. only (office leasing and travel authorizations). Its history was enlightening too. The organization was created two weeks after the first Trade Towers bombing in New York in the 1990s, and their budget and personnel were doubled after the African

embassy bombings and tripled after the
attack on the *Cole.*

After 9/11 the budget increased ten
times.

But the real key was that in the archives duBois had found unsigned legal
opinion letters from government attorneys. They discussed at length the standards for justifiable homicide in all states
and the District of Columbia. And general guidelines for deciding when to refer a death to the prosecutor's office
and when not to. There were also memos
about procedures at hundreds of coro-
ners' and medical examiners' offices
around the country.

Joanne's operations would have involved staging deaths to appear to be
suicides, accidents, random crimes of
violence and self-defense.

I thought back to what Ryan had told
me when I'd first arrived at their house
on Saturday morning.

*You know, Corte, this world . . . what
you and I do? Joanne can't handle it
well. Things freak her out, things we
don't even think about. . . .*

Ryan whispered, "Did you . . . did you do it yourself?"

"No." Shaking her head, Joanne sucked in a great breath. She started to speak and her voice caught. Then she started again. "We were anchors—two-person teams. We ran a third-party contractor. He was the . . . active party. But I was on site. I gave the order."

"Jo," her sister gasped. "You didn't. You couldn't have."

"Yes, I did, Mar. Yes, I did. I was there when it happened. A dozen times, more. I was there."

Absolute silence. Ryan seemed paralyzed. It was Maree who moved closer and took her sister's arm. "It's all right, it's okay. You didn't want to do it. You got sucked in. They do that. See, businesses and government—what I tell you all the time. They suck you right in. Get you to do things you don't want to do."

Joanne was looking at her sister's hand as it kneaded her forearm. She said, "Oh, but I *did* want to do it, Mar. It's what Dad wanted me to do, and what I wanted. Be a patriot, doing something good."

Ryan asked, "A dozen times? More?"

"I ran twenty-two assignments."

"You killed twenty-two people?"

"Some were multiple target assignments but some were also renditions for interrogation."

"Oh, Jesus Christ," Ryan muttered. "Jesus." Then some silence passed and he asked, "After we met . . . did you keep doing it?"

"No. Well, for about a year I was active but I didn't run any operations. I told them no. They wanted me to. But I told them no."

They'd want her because she was good, I surmised.

Then she turned to me. "Really, Corte, the people in my organization have looked into everything. There's no connection between any of my assignments and Henry Loving. I left six years ago. It makes no sense for anybody to target me now."

Ryan Kessler was then staring out the window and from the icy smile on his face I saw that his thoughts had arrived where mine had been for the past ten minutes or so. He asked his wife, "Were you doing this when I met you?"

Joanne swallowed, her face flushed. "I told you I was active for a year but I didn't—"

"No, I mean the day I met you, Jo?"

When she said nothing he continued, "Oh, my God. At the deli. You were on assignment."

Joanne lowered her eyes.

I supposed that the owner and his wife were probably key in some terrorist cell. Joanne and the partner had been ordered to eliminate them. They had gone into the deli and as soon as it was clear they called in the contractor, who was fronting as a robber for the security camera. He killed the couple. The plan would have been for him to flee, and Joanne and the partner would give statements to the police describing the incident as a robbery gone bad.

Only, Detective Ryan Kessler had heard the shots and raced into the store.

The hero . . .

"It wasn't some crankhead from South East who shot me; it was your fucking hit man."

Now emotion bled into Joanne's voice. "I checked the police schedule a dozen times! Nobody was supposed to be nearby."

"You were the one in charge?"

She sighed. Like me, she knew what was coming. "I was primary anchor on that one, yes."

"The anchor gives the . . . what'd you call it? A shoot order?"

"We don't call it that but I gave the order, yes."

"And you also gave him the order to shoot me?"

Joanne started to speak but her voice choked to a stop. "We had to get our contractor out of there. I used a code. It means to use nonlethal force on an innocent. We never would have done it if you hadn't been armed. But all of a sudden there you were."

There was a crash, and I jumped at the sound. Maree had leapt to her feet and a wineglass and coffee cup had tumbled to the floor and shattered. She stepped forward and leaned into her sister's face. Joanne looked down as Maree raged, "You go off on me because I end up with a boyfriend you don't like. You say those terrible things about me, being irresponsible. And you . . ." Her voice choked. "You murdered people for a living!"

Joanne said nothing but looked away. I saw her fists were kneading and fingers white. Maree spun around and stomped up the hallway to the bedroom.

Ryan shook his head and said to Joanne, "I didn't rescue you. I didn't rescue anybody."

"I . . . Oh, honey. A million times I tried to tell you. I—"

"So you went out with me for sympathy. Out of guilt."

"No! I went out with you because I wanted to change. I wanted a real life, a normal life. I wanted you. You were good. You did the right thing! I couldn't live with what my organization was doing anymore." She moved her hand toward him. He eased away. He stepped into the kitchen, snagged the whiskey bottle that had been untouched for a day and vanished down the hall.

The bedroom door closed. Though I expected a slam, I knew it was shut only because the wedge of light faded to black. I didn't hear so much as a latch click.

Chapter 46

I was in the den with Joanne, alone.

Looking over the top-secret sheets duBois had emailed me. Much was redacted, including the name of her organization, which was far less public even than mine. Though one thing that wasn't redacted was a picture of Joanne from eight or ten years ago. And her name within the organization, Lily Hawthorne. The woman in the picture looked much like the woman in front of me. Handsome but not pretty, unsmiling, slim.

Reserved and secretive too.

I realized a lot of other curiosities over the past few days made sense now. Joanne's desperation to get her step-daughter away from her, afraid that she was in fact the reason the girl might be kidnapped or hurt. And her concern about the neighbors in Fairfax, the

Knoxes—a worry at the time that seemed out of proportion to the situation. She'd been horrified at the chance that *she* was the cause of Teddy's wife's death at the hand of Henry Loving. I recalled too how hard she'd been pressing me for information about which of Ryan's cases could be the reason Loving had been hired. And her searching Maree's computer, hoping to find any clues that she wasn't the cause.

She'd also supported my choices in the tactical situations, pleading or even ordering her husband to follow what I'd decided—because, as a pro, she knew I was right.

In a matter-of-fact voice, she said to me, "Have you found out anything more than that?" She glanced toward the documents, which said nothing directly about her job.

"Only that you were with the Sickle project. My associate's good but she couldn't get much more than that. Your archives're locked pretty tight. As for active files—if the group is still active . . ." She said nothing. "If it's still active, she didn't find anything on record."

Though the nickname of the group was anglicized to the name of the farm implement, in fact it came from the Israeli Defense Force's name for assassination—in Hebrew, *sikul memukad,* which means "focused foiling."

"My associate found you've been a target before."

"Corte, everybody in Sickle was permanently targeted. Because of what we did. There were never any operations, though. Just surveillance. That report is five years old." She continued, "Yes, I'm sure I have enemies. But there wasn't a shred of intelligence that suggested I'd have any information that somebody wanted—certainly nothing that would justify hiring a lifter like Henry Loving."

The past . . .

I said, "You've been in touch with your people? How?" I'd monitored their phone use.

"I have another phone," she said. "It's untraceable. Believe me, it's untraceable."

"You uploaded the pictures to them on it—the ones from Maree's computer?"

Her eyes took in her purse, where I

supposed the very fancy, shielded device rested. Now I understood why she
kept the handbag so close. "I transferred
them, yes. Everything went encrypted
through a half dozen proxies. There
won't even be bulges in the Internet traffic in the area here. The system takes
care of that."

My immediate impression was that,
despite the trauma of being caught,
Joanne was more comfortable now,
more at peace. She'd been living a lie
for a long time. At least she wouldn't
have the burden of carting around that
secret anymore. I understood too that
you don't hook up with organizations
that run operations like Sickle unless the
work is at least partly in your blood.
She'd undoubtedly been a good wife
and stepmother but I wasn't sure I believed her denials that she was so eager
to give up her clandestine side. I knew
how I'd feel if I had to abandon the job
of being a shepherd. It would have destroyed something within me.

"All right, you tell me there're no leads.
But it's my job to keep you and your

family alive. I want to know exactly what your people have focused on."

"Every case I worked is closed. All the principals were either abducted and re-settled . . . or zeroed," she said, using a verb that I'd heard from time to time if my principal was in a similar line of work. It had become popular among the Mossad. They liked to use shorthand they thought was American.

Zero . . .

"The only assignment with a residual actor was my last one. In the deli. He was a friend of the deli owners we tar-geted. He was a minor player. A liaison and runner basically. . . . He was cleared years ago."

"Tell me about him anyway."

"The couple were collecting and sell-ing nuclear arms intelligence. This man put them in contact with a few govern-ment contractors and people in helpful positions, academics. He delivered some files and software to them. That was it. When they were zeroed he pan-icked and went completely straight, gave us names. We monitored him for years. Then took him off the list."

"Name?"

"That I can't do, Corte."

"Surveillance on him yesterday and today?"

"Yes. Nothing puts him together with Loving."

I considered what she'd told me. I considered the dwindling leads in the case that might reveal the primary who'd hired Henry Loving. Alone, I stepped into the back, enclosed porch of the house, gesturing Tony Barr and Lyle Ahmad to join me.

"We have a situation."

I gave them the news about Joanne. I explained that she was what in our organization would be called point control officer, running a small tactical team. In her case, though, she wasn't protecting lives but eliminating them.

Lyle Ahmad took the news as unemotionally as I would have expected, as if I'd told him the stock market had dropped a few points or a baseball team score was tied in the third. The reaction of Freddy's FBI agent was different. Tony Barr's face flashed with anger. "She didn't tell us?" he whispered. He was undoubtedly used to suspects who regularly lied. But this deception was from somebody he was risking his life to protect.

This meeting, though, wasn't to debate the sin of our principal; it was to consider how the new information affected our protection strategy. I said, "She's positive she isn't the target. But I think for the time being we have to assume she is and that the primary who hired Loving could be funded with big money and has the support of significant foreign interests." I reminded the two men about the helicopter at Carter's house near the Potomac.

Ahmad said, "So it's possible they could use a chopper for a tactical assault, not just extraction."

"Wouldn't be surprised," I told him.

Barr said, "We should liaise with local air traffic control."

"Good idea, and shift to sixty percent outside patrol. And look up, a lot. Lyle, run the perimeter now."

He punched the door code and stepped outside.

Barr and I returned. Joanne was in the

living room, looking into the hallway toward the closed bedroom door.

"The director of your group," I said. "The same one you worked for back then?"

"Yes."

"I want to talk to him."

She gave a resigned nod. She understood it was useless to argue. Which it was.

We walked into the den. She took her own phone from her purse. She set it on my desk and hit SPEAKER then a speed-dial button. Although today's scrambled phones no longer sound like a fax machine, I imagined I heard a clatter as there was a click, and a voice rose from the black box in front of us. "This is Williams."

"It's me," Joanne said. There was a momentary pause while, presumably, some electronics verified that this was her voice. "On speaker."

"On speaker," Williams grumbled. "That says a lot."

Meaning that we'd figured it all out.

"Yessir."

I identified myself and explained that I was in charge of the protection detail for the Kesslers.

Williams of the elusive first name said, "I know who you are. I figured it was just a matter of time. Somebody's been tickling our servers."

I was certainly angry at the withholding of the information about her prior career but I recalled my mantra about defining goals and coming up with efficient solutions. There might be a time for recrimination but the task now was to keep the Kesslers safe and to find the primary who had hired Loving. So I said, "I need all the details on this man who was involved in Joanne's last case."

A pause on the other end, which might have been a reaction to my request. Or it might have arisen because the woman in question wasn't Joanne to him but Lily Hawthorne.

"There is absolutely no shred of evidence that he's involved. Or anybody else that Joanne came in contact with. We've been monitoring the situation from the beginning."

"Even so, I want the name."

"I can't do that."

I said firmly, "I hope you understand that I have a job to do. Part of that is assessing threats on my own. I can't just take your word for it."

"Part of my job is keeping matters like this very, very private."

"I know that," I said slowly.

And let my threat register and spread. Public announcements can often be a very effective edge.

Williams sighed. "His name is Aslan Zagaev. He is a Chechnyan Muslim. Naturalized as part of the plea deal."

"You've been monitoring him. Where is he?"

"At the moment? At home in Alexandria."

"What're his details?"

"Owns a half dozen carpet stores. A restaurant. My people have been through everything, Corte. I mean everything. Com profiles, banking accounts, travel records, corporate holdings, investments, family, brother and sisters, associates. Nothing. He's absolutely clean."

"Chechnyan Muslim. Does he go to the Middle East?"

"Yes. On business to buy rugs. But we don't have GPS around his neck. The folks he was dealing with here, the couple in the deli? They were Pakistani, not Arabs. And recently? No phone calls in the past two weeks. Routine at his office hasn't been affected, best as we can tell. Christ, Corte, we're taking this seriously. We know what we're doing."

I asked, "Could he be deep cover, a sleeper?"

Williams asked, "After six years? They don't really work that way." He said this with some authority. "Besides, sleepers don't volunteer at the Georgetown Islamic Youth Center. Or go near anyplace with the *I* word in it. He'd be at Presbyterian bake sales."

"You have no other actors it could be?"

"That's right."

Presumably because they were dead.

I said, "I want the names of your security man and analyst on Zagaev."

"Corte, what could Lily . . . what could *Joanne* possibly know that he'd have any interest in, after all these years?"

The answer seemed obvious to me. "She knows where to find you, doesn't she?"

Chapter 47

After we disconnected, Joanne stood for a long moment looking toward the hallway that led to the closed bedroom door behind which her husband un-doubtedly was fuming.

She took several steps down the hall and then stopped and returned to the couch.

I called Williams's case analyst. The director had given him the okay to talk to me—about the Joanne Kessler secu-rity matter only, of course, not about the Sickle part—and I got addresses and phone numbers and corporate informa-tion about Aslan Zagaev and his busi-nesses. He told me that neither he or the security officer Williams had ordered into the field on Saturday morning had found anything linking Zagaev to Loving, confirming what Joanne and Williams had stated.

I thought, Well, obviously he's not going to be making incriminating calls from those phones. Did they even think about prepaid mobiles? There were limits as to how much digging Williams's people could do, sure, but these were basic elements of tradecraft.

I disconnected, called Claire duBois and explained the situation to her. "Drop everything and start running background on Zagaev," I told her. "I want everything."

"Shoe size to what's on his TiVo," she said.

"Family, employees, family *of* his employees, travel records. Concentrate on the past couple of days, then go on from there. Any connection to Loving, anything that *could be* a connection to Loving."

I then asked her to transfer me to Aaron Ellis. I briefed him and he coughed a surprised laugh. "Joanne?"

"Seems so. At least Ryan's cases haven't led us anywhere. There's one actor still around from her past. We're going to follow up on it."

"But Westerfield called, all excited about some D.C. police scandal. He was saying you thought that that was why Ryan was targeted. Some senior official in the department or city hall hired Loving."

"I'd just as soon he kept thinking that, Aaron."

Silence for a moment. "Corte . . . you mean the police scandal's fake too?"

"Not fake. It was a valid theory."

"Was."

"Correct."

"But by the time you suggested to Westerfield it was a possibility, you knew it wasn't?"

"Aaron, just try to keep him off me for a while."

"I'll do the best I can."

Finally, I called and briefed Freddy about Joanne's deception.

The jokey facade was gone. "Why the fuck didn't the bitch tell us? She didn't have an inkling this whole tidal wave of crap might have something to do with the fact she was an assassin?"

"I don't think they like to use that word."

"I care?"

"This Williams—"

"Just for the record," Freddy grunted, "he's not as clever as he thinks he is. Or would like to be. A bunch of us know about him and his Sickle band of brothers . . . and sisters, I guess. We thought it was more dirty tricks. But, when you think about it, shooting somebody in the head is about as dirty as it gets. How're you handling it?"

"Claire's doing homework." I debated. "I'll need some warrants. She'll get you the details. Who and where."

"All right, will do." Then he asked, "What's Zagaev's game, you think?"

"I don't know. Williams said sleepers don't work that way. But it works that way if it works."

"Now, that's quotable, son."

"Think about it. Williams cleared him five, six years ago. They drop surveillance. That leaves him free to hire Loving to snatch Joanne and get all kinds of information. That sounds like a pretty successful sleeper cell to me. He isn't exactly dripping guilt but it's all we've got."

"That's my second fastest man theory."

"The second . . . what?" I asked.

"You know how fast you have to be to outrun a bear, Corte?"

I was watching Joanne stare out the window. "How fast?"

"Just a little faster than the guy with you." Freddy seemed to be waiting. When I didn't say anything he said, "I mean that Zagaev doesn't have to be a *perfect* suspect. He just has to be good enough."

"I'll have Claire call you with what she's learned."

Chapter 48

Twenty minutes later Claire duBois called with information about Aslan Zagaev. This was perhaps a new record for her.

"I sent Freddy everything," she explained. "He's getting the warrants now."

"Good. Brief me."

"He was born outside of Grozny, came over here to study at American University when he was twenty-two. He did postgrad work at MIT and came back to the D.C. area. He started to spend some time at a radical mosque in our hometown, Alexandria. He broke with them—he wasn't religious enough, apparently—but what he was good at was being an entrepreneur. With his science background and connections he made on Embassy Row and among government contractors, he found there was a market—selling trade secrets."

"Why'd he get off with a plea?"

"The crime was industrial espionage. What he did was illegal, yes, but very clever. Technically he didn't steal anything that was directly against national security. The Pakistani couple that Joanne and her partner took out? They were consolidators. They assembled information from Zagaev and others into something more useful. I mean, something useful in the *dangerous* sense. I've learned a lot about nuclear fuel rods. And centrifuges. Enrichment is fascinating."

All in twenty minutes.

Before she could start the physics lecture, though, I asked, "So Zagaev cooperated and went on to live the American dream life?"

"He got married, had a couple of kids and didn't have anything to do with his old life."

A lot of that going around nowadays, I reflected, looking at Joanne.

"But for the last few years he seemed to become more religious, though the mosque he and his family go to now is moderate. He seems to lead a fairly secular life. He owns some carpet stores and a restaurant. His kids are in a good private school. He has been taking a few more trips overseas, Turkey a lot. The rugs, I guess. Saudi and Jordan."

"Any watchlists?"

"No, none of ours and none in the U.K., Pakistani, India, Jordanian, Saudi or Israeli databases."

On the surface, yes, innocent. But I still liked my idea of a deep sleeper cell.

DuBois continued with the rest of the information she knew I would want. She rattled off details about gun registrations (none, because he'd pled to a felony years ago and could not own firearms), state criminal convictions (none), traffic stops (one, crossing the white line prematurely to make a right turn), incriminating posts on social networking sites (none), cars, mortgages, medical records, unusual consumer product purchases, travel records and information about his rug operation and the restaurant.

I knew Williams's people had given

him a pass, but I still wasn't convinced he was clean.

I disconnected. Joanne looked at me. She'd overheard everything. "You think it's Zagaev?"

"I don't know. We're looking."

"He seemed so inconsequential. I can't see it."

I sat in an armchair; the smell of ancient upholstery rose.

After a moment she said, "Thank you."

I lifted an eyebrow.

"About Maree. You didn't have to go after her. That wasn't your job."

"It was, yes. It's not efficient to have your principals separated. Too much of a risk."

She looked at me knowingly. "It was sure a risk to her, right?"

My voice lowered, though I knew Maree couldn't hear. "She ran to the cliff by the river. But I don't think she was going to jump."

"But you couldn't tell."

"No, I couldn't tell. She's vulnerable. But not hopelessly lost."

"Not like me."

I said nothing; what was there to say?

It was my task to keep my principals' physical incarnations alive and theirs to protect their own souls and hearts.

"You know what my biggest mistake was, Corte? Thinking I could have it all. Doing what I did for Williams and then dropping the job cold, like it had never existed, and going for a family." A nod toward the bedroom. "When I started running the teams, I thought a normal life was out of the question." A sigh. "A while ago, one of my jobs went bad. I was shot. Pretty seriously."

"Showed up as the car crash in the official documents."

Joanne no longer seemed surprised at what I knew or surmised. "Plastic surgery on the entrance would so it looked like I'd been cut by a piece of wreckage." A shallow smile. "They think of everything." Then her mouth straightened. "But that was it for me having children."

"I see. I'm sorry."

A shake of her head, surely reflecting dismay at what Ryan's reaction would be to this news. "After it happened, and I was in therapy, I didn't care. It was like getting shot was a sign that I was meant to keep going with Sickle. But then I met Ryan and his daughter. I realized what I'd missed. So I went for it. But it was stupid. I should never've gone with the organization in the first place or I should've stayed and never gotten married, tried to be a wife and mother." A weak smile. "I'm surprised I lasted six years before I got busted. You can't have both lives, Corte. You know that too. The difference is you're honest about it. You didn't even try."

I found myself looking down, involuntarily. Joanne added, "Or maybe you did try and it didn't work out either. . . . I'm sorry. That was out of line."

I gave no reaction. I was relieved when my phone buzzed. "I have to take this."

"Sure."

I rose, stepped away and hit ANSWER. "Freddy? What do you have?"

"Something good, Corte. The bear theory worked out. You were right. Listen to this. About fifteen minutes ago we had a SIG-INT hit on a mobile registered to the brother of somebody who works for Annandale Carpet—Zagaev's company. Our boxes ran a voice print analysis of both callers. We had Zagaev's voice on tape from way back when and it registered positive, which we expected. But what we *didn't* expect was that the fellow he was chatting away with was a guy you might've heard of. Henry Loving."

I froze, hunched over the desk.

"We ran it through three computers and tested the sample against four snippets from Loving in the past. There's no doubt it's him."

"What'd they say?"

"It was typical code. Zagaev asked how was the delivery coming. Loving said, 'There've been a few delays. The job site in Loudoun, White's Ferry, was closed down. That deal fell through.'"

Trying to kidnap Amanda, they meant.

"Zagaev said he'd told Loving he didn't want to pursue that part of the job in the first place. Loving said it didn't matter now anyway; he'd given up on it. Then he said he was working hard to find some other options in Virginia. They would talk again in a few hours. He might want to pick up what they'd talked about before. Just to be safe."

"Any triangulation at all?"

"No, happened too fast. They both took their batteries out when they were through talking. But we've got Zagaev's GPS, and five minutes after he hung up, he started driving. We've got people headed in his direction."

"He's going to pick up something," I mused. "What?"

"We'll find out."

I considered this information. "Okay, so he's given up trying for Amanda as his edge."

Joanne turned toward me at this.

I continued to Freddy, "But what does he mean by 'other options' in Virginia?"

"Maybe that Loving and his partner are going after friends or relatives of Joanne. That could be it. Maybe he's looking for the sister right now, Maree. He might not know she's with you. I'll let you know when we get a visual."

We disconnected.

I said to Joanne, "It's Zagaev. He's been talking to Loving. Positive voice prints."

A brief flash of dismay in her face, recognition of the confirmation that she was in fact responsible for what had happened. Yet then her eyes grew hopeful; the corollary of Zagaev's guilt, of course, was that we had a solid lead. "Whereabouts?"

"Freddy's putting surveillance in place. SIG-INT and on the ground. For now we wait."

Her laugh was colored with cynicism and perhaps a bit of sorrow. "Waiting. I've done my share of that in this business. I suppose it's the same for you. . . . And you mentioned Amanda?"

"Loving's given up looking for her. He's going for another edge. We don't know who or what."

Joanne was staring at an old photograph on the wall: a family in nineteenth-century clothing.

Ten long, long minutes later the phone rang again.

"Go ahead, Freddy," I said urgently.

"Corte, listen to this." The man's voice was surprisingly animated, for a change. "Getting better. We tracked Zagaev to a warehouse in Springfield. He goes inside, gets some weapons."

My heart was racing. "He can't touch a gun, not with his felony plea."

"Exactly, son. Hold on." A pause. Freddy then said, "Okay, he just left and our people're with him."

"Where is he headed?"

"North. Inner loop of the Beltway."

"Was anybody with him? Even a shadow?" I asked.

"You mean Loving?"

"I mean was anybody with him, even a shadow."

"Feisty as ever, Corte."

"Freddy."

"No, he was all by his little old lonesome. So what do you think? It's your call."

I'd been considering my strategy all along. I said quickly, "Continue the surveillance and let me know the minute he changes direction. I'll be on the road in three minutes."

Chapter 49

What would my opponent do here?

I wasn't thinking of Henry Loving at the moment, but of his primary, Aslan Zagaev. He'd collected weapons. He'd made this unexpected and purposeful drive after a call from Loving. What did that mean, what did he have in mind?

I was on Route 7, moving south, aiming for the same residential and commercial cluster—Tysons Corner—that Zagaev seemed to be driving toward from the opposite direction.

My opponent . . . what is he going to do?

In game theory analysis the followers of eighteenth-century statistician Thomas Bayes hold that the world is made up of constantly changing knowledge, and in determining the probability of an event—what Zagaev was planning, in this case—you have to continually readjust your predictions as you learn new bits of information. The odds that he'll play rock, as opposed to paper or scissors, change from 33⅓ percent, for instance, if you learn that your opponent has a muscle problem that makes it painful for him to form a fist.

But with Zagaev, there was very little information at all to narrow my predictions of what he was doing and to come up with a rational strategy on how to deal with him. He'd have the answers to what Joanne Kessler knew, the identities of other primaries, if he wasn't working alone. And, of course, he'd know where Henry Loving was or how to find him.

Should we continue to follow, should we arrest him, should we set up surveillance on his employees?

I blew through a red light, grateful the county police were busy elsewhere. I plugged in the earbud and called Freddy.

"Yeah? Corte? Yeah?"

"Where is he?"

"Route Seven, heading north. About five minutes from Tysons."

I was on Route 7, heading south. And about five minutes from Tysons.

Freddy added, "We're a half mile behind him. He's being a good citizen. Stopping for yellows, yielding to pedestrians."

So being inconspicuous was more important to the Chechnyan than getting wherever he was going quickly with his weapons. This was more information but it wasn't particularly helpful.

"Teams?" I asked.

"Two. We're keeping back. Relying on GPS."

"Zagaev make any calls?"

"We haven't picked up anything since he hung up with Loving forty minutes ago."

"You're scanning all his employees' phones and their relatives?"

"Hey, Corte, guess what? We've done this before."

I didn't remind him that nobody at Williams's organization or the Bureau thought to consider employees' family members until I suggested doing so.

"Okay," Freddy said. "He's still moving

steady. Taking us right into Loving's arms."

Was he?

Imperfect information . . .

"Something's bothering me," I said.

"You'd be a bad person to go to a ball game with, Corte. You're so negative. You ever been to a ball game?"

"I don't think he's going to Loving."

"Why not?"

"Most primaries want to keep some distance from their lifters. Safer for them."

"He's delivering the guns."

I pointed out, "Loving doesn't need armament from a primary. He's got plenty of his own. His partner certainly does."

"So what're you saying?"

I made a decision. "I want to take Zagaev, not tail him."

"Why?"

Bayesian game theory analysis wasn't much help. I didn't have *any* information, perfect or otherwise. I told him the truth. "A hunch."

There was silence for a moment.

Freddy said, "But if we don't stop him

fast, he'll call or text Loving and any other primaries. They'll vanish. We stink of federal cars. He'll see us coming."

He was right.

I asked, "What's Zagaev's vehicle?"

"Silver BMW seven-forty." He gave me the tag numbers.

"And his location now?"

"Just getting to Tysons. He's bypassing the business district, turning onto Holly Lane. I think he's making for the tollway."

"If he gets on that, there's no way you can take him before he gets a message to Loving. He'll see you coming."

I was now at Tysons myself. I sped up and turned onto a road that crossed over Holly. I skidded to a stop, climbed out and pretended to look over a roadside produce stand as I scanned the road that Zagaev would be approaching on.

"I'll call you back, Freddy."

In a moment I saw a silver Beemer heading toward me. In about two minutes he'd pass underneath and make the turn that would put him on the Dulles Tollway. I squinted and checked the tag number—Virginia conveniently includes both rear and front plates. I caught a fast glimpse of Zagaev's bearded, unsmiling face. I confirmed it was he; Freddie had uploaded a picture to my mobile. There seemed to be nobody else in the car.

I'm not known for making spontaneous, let alone rash decisions. But a game player recognizes that sometimes a bold choice is necessary. I turned and began to sprint.

Chapter 50

"A pumpkin bomb, Corte. You *do* have a sense of humor. Despite what everybody says." Freddy kicked at a piece of slimy vegetable. "You just express it different than most people."

There were two FBI cars in the underpass, bracketing Zagaev's yellow-and-orange-smeared vehicle, the windshield messy but intact; the folks in Munich make a solid machine.

Since a traditional takedown wasn't an option—because Zagaev could warn Loving—I'd decided to stop him myself as he cruised under the overpass I was parked near. I'd bought a ripe pumpkin from the produce stand beside the road and, when Zagaev sped underneath me, I dropped it into the middle of his windshield. I then slid down the incline, gun drawn, and got him out of the car. He was stunned but unhurt. A fast check of the phone revealed he'd placed no calls or sent any texts in the past five minutes.

I was pretty sure that neither Loving nor the partner would be present, but not positive, so I asked Freddy, "Your people notice anybody peel off when he didn't make the turn on the tollway?"

"'Peel.' That's funny. Like with fruits and vegetables. But I don't suppose you meant it that way."

I lifted an impatient eyebrow.

"No. He was alone."

In a faintly accented voice, Zagaev muttered, "Who are you? Why you did this to me? Look at my car! It's ruined."

I wasn't interested in his complaints. I was sore from my jog along the shoulder of the road with my ripe, twenty-five-pound projectile.

Another agent had gone through the BMW's trunk and had assessed the arms haul. He reported, "Nothing spectacular. M-four rip-offs from Russia, with magical disappearing serial numbers. And a couple of Beretta nine mils, *with* numbers. They're stolen, surprise, surprise. Lot of bullets. Nothing that goes bang in the night." He transferred the lot of it into the trunk of Freddy's car.

"I want my lawyer."

Ignoring him still, I said to Freddy, "What's around here for a chat?"

The Washington, D.C., area is home to dozens of police and national security organizations, some as public and visible as the CIA, some of them sort of anonymous, like ours, others so anonymous they don't exist. Like Williams's. But one thing they all have in common: They need facilities—buildings to operate from, just like insurance companies or computer software start-ups. Many of even the most secret take space in high- and low-rises in and around Tysons, where we were now. It's plenty overbuilt—so the general service managers can get good bargains. Saving us taxpayer dollars.

Besides the area's got Clyde's and Starbucks and Arigato sushi; even spies need to eat franchise food like the rest of us.

Freddy thought for a moment and turned around, nodding at a boring-looking white office building on the other side of the tollway, only two hundred yards away.

"That's convenient," I said. "You have a hood?"

The agent produced one.

"No, no!" Zagaev blustered. "You can't do that. I'm a citizen."

I pulled the hood over his head and guided him to the backseat of Freddy's car, mindful of his head. Another agent slipped in beside him and asked, "Can you breathe?"

"You fucker!" he shouted. "Motherfucker. You can't do this. I will see my lawyer now."

I turned to Freddy. "He can breathe."

A half hour later I was through security at the building that Freddy had indicated. It was, as it turned out, one of the more public federal organizations. Because of which, the FBI agents explained, Zagaev had been taken through the back.

I went downstairs and met a slim woman of around forty, short dark hair. Sharp eyes. She was wearing a black suit and had a heavy bag slung over her shoulder. She worked for our organization and helped us out in what I'd call unusual situations, like this one. Her name was Roberta Santoro, though she was known around the office simply as Bert.

I greeted her. She was characteristically silent. I asked, "Ready?"

A nod.

We went into a conference room and found Aslan Zagaev sitting in a chair, wrists shackled behind him. A video camera on a tripod was focused on him. The red light glowed. He looked up at us indignantly. "You could have killed me!"

"It was a pumpkin," I pointed out. "It wouldn't've killed you."

"Yes, it could have. It could have come through the windshield and killed me." He snapped, "Why do I not have a lawyer?"

Bert walked to the end of the table and sat. Her hands rested in her lap and her face was passive. I didn't say anything about her to Zagaev, nor did she proffer any ID. He looked at her once then back to me. Snuck a glance again and told me, "You have no right to do this. I know how those guns got there. You planted them."

In game theory your opponent's personality is irrelevant. There's even a type of game in which it's understood you can substitute any human being for the other player. But for me, when playing a board game, seeing the person sitting across from me is everything. Sometimes on my lunch hours or after work I'll go to my gaming club in Old Town, and if I'm not in top form I'll just sit and watch others play. I study mannerisms, their eyes, how they hold their cards or roll the die or move their markers or chess pieces. I'm not trying to spot tells—those are either obvious, in unskilled players, or nonexistent, among the talented—but I watch to see how players act and react, what they enjoy and what they dislike.

I watch for responses to victory and to defeat.

I watch for trembling hands.

Now, I regarded my opponent carefully, as if we were sitting across from each other over a chessboard. Zagaev had a round head, a double chin that his beard obscured pretty well and bristly hair that couldn't decide to be gray or less gray. His age, duBois had reported, was only forty-three. His head was large, his pallor anemic. He nervously gripped and ungripped his hands every few seconds. I knew this only because I heard the tinkle of cuffs behind his back. He wore a thick gold chain around his neck and an amulet on which was an unlikely icon. I was pretty sure it was Tsar Alexander II, who I knew from my studies was a moderate reformer— by absolute-ruler standards—in mid-nineteenth-century Russia. Still, it was curious that a Chechnyan would choose this particular image.

Zagaev's clothes were expensive, more than I could afford, more than I wanted to. His suit was cut from vibrant blue silk, the color of the sky in a child's fantasy book. His snakeskin shoes glittered in the jarring overhead light. His sweat was repulsive; I could smell body odor and onions from across the table.

I leaned forward. I am not large, that's true. But I've learned something interesting in my years as a shepherd. People tend to fear you more if you're not physically imposing. Perhaps they're thinking that the damage I can do to their lives is worse than that of somebody with a lead pipe. Zagaev, who outweighed me by fifty pounds, now eased back.

"I need to know who you're working with."

"I'm not a bad person." Zagaev looked up at me with imploring eyes. Claims of ethical purity are a common strategy in games like this. But they're paper, forever losing to scissors.

"That doesn't enter into our discussion. Who are you working with?"

He then grew angry and the softer expression of a moment ago vanished. "There is no one! No conspiracy, no airplane hijackers, no subway riders with backpacks . . ."

I glanced toward Bert. Not a blink of response.

Zagaev noticed, discomfited. He'd be wondering who she was.

I continued, "We know one person you're working with. You were speaking to him on one of your employee's relative's phones not long ago."

His face filled with disgust. He muttered some words to himself. "It was not me! An impersonator. You people do this all the time."

Ignoring the tired denials, I said, "Well, Aslan, we have to assume you're working with a cell and that it's a threat to our national security. Given your misstep six years ago—your relation with the Pakistani couple."

"Murdered by you! I wasn't guilty of anything. I confessed only so I wouldn't be hounded. Or murdered myself."

I continued calmly, "We need to know who else is involved."

"Involved in what?"

I continued, "Understand me, Aslan, I'm not an interrogator. I'm just asking you the questions that the interrogators will ask. I'm not trying to trick you. It's not a strategy. I'm explaining to you."

"That in itself could be a strategy," he offered with an oily smile.

"Your life as you've lived it is over. We can make the case against you. The guns, the connection with Henry Loving, the fact you want to extract information from Joanne Kessler."

The smile faded some, hearing what I knew.

Bert continued to watch, passively.

Zagaev's eyes slipped to her and back. "Who is your friend?" he asked me. "Why doesn't she say anything?"

"Who are you working with?"

"I *work* in my carpet stores and in my restaurant. Why are you persecuting me? You plant guns in my trunk, you try to kill me with that projectile. You will be in very bad trouble over this. I have a right to a lawyer."

"We have you on tape."

"Fake, as I was saying. I'm bored with this now. You are very tedious, sir."

I sighed.

I looked toward Bert. She lifted her index finger, ever so slightly.

Grimacing, I paused then nodded.

I pushed back and stood.

Bert glanced toward the camera.

I stepped forward and shut it off, unplugged and wound up the cord and started for the door, with the camera under my arm.

Zagaev said nothing but his eyes widened. He'd be wondering why I was taking the camera with me. What did I not want preserved for posterity?

As I pulled the door open, Bert rose and circled behind Zagaev. She drew the blinds over the one-way mirror. She looked at Zagaev's shackled hands, then his lap. Her face revealed some satisfaction. Then she sat beside him and extracted from her jacket pocket a vinyl box about the size of a paperback book. It was bright red, as if warning that the contents were very dangerous.

As she drew the zipper open loudly, Zagaev gasped.

I stepped outside, letting the door swing shut behind me.

Chapter 51

"Wait!" the prisoner cried.

His face had gone ruddy. "Please, you must be patient! Have a little patience! This is all very disorienting to me. One moment I'm driving along and the next, bang, here I am, my life threatened. You can understand that. Surely you can understand!"

I turned just before the door closed. I slipped my foot into the jamb, stopping it. I looked back. Zagaev stared at the red box.

Bert regarded me, her face completely impassive.

"You're stalling," I said to Zagaev.

"No, no! I will not waste your time." His face collapsed. "Please . . ."

I stepped back into the room, left the camera beside the door and leaned across the table. "If you help us out, I'm in a position to make sure that no one troubles your family, other than to interview them, provided none of them has committed any crimes."

"No, no, my family is innocent."

"You won't have to worry about reprisals against them. I can arrange for them to be relocated. I'll protect you too through trial and, if you fully cooperate, I'll recommend to the FBI and the prosecutor that they take that into account in charging and sentencing."

"Can you protect my family," he whispered, "from Henry Loving?"

"Yes," I said firmly. "I'll protect you from him too."

A long moment of debate. I looked at Zagaev's amulet, Alexander II with his impressive mustache. Though arguably the most liberal of the tsars, the emancipator of the serfs, he was assassinated by revolutionaries.

"All right, yes. All right." He slumped.

I sat in my original chair and Bert returned to hers.

Our organization didn't torture to get information. Not even water boarding. We made this decision for two reasons.

First, it was illegal—this is a country of laws, after all. Second, we'd studied the subject and found it largely inefficient, since processing all the information you got from a tortured prisoner and reassembling it into the truth generally took much longer than using softer methods of interrogation. Even then torture tends to work with only a small number of subjects.

Nor was Bert Santoro our resident grand inquisitor. She was the office manager of our headquarters in Old Town, the woman who reviewed expense accounts and budgets and ordered furniture and computers. She had nothing to do with operations. With four wonderful kids and a great husband, Bert was like any one of thousands of government workers in the D.C. area. But she had a cold beauty that made her perfect to play the steely operative role, someone who enjoyed pulling out fingernails or using electrodes to extract information from my interogatees.

Zagaev whispered to me, "Who is she?" He turned to her. "Why don't you say anything?"

Bert, probably thinking about something like my overdue expense account, silenced him with a look.

I said, "Aslan?"

With a last glance at the red vinyl case, which I knew happened to contain only makeup, he sighed and I heard chain tinkle as he lowered his shoulders and hands. "Naturally you thought I was part of some plot, some terrible plan to bring down the infidels. What nonsense! No, no, my plan was about business. You see how much of an American I have become? That's what I care about. The all-powerful dollar."

He seemed concerned that my notebook was closed. "Please, this is my story. Please, you can write it down."

Every syllable was, of course, being recorded by a hidden video and audio system—the Sony video by the door was more of a dramatic prop. Still, I thought it best not to remind him he was being taped surreptitiously and so I opened my notebook.

"Years ago, yes, I knew the couple who worked in the deli, the couple murdered . . . the couple who died. I did not respect them. I had no interest in their cause. But I did have an interest in the money they paid me. Which was not in-considerable. You have seen the record, yes? You know. After they died, I grieved—but only for the loss of the in-come.

"I led a more or less successful life here. Ah, but isn't success a moving target? I have been having some prob-lems, financial in nature. The economy? Who needs rugs when you can't afford your mortgage payments? Who goes to eat at my wonderful restaurant when you must buy bulk frozen dinners at Sam's Club to feed your children? How could I make more money? Did I have any service I could perform? Did I have anything valuable that I could sell? Then it occurred to me. What if I could learn more about the operation behind the deaths of the Pakistanis in the deli six years ago? How valuable would that be? I remembered the woman who was the point control officer behind the opera-tion to kill them: Joanne Kessler. Even if she had retired she would surely have valuable information or lead me to people who did.

"I made some phone calls, discreet phone calls, to a connection of mine in Damascus. I learned there was indeed an interest in information of this sort. A multimillion-dollar interest. A man there gave me Henry Loving's name."

So that was the answer. I'd anticipated part of it—targeting Joanne because of information she'd have about secret government organizations. I had posited a terrorist motive and sleeper cell; in fact, it was just business. Given Zagaev's entrepreneurial life, I should have guessed.

"What're you paying Loving?"

"One million dollars, half up front. Half when we got good information from Joanne."

"If you cancel the job?"

"I still must pay everything."

I asked, "Where is Loving now?"

"I don't know, I swear to God, praise be to Him. I've met Loving once—last week in West Virginia."

"Why there?"

Zagaev shrugged. "Out of the way. He

was afraid he'd be recognized if he flew into Dulles."

"Go on."

"I gave him a deposit. He doesn't like wire transfers." A mirthless laugh. "Much less a personal check."

"And you haven't seen him since then?"

"No. We leave text messages or speak on the phone. He gave me a code to use when we talk. About construction jobs and the like."

"What number do you call?"

Zagaev gave it to me and I recognized immediately that it was a rerouting service. It would be impossible to trace. The area code was in the Caribbean.

"The helicopter? Is it yours?"

"One of my partners in the restaurant. It's his."

"What were you doing with the guns?"

"He gave them to me for my protection. But, when he called, he gave the code that I should dispose of them. He was probably concerned that the people guarding Joanne might find them." Zagaev chewed on his lip, staring at the red makeup case. "I swear I didn't know how dangerous this Loving was. If I could have gotten the information from that woman, the point control woman, any other way, I would have. I swear to God, praise be to Him, that I didn't know he would use the daughter as leverage."

I remembered he'd said something of the sort, according to the tap Freddy'd put on the phone.

I asked, "Who else is working with him? Partners?"

"He's working with one man, former military. I've seen him once. Tall, dark blond hair. Wears a green jacket. I don't know his name."

"Anyone else?"

"Not that I know of."

I said, "I'll be right back." I stepped outside, leaving Zagaev to stare uneasily at Bert.

I found Freddy, who said, "He's singing like Britney."

"It's good. He's working solo and the idea originated with him. The Syrians might buy the finished product but *he* approached them, not the other way around. They probably don't even know Joanne's identity."

With the Chechnyan in custody that

meant the only threats to the Kesslers were Loving and his partner and they wouldn't be much of a threat at all as soon as they found Zagaev was in custody. They'd probably flee.

"What're you planning?" the agent asked.

There were two strategies to play.

I debated a moment and decided I really had no choice.

Chapter 52

Waiting again.

At 4:00 p.m. we were in a deserted field near the park embracing the site of the First Battle of Manassas or—if you're a Northerner—the First Battle of Bull Run.

Not far from where Thomas Jonathan Jackson fought his way through the brush—and grape and chain shot—to earn the name Stonewall.

In the still, overcast day, waiting.

"It's the most dangerous time of all," Abe would tell me, as I would later lecture my protégés. "Waiting. Because if you're in this line of work, if you're a shepherd, you're smart. And smart minds need stimulants—crack, speed, puzzles, Rubik's Cubes. Waiting's going to make you dull. But you can't afford to become dull, because the hitter or lifter never waits. Why? Because he's using all his energy to move in close to you."

It was a lesson I took to heart. Especially since Loving had the tendency to appear unexpectedly. But it didn't lessen the difficulty of waiting. I scanned the ground. Even on short notice, Freddy had managed to pull together four teams of special ops experts, all with military backgrounds, and chopper them into a staging area nearby but not so close Loving might notice. We'd arrived a half hour earlier and left our cars in a suburban strip mall parking lot a hundred yards away, then had made our way here through bushes and reedy fields. Birds zipped into the air and grasshoppers sprang away startlingly.

We assembled near the battlefield—it was surprisingly small, hardly able to have hosted the carnage of 150 years ago—and moved silently into position in a field and a stand of trees surrounding the deserted parking lot where Zagaev had agreed to meet with Loving. The lot was next to the site of a demolished warehouse or small factory. Freddy and the tactical officers and I were linked with special com devices, earbuds and invisible stalk mikes that could pick up the faintest of whispers. The brand name was Micro-Mike and they cost two thousand each.

But as we deployed, there was no chatter. The ops teams were consummate professionals.

At the far end of the lot Zagaev's car was parked, the silhouette of a man's head just visible in the driver's seat. The Chechnyan had panicked when I told him he was going to call The lifter, cancel the job and meet him here to pay the remainder of his fee.

But I wasn't going to put him in danger. I didn't dare risk Zagaev's life—for humanitarian reasons, of course, but primarily so that he would be able to testify in the eventual prosecution of Loving. Also, I liked the idea of handing him over alive to Westerfield, to keep the prosecutor from devouring me. Zagaev wasn't exactly behind a front-page terrorist plot but it would be a good win for the vindictive man who would soon be deprived of his juicy Metropolitan Police corruption case.

Accordingly, the occupant of the car was not Aslan Zagaev, nor was it one of the tactical agents. It was Omar, essentially a robotic head and torso, with a few servo motors inside that let him—well, it—mimic pretty well the movement and gestures of a human being. You could program the system so that Omar would act bored or drunk or—the most-used setting—nervous and fidgety. The features weren't as good as Disney animatronics but inside a vehicle or in the dark, he could usually trick a shooter. Omar—and Omarina (brunette or blonde and 36D)—came in white, black and Latino.

"No Chechnyan models, son," Freddy had told me.

The best part about Omar was that he wasn't simply a decoy. Surrounding the robot was a grid of ultraviolet and microwave beams. When Loving or his partner, presumably from some distance, took up position and fired the typical three-burst round into Omar's head, empty and inexpensively replaceable, a computer would instantly correlate trajectory, speed and GPS coordinates and indicate on our handhelds where the shooter was, down to three feet.

Would Loving take the bait?

I believed so. Back in Tysons, Zagaev had gotten in touch with the lifter. In the script I prepared I had him tell Loving that he wanted to terminate the job. He'd pay him the rest of the money and they could go their own ways. As I'd listened in on the conversation, I'd noted what seemed to be disappointment in Loving's voice. I wondered if that was due to his reluctance to cease playing this game with me personally.

But that was perhaps projecting my feelings onto him.

I'd also had Zagaev inquire casually if anybody else knew that he was the one who'd hired Loving. The lifter assured him that he hadn't said anything; he never did. That would be unprofessional.

Of course, I'd had Zagaev ask this seemingly innocent question for a very specific purpose: to make Loving believe that Zagaev might try to kill him and save the rest of the fee.

So, I was betting that Loving would meet him here to eliminate the man who knew his identity and perhaps a few other incriminating facts about him.

Was I right?

You never knew with Loving.

As in the Prisoners' Dilemma, Prisoner One could never be sure that Prisoner Two was going to refuse to confess. The bank depositor would never be sure that all the other depositors would stand firm and not withdraw their savings.

But, though economists and mathematicians don't admit it, game theory is about playing the odds. I don't believe in luck but I do believe in circumstance. It had not worked to my advantage in Rhode Island. Perhaps it would here.

We heard distant traffic, immediate insects, a barking dog, the cheerful shouting of children at the battlefield where more than thirty-five thousand men engaged in the summer of 1861, and five thousand died or were wounded. I was in cover behind thick trees that had not even been seeds when those soldiers fell.

The meeting had been arranged for 4:45. We were now a few minutes past that.

In the distance, a light-colored vehicle quickly turned onto the road that led to the deserted parking lot we surrounded. The skidding turn was a standard tactical maneuver, not to evade any following cars but to see if you were in fact being followed. If you signal your intention to turn, a tail will do the same. If you skid around a corner, keeping an eye in the rearview mirror, you can easily judge from the reaction of the driver behind you if it's a tail, even if he decides to stay on the road. The car's rapid turn now suggested that it might be Loving's.

Some of the tactical officers weren't in view of the road, and the commander—Freddy's lieutenant—alerted everyone to the newly arrived car. I found myself tensing, flashing back to the sight of Loving earlier—at the flytrap. I reached behind me and rested my hand on my Glock. This was instinct only; there were people present who were more talented at this sort of thing than I. Lowering my hand, I watched the transit of the light-colored car.

Was it the lifter? This road didn't lead

to the battlefield; it didn't lead anywhere, really. The occupants could be kids here to smoke grass or drink or make out. It could be a Civil War buff who wanted to experience the historic site from this angle. Manassas also had its share of meth cookers. Maybe a deal was going down.

Before reaching the parking lot where Zagaev's car was idling, the new vehicle pulled off into the bushes.

Then came a whisper through my earbud: "Team Three. Two males exiting vehicle, civilian clothing. One is armed, handgun. Proceeding toward parking lot through brush."

Loving and his partner. I'd hoped they'd both be here.

"Roger. All teams, stay in position. No motion, no sound. Sniper one, can you target the subject vehicle?"

"Negative."

"Roger."

I wondered momentarily if the partner was Loving's protégé, as I had been Abe's and Claire duBois mine. Did Loving lecture about the rules of play the way I had been lectured and I lectured now? This seemed at first a crazy thought but then I asked myself, why? Tradecraft of all types had to be mastered.

"Team Two. Subjects are on western perimeter of the parking lot, observing Zagaev's vehicle."

Freddy's voice whispered, "Move Omar's head around but not so he's looking back toward them."

"Roger that."

The robot glanced to the side. The head dipped. Whoever guided the mannequin was an artist.

"Subjects're checking out the park. Okay, they're separating, moving up on either side of the car. Be advised, both have weapons now. Autoloader handguns."

"Copy that."

So they weren't going for a sniper shot; they were going to take him from behind, close. Just shoot him and have done with it.

Or, I reflected, this might not be a kill at all. Maybe their intention was for the partner to cover the transaction as Loving collected the money. They would shake hands and leave.

I was breathing hard, forcing myself not to strain forward for a glimpse but staying low in the brush. Suddenly I felt a trickle down my spine and looked behind me fast, though I knew Loving couldn't have come up behind me here, not with the tactical agents arrayed as they were.

I saw nothing but saplings and brush.

"Tac Op Leader. We've got a visual. Both suspects are in confinement positions."

Freddy said, "You're greenlighted."

"Roger. Greenlighted. On my command, Teams Three and One, flashbangs . . . then move in, flanking and rear. Hold . . . hold . . ."

I wondered what the communications here had been like in July of 1861 when troops had been preparing to engage.

"Now. Move in, move in!"

I heard a series of explosions and saw flashes as the tactical ops teams sped forward.

My hand was cramping—my left hand, not the one I used for shooting—and I was half rising from cover. I sucked in air. I realized that I hadn't been breathing for a good thirty seconds or more.

The teams converged, screaming, as they were instructed to do, "FBI, FBI, on the ground, let me see your hands! Let me see your hands!"

"We've got—" one started to radio.

A long pause. "Team Three to Tac Op Leader. Need you here. Now."

What was going on?

"I don't get it. . . ."

"Shit."

My heart sank at the transmissions, hardly what you would have hoped for in a successful operation.

And, moving from cover, I made a deduction that proved to be true. The two men sneaking up on Omar were displaying what appeared to be law enforcement shields. They were, of course, detectives from Prince William County, here to investigate the reports of a drug deal or cries for help that Loving had undoubtedly called in the minute he hung up from speaking with Zagaev.

A call made to distract us while he orchestrated his escape.

Chapter 53

I was speaking to Claire duBois.

"Loving's on the run. He might be driving but I think he wants to get clear of the area. Data mine flight reservations. I want to know anybody who bought a ticket, after he talked to Zagaev—about three p.m.—for travel today. Maybe from Dulles, National or BWI but I think he's still going to be avoiding them, especially now that he suspects we've turned Zagaev."

"Amtrak?" duBois asked.

"Freddy's told the police at Union Station to look for him. But I'm betting he wants to put more distance between us faster than taking a train."

"I'll get right on it."

Zagaev had no clue where Loving might have gone, except to add that the flight to Charleston, West Virginia, had taken him about five hours, which suggested he was based somewhere on the West Coast, though possibly Mexico, the Caribbean or Canada.

The tactical officers were assembling their gear. We talked to the county detectives but it was no surprise that the call that had brought them here had been anonymous and from an untraceable phone. "The caller said he'd seen somebody selling 'army guns' from the back of his car. What were we supposed to do? Jesus, you guys scared the shit out of us. Flash-bangs? Messed up my eyes, I'll tell you. I'm talking to my commander about this."

I realized Loving's choice of a crime was smart. Had he reported a drug deal or a girl's shouting for help, as I'd thought originally, a standard patrol car with uniformed officers would have shown up. Selling weapons brought plainclothes detectives, which tricked us into believing they were Loving and the partner and prolonged his chance to escape.

Freddy said, "How'd he know we turned Zagaev?"

"Years and years of doing this shit."

The agent lifted an eyebrow. "A sense of humor *and* you're cursing, son."

Ten minutes later duBois called back. "Five minutes after Zagaev and Loving hung up, a man named Richard Hill bought an e-ticket to Seattle from Philly. It was the next available flight."

"Why do you think it's Loving? That's not a known alias of his."

"Well, for one thing, because Richard Hill is dead. His birth certificate was used to get a driver's license two years after he died."

"Ghosting." This was a common technique for establishing a false identity.

"Exactly. But mostly we know because the airline records the calls; I got the clip. Voice print matches."

"Flight time?"

"Little under three hours from now."

"One ticket?" I was thinking of the sandy-haired partner.

"No, two. Another fake name. That person's dead too."

I told her I'd get back to her, disconnected and then gestured Freddy over and told him. He grunted. "Your girl data mines better'n my girl. Tell you, Corte, I might hire her away from you." He called the Bureau's Philly field office and briefed them. He disconnected and turned back to me. "They'll be on site in twenty minutes."

"Subtle, Freddy. Call them back and tell them to be subtle. They need to stay invisible till the last minute."

"They'll be subtle."

I cocked my eyebrow.

"I'll call 'em back." Then he gave me a rare grin. "You coming along for the hunting party?"

I thought of Rhode Island. I thought of Abe. The idea of being present at Loving's arrest was immensely appealing.

How badly I wanted to go . . .

But I said, "I'll leave that to you folks. I'm going to head back to the safe house, keep an eye on my principals."

"What for? The case's over with, Corte."

"That's true, Freddy. But the fact is they still need guarding."

"We got the sole primary in custody and the lifter's headed for the hills. Who'd they need protecting from?"

"Themselves."

Chapter 54

The atmosphere in the Great Falls safe house suggested that what I'd told Freddy was true.

I walked into the middle of a fight between the sisters. It was intense and even my arrival, presumably with vital information about the case, didn't deflect the jousting. Ryan was nowhere to be seen.

"I was upset." Joanne slapped her thighs. "What do you think? People say things when they're upset they don't mean. Come on. How can you move out?"

"I'd planned it already."

"Not with Andrew," Joanne said.

"He's changed."

"Oh, please, Mar. Men like that don't change. They say they do, they recite crap from twelve-step programs. But they don't change."

"I don't want to talk about it."

"He put you in the hospital."

"Enough!" Maree snapped, waving her hand.

After a dense silence both women turned toward me.

I said, "I'd like to talk to you for a few minutes, tell you what's happened."

Joanne looked once more at her sister, a glance both sorrowful and frustrated, and turned to me, dropping onto the couch.

"Where's Ryan?" I asked.

"Here," he said, walking into the living room. He was drinking coffee, it seemed, though I supposed it could have had whiskey in it. I couldn't smell any, though. He walked past his sister-in-law and his wife and took a straight-back chair in the corner of the room. He ignored the women and kept his attention on me.

I called Lyle Ahmad and Tony Barr in as well and told the assembly, "We've got the primary and Loving's on his way out of town. We confirmed it was Zagaev. Not a terrorist issue, not directly."

I looked toward Joanne. "He was trying to extract information from you and then sell it."

Ryan Kessler said nothing, didn't even look at his wife.

"So it's over with," Maree said. Then she added, "I'd like to go home—go back to their house—and get my things."

I said to her, "I'm sorry, not quite yet. We don't have Loving or the partner in custody yet. I'm ninety-nine percent sure it's okay but I want to keep you here, until we do."

I expected to receive a taste of the testy attitude Maree was serving up to her sister, or at least another Tour Guide comment, but she looked me over with a softening face. "Whatever you think best."

I didn't know what to make of her agreeable nature.

Or the coy smile.

Ryan asked, "And my daughter?"

I noted the singular possessive. Joanne must have too.

"She can join us. Bill Carter too. I've already called him, and one of the guards I know there is driving them to a pickup location. I'll go get them myself and bring them here."

Joanne's eyes grew still and I guessed she was thinking that either she or her husband would have to have some serious discussions with the girl about Stepmom's former career.

I went into the den and sat in the office chair, which gave a comforting squeak. I learned from Freddy that the chopper had landed at the Philadelphia airport with the Bureau tactical team and that they were deploying in the garage and inside and around the terminal to begin surveillance. Assuming Loving was driving at legal speeds to the airport in Philadelphia, which I was sure he would be, he'd arrive within about ninety minutes.

I then called Aaron Ellis, to whom I gave the final details of the case.

He said, "Guess congratulations are in order."

The word seemed to jar. I heard gravity in my boss's voice when he asked, "Corte?"

"Go ahead."

"Senator Stevenson."

"Yes?"

"He called me."

I asked, "Directly? Not Sandy Alberts?"

"That's right. He called about you."

"Hold on." I rose, shut the door to the den and sat down again. Took a deep breath. Another. Then: "Go ahead, Aaron."

"He was asking me questions I didn't know the answers to." Ellis paused. "I need the truth, Corte. Are you in Stevenson's sights?"

I couldn't forestall it any longer. "I'm in his sights."

"Go on," Ellis said grimly.

I organized my response. Finally, I said, "After Abe was killed, I wanted to get Loving really bad. But he operates off the grid better than anybody I've ever seen. So I managed to get Loving's name on some lists."

"So?"

"It wasn't just watchlists. I added him to some wiretap warrant databases."

"*You* added him." Ellis was nearly whispering. "You mean, there was no judge involved?"

"No. I got into the integrated system

myself. If I'd waited to go to a judge until we found him, it would have been too
late. Look, it wasn't to collect evidence,
Aaron. It wasn't for trial. It was just to
find him."

"Jesus . . . In the meeting on Saturday
with Westerfield? He said they picked
up the go-ahead order on a warranted
tap. That was one of yours?"

My *illegally* warranted tap.

"That's right."

"So when Alberts came in to my office to talk to you, what? He was fishing?"

"I would guess so." I'd covered my
tracks pretty well but in my zeal to get
Loving I would have left behind trails
about what I'd done. "He or Stevenson
are probably tracking down instances of
dicey warrants and some of them
must've pointed to me. Alberts called
Freddy too. About me specifically."

I heard a creak. I pictured my boss
rocking in his office chair. His shoulders
were exactly as wide as the leather back.

I said, "It's not going to matter to Stevenson that the Kesslers'd be dead now
if I hadn't had the wiretap orders in

place. I've been reading up on him. He's ideological. He's not holding the hearings because of reelection and he's not doing it to boost his party or for the press. He genuinely believes in law and order. And warrantless surveillance is a crime."

As was, of course, forging warrants.

I remembered my dismay when I read what I'd learned about Stevenson and realized he was the worst possible enemy: a powerful man with a deeply held conviction that he was in the right. Especially when the person he was targeting, me, was so clearly wrong.

I'd felt dismay too at the fact that I'd found myself searching for a scandal or impropriety in Stevenson's life, anything I could use to discourage him from subpoenaing me—no, I'm not above using an edge like that myself. But there'd been nothing. He liked dating younger women, but he was single, so there was no problem there. His campaigns were largely funded by one of the biggest conservative political action committees in Washington. But all politicians' campaigns were backed by PACs; his just happened to be more flush than many others. Even his aide, Sandy Alberts, had been meticulous about severing all ties to all lobbying firms before coming to work for Stevenson.

No edge to threaten him with.

And there was nothing I could offer him to make him forget about me. I was exactly what he wanted to expose: an agent of the government working for a shadowy organization and playing fast and loose with the laws of the country.

"Where did Stevenson leave it?" I asked.

"He wants to know about cases you've run in the past few years, where perps went to trial."

To find out if any lifters or hitters I helped arrest were convicted on the basis of illegal taps. I told my boss, "It was only Loving. There weren't any others."

"Apparently that won't matter to him."

No, it wouldn't. A single incident of a crime is still a crime.

Aaron said, "You know if I don't deliver case files, he'll subpoena them. And he's going get you on the stand in the hearings."

Which would be the end of my career as a shepherd.

And perhaps the start of a very embarrassing trial, which would possibly end in a prison sentence.

"We're so close to Loving," I said, sitting forward tensely in the chair. "Please. Do the best you can to keep Stevenson—"

My boss, normally as calm as I was, now snapped, "I'm doing a lot of fucking interference-running for you on this job, Corte."

"I know. I'll cooperate with Stevenson completely—when Loving's in the can. I'll take whatever the consequences are."

"You know this has put the whole organization in a real awkward position. We can't afford to be public, Corte."

"I know, yes."

"I'll stall for a day or two, if I can. But if the subpoena's delivered, there's nothing I can do."

"I understand. Thanks, Aaron."

I hung up and sat back, rubbing my eyes, feeling utterly depleted. What could I salvage from this mess? Even if I avoided jail, it seemed my career as a shepherd was soon to be over. I couldn't help but think about some of the assignments I'd run, about some of my principals.

About Claire duBois.

About Abe Fallow too.

But then I recalled that, whatever happened in the future, the Kessler job wasn't finished yet. We still had Loving and the partner to nail. And we still had a case to make against the primary—and I'd make damn sure that it was completely buttoned up, independent of any bogus warrants.

I found the transcript of Aslan Zagaev's statement, opened it and began to read.

> *I led a more or less successful life here. Ah, but isn't success a moving target? I have been having some problems, financial in nature. The economy? Who needs rugs when you can't afford your mortgage payments? Who goes to eat at my wonderful restaurant when you must buy bulk frozen dinners at Sam's*

Club to feed your children? How could I make more money? Did I have any service I could perform? Did I have anything valuable that I could sell? Then it occurred to me. What if I could learn more about the operation behind the deaths of the Pakistanis in the deli six years ago? How valuable would that be? I remembered the woman who was the point control officer behind the operation to kill them: Joanne Kessler. Even if she had retired she would surely have valuable information or lead me to people who did.

I made some phone calls, discreet phone calls to a connection of mine in Damascus. I learned there was indeed an interest in information of this sort. A multimillion-dollar interest. A man there gave me Henry Loving's name.

When I finished I sat back. He seemed pathetic. More than that, though, he was a fool. Why risk prison, where he'd be spending the rest of his life, for a bit more money? It seemed like a curious motive for somebody who wasn't destitute and who had a family, whom he will see, from now on, only through bars or bullet-proof windows. I could understand it if he were a true terrorist, or if he were being blackmailed . . .

A thought occurred to me, resulting in a ping in my gut. I leaned forward fast and reread a portion of the transcript again.

I remembered the woman who was the point control officer behind the operation to kill them: Joanne Kessler.

Oh, no . . .

I grabbed my com device and called Lyle Ahmad.

"Now," I said. "I need you now."

The young clone showed up a moment later, his face impassive, eyes watchful.

"Yessir?"

"Close the door. Where're the principals?"

He eased the thick oak panel shut and stepped to the desk. "Ryan's in the back den, reading. Pretending to. He's been drinking. Joanne's in the bedroom. Maree's on her computer. In her room."

"And Barr?"

"Patrolling the back perimeter."

I lowered my voice. "We have a situation. About Barr . . . I think he's either been turned or he's a plant."

The officer's eyes were still. He was undoubtedly as alarmed as I was but, like me, he was approaching the situation calmly. The way I'd taught him. "All right."

I explained my thinking. "When I told you and Barr about Joanne's job with Sickle, I described her as a point control officer."

"I remember."

"But that's unique to our organization; Joanne called herself 'anchor' on the hit teams. Zagaev, though, referred to her as 'point control.'"

Ahmad was nodding. "How did he hear that term?"

"Exactly. The only way was if somebody here had told him."

"Barr."

"And," I added, "Zagaev used Joanne's

name. Sure, he may have been involved with the couple killed at the deli, but how could he have learned her name? Williams and the Sickle people would've kept it secret."

I continued, "So Loving got to somebody inside Justice and learned that Freddy was sending Tony Barr to the safe house."

"He got to Barr and turned him."

Another grim possibility had occurred to me. "Or he's not Barr. He's an imposter."

"And the real Barr is dead."

The unfortunate but logical conclusion.

I said to Ahmad, "Barr—or whoever he is—called Loving and told him we suspected Joanne was the principal and Zagaev might be the primary."

The lifter would have realized he'd been handed the perfect misdirection. He'd tracked down Zagaev and forced him into agreeing to play the role of primary—probably using his family as an edge. Loving had briefed Zagaev about all aspects of the operation—the helicopter, for instance—and told him to convince us that Joanne was in fact the target. The Chechnyan had made calls implicating himself and then, when we caught up with him, confessed.

Taking the pressure off Loving and the real primary.

"But if it's true," the young officer pointed out, "why hasn't Barr done anything more than give information to Loving? He could've told him where the safe house is. He could've shot us all in the back."

This was true. "I don't know. I've got to find out more. But for now, we've got to assume we have a hostile on the premises. Get all the principals into the den and stay with them. And call the detention center and get a message to Bill Carter. Tell them I'm not going to pick him and Amanda up yet. I want them back in the slammer until I figure out what's going on."

"Yessir." He headed out the door.

I stared at the transcript.

Point control officer . . .

How could I verify my theory? In order to get into the safe house Barr had passed fingerprint and facial recognition scans. So either he really was Tony Barr or somebody had gotten into the Justice Department's security servers— possibly an FBI employee or someone from any law-enforcement-related federal organization. I logged on to the Bureau personnel server, punched in the appropriate pass codes and looked over Barr's profile. The picture was identical, distinguishing characteristics, age. His prints were there—they were the sample that Geoff would have used to verify his identity. Everything pointed to the fact that the man here in the compound was Tony Barr.

I called up another screen and began searching social networking sites, typing in "Tony Barr" along with relevant demographic information.

The world of Google . . .

It took no more than three minutes to verify that we indeed had an imposter. The real Barr bore only a faint resemblance to the man in our back-forty at the moment.

So Barr was dead and the imposter was one of Loving's partners. I tucked away the shock at this confirmation and tried to figure out what his purpose here was or what Loving was really up to. I had no answers.

And to learn this I decided I needed some help.

I debated for a moment and then placed a call.

"This's Williams," rasped the voice.

"It's Corte."

"I know. Saw the number. I'm watching the dispatches. You got things taken care of."

Meaning: Why're you bothering me?

"There's a possibility they're not as taken care of as we'd hoped."

A grunt.

I explained the situation.

Williams took this in silently. "You're still alive. So what's your fake agent up to?"

"That's the question. I need to find out. But I can't trust anybody in the Bureau. There's a mole there, and they're probably monitoring what's going on at my outfit. . . . Do you have somebody we can use?"

I found it curious he didn't hesitate.

"Matter of fact, I do." He gave me a phone number. "Call him."

"Time's critical," I said. "How close are they?"

Williams offered a very expected chuckle. "A lot closer than you think."

Chapter 55

Twenty minutes later I stepped outside, smelling the chill moist air, the aroma from a wood fire in the distance. Kids sometimes lit campfires in the park overlooking the Potomac falls.

I recalled Maree and me, sitting uneasily—in my case, at least—on the rock shelf forty feet above the raging water earlier this morning. I recalled her kissing me.

Then I forced myself to concentrate.

Because the man fronting as Tony Barr was now approaching, vigilant as ever and armed with an impressive automatic weapon. I needed him to believe I had no inkling he was a partner of Henry Loving.

"Tony," I said, nodding. The intense, quiet man joined me. His eyes kept scanning the property. I asked, "Lyle's inside?" So far I was keeping my voice calm and looking at him in ways I thought appropriate to these circumstance.

"Yessir. . . . Any word from Philly?" he asked.

What the hell was Loving up to? I wondered. I said, "Nothing yet. Loving won't be there for another half hour or so, at the earliest." Car keys jangled in my hand. "I'm going to pick up the Kesslers' daughter and their friend."

A sliver of moon kept appearing and vanishing, as the thick clouds scooted by above us. Maple and oak sloughed silver leaves in the breeze and the tall hemlocks in the side yard swayed. The wind breathed easily.

I looked around the property. "It's a lot different here now, with the primary in custody and the lifter about to be nailed. You can almost enjoy it." I glanced at the imposter's black angular machine gun. It wasn't pointed near me but if he caught on that I knew who he was I'd be dead before I could move an inch.

The man said, "That's true—except for some deer with a suicidal personality who jumped out of the bushes over there a little while ago. We almost had venison for breakfast. Just heard him again, the same place. They're not really very bright, are they?"

"I don't think that's why God made them." Was he suspicious? I couldn't tell. I continued, "Listen, Tony, when I get back I want to coordinate getting the Kesslers to Fairfax in the morning. Loving'll be in custody by then. But I want some protection on them for the next couple of days, until everything's resolved. Agent Frederick said you might be willing to take that on." I was vamping. Overdoing it? I wondered. I wasn't sure. A bad performance would kill me.

"Yessir . . . if he'd like."

I smiled. "Meaning you're not all that crazy about baby-sitting detail."

He grinned too. "I'm happy to be of help, sir."

"Appreciate it."

Then a faint snap came from the front yard.

Both of us shared a troubled look and turned toward the sound. Tense, squinting.

"What do you think that was?" I asked.

"Our deer?" he asked in a whisper.

I shook my head. "Not in the front. They don't go there."

The sound was repeated, louder.

We trained the muzzles of our weapons in the direction of the snap.

"The hell is it?" he asked.

We got the answer a moment later as we saw another rock sail over the house and land in the driveway.

"Diversion," I rasped with alarm in my voice. We both spun around fast—to see a man covering us with a silenced semiautomatic pistol. He'd come up behind us quietly, as we were staring toward the sound, after flinging the stones over the roof to distract us.

The lean sandy-haired man was wearing the same green jacket he'd been wearing on Saturday at the assault on the Kesslers' house and at the flytrap.

I whispered, "It's Loving's partner!"

"His—?" the Barr-imposter began to ask. But before he finished the sentence the man in the green jacket squinted, lifted his weapon toward my leg and fired three times.

I cried out and went down hard.

Chapter 56

The bullets, in fact, hadn't hit me at all.

And the man in the jacket wasn't Loving's partner.

He was Williams's security expert, a man named Jonny Pogue—the one who was indeed closer than I would have thought, as Williams had said, after his grunting chuckle. Pogue had been stationed directly across the road and had been shadowing us for days to make certain that Joanne and her dark secrets didn't fall into the wrong hands. That's what he'd been doing at the Kesslers' house and at the flytrap, but since he was operating undercover, he never contacted us and we'd assumed he was the partner.

Over the phone shortly before, Pogue and I had worked out the ruse that was now unfolding, a strategy that might get to the truth about the imposter and what Loving's true plan was.

A strategy that might also get both Pogue and me killed.

Pogue knelt down and pretended to search me carefully; as he did so he turned his back to the imposter and was completely vulnerable. But the man, who could have shot him at any moment, was confused that Pogue was ignoring him. And further disarmed by Pogue's picking up my Glock and handing it to the phony FBI agent. "Here."

"I'm sorry," he said, taking the weapons uncertainly, "but who the fuck are you?"

"Pogue."

"Henry never said—"

"Loving doesn't know about me. I work for the man who hired him."

This was a gamble that Pogue and I had discussed. If the imposter himself worked for the primary, the whole play would end right now—maybe bloodily.

But then I heard him give a brief laugh and say, "Oh, sure. That explains it."

"I've been keeping an eye on you and Henry just to make sure things go according to plan." Pogue rose and extended his hand. "What's the name?"

"McCall."

They shook hands briefly. Then Pogue muttered, "Well, McCall, we got a problem. You know the insider—got you the info about Barr and your picture up on the Bureau website."

McCall nodded absently, looking around. "I don't know who it is, just somebody in that asshole Fredericks' office."

So the mole *was* in Freddy's department. This was bad. I didn't react, however, just clutched my leg and moaned. McCall seemed to enjoy it.

"Well, whoever they are, they changed their fucking mind," Pogue spat out. "They're talking."

"Shit, no."

"Shit, yeah." There was a mocking quality about the comment, the sort you'd hear between two soldiers on allied armies. Pogue was acting in top form.

Sickle . . .

McCall asked, "They know about me?"

"I don't know. Maybe not yet but they

will. It's just a matter of time till they figure out that you clipped Barr."

Defensively McCall said, "The body's
in a storm drain. Take 'em days to find
it."

"You can fucking hope. But the point
is we've gotta bail. Get to Henry and
warn him—we can't use the phones or
radio. They have all our numbers and
frequencies."

"What about him?" McCall pointed
my own Glock at me.

"He's coming with us. There's things
my boss wants to know. But the priority
is we've got to get to Henry. I mean,
now. Where is he?"

"Last time I talked to him he was pretty
close." McCall smirked, "They bought
all that crap about him going to Philly."

"Well, let's get to him. Before they
track him down. Where is he exactly?"

Careful, I thought to Pogue. I was worried he might be overdoing it.

"He was going to facility, after he and
the crew picked up the target."

Pogue asked, "The target? Joanne
Kessler?"

McCall frowned. "No, no, man. She doesn't have anything to do with this. . . . I mean, the *real* target. Amanda, the daughter."

Chapter 57

Amanda . . .

She was the Kessler they were after? Not Ryan or his wife?

I desperately tried to piece together how this could be.

Recovering, Pogue said, "I know *that.* I just thought Henry'd want to take Joanne and her husband out."

McCall shrugged. "Maybe. But he didn't say anything to me about it."

Pogue muttered, "I want to get the fuck out of here now. We'll meet him at the facility. Where is it again?"

This was a good try. I probably would have waited a little longer to pry some more details out, but there it was.

And I could tell by the thick silence that followed that the ruse was over. McCall had grown suspicious.

I couldn't take a chance he'd discard

my Glock—it was unloaded—and go for his machine gun. I rolled to my feet. "Now. Take him."

Gasping, McCall reacted fast, lifting the only weapon in his grip, my Glock, toward us.

Pogue muttered calmly, "It's empty." He targeted McCall with the suppressed Beretta. I stepped forward and grabbed my Glock from McCall's hand, reloaded, drew the slide and released it.

I covered McCall, gaping at us in shock, as Pogue slipped restraints onto his hands, cinching them tight. I took my phone and quickly dialed the detention center.

Lyle Ahmad now appeared from the bushes, where he'd been stationed with his own M4, a night scope mounted. I'd sent Ahmad into the woods to target the imposter while Pogue and I put on our little performance to see what we could learn from the man.

Grasping how completely he'd been suckered, McCall muttered, "I'm fucked." He was staring at my leg, where the bullet holes should have been. "I am so fucked."

I spoke to the supervisor at the detention center and learned that he still couldn't get in touch with the guards who were escorting Bill Carter and Amanda back from the rendezvous point.

I exhaled slowly between gritted teeth. Now that I realized Amanda was the target I knew that McCall would have told Loving the girl and Bill Carter were leaving the detention center. He wouldn't know the rendezvous spot specifically but Loving or other partners could have been waiting outside the prison for the car to emerge.

"Call me the minute you hear anything."

"Yessir."

I disconnected. I knew the mole was in the Bureau so I couldn't call Freddy for a tactical team. And I couldn't contact anybody in our organization, even Claire, in case the traitor was in touch with someone there.

I debated and decided to call local police and county troopers, sending them to search the road between the detention center and the rendezvous spot—a strip mall in Sterling, Virginia.

There was a possibility of a kidnapping, I told them. I warned them that the suspect or suspects were armed.

I slipped the phone away and crouched beside McCall, who was sitting slumped forward on the grass. His eyes met mine every fourth heartbeat.

"You were the one shooting at us in North East, at the warehouse?" I asked. "And you were the one who got the trackers onto my car?"

He said nothing but a flicker in his eyes told me that I was on the money.

"And at Bill Carter's place, you were in the woods across the road?"

McCall's lips tightened but still he remained silent.

"Why do they want Amanda?"

No response.

"Where is this facility? What is it?"

"I'm not saying anything."

In a raspy voice, Pogue said, "You just admitted killing Tony Barr, a federal agent. You have no leverage here."

McCall whispered, miserable, "Whatever you'd do to me, it doesn't come close to what Loving would do if he found out I talked. I've got family, friends—Loving'd take them out in a minute. Or do worse."

"We'll protect them," I said.

"From Loving?" McCall laughed coldly. "Right."

"You said you didn't know the primary's name. What *do* you know about him?"

Silence.

My phone buzzed. I stepped away and quickly hit ANSWER. "Corte."

It was a captain with the state police. "Sir, some of my troopers found William Carter. He's alive. Wounded but alive. A security guard from Northern Virginia Detention is dead."

"And the girl?"

"Afraid she's gone. They were about six miles from the prison. Carter said a black SUV ran them onto the shoulder, shot out the tires. Three men inside. None of them fit the description of the suspect, Loving."

Three *other* actors?

"Carter didn't get any look at the tag."

"What happened there?"

"Amanda kicked one of the suspects you know where. . . . Then she turned

around and shoved Carter down a steep
hill into a creek—to save him, you know.
Kid was a real hero, Carter said. She
started to jump after him but they got
her."

A hero, like her father.

"They fired on him but they didn't want
to wait around. And took off. Winged
him in the ankle but he'll live."

"Which direction did they go?"

"No idea, sir. We put it out on the wire
but so far, nothing. Follow up?"

"No. Keep it quiet for the time being."

"Yessir."

After we disconnected I looked at the
house, where the girl's father and stepmother waited. I looked over the fields
around the house, growing lighter and
darker as passing clouds squelched the
moonlight from time to time. Debating.
Were the three men in the SUV the primaries? Or were they muscle too? Or
other partners of Loving?

I wondered again, what information
could a primary possibly want to extract
from a sixteen-year-old girl?

I glanced at Pogue, then crouched
down in front of McCall.

Calm, Corte. Whatever happens you have to stay calm. When you look into your opponent's face, when you talk to him, it should be like you're discussing cornflakes. Never more emotional than that. . . . Emotion's deadly.

What's the goal? I asked myself.

What's the most efficient way to achieve it?

I knew these questions. I knew them in my heart. Yet for some reason now I grabbed McCall by the collar, gripped until he started to choke and shouted, "Where did they take her?"

He shook his head, as best he could.

"What's the facility, where is it?" Twisting harder. I felt Ahmad's eyes on me. He'd never seen me like this.

Spittle formed in the corners of McCall's lips.

"Where?" I raged.

His terrified eyes turned toward me. But he still remained silent.

I released him, stood up. I didn't want to take him into the house with my principals. I glanced toward the panic house, a small outbuilding about the size of a detached three-car garage. It didn't look substantial but it was. People could flee inside, seal the doors and be safe from any kind of armament up to the level of a rocket-propelled grenade.

"Get him inside."

Ahmad and Pogue dragged McCall roughly into the outbuilding.

I remained on the dewy grass and looked toward the panic house. The heavy steel door was open and the lights were on inside. I could see McCall shackled to a kitchen chair. His face wasn't defiant; he was scared.

The place was brightly lit and painted in easy colors—yellow and pastel blue—on the theory that if there was an extended siege, the occupants might be less inclined to surrender if the setting was cheery. Little things like that make a difference.

I turned away and walked to the main house. I punched in the key to the door. I wasn't looking forward to delivering the news.

All of my principals were clustered around a window, staring out. I hadn't explained to them about my suspicions of the man posing as Barr. But I now gave them the details of how he'd gotten inside and how Zagaev was a feint.

"Oh, Christ," Maree said. "He could've killed us. While we were asleep he could've, like, cut our throats."

Ryan asked, "Who's the other one, the tall guy?"

It was Joanne who spoke. "His name's Jon Pogue. He works for my organization." Then her voice faded, as she looked at me. "Why would they need a feint, though, Corte? Getting a mole inside here should've been enough. What else is going on?"

I inhaled a little deeper than usual. "It's Amanda they're after. And they've got her."

Joanne's mouth tightened and Ryan growled, "Where, where is she?"

"We don't know. But there's no doubt. Amanda was the Kessler they wanted."

"No, no," Maree whispered.

Joanne said in a voice as calm as mine, "Why? What does she know?"

I shook my head.

Ryan's face was red. "Those pricks! My little girl . . . what . . . ?" Then, it seemed, forming words became too much for him.

"And Bill?" Joanne asked.

"Minor injuries. He'll be okay. They killed the detention center guard who was with them. We believe they've taken Amanda to a rendezvous site nearby. Loving's on his way there. But we don't know where. We tried to find out from McCall but he caught on and he's not saying anything."

Ryan muttered, "Well, Jesus, what're we going to do?"

I said, "I could use some help." My eyes on Joanne.

She lifted an eyebrow.

I said, "Part of McCall wants to cooperate. I can tell. He's on the borderline. I'm thinking if you could talk to him, he might help us out."

"Appeal to his sense of decency?" she asked.

"As Amanda's stepmother, yes."

Her eyes swung to the wedge of light falling on the grass from the open door of the panic building. "I'll give it a try."

Chapter 58

Pogue and I stood outside the closed door to the outbuilding.

I observed him closely for the first time.

The head beneath that sandy hair was long, a predator's skull. His features were pinched—they'd circled in on themselves—and a scar curved forward from his chin, short and narrow, from a knife, not shrapnel. He didn't smile or offer much expression and I doubted that he ever did. No wedding ring, no jewelry. I noted remnants of stitching where insignias had been removed from his green jacket. I supposed that it was a personal favorite and that he'd had the garment for years.

His narrow hips were encircled by a worn canvas belt. It held a special holster—a clamp basically, fitted for a si-

lenced pistol—and a number of magazine holders, along with a knife and
several small boxes whose purpose I
couldn't guess.

Unlike Ryan Kessler, Pogue didn't
constantly tap or fidget with his weapons. He knew where they were if he
needed them. On the ground beside
him was a battered dark nylon rucksack,
whose contents were heavy. I'd heard a
clank when he'd set it down.

He stood with his arms crossed, looking over the property with the eye of a
shepherd, as if he weren't aware of my
presence. Finally he said, "Missed this
one."

Meaning Barr, I assumed.

He continued, "I had information. Bits
of it. But nothing fit together."

Though that wasn't completely true.
The bits *did* fit together, like a machine-
cut jigsaw puzzle. I'd been focused on
the individual pieces, though. Not the
image as a whole. I'm not much of a
jigsaw player—it's not really a game—
but I know the strategy generally is to
do the outer border first, so that you
have a framework, and then fill in.

Exactly what I hadn't done here. I'd made a lot of assumptions.

He looked at my back. "You like that Glock?"

"I do."

"They're fine firearms." Then, with a hint of criticism: "Prefer a little longer barrel myself."

"Interesting holster." Nodding down at his hip.

"Hmm," he replied.

More silence. Pogue said, "Evolution." There was some thoughtfulness in his voice.

While pursuing my various college degrees I usually found time to take some courses for no reason other than that I was curious about the topic. Once I'd taken a very good class in medical school, called Darwin and the History of Biology (also because the lecture hall was next to where Peggy was taking Anatomy). I was curious what Pogue meant and I glanced his way.

"Weapons reflect efficient evolution more than anything else in society, don't you think?"

Survival of the fittest, in a way, but not quite what Darwin was thinking of.

But it proved to be an interesting idea. Pogue continued, "You've got medicine and vehicles and paint and clocks, computers, processed food, you name it. Think about them. Giving mercury as medicine or leaching blood out of people. Or making airplanes that crash and bridges that collapse. Engineers and scientists just flailing around, trying to get it right, killing people, themselves included, in the process. Failure after failure after failure."

"I suppose that's true."

"But weapons? They're efficient from the git-go." An accent, slightly Southern, protruded.

Efficient . . .

"You couldn't have a sword that broke the first time you used it. You couldn't have a musket that blew up in your face—the men who made those made 'em right the first time. No luxury for error. That's why you can still shoot guns're two hundred years old and some of 'em are pretty damn accurate."

"Natural selection."

Pogue said, "Darwinian gunsmithing."

Some heady thinking from a man who, even if he wasn't technically a government killer, protected them for a living.

We fell silent, not because of the conversation, but because Ryan Kessler was limping down from the house like a bear just out of hibernation.

Pogue and I nodded toward him.

"Anything?" The detective eyed the outbuilding.

"Not yet."

We stood in silence. Ryan's hands were in his pockets. He stared down. His eyes were red.

"How's Maree?"

"Holding up okay."

More silence.

Then came the snap of a lock as the door opened. Ryan jumped. Pogue and I did not.

Joanne stepped out and announced, "I've got it. I know where Amanda is."

Without another word she started for the house, walking ahead of us, as she used disinfectant wipes to clean the blood off her hands.

Chapter 59

In game theory the concept of the grim trigger is an interesting one.

This occurs in "iterated" games—those in which the same opponents play the same game against each other over and over again. Eventually players settle into strategies that achieve the best common good, even if it's less than perfect for their own self-interest. For instance, they learn in the Prisoners' Dilemma the best outcome is to refuse to confess.

But sometimes Player A "defects," breaks the pattern, by confessing, which means he gets off scot-free while Prisoner B gets a much longer sentence.

Player B then might play grim trigger, abandoning any semblance of cooperation and defecting forever.

Another way to put it is that if one

player decides even one time not to play by the rules, the opponent from then on plays exclusively—and ruthlessly—for his own self-interest.

There was no cooperation involved between Henry Loving and me, of course, in this deadly game we were playing but the same theory applied. By kidnapping a teenager to torture her and extract information, as far as I was concerned, Loving had defected.

I was now playing grim trigger.

Which meant unleashing Joanne Kessler—in her incarnation as Lily Hawthorne—on Loving's associate, McCall, to lift the information from him. Whatever that took. My interrogation skills are good but it would take time to get somebody like McCall, terrified of Henry Loving, to talk.

I needed somebody he would fear more.

Hence my subtle request to Joanne in the living room twenty minutes before, using chilling euphemisms, which she picked up on instantly. I could see from her eyes.

Appeal to his sense of decency?

As Amanda's stepmother, yes.

She and I had then gone to the out-building. We'd found McCall looking up from the heavy chair, scared, yes, but resolute in not betraying Loving. As I'd gestured Ahmad out, McCall had barked an uneasy laugh. "You're giving me that voodoo look, Corte. What's this about?"

Joanne Kessler definitely wasn't giving him any looks. She was just studying him.

"Why isn't anybody saying anything?" His voice caught.

The sense of threat in the room reminded me of the Zagaev interrogation Bert Santoro and I had conducted not long ago.

Only this was real.

Joanne had nodded to me and I'd gone to a control panel in the wall and inserted a key and hit several buttons. I'd told her, "No communication out or in. The video's off. You're invisible."

"Look, Joanne," McCall had said desperately. "I just can't help you out, I'm sorry. I wish I could but I can't. I feel for you, I really do. If there was any way . . ."

She wasn't paying any attention to

him. She'd turned back to me and asked, "Any tools here?"

"Under the sink. Nothing fancy."

"That's all I need." Joanne had then closed the door.

Another thing about the outbuilding. The designers completely soundproofed the place. The reason for this was so that the principals couldn't hear threats or demands coming from the outside.

The corollary was that neither could you hear screams from inside.

Night was around the compound as we gathered on the front porch of the safe house. Joanne seemed no more agitated than someone who'd survived a bargain basement sale at a mall store, standing her ground at the popular sizes and snagging the best.

She said to me, "They've taken her to an old military installation on Route Fifteen near Leesburg, a mile south of Oatlands."

I knew Oatlands. A venue for Renaissance fairs and dog shows. Peggy and I had taken the boys there once.

She continued, "The facility's about a hundred yards west of Fifteen down an unmarked dirt road, in the side of a hill, like a bunker. McCall doesn't know why they want her. It's very secret. He would've told me if he did."

Joanne was speaking loudly. She realized this and reached up and extracted the cotton balls from her ears.

"Loving'll be there soon and in about an hour the primary or the people who work for him will too."

"Nothing at all about why they want her?"

"No. He said it wasn't hard to find or kidnap Amanda. Anybody could have done that." Her voice was rock steady as she said, "The reason they hired Loving was that nobody else was willing to torture a teenager, if it came to that."

Ryan gasped. I noted that Joanne and her husband had not looked at each other since she'd left the outbuilding. He'd glanced inside to see her handiwork. There was a lot of blood on the floor. The reaction on her husband's face was one you don't see often in a police officer.

Joanne continued, "The three men who took her are minders. They might work for the primary or maybe Loving hired them. McCall doesn't know. Only the primary knows what information to extract. Even Loving doesn't."

I asked, "Does Loving expect McCall?"

"No. He's supposed to stay here, within cover."

This was good. If he'd been required to, say, report to Loving every fifteen minutes, that would have been a tactical problem.

But now it was our move.

What strategy was best?

Rock, paper or scissors?

Joanne turned to Pogue. "A G team?"

I'd never heard the term but it wasn't hard to deduce.

The operative said, "Two, three hours. We're not as mobile here as we used to be. More New York and L.A."

I glanced at Pogue. "You and me?"

"I'd say." He cast an eye toward Joanne and for a moment it occurred to me that while he may not have been the partner on the Pakistani deli hit, there was history between them.

A voice said firmly, "I'm going too."

Ryan Kessler.

I said, not unsympathetically, "This isn't your expertise, Ryan."

"Because I've been sitting behind a desk for six years, watching my ass spread? I've been on tac ops in the past. I know what I'm doing."

"No. Because you're involved. She's your daughter. You can't engage a hostile if you're involved. It's not efficient."

"Look," the man said, sounding reasonable. "It's no risk my being there. He doesn't want me, Corte."

I pointed out, "He could use you as an edge to get Amanda to talk."

"She's a sixteen-year-old girl," Ryan muttered. "He doesn't need an edge. He barks at her and she tells him what he wants to know."

That wasn't the Amanda Kessler I'd seen.

"You're too emotional. There's nothing wrong with that. But you'll have to stand down."

"That's a dirty word to you, Corte, isn't it? 'Emotion.' Tough being a robot, isn't it?"

"Ryan, honey, please," Joanne said,

reverting to the good wife she'd been earlier. Or, more accurately, the *role* of the good wife she'd been playing.

I didn't argue with Ryan. How could I? He was 100 percent right.

He walked close. "Maybe it's time to take the gloves off, Corte. And be honest. It was all bullshit, wasn't it? What you said?"

I could see what was coming.

"You've just been patting me on the head, haven't you? The way you've been handling me? Is it out of the bodyguard's manual of tricks? Give your principal some busywork. Lie to him. Tell him he's going to help you save the day. 'We'll take down Loving together, just wait till we're someplace else.' Then send him off to guard a field of fucking daisies and ragweed. In Fairfax, at my house, you knew Loving wasn't going to come at us from that direction, didn't you? You had me guard it to keep me occupied."

I hesitated. "Yes, I did."

"And you still had the balls to tell me what a great job I'd done." He shook his head. "Oh, fuck, Corte. And when there actually *was* somebody to take down here—McCall—you didn't consider me, did you? You called in our friend." A contemptuous glance at Pogue. "You have a term for it, for keeping us principals busy? Making sure we sit in the corner with our toys and don't bug the adults? Come on, Corte."

"Ry, honey, please. You—"

"Shut up!" he snapped to Joanne. Then turned back. "So what do you call it?"

"Bait-and-switch."

"You son of a bitch," he muttered. "Guard the side yard, Ryan. Aim low, avoid his femoral artery. You're probably a great shot. . . . '"

"I needed to get you on my side."

"And sharing your war stories. How you got started in the business . . . your sign cutting, your orienteering. All lies?"

"No."

"Bullshit."

My heart went out to him. How could it not? A man who'd been robbed of a career he loved—and by his wife, no less.

Who'd been robbed of his status as a hero.

And lied to by me.

He whispered, "Give me this chance. I'm a good shot and the limp's nothing. I can move fast, if I have to."

Joanne said, "No, Ry. Let them handle it."

"I'm sorry," I told him.

"Well, I'm going anyway." He was speaking to me. "You can't stop me. I know where she is. After you're gone I'll just get in somebody's fucking car and go anyway." His hand strayed to his weapon.

A moment of dense silence. My eyes needed only to slip toward Lyle Ahmad, and the former marine stepped up behind, easing Ryan to the floor with a basic wrist grip on his gun hand. There was a countermove, by which Ryan, the larger of the men, could have escaped but, if he'd ever known it, he'd forgotten.

His eyes on mine, he growled, "Fucking coward. You couldn't even take me yourself, could you? Had to have somebody get me from behind."

I stepped forward and slipped nylon restraints around his wrists.

"No!" he cried.

"I'm sorry."

"She's my daughter!"

It was Joanne I was looking at, though. For the first time since I'd met her, tears were now streaking down her cheeks.

Ahmad got Ryan into a sitting position. I leaned down toward his thick, damp face, dark with anger. I said firmly, "I'm going to bring her back to you. This is what I do. I'll bring her back safe."

Chapter 60

Route 15 is a hilly road through the heart of Civil War Virginia, forty miles outside of Washington. Large, private estates on the capillaries of horse country fight against the encroaching cookie-cutter developments with streets named according to themes, like Camelot, flora, colonial New England.

You'll find oddities along the highway. Decrepit, abandoned farms whose owners aren't willing to sell to salivating developers or who have simply disappeared—often because they prefer staying off the grid for any number of reasons. There are also ominous structures, stained concrete or rusting steel, ringed with dire warning signs and sharp, equally rusty wire, blanketed with kudzu. They once supported various attempts at defense systems during the Cold War.

We can't take down intercontinental ballistic missiles nowadays, much less fifty years ago, but that didn't stop the army or air force from trying. Some of these buildings were actually for sale but since most of them had served as weapons storage facilities, the toxic cleanup costs would be prohibitive.

I'd done a thorough run-down of our destination, USAF-LC Facility 193, a large concrete building only thirty or forty minutes from the safe house in Great Falls.

I piloted my car past the facility now and noted the concrete facade and the forty- or fifty-foot mound of earth, grass covered, that the building disappeared into. It was, as McCall had told Joanne, set back about one hundred yards. The gate was closed but the fences around the front and sides weren't imposing and didn't appear to be electrified or mounted with sensors.

I eased to a stop. Examining the place through my Xenonics night vision monocular, Pogue said, "Two SUVs, can't tell the tags. Some lights inside the building. One person outside, can't tell if he's armed. Assume he is."

I continued, pulling off the shoulder into bushes, then shut the engine off. It was 8:45 and dark. Normally the stars were striking here but tonight they were invisible, thanks to the blanketing clouds. Pogue and I climbed out, waited for a semi to burn along the road, spinning up dust and limp leaves in its wake. We crossed the road and moved toward the facility, using the dense brush and trees for cover. Pogue studied the place again through the monocular and held up a single index finger. Only one guard still.

I looked too. A youngish man with a close crew cut. He wore dark jeans and a sweatshirt. He kept his hand at his side and when he turned and made some brief rounds, I could see that he wore a semiautomatic pistol on his hip.

Still thirty yards away, Pogue slipped an earpiece in and spoke into his collar. I couldn't hear the words clearly but I deduced he was reporting in to Williams, Joanne's former boss.

If McCall was right about the times, the primary had not yet arrived. This conclusion was reasonable since there were only two vehicles here—Loving's and the SUV the minders had used to kidnap the girl. Amanda would be held for the time being, until the primary who wanted the information from her arrived.

The reason they hired Loving was that nobody else was willing to torture a teenager, if it came to that. . . .

What on earth could she possibly know? Something she'd learned about one of her father's earlier cases? Or something else? Like all teens in the D.C. area she'd have friends whose mothers or fathers worked for the government and for government contractors. Had she and a girlfriend read through files in a parent's computer, something classified?

But that question would have to wait.

Our job now was simple: Save the girl.

Pogue listened for a moment and whispered a few more words. Then he signed off. He eased closer to me and whispered, "Williams says you're in charge. How do we handle it?"

"I don't want to wait for the primary. I

want to extract her now. Use nonlethal if possible . . . at least on one of them."

I wanted somebody alive to learn who was behind this.

"All right." He glanced at my gun. "You tapped?"

Meaning: Was my Glock threaded for a silencer? I rarely had reason even to draw my weapon, let alone make sure it fired in a whisper. "No."

He handed me his. "One in the bedroom. Safety's on."

He'd tell me this because Glocks don't have a safety lever; they have a double trigger that prevents accidental discharges. I was familiar with the Beretta, though, and slid the lever smoothly to the fire position. The Italians made as efficient weapons as the Austrians.

I was curious why he'd given me his gun. Then he said, "Cover me."

He opened his backpack and extracted some metal and plastic pieces. He assembled them into a small crossbow, steel.

The evolution of weapons . . .

It took two strokes to cock it. The bolt

he loaded didn't have a sharp tip but instead an elongated tube.

"I should be a little closer," he whispered.

We moved forward. I was in the lead, using my training as an orienteer and amateur sign cutter yet again to keep our transit silent. I thought back briefly to that very long, very hot day outside San Antonio, leading the illegals to safety as quietly and as unobtrusively as I could.

Pogue and I eased into a compacted stand of weeds about forty feet from the guard. With a nod at the bow, Pogue said, "Stun gun. It'll immobilize him for about twenty seconds, so we'll have to get to him fast. I'll go first, you come behind and cover me with the Beretta. You're okay with that, right?"

Meaning killing somebody. I said, "Yes."

I aimed toward the doorway, where any reinforcements would come from.

"Go," I whispered.

Chapter 61

Pogue lifted the weapon, looking completely at ease, like a man about to cast a fly into a clear stream.

He was compensating for gravity and the slight breeze. When the guard turned away from us, Pogue pulled the trigger. With a faint snap, the bolt zipped into the air in a perfect arc, hitting the man somewhere in the middle of the back. I didn't know how many volts the flying Taser had but it was enough. The guard went down, shivering.

Then we were on our feet, running in tandem. Pogue had dropped the bow and had a backup pistol in his hand. With the silenced automatic, I scanned the doorway, the building's windows and the area around us for signs of hostiles. There were none. Pogue hog-tied the guard with plastic restraints and slapped an adhesive gag over his mouth. He bent down and pocketed the man's phone and radio, after shutting them off, as well as his pistol, while I patted him down for other weapons. Even though tactical ops aren't my specialty, I knew you never left weapons for the other side to pick up later.

Take or trash, the saying went.

I dug the man's wallet out of his pocket. I was disappointed but not surprised to see he was a pro and there was no evidence of his employer or affiliation. He had four driver's licenses—different names, same picture—money and credit cards in those various names.

In a moment the man revived. He looked up at us, fearfully, and began to retch. Pogue and I dragged him around the corner of the building and I ripped the gag off and let him vomit. When he was done Pogue slapped another gag on him. I crouched down and pulled out the small locking-blade Buck knife I carry.

I opened it with a soft click. The man stirred. I pointed to the gag and held up two fingers. Terrifying the man even more, Pogue applied a second.

I bent close and said, "Is Loving here?"

A hesitation. Pogue gripped one of the man's hands and I scraped the blade across the top of a nail. Painless but persuasive, even with the gag, you could hear the terrified scream.

A yes nod.

"How many people inside, total?" I began to count. At four, he bobbed his head up and down vigorously.

"And the man who hired Loving? We know he's on his way. When will he get here? Blink—each blink is five minutes."

I tallied them up. It came to a half hour.

"Who is he?"

A series of desperate nos. I believed he didn't know the primary's identity.

"Inside, those four . . . are they all with the girl?"

A shrug but a terrified one and I suspected he didn't know.

"Where?" I began running through various directions, at which he either nodded or shook his head. Once or twice he shrugged.

Apparently they were in the back of the facility, straight down the main corridor, though he didn't know or couldn't remember if it was upstairs or down. While just one story here at the entrance, farther inside the hill there were multiple floors, duBois had learned.

I nodded to Pogue and closed my eyes and tilted my head briefly. The man extracted a heavy-duty hypodermic syringe. The guard stirred violently, probably thinking we were going to kill him, but Pogue got the needle into a vein skillfully and a moment later he was asleep. "How long?" I whispered.

"Two hours, give or take."

I ripped the gag off, fearful that the guard might vomit again and choke to death. Pogue looked at me questioningly, as if he didn't care what happened to the man, but said nothing.

At the front door I spit on the hinges to keep them from squealing and we eased it silently open. I expected to find battery-powered lamps but the overhead lights were working. Pogue shrugged at what could be deduced from the functioning power: Perhaps the facility had been taken over by Henry Loving. A place of business—to ply his trade as a lifter. It was intimidating; subjects would be terrified to be brought here. Also, the walls were thick enough to withstand a Russian assault—which meant that any locals passing nearby couldn't hear the screams from inside.

The linoleum-floored corridor, stained from water seepage, extended straight to the back of the facility. I looked for cameras or other security systems and found none.

I returned the silenced Beretta to Pogue and drew my Glock. We started down the hundred-foot-long hallway, keeping to the shadows. Pogue was in front and I watched the rear regularly. He tried doorknobs occasionally but the doors were locked. Apparently there was only this one main way in and out of the facility, though there would have to be some fire exits.

Escape would come later, though. First, I had to find the principal that I'd lost.

Where the corridor ended there were stairs leading both down and up.

Which way?

I played another game. I mentally flipped a coin.

Up won.

Chapter 62

Pausing to listen, on the second-floor landing.

Faint noises, the source impossible to guess, came from unknown directions. Taps, clicks, water dripping? The air here was raw with the scent of mold and very chill. I knew that interrogators regularly use underheated interview rooms.

The door to the second floor was locked and we continued to the third floor, the top. At the far end of this corridor we could see illumination, about fifty feet ahead. We moved quickly along the shabby linoleum to the doorway from which the light filtered. We paused outside and glanced in. The door opened onto a wide balcony overlooking the second floor, a very large room, seventy-five by a hundred feet or so. The place was a control room of some sort, filled with gray desks, partitions and metal electronics consoles from which the guts had been removed. The smell of musty paper joined that of the mold. The overhead lights were off but at the far end, on the other side of high partitions, were pools of illumination.

I pointed and, with Pogue now covering me, we went in the direction of the light, crouching, practically on our knees. We came to a stairwell heading down to the main floor but stayed on the balcony. Soon we could hear voices rising and falling softly from the far end of the room, in the direction in which we were headed. Men's voices, I couldn't make out the words. But there were some tones of impatience, followed by a calm utterance, perhaps reassurance.

If Amanda was there, she wasn't speaking.

We continued farther down the balcony, moving slowly. There was a lot of trash up here, including broken glass and scraps of sheet metal, which we had to avoid. The men were speaking softly; they would easily hear the sound made by a careless footfall.

Finally we got to the end of the balcony. Below us were the pools of light we'd seen. I rose slowly and peeked over the edge. The light, I saw, was cast by two cheap, mismatched lamps sitting on desks. Incongruously, one sported a Disney shade, torn and stained. Nemo, I noted.

Only ten feet from it sat Amanda Kessler.

In dusty jeans and dark blue sweatshirt the girl huddled in a gray metal office chair, face grim and defiant. Her knees were drawn up. Her wrists were duct taped but they'd let her keep her bear purse with its silly grin.

Her captors were underneath us, obscured by the overhanging balcony. Loving and the three others. If we could get the four of them into the open, out from under the balcony, we'd be in an excellent shooting position. I raised two fingers and drew my hand across my throat. Two more raised fingers, then the letter *L*, to indicate Loving, and I pointed to my shoulder.

I wanted two dead and Loving and one other wounded, to keep them alive for interrogation. A shattered clavicle or scapula will completely disable a hostile, unlike a leg shot.

Pogue acknowledged my message while I looked around the floor to find something to fling into the shadows to draw them out—as Pogue himself had done at the safe house just hours before.

One of the kidnappers entered our line of sight below, walking toward the girl. He paused before he got to Amanda, who watched him with narrowed eyes. He picked up a coffee cup. The bulky man was in a suit. He sipped and looked around the room. "They fired missiles from here?"

"I don't know," came another voice. Not Loving's.

"It was Nikes."

"What, like the shoe?"

"Like the Greek god."

The voices had no Southern drawl.

"There are silos around here someplace. In Clifton. In case the Russians attacked."

"The Russians? Why would they attack us?"

"Jesus."

I picked up a few bits of broken glass. Pogue saw and silently took a second magazine for the Beretta out of his holster and set it on the floor in front of him. I kept my second in my pocket. I only had one extra, unlike Pogue, who seemed to have about a hundred rounds on him, and if the operation became one of pursuit or escape under fire I didn't want to leave any ammunition behind.

"Where is he?" another voice called.

"Be patient."

I felt a chill, hearing the calm voice of Henry Loving.

"You think they know?"

"That we have her? Not yet. McCall would've let us know."

The girl said suddenly, "You're going to get arrested. All of you. Or shot." Amanda Kessler was not, unlike the others, whispering. Her voice was strident.

The man with the coffee glanced at her but said nothing.

Neither did anybody else.

"My father's a policeman."

"We know," came another voice.

But Loving shushed him. "Chat's inefficient. Be quiet."

I glanced at Pogue. From his pocket he withdrew earplugs. I was familiar with them. They block out the high decibels and pitch of gunfire but allow human voices through. He handed a pair to me. I shoved them in. I took a deep breath and let fly the piece of glass, which landed with a *tink* in the far corner of the room.

The hostile in view set down the coffee and drew his pistol. "Fuck was that?"

Two others appeared from below the balcony, one with a dark automatic in his hand, moving forward slowly.

That was three. We needed the fourth to make our plan work. Where was Loving?

Come on. . . .

From directly underneath us, the lifter calmly ordered, "Call out front."

As the three men in front of us looked around, one lifted a radio. "Jamie, what's up? Is he here yet? We heard something inside."

Receiving no response, he looked back uncertainly.

I let fly another bit of glass and it skidded across the floor.

Both of the armed men below us lifted their weapons.

"Shut the radio off," Loving commanded.

And stepped into view.

We now had all four targets in front of us, bracketing Amanda. Loving and the man with the radio were to the right of her and the two armed captors on the left.

Pogue pointed to the two with the weapons and drew his finger over his throat, then to himself.

He was, after all, a professional killer and I was, in effect, the opposite. I prepared to shoot into the shoulder of the man on the right and Henry Loving.

I aimed. Pogue held up three fingers of his left hand and began counting down.

I trained my sights on Loving. The image in my mind was Abe Fallow.

Two . . .

It was then that Amanda gave a gasp

and jerked back. "Oh, shit." She screamed, "No!" She was staring down. The men crouched and separated and we momentarily lost our targets. One stepped back, just out of view.

Pogue and I froze.

The girl said, "A rat. There's a rat under the chair! Get it away!"

"A—"

The captor nearest her muttered, "Fuck, scared the shit out of me." He stood and stepped forward, close to Amanda, looking under the chair.

Pogue and I started to aim once more.

Which was when the girl's bound hands lifted the bear purse to her mouth. She unzipped it with her teeth and manage to pull out a small black canister. She aimed awkwardly but fired a stream of orange pepper spray directly into the startled face of her captor. From two feet away it shot straight into his eyes. He screamed and dropped his gun, which Amanda dove for. The man beside him swung his gun toward her.

Loving shouted, "No!"

Pogue and I simultaneously shot the man who was about to fire at Amanda.

Henry Loving knew instantly what had happened and, as we turned our guns toward him and the others, he swept his arm into the lamps, which shattered on the floor, plunging the room into darkness. The only illumination now was the ruddy glow from the three exit signs.

Pogue and I stared down into the murky scene, where I had a vague image of Amanda scrabbling away from the men into the obstacle course of the room.

Then, beneath me, I heard the whispers of the three remaining captors as they planned their strategy.

Chapter 63

Now it didn't matter if there was a mole in Freddy's office or not, since Loving knew about our presence. So I hit SEND, transmitting the text I'd prepared earlier. It gave Freddy a brief explanation and an urgent request for backup. I told him too that the primary was en route, so to set up roadblocks around the facility.

Amanda's heroics had guaranteed that we now needed all the help we could get.

Eyes growing accustomed to the darkness, we made our way down the stairway to the floor of the control room. I saw a dim form but whether it was a shadow or a silhouette, I didn't know. I aimed but was well aware it might be Amanda and waited for a clear image.

I never got one. He, or she, disappeared.

I heard hard breathing and faint groans from the man Amanda had sprayed. "Fuck, that hurts. . . . Okay, okay. I can see. I've got my weapon. Who the fuck's here?"

From somewhere, not that far away, Loving hissed for their silence.

Where was Amanda?

A moment later I heard more whispering.

Loving was playing a Bayesian game now, one modeled on imperfect information. He wouldn't know whom he was up against. How many we were, who we were, what our agenda was. But he'd be making instantaneous adjustments in assessing the probability of what his enemy would do.

He'd think there might be just one adversary here—he wouldn't have heard the second shot, from Pogue's silenced weapon. He knew that the attacker had eliminated the guard out front. He knew that the opponent was willing to fire without surrender demands. Another bit of information was that to distract them we'd flung glass into the corner of the control room, meaning this was a very limited operation, with no SWAT backup. Had the Bureau's hostage rescue team been on hand, this place would have been lit up like Times Square.

Loving would be thinking he and his men outnumbered the opponents and that they still had some time. Enough to find the girl and escape.

A piercing scream filled the black space. Amanda. She was near me. I could hear the sounds of a struggle. Then a loud clank and a man shouted in pain, "Need some help. She got me with that fucking spray shit. I'm in the northwest corner—"

"Quiet," Loving shouted, as Pogue and I separated instinctively and moved fast in that direction. I fired covering shots high.

The shadowy figure by the door lifted his gun and fired a round in my general direction. Pogue returned fire, a burst of three, and sent the man to the floor, though he wasn't hit—not badly at least—since he continued to fire.

I tallied one dead, one or two hit by pepper spray.

"Fuck, she got away," another voice called.

"We're federal agents," I called, "we've got teams outside too."

Pogue shouted, "We know there are three of you. I want all three with hands up standing in the light of the exit door. Do it now. Or we will engage you."

Then Henry Loving spoke again: "Corte, you're running a rogue operation. We won't kill the girl. We just need some information. Back out."

"Fuck you," Amanda cried.

"Amanda!" I called. "Get on the floor. Lie down, wherever you are. Stay down, be quiet."

This was greeted with several more shots in my direction.

"Stop the firing," Loving said adamantly.

"Where are you?" Amanda cried.

"Just get on the floor. There are—"

A huge crack of explosion and I was rolling backward, blinded.

A flash-bang grenade.

Underestimated them, I thought. Even

the earplugs didn't save my hearing this time. Pogue too hadn't expected the grenade and had been slammed into the desk hard. Still, he struggled to his knees again and looked for a target, though the flash had been so bright our vision was fuzzy.

We both scrabbled away from the place where one of the kidnappers had lobbed the nonlethal stun grenade. I was desperate to find Amanda but didn't dare call again for fear of giving away my position; I could tell from their shadows they were moving in, flanking us.

It was then that I heard a noise behind me and spun around, as the attacker, only a few feet away, lunged forward, slamming me to the floor.

Chapter 64

The attacker was kicking and trying desperately to get to my weapon.

At the same time as my vision began to return I caught a whiff of sweat and perfume.

"Amanda!" I whispered. "It's me, Corte." I pushed her off me.

The girl backed up, squinting and aiming the pepper spray into my face. In the red light from the exit sign I could see her grim eyes.

She's got some grit, your daughter. It'd take a lot to get her rattled. . . .

The panic bled from her expression. "Oh . . . Mr. Corte." Her cheeks were damp but not from crying; the residual gas from the spray was irritating her, like everybody else here. I pulled the duct tape off her wrists.

Pogue looked our way and gestured

us down, then scanned the nearby portions of the office.

The girl collapsed against me, not in panic, though. She was exhausted.

Nearby: the sound of metal hitting the concrete floor.

"Eyes and ears," Pogue snapped.

I closed my eyes and pulled Amanda close, her face in my chest, covering her ears. When the grenade went off, this time we were prepared.

Except that this grenade was different.

There was a hiss and pop, rather than an explosion. I looked up to see a brilliant white light fill the entire room, shooting stark shadows onto the walls. At the same time the phosphorous burst out in a small dome and ignited the nearby portion of floor, the partitions and the upholstery of the office chairs. The brilliant white light died but the fire continued—and it grew—and we could just make out shadowy forms moving briefly on the far side of the room, then vanishing.

A moment later another grenade landed, closer to us. We scrabbled away before it detonated and another sphere of the sticky incendiary rose. Phosphorous is like napalm. It sticks like glue and will burn through clothing and skin.

"We can't stay here," Pogue whispered, looking right and left. Eyes scanning constantly. "Okay, here's what we do. We can't all run a defense going back out the main corridor, so I'm going to keep them pinned. You and the girl go out the front. When help comes tell 'em where I am."

Pogue's approach was the only logical one. I said, "Freddy's on his way. Shouldn't be long."

Another grenade flew toward us and we were just able to get out of the way in time. It detonated, starting a third fire.

I considered a possible strategy. I whispered, "One minute."

I eased Amanda down under a desk and gestured for Pogue to cover her. He acknowledged this. I made my way a little closer to where I believed the latest grenade had come from. I knew the flash-bang grenades would have stunned the others' hearing too and I was betting that Loving might not recognize my voice.

I took a deep breath and shouted, "Henry, he's behind you! Ten feet."

Loving didn't fall for it, in fact he instantly anticipated the strategy and called, "No! Everybody down." But one of his colleagues had risen from cover and spun around, lifting his gun.

A perfect target. I fired a group of three. Two in the chest, one in the head. He dropped hard.

Pogue acknowledged this with a nod. Two down.

I ducked to cover, as the other associate of Loving's fired blindly in my direction. I bent down. "You ready, Amanda?"

"I'm totally ready."

Pogue moved twenty feet away from us, to a spot where he'd draw their fire. He unscrewed the silencer and let go with five or six rounds throughout the room. The Beretta roared.

Crouching, Amanda and I dodged sputtering, white-hot fires and pushed through the exit door on the second-floor hallway. I was afraid that the door was locked from this side too but it wasn't and I kicked it open.

A machine pistol started firing, along with another flash-bang, then another. Loving understood that Amanda and I had escaped and the two remaining hostiles were doing all they could to take Pogue out and get past him.

Then the girl and I were in the stairwell and speeding down the steps. We made it to the corridor on the main floor and started down the endless hallway toward the exit ahead of us. I was dizzy from scanning the doorways, scanning the corridor behind, scanning the corridor ahead. Mostly looking behind, though, which was the direction Loving or his surviving partner would come from.

More explosions and automatic weapon fire but growing more muted as we hurried for the exit.

Then I heard a hollow cry of pain.

It was Pogue's voice. There was no doubt. It continued for a moment or two as, I supposed, the phosphorous burned through his jacket and slacks to the skin. Finally there was a single shot and the screams and gunfire stopped.

I wondered if he'd ended his own life.

A horrific thought but I couldn't dwell on it. This meant Loving and the other man would be after us at any moment. We pressed forward. The doorways were bothering me. They were recessed slightly and as we came to each one, I had no way of knowing if a door was ajar. I believed the guard outside that there were four people with the girl but it would have been possible that the primary along with other minders had arrived and, hearing the shots, were hiding here, behind one of the doors.

I decided, though, that it really didn't matter. We had to move forward fast.

But now Amanda was starting to lose it. With her adrenaline fading, hysteria was flowing in like a riptide. She was crying, breathing hard and stumbling.

"Come on, Amanda. Are you with me?" I gripped her arm.

She took a deep breath. The tears ceased. "Yeah. I'm with you."

Looking behind . . .

Nothing.

I could detect the horrific smell of

burning flesh and I tried not to think about Pogue.

Ten feet from the front door. Five feet.

A glance behind. The corridor was still empty. Maybe Pogue had taken out Loving and the remaining hostile.

I pushed through the door fast, inhaling the sweet damp air. My strategy was to shoot the tires out of the other cars and SUVs here, then get to mine. And drive fast. I'd call Freddy from the road. Coordinate the assault here. Amanda clung to my arm with one hand and clutched her pepper spray in the other. I saw a Metropolitan Police Department label on the side.

My phone buzzed with a text. It was Freddy, reporting that the troops would be here in twenty minutes or so.

I paused in front of the building and glanced back down the corridor again. It was still empty. Then I turned toward the vehicles. I lifted my Glock toward the tires, whispering, "Cover your ears."

Before I could shoot, though, I heard a noise behind me. I turned fast but saw nothing. The corridor was still empty.

I realized then that the noise was coming from *above* us.

I looked up to see Henry Loving launch himself from the roof. He crashed down onto Amanda and me, sending us sprawling on the concrete apron. I landed hard with a stunning, painful jolt in my spine. Air spurted from my lungs, and the Glock tumbled out of reach through the dirt and weeds.

Chapter 65

His clothing scorched—some skin too—Loving rolled off me onto the sidewalk that led to the facility's parking lot. He'd lost his weapon inside and his face was bleeding, though the wound didn't seem bad. He winced as he gripped his side, where his cousin had stitched him up from my gunshot at Carter's lake house.

As he struggled to get to the gun, I grabbed his leg and jacket.

I realized he'd used a fire door on the other side of the hill and had sprinted here through the grass and foliage of the camouflaged roof.

Amanda crawled forward toward him, brandishing her pepper spray. I started to tell her not to but it was too late. She cried out in rage and pushed it close to his face.

As he'd been expecting.

His hand shot out, grabbed the canister and twisted the nozzle toward us both. Amanda's battle cry turned to a scream of pain as a stream of the orange liquid shot out between us, catching both the girl and me in the peripheral mist.

The pain was excruciating. I jammed my eyes shut as the tears started and then opened them, squinting. Amanda had rolled to the ground and was wiping at her face frantically. Through the damp slit of vision I could see the lump of my weapon ahead of us, no more than five feet away from Loving's hand. He dropped the spray and began to pound on my arm with one hand and claw his way toward the gun with the other.

He dragged me a foot closer to the weapon. How could the unimposing man be so strong? I thought at first desperation was driving him but then I realized it was calm determination. He began kicking. One shoe caught my cheek and I tasted blood. Loving's whole purpose in life had become reaching that gun.

Which he did just a moment later.

As he spun toward me, I dug my feet into the ground and leapt forward. Gripping his wrist with one hand, I pulled car keys from my pocket with the other. "Can you drive?" I called to Amanda.

The girl said nothing but was staggering to her feet. She looked defiantly at Loving.

I repeated my question, shouting.

"Yes," she gasped, wiping her eyes.

I flung the keys to her. "My car's up the road. The Honda. There's an address on the front seat. Go there and wait!"

"I—"

"Now! Do it!"

She paused only a moment longer and then fled.

Loving's efforts grew more ferocious as he tried to shake me off. We were locked in a sweaty, agonizing wrestling match, fighting fiercely for control of the weapon. A moment later I heard my car start and the tires squeal as the girl sped into the night.

The lifter glanced toward the vanish-

ing taillights without reaction and renewed his battle to escape my grip.

Then I began to feel my grip loosen . . .
and finally Loving wrenched his gun
hand free and swung the boxy Glock
toward me hard. I felt the metal barrel
slam in my temple and I was suddenly
on my back, blood in my eyes, making
them sting all the more. In seconds,
Loving had my hands in restraints, then
pulled me into a sitting position.

The lifter staggered to his feet, he too
nearly spent. Breathing deeply, he
hawked and spat. He looked in the direction that the girl had gone and gave
a blink. His expression was as if he'd
missed a parking space close to his
destination. He pulled out a phone and
placed a call, stepping away but watching closely. I couldn't hear what he said
but I knew the message was to explain
to the primary what had happened and
tell him not to come here. He disconnected.

We regarded each other for a few
seconds. He looked around again and
then said, "I know you've called people

in. But I estimate I've got twenty minutes."

I recalled that it had taken him only
seven to get all the names he needed
from Abe Fallow, lying beside that creek
in North Carolina.

He continued softly, "Now, the address in your car, where the girl's going? It's not the safe house. You wouldn't
write that down. Where?"

I thought of Amanda, getting away,
speeding through the night, up and
down the hills on Route 15.

A distant memory of Peggy and the
boys surfaced. Sam and Jeremy. This
time I couldn't dispose of it. Nor did I
want to.

I said nothing to Loving.

He slipped my gun into his waistband
and stepped closer. He pushed me onto
my back and put restraints on my feet
too, keeping his face back in case I tried
to kick him, which wasn't going to happen. I just didn't have the strength.

He looked around once more and took
a small, well-worn manila envelope from
his pocket and shook the contents onto
the ground.

So there it was. His tools of the trade to get subjects to talk. The alcohol was in a small bottle, not much bigger than one allowed on airplanes by TSA. The sandpaper was fine grained. The sort you'd use near the end of a refinishing job. It all looked so innocent.

For a moment I expected we would fall into a conversation. Some repartee. After all, we'd been opponents for years and had in the past two days been playing a game of Rock, Paper, Scissors over and over again.

But he was as serious a player as I was and went about his task skillfully.

What's his goal?

To find Amanda.

What's the most efficient way to achieve it?

He pulled my right shoe off, then the sock. Toes, like fingers, I knew, had a plentitude of nerves. They're among the most sensitive parts of the human body. He knelt on my calf to keep my leg immobile—which was in itself excruciating—and then selected a piece of sandpaper. He began to work on the front of my big toe.

Nothing for a moment, then I felt discomfort and finally an intense searing burn that coursed straight up into my face. I gasped involuntarily and finally shouted out in pain.

My nose hurt, my teeth, my throat.

All from his gentle sanding.

Loving reached for the bottle of alcohol and unscrewed the top, which he carefully put into his pocket. He didn't bother to look at me or say a word. The rules of play were obvious. Either I'd tell him where Amanda had gone or I wouldn't.

He tilted the bottle and I felt a burst of cold—this too merely irritating at first. But then the excruciating agony rose again to my jaw. Pain like pain I'd never felt. It was a creature, moving where it wanted throughout my body. Living, pulsing. Clever and driven. I could see it as colors, I could hear it.

"Rock, paper, scissors," I muttered between teeth jammed together. "Rock, paper, scissors," Through tear-filled eyes, I noticed Loving put the bottle down and pick up the sandpaper again.

"Rock, paper, scissors."

Peggy, Peggy, Peggy . . .
"Rock, paper, scissors . . ."
He started on a second toe.
I screamed.
Rock paper scissors rock paper . . .
Another scream.
He picked up the alcohol once again.

Then, as I gasped for breath, I heard two noises. The first was the snap of a branch not far away, in the direction of the road.

The second was a metallic click. A particular click that nobody in my line of work would mistake.

Loving knew it too, of course, and in an instant he'd dropped his implements of torture and was pulling my Glock from his waistband. He fell to his belly, wincing, as the first shot shook the night. It was a miss—but close. Dirt kicked up behind us.

The lifter rolled away from me seven or eight feet—he couldn't afford for me to get killed by a stray shot before he learned where Amanda was headed—and went prone again. We were in a lawn of low grass, which offered very poor cover.

Another shot. I glanced in the direction it came from and saw a man lumbering through the bushes, a revolver held forward in his hand, cocking and firing toward Loving. Initially I was surprised to see the newcomer's identity. But then I realized I shouldn't have been.

Ryan Kessler was one of the few people who knew where Pogue and I had been going.

The cop wasn't dodging or crouching. He didn't even slow down or cringe when Loving fired a burst of three. I couldn't see if Ryan had been hit; he just kept moving forward, squinting into the dark to find a clear target.

Then there was silence. Even in the dim light he was well within range of the Glock and yet Loving didn't fire again. I glanced up and saw why. Shooting my gun, he hadn't known how many rounds were left. He'd emptied the magazine; the slide was locked back, awaiting reloading.

Loving realized that I might have a fresh magazine on me, which in fact I did. He glanced toward Ryan, making steady progress, limping forward, trying to find a target.

Loving moved and Ryan fired. Then he too was out of ammo. I heard the click of the hammer on spent brass. He pulled a speed loader off his belt and flipped open the cylinder of the gun to eject and reload.

Loving scrabbled toward me and reached for my jacket pocket. I immediately spun over on my belly, ignoring the excruciating pain in my toe, to keep him from getting the extra ammo. Loving glanced at Ryan, who was inserting the round rack of shells, and then he tugged my jacket out from underneath me, reaching for the pocket. Ryan started walking closer.

Now, Loving was desperate.

I summoned whatever strength I had left and jerked my knees up, striking Loving hard in the side, where I'd shot him earlier. He gasped in pain and, off balance, sat back.

Then, grimacing, he blinked and leaned forward once more for my jacket. He fished for and found my full clip. He yanked it out and reloaded.

His face was only a few feet from mine when Ryan Kessler shot the lifter twice in the chest. Henry Loving blinked and slumped, then fell to his side. And as he died, it was my eyes, not the cop's, he was staring into.

Then Ryan Kessler too sat down, studying a bloody tear in his belly. His eyes were dismayed. Though not, it seemed, at this wound—which looked bad to me; it was Loving's second hit that troubled him most. He gave a disgusted sigh as he pressed his bleeding thigh. "My other leg." He looked at me. "My good one. Son of a bitch." Then he passed out.

Chapter 66

A half hour later—the old government facility lit up like a carnival and populated with a hundred agents and emergency workers—I was standing near the front of the compound.

Freddy's tac people, in respirators and masks, were working their way through the building and over the grounds, clearing the place for the fire crews. They'd found the other three hostiles, all dead, but the flames were still raging where Pogue had made his last stand and they couldn't get to his body yet. The guard out front was now conscious and in cuffs.

Nearby, medics were preparing to take Ryan Kessler to Leesburg Hospital for surgery. He'd regained consciousness and didn't seem as badly injured as I'd thought. "In and out," he told me, the same phrase Dr. Frank Loving had used to describe the course of my bullet through his cousin's side.

I'd called Joanne and told her that her stepdaughter was fine and that her husband had been shot. "He's stable," I told her. I gave her the name of a doctor to call. Then I broke the news to her about Pogue. There was a beat of a pause and then she thanked me for letting her know.

I wondered again about their history.

I asked, "You let Ryan out, didn't you?"

Another pause. "Yes. I kept Lyle distracted."

She must have watched one of us punch the code to deactivate the alarm to the door and memorized the number. Or maybe she had some special app in her security-blanket purse that cracked locks.

I explained to her, "He saved my life."

I saw Freddy approach. I told Joanne I'd call her back.

"Wait, Corte," she said.

"Yes?"

"Hold on."

A moment later I heard Maree's voice. "Corte?"

"Yes."

"You get hurt?"

"Nothing serious."

Silence.

"I'm glad." Then, incongruously, she added, "I just wanted to say . . . I got an image of you. When we were by the river? Remember?"

I digested this for a moment. "Yes."

"It's really good."

"An image."

She hesitated. "You're sure you're all right?"

"I'm fine, yes. I have to go."

"All right. Call me when you can."

Now I hesitated. "Sure." We disconnected. Freddy now joined me.

I asked, "What'd you find?"

"This's a mystery wrapped in whatever else that expression says."

I glanced his way impatiently.

"Okay, here we go. Loving we know. The others?" He swept his hand around the compound. "They were capital *C* contractors. As in former-Blackwatertype contractors. Not that outfit but you get the meaning."

Mercenaries, security forces. I wasn't surprised, given what I'd seen in the wallet of the guard we'd knocked out. But I was discouraged. Groups like that were expert at leaving no traces back to their primaries. "So we just don't know," I offered.

"That pretty much says it, son."

"And him?" I looked toward the re-vived guard.

Freddy said, "Wants a lawyer like a baby wants a bottle."

"Loving made a call. I'm sure he warned the primary off. You check his phone?"

"No record of anything. You didn't ex-pect there would be, did you?"

"No."

"We got Loving," Freddy pointed out. Probably thinking I'd consider this a ma-jor victory.

I muttered, "But I want the primary." I found myself gazing at the tarp covering Loving's body.

I asked the agent, "You clean out your department?"

Freddy's lips tightened. "An assistant in Communications. I checked her phone records. She'd been making calls through a dead letter line in the Caribbean over the past day. Loving got the names of her kids and the school they go to, so she fed him everything he wanted."

Edge . . .

"Her kids are okay?"

"Yeah. Sometimes all you need is to mention a name or two. You don't need implements of torture."

"That'll do it." Aware my toe was still in agony.

"I don't know about bringing charges against her. I don't like the idea but I may have to."

"And Zagaev? His family?"

"You were right. Loving paid them a visit, too—to get him to pretend he was the primary. But they're fine." A shrug. "The guy didn't do anything wrong, either, except lie to us and cart around some guns he shouldn't've. So . . . I don't know, we'll have to see about charges for him too." Freddy laughed. "He apologized for saying bad things to you about the pumpkin. He didn't want to. He said you seemed like a nice man."

Freddy headed off to consult with his teams and the state police.

I found myself looking over at Henry Loving's body. All his personal effects had been gathered and were sitting on a tarp next to him. I walked over and looked down at them. A wallet, a small wad of cash. A knife. The sandpaper and alcohol. An empty pistol magazine. Maps and pens, scraps of paper. Six cell phones. All encrypted and missing call logs. I knew the models and the software; it would take Hermes weeks to get information from them—if at all.

And I noted too the shoe box, the one he'd taken from his family house just before he'd burned it to the ground.

My heart thudded with anticipation as I walked over to one of the Bureau's Evidence Response Team agents and asked for a pair of latex gloves. I pulled them on and returned to the cache. I stood for a moment, then crouched over the box. Did it indeed contain more pictures? Or was it something else, something his sister had given him? His father or mother?

I peeled off several strips of yellowed tape and began to lift the lid.

Then I stopped.

Painfully I rose to my feet and left the box with the rest of the effects. Taking the gloves off and returning to my car, I reflected that whatever might be inside, it was nothing that I truly needed to know.

Chapter 67

I saw my Honda—the one Amanda had escaped in—approach. I waved to the driver, an FBI agent I knew. I couldn't see through the tinted glass but I knew the girl was in the backseat.

I hadn't, in fact, given her any directions about where to drive. There was no address in the vehicle. I figured that even if she didn't find anything she'd still drive as fast as she could to the nearest 7-Eleven or gas station to call 911. Giving her those instructions was the only way I could think of to keep myself alive long enough for Freddy to arrive with the troops and take Loving into custody. I'd made him believe that only I knew where she was going. I'd turned myself into the principal.

As it turned out, she hadn't gotten very far at all. At a gas station a few miles north on Route 15 she'd pulled in a little fast and taken out a rack of tires. The local police had been apprised of the situation and they got in touch with Freddy, who sent a car to protect her.

I didn't want Amanda to see the bodies. I also knew the primary was unaccounted for so I wanted to keep her out of sight. I climbed into the backseat with her and shut the door.

Breathlessly she said, "You're all right! I heard you were but I didn't know. What's wrong with your foot?"

"Stubbed my toe. Your dad's going to be okay."

"I know. I heard." The girl grew silent, looking at the compound. "That's the man we were fighting with, Loving?" A glance at the tarp covering the body.

"Yes."

"I'm glad he's dead." She said this firmly. She meant it.

Got some grit . . .

"Can I go see my dad?"

"Not quite yet. Somebody from my office's going to take you to a place to stay with your stepmother and aunt."

The Great Falls safe house was compromised, so I'd arranged for Ahmad to take Joanne and Maree to another one. The house was in Loudoun County, not too far away from here, also on an old estate. Though it wasn't as nice as the Great Falls one.

"Uncle Bill's all right too."

"He had a little problem with his foot too. But he'll be fine."

Her face was still. "I was really worried when they were shooting at him, by the roadside."

"You saved his life."

She didn't say anything but was looking at the compound. "All those guns . . . they're so loud. They don't sound like that in the movies. Or like the ones we shot at camp. That other man who was with you?"

I shook my head. "He didn't make it."

"I'm sorry," she whispered. "Did he have a family?"

"I don't know."

Amanda wiped tears.

I wished she hadn't attacked the minder but she wouldn't have known Pogue and I were there. I couldn't help but admire her courage. I told her, "That was good, the way you handled yourself in there. The pepper spray."

The girl's face, ruddy with subtle dots of acne, gave a wan smile. "Dad taught me to look out for myself. Before I left with Uncle Bill I kind of borrowed some Mace from Dad's dresser to take with me. I kept it hidden in my bear bag."

"Smart. You're sure you're just sixteen?"

"That's why I had it," she said matter-of-factly. "They didn't bother to search me. They were stupid."

"They were."

"Like, Agent Corte, I kind of messed up your car. I hit some tires. Like, I'm really, really sorry."

"We've got insurance."

She gave a weak smile.

I gritted my teeth from the toe pain and sat forward, taking a pad and pen from my pocket. "I need to ask you some questions."

"Sure."

"You know, we thought at first they wanted to kidnap you to get your father to tell them something about one of his cases."

"But it was me they wanted."

"Right. The people here were just hired—and we need to find out by who."

"So you can throw their ass in jail."

"Exactly. Now, did those men mention anything after they kidnapped you? Anything that might give us an idea of who hired them or why they wanted you."

She thought for a moment. "Like, after they got me in the truck and we were driving here, they were talking some. But it was like they didn't know anything about me. Or say anything about anybody else."

I asked her to tell me essentially everything she'd done for the past month. Amanda understood that her father had been shot and she nearly killed because of some occurrence or someone she'd come in contact with recently, and she took her assignment seriously, launching into a lengthy recitation of her activities. The girl led an astonishingly busy life. And had a very good memory. I took voluminous notes as she described time with friends and their parents, her high school classes, sporting events, concerts, trips to shopping malls, her involvement on the yearbook, a French Club outing to the embassy in D.C., a cooking class, a picture-taking expedition with her aunt in Rock Creek Park, reporting for her blog about AIDS awareness and the fellow student who'd killed herself despite seeking help in the school's self-harm clinic, her Facebook activities and friends (a *lot* of notes there), her college-level computer course in which her "weird and totally brilliant" Chinese professor let the students try out software programs and evaluate them. A dozen other entries.

Finally, I sat back, letting my mind consider possible reasons the girl had been targeted.

I noted an armored SUV arrive, driven by Geoff, the clone from our organization. I rolled down the window and waved. He pulled up.

I said to Amanda, "I think I have all I need. I'm going to have my associate here take you to your stepmother and aunt."

"Yeah, I kinda want to see them."

"I'm sure you do."

She surprised me by giving me a hug

and we climbed out. She got into the SUV and, with a nod from me, Geoff eased the big vehicle away from the site.

I sat down on a log and read through my notes of my interview with Amanda a few minutes before. Closed my eyes. Partly from the sting, partly to help me concentrate. Then I sent Claire duBois an email asking her to do what she did best. The replay—seconds later—assured me that she'd get to the requests immediately.

I rose and walked stiffly to a fire truck, where I got a bottle of water from a cooler and drank most of it down.

Just as I'd finished, I heard a voice behind me gruffly ask, "You got another one of those?"

I turned and found myself staring at Jonny Pogue, who was examining the cloth and skin on his left forearm, more troubled, it seemed, by his scorched green jacket than the seared flesh.

Chapter 68

"Pogue . . . What happened?" I was as delighted to see him as I was surprised he'd survived.

He said nothing and when I continued to look him over he repeated his request: "Water?"

"Sure. Sorry." I handed him a bottle. He drank about half and upended the rest over his head. He rubbed his eyes and looked past me at a med tech. "Any chance you could take a look at this?" A nod at his burned arm. He coughed hard and spat. Made a face at the taste of scorch in his mouth.

Two medics got him sitting. He refused requests both to lie down and to take a painkiller. A tech began to cut his sleeve. "Don't do that!" Pogue barked and unzipped then pulled off the jacket. "Why cut it?"

The burn looked bad but Pogue lost interest as the men went to work.

"What happened?" I repeated. "How did you . . . ?"

"I got trapped in the corner, 'cause of the fire. Managed to make it up the stairs on the balcony but they tossed another phos grenade up there. I took the last hostile out but the flames were pretty intense by then. I went down an elevator shaft to the basement, conked my noggin. Came to about a half hour ago and didn't know what I'd find out front so I tracked down a back fire exit."

I told him that Loving had done much the same.

"Why're you limping?"

I explained.

"Ouch. You nailed his ass, though, I heard."

"Not me. Ryan Kessler."

A snicker. "Well now. How'd that happen?"

"Joanne."

Pogue grunted. "Hm . . . The wife sprung him. He going to be okay?"

"Seems so."

Pogue's face wrinkled up, maybe from

the pain as the dressing went on his burned arm or maybe from seeing my smile that he was alive.

"That's one feisty girl. Pepper spray. Fucked up our plans. But it was good to see that prick hurt, have to say."

Grit . . .

"The primary?" he asked, looking over the expanse of fields, with a dozen highways beyond.

"Loving warned him off. But I've got some good leads. My associate's following them up right now." I thanked him again for everything and we agreed to stay in touch. If he ever wanted to leave his organization, I'd hire him in a minute. Though he didn't seem the sort to run away from a threat as a first impulse, which is what we shepherds are trained to do.

I pushed off from the fire truck, which I was leaning on for support, and put some weight on my foot with the raw toe.

Damn, it hurt. I exhaled softly. Thinking, if I actually had had information about Amanda's whereabouts, how long could I have held out before I talked? I would have talked, of course. There are differing opinions about whether torture leads to valid information. But one thing it definitely leads to is talking. People may be intent on remaining silent but in the face of pain they will talk.

I returned to my car and sat in the driver's seat, eyes closed, and let the tears from the stinging pepper spray flow, which for some reason eased the pain. Bottled water didn't do much but tears helped.

Fifteen minutes later I got an email. I wiped my face and, squinting, read what Claire duBois had sent in response to my request not long before.

As I read it I was thinking of the phenomenon of endgame.

Although the concept can apply to many games, it is most common in chess, which is where I study the subject exhaustively.

As the middle game draws to a close and the endgame approaches, a fundamental change occurs in the players' attitudes, and, I swear, a macabre eeriness descends over the board. The surviving pieces take on different roles and importance. For instance, pawns become vital; not only can they move to the opponent's first line and become queens but they provide important defensive barriers that limit the other player's moves. Similarly the king spends most of the game in hiding, protected by his minions. But in endgame, he often must go on the offensive himself.

Each move is intensified. The odds of a single error leading to defeat rise dramatically as the match draws to a close.

Endgame is rife with improvisation, desperation, flashes of brilliance and instances of fatal panic.

There are many surprises too.

I stared at my notes from Amanda and at Claire's email for some minutes. As Pogue had said earlier, I'd had all the bits of information as to why Amanda was the target; I just hadn't put them together . . . until now. I considered my endgame strategy and I composed another email that began with a stern warning to keep the contents absolutely secret. The subject had to do with the Saturday course that Amanda Kessler took at a local community college, taught by a part-time professor named Peter Yu. He worked during the week for a software developer, Global Software Innovations, and it was he who distributed to Amanda and the other students beta copies of software to try out—like the picture editing program that Amanda had given Maree.

But the most interesting fact about Yu was that GSI did more than create commercial and consumer software. The company—and Yu's specialty, as it turned out—happened to be developing military programs for cutting-edge battlefield imagery analysis. The software for those applications was classified at the highest level.

I finished my email and read through it once more.

My finger hovered for a moment. Then I clicked SEND and sent my words into the ozone.

TUESDAY

The object of the game is to discover the answer to these three questions:

1st. Who? Which one of the several suspects did it?
2nd. Where?
3rd. How?

—FROM THE INSTRUCTIONS TO THE
BOARD GAME CLUE

Chapter 69

At 9:00 a.m. my protégée and I were sitting in one of my organization's SUVs on a sedate street in Fair Oaks, Virginia, a section of Fairfax.

"And?" I asked Claire duBois, as she was moving her thumb to the DISCONNECT button on her BlackBerry. She'd been calling about Ryan Kessler.

"He's doing okay. The doctor said he was stable. I never understood those medical condition terms. Stable. Serious. Critical. They're like the Homeland Security threat warnings. Orange, yellow, green, taupe. Or whatever they are. Is that really helpful? I don't think so. Somebody sits in a room and thinks those up. Our taxpayer dollars." She tucked her trimmed, shiny brunette strands behind an ear. The gesture was silent; she wasn't wearing the jingling charm bracelet this morning. For safety's sake. Jewelry and tac ops don't mix.

Ryan was in a federal detention hospital. Amanda, Joanne and Maree were tucked away in the new safe house, with Ahmad and the clone who'd collected Amanda last night watching over them.

DuBois and I were on the trail of the primary.

I returned to our surveillance. The houses around us reminded me of Ryan Kessler's place. About every fifth one was, if not identical, then designed from the same mold. We were staring through bushes at a split-level colonial, on the other side of a dog-park-cum-playground. It was the house of Peter Yu, the part-time professor of computer science at Northern Virginia College and a software designer for Global Software Innovations. The company was headquartered along the Dulles "technology corridor," which was really just a dozen office buildings on the tollway, housing corporations whose claim to tech fame was mostly that they were listed on the NASDAQ stock exchange.

I was watching through binoculars,

observing some ambiguous movement in the backyard of the house.

I lifted the Motorola and asked Freddy, who was parked nearby, "We ready to move in?"

"I'm not sure what I'm looking at."

I squinted. "It's him. I'm sure."

"You're younger than I am, son. The eyes are the first to go. Well, not the first, unfortunately, but pretty close. Hold on, our surveillance boys're calling. . . . Okay, there're two of them at the house."

"I see the second one," I told the agent.

"Some muscle, looks like. You in armor?"

I glanced toward Claire duBois's navy blue blazer, specifically her chest. It wasn't the first time, I had to admit, but the circumstances now were such that there was nothing remotely sexual about the look. I was checking that the thick nylon plates Velcroed around her were secure. I knew that my American Body Armor vest was.

"We're good," I told Freddy.

"All right. Let's go. My guys and gals

tell me they have a visual on the evidence. Oh, and the muscle's armed. Autoloader. In a hip holster."

"We're moving." I disconnected.

I said to duBois, "You won't need it but keep your jacket unbuttoned."

"Okay."

The "it" was her Glock.

In fact, I was *pretty* sure she wouldn't need it. But I remembered the men in the old military facility in Leesburg. I remembered Henry Loving. I knew from my studies—history, not my other degrees—that people can behave unpredictably at desperate times. Besides, even though we believed there were only two individuals here, this entire job had been fraught with surprise.

Our SUV and four other cars accelerated fast and skidded up over the grass on Professor Peter Yu's property, tearing up the lawn and destroying shrubs. I'm told that this dramatic entrance, which you'd think was made up by TV-movie directors, is in fact the most efficient way to approach a suspect. It's all about intimidation.

We tugged on door levers and jumped

out, all our jackets fluttering in the wet breeze. I was limping—the toe still stung like crazy. DuBois and I moved in slowly, behind the eight armed tactical officers, who were sprinting into Yu's open garage, brandishing weapons.

"On the ground, FBI! FBI!"

Screaming is standard operating procedure too. Intimidation, again.

In a moment the two men were on their bellies, hands bound behind them with Monadnock restraints. Other agents entered the house, searched it and then returned, calling, "Clear."

Claire and I approached the two suspects, now being helped to their feet.

One of the men stared at me with a gaze of disbelief that immediately turned to pure hated. Sandy Alberts, Senator Lionel Stevenson's chief of staff, spat out, "Corte? I . . . Corte?"

His partner, the muscle, was a pro, probably connected with the same outfit as the people Pogue and I had engaged in the facility on Route 15. He simply grimaced and said nothing.

Freddy, the senior official law enforcer among us, said, "Mr. Alberts, you're un-

der arrest for the kidnapping of a Fairfax County resident, Amanda Kessler,
yesterday, and conspiracy counts, involving the homicide of a federal agent."

Alberts gasped. I don't think I'd ever
heard anything other than a threatened
animal make a noise like that. "But . . ."

Agents searched his partner's slacks
and jacket but came up with no ID. "You
going to tell me who you are?" Freddy
asked him.

The man was completely silent.

The senior agent shrugged. He said
to an associate, "We'll get his prints,
track him down. Conspiracy for him too.
We'll add more goodies later." Freddy
then turned to Alberts, saying, "There'll
be state charges too but those are Virginia's. You'll be hearing from the commonwealth's attorney about them."

A crime scene tech was inventorying
the contents of Alberts's shoulder bag,
which had been upended on the floor of
Yu's garage. I too looked over the stash.
Documents and pictures and some
plastic bags that would have physical
evidence—probably some strands of
Amanda Kessler's hair or something

else with her DNA on it. Alberts and his thug had come here to plant the clues to suggest that Professor Yu was the primary who had hired Henry Loving.

"Sandy," I said. "Senator Stevenson. Let's talk about him for a minute."

Desperately the aide said, "I don't know what you mean."

Freddy snorted a laugh.

I said, "We know everything."

"What are you talking about?"

"Well, let's start with: We know that the senator likes lecturing at schools. We know he likes the company of young ladies."

Alberts's eyes grew wide. Then he recovered and looked down.

I continued, "Sometime in the past year Stevenson met a student after a speaking engagement—at a community college in Northern Virginia. Her name was Susan Markus. He thought she was a college student. But she actually was in high school. Sixteen years old. A classmate of Amanda Kessler's."

As duBois had pieced things together, it seemed to be the same event that I'd read about in my research on Stevenson: the community college where he'd given his popular "rule of law" speech.

I told Alberts, "Whether he invited her to his office or a motel or the back of his limo, we don't know."

"Yet," Freddy added. "We don't know yet."

"But we're pretty sure there was some . . . inappropriate behavior on the senator's part."

"That's a lie!" But there was no conviction behind Alberts's protest.

I said, "The senator can't be stupid. He didn't think she was under age. He met her at a community college and he probably assumed she was a student there, not a high school girl. In any case, whatever happened was statutory rape at the minimum. Amanda Kessler was a volunteer at her school's self-harm prevention program. Susan was depressed about what happened and she came in to get some help. Amanda was the girl she talked to. Susan told her she'd been involved with an older man and he was pressuring her not to say anything about the incident. Amanda set Susan up with an adult counselor but before she went to the appointment she killed herself. Amanda took the death hard and planned to devote her blog to the girl's suicide, looking into why she killed herself, what led up to it. She was going to be talking to Susan's friends, her family. It was just a matter of time before Amanda got to the truth."

"And," Freddy said, "we're not completely sure that Susan actually did take her own life. She might've been . . . helped."

Alberts began to speak but then fell silent.

Freddy, better at the dramatics than I, said, "Oh, going to say something about the coroner's report ruling the death a suicide? Going to say you've looked into it? Why would you've done that?"

Still, silence.

I continued, "Your job was to hire somebody like Loving to find out the names of everybody Amanda had talked to about Susan's death. Get all of Amanda's notes, everything. And then kill her too."

Alberts's shoulders sagged and he glanced around Yu's house.

I gave voice to his thought, which was too incriminating for Alberts to utter. "I know, you thought we were looking at Global Software Innovations and Peter Yu. . . . No, that was just bait to draw you out into the open. I suspected you and the senator but I didn't have any real proof. I made sure you were on the list to get the interagency alert about Global. If you were guilty I figured you'd come here to plant evidence implicating Yu."

"I'm completely innocent of any wrongdoing. That's all I'll say. I want an attorney."

"Help us out here, Sandy," I said in a reasonable voice. "We've got you cold. Come on." I glanced toward the solid, unsmiling suspect with him. "I know you found *him* and the other mercenaries through your contacts at the Armed Services Committee, right? They put you in touch with Henry Loving. They arranged for the helicopter. And you were desperate to find out what we knew so you came up with the story about the investigation into warrantless taps."

His eyes swung desperately.

I said, "Don't take the heat for this, Sandy. Work with us. . . . We know you cut your ties to your lobbying outfit before you went to work with Stevenson but they were involved too, weren't they?"

A paltry shake of his head.

"And the political action committee backing Stevenson? They need him to be the darling of the party. They couldn't afford a scandal. Who there—at the PAC—was involved?"

Alberts, near tears, blurted, "Senator Stevenson is a great man." The protest was both humorous and remarkably sad. "He didn't know. . . ."

"What?" I asked firmly. "What didn't he know?"

Alberts's shoulders slumped.

I gazed at an FBI van up the street. Inside was the man whose house this was, Professor Peter Yu, and his wife. They'd agreed to let us use their place as a takedown set after they pretended to leave for work. Alberts looked that way too and it seemed he finally understood how completely scammed he'd been.

Glancing at Freddy, whose nod gave me carte blanche to take over, I stepped a bit closer to Alberts. "We can work a deal, if you cooperate."

Alberts muttered, "To implicate the senator."

Freddy barked a laugh. "What else would we be interested in?"

"I don't think I can do that."

The word "think" was critical, since it told me he had acknowledged we had an edge over him. I articulated my position in general terms. "All I know is that you could spend the rest of your life in jail or you could spend a lot less than that." I let the thought register. Then I gestured toward another agent, who approached. To Alberts I said, "We're going to take you to detention now. Just think about what I said."

His lips tightened and his eyes closed momentarily.

As he and his partner were led off, Claire duBois turned to me and actually managed to make me smile, nodding toward Alberts's back and saying, "What you were telling me about game theory? How's that for the Prisoners' Dilemma?"

Chapter 70

I was sitting in Aaron Ellis's office, again focused on one of the pictures his child had painted. Maybe it was a haystack with turrets. Maybe a yellow castle, gold or brass. Hard to say.

The time was 10:30 a.m. Claire duBois was pulling up a chair beside me. My boss said, "He's on his way up."

"In fact," another voice filled the room, "*voilà*! He's here." U.S. Attorney Jason Westerfield paused in the doorway. "Was that a dark tone you were speaking in, Aaron? Ha, just being amusing. Okay *pour entrer*?" Today he was dressed like an attorney, very different from his Saturday suburban-warrior guise.

Ellis waved to the chairs across from the coffee table.

The slim man entered, trailed by his

assistant, Chris Teasley. Interesting, I couldn't help but observe: Here were Westerfield and I, flanked by our seconds, attractive women both, and a decade-plus younger. I noticed that Chris Teasley slipped her eyes toward duBois's Macy's suit and silver bracelet. I regretted to note also that the loaded glance had also registered with my protégée.

"Well, to the matter at hand," Westerfield said. "I was pretty surprised the whole morass rose as high as it did." He caught *that* mixed metaphor, at least, and hesitated. Then: "A U.S. senator. Hm." His voice and attitude continued to be as irritating as I remembered from the last time we met. Well, *every time* we'd met.

I shifted my foot gingerly. Inhaled at the pain. Focused again.

"So, Corte. Dish . . . *s'il vous plaît*."

I explained to him what I'd told Sandy Alberts not long before: that Loving had been hired because of Amanda's intention to blog about the death of a student Stevenson had molested.

"How'd you figure it out?"

The idea had occurred to me, I said, when I'd been speaking to Amanda last night in my car at the abandoned government facility. Of everything she'd told me about her recent life, one thing that stood out as a possible reason for Henry Loving's assignment was her job as a student volunteer at the self-harm prevention program and the blog about Susan's suicide.

Teasley asked, "But how'd you make the leap to Stevenson?"

"The senator himself helped me there. It just seemed a little curious that a senatorial aide would contact us about illegal eavesdropping right after we'd gotten the assignment. Last night I had Claire find out if Stevenson had actually scheduled committee hearings into wiretaps. He hadn't."

I'd realized that *I* was the one who'd speculated that Stevenson had come out against illegal surveillance from an ideological standpoint; the senator himself had never even commented on it. His speech at the college—possibly where he met Susan—was nothing more than classic rhetoric about the rule of law.

"He and Alberts had just made up the issue to look over my shoulder on the Kessler job."

My boss and I shared a glance. Westerfield apparently didn't know about my lapse in arranging for the illegal taps on Loving a few years ago. And perhaps Stevenson didn't either. The issue might arise, but then again it might already be dead.

"So I thought more about Stevenson: a man with a reputation for dating younger women. And lecturing regularly at schools. He's from Ohio, which isn't far from Charleston, West Virginia. That'd be a good central place for Alberts and him to have met Loving. I had Claire look into it. Checked phone and travel records, incidents of complaints in the past about him groping women, paying them off afterward." I shrugged. "It was a theory, not 100 percent certain, so I set up a sting about Global Software to see if Alberts would take the bait and try to lead us toward Peter Yu."

"Yes, saw the alert about Global,"

Westerfield said sourly, probably thinking that I'd yet again taken him in too, though in this instance it had nothing to do with keeping him off my back.

I said, "Alberts. I'm pretty sure he's going to roll over."

The Prisoners' Dilemma . . .

Ellis said, "But kidnapping a girl, planning to torture her . . . and security contractors. This was a big operation, extreme. Why? And what was the deadline all about? They needed the information by last night."

That was obvious to me. I explained, "Well, in the first place, Stevenson didn't want to go to jail, of course, so he'd try to silence any witnesses who could tie him to Susan's death. But there're more people involved in this than just Stevenson and Alberts."

This perked up Westerfield's attention. Conspiracy theories often do. "How do you mean?"

"For one thing, the Supreme Court nominee. The confirmation vote in the Senate's tomorrow. Amanda was going to be blogging about Susan all week, looking into her suicide."

The U.S. attorney said, "I still don't get the connection."

I explained that Stevenson was the one who'd built the coalition of votes to win the confirmation of the right-wing justice. "He'd managed to get a one-vote majority. If he got arrested or even implicated in a sex abuse scandal, that coalition would fall apart and the Republican's dream justice doesn't get confirmed. I'm pretty sure some people from the PAC supporting Stevenson and somebody from Alberts's lobbying firm were involved."

A wolf's gleam in Westerfield's eye. "That's good."

I said, "Look at the anger out there, look at the partisanship. People seem willing to do whatever they need to for their side to win."

Too much screaming in Congress. Too much screaming everywhere.

Westerfield looked toward Teasley, who wrote furiously in her notebook, and then he repeated, "That's good, Corte. Good . . ."

But he didn't exactly mean good. Something more was coming.

"Only . . ." He rocked back on his skinny butt and gazed at the ceiling momentarily. Regret—real or faux—filled his face. "How'd you like to retire in a blaze of glory?"

"Retire?" Aaron Ellis asked.

"See, you kind of played us."

The U.S. attorney's office, I assumed he meant.

"What're you saying, Jason?" Ellis asked.

"That incident about sending the Kesslers to the slammer? It was pretty awkward."

There'll be some fallout. You outright lied to me. . . .

I supposed that the attorney general himself had been there or some other higher-up in Justice. Perhaps hoping to interview Ryan Kessler, the hero cop. There'd been some damage to Westerfield's career.

"I'm thinking your resignation would be in order. Letter of apology. Let the powers that be know you intentionally pulled the wool over our eyes."

Clichés again. Did judges ever reprimand him in court for his clunky figures of speech?

Westerfield continued, "I'll make sure you get full benefits, of course. But a slip-slide into a private security company might be a good idea. Hey, you'll double your salary. I can even set you up with some nice prospects."

"Jason," Ellis began.

"I'm sorry. I really am," Westerfield said. Again a dark face, a troubled face. "But if that doesn't happen . . . hate to say it, but there is some issue I heard tell about: surveillance warrants."

I felt several pairs of eyes slide toward me.

So, Westerfield did know about them, which meant he had an edge on me. A pretty damn good one.

The prosecutor said, "How 'bout we shake on it? Go our separate ways? Aren't you tired of getting shot at, Corte?"

The Nash bargaining game, named after the famous mathematician John Nash, is a favorite among game theorists and one of my favorites too. It works this way: There are two players who each want a portion of something that can be divided. Say, two bosses who need to share an administrative assistant, who can work only forty hours a week total. Each player writes down on a slip of paper how many hours he wants the assistant to work for him, without knowing what the other is asking for. If the total amount equals forty hours or less, each gets the assistant for the time he's asked. If the total exceeds forty hours, neither gets the assistant at all.

I was now, apparently, the subject of the bargaining game being played between Ellis and Westerfield.

But game theory only works when the rules are clearly set out ahead of time. In the Nash bargaining game here, neither of the players was aware of another rule presently at work: that what they were bargaining over—me—might be a player in the game too.

As Westerfield and Ellis were proposing some face-saving compromise—I wasn't paying attention—I interrupted. "Jason?"

He paused and looked at me.

I said, "I'm not leaving. I'm not writing

any letters of resignation. You're going to drop the matter."

Both my boss and Westerfield blinked. The prosecutor glanced at his equally startled assistant, who was fondling her pearls.

A cool smile parted Westerfield's tiny lips. "Now, you're not . . ."

He didn't want to say "threatening me, are you?" But that was where his ominous sentence flared for a landing.

Ellis said, "Corte, it's okay. We can work out something. There's room for compromise here."

I rose and walked to the door, closed it.

Westerfield looked mystified. Ellis wanted to be elsewhere. DuBois gave what passed for a smile. My kind of smile. "Go ahead," I said to her and sat back. I teach my protégées about dealing with lifters and hitters and primaries. I also teach them about dealing with our compatriots.

She turned to Westerfield and said respectfully, "Sir, we thought it would be prudent—in shoring up the case against Mr. Alberts and Senator Stevenson—to

find out exactly when and how they became aware that our organization was
running the protection operation for the
Kesslers. That was the big unanswered
question that Officer Corte and I were
wondering about. Of course, there are
no official announcements when we
take on an assignment. It's vital that our
organization remain as anonymous as
possible. As you can imagine, we can
hardly function efficiently if people are
dropping in and poking their noses into
our work. In fact, the guidelines that all
law enforcement agencies are given
specifically state that they're prohibited
from mentioning our existence, let alone
that we're engaged in a specific assignment."

"Poking noses?" Westerfield lifted his
hands in an irritated fashion, meaning:
Your point?

"It seems, based on phone records—
obtained with duly issued warrants, of
course—that Sandy Alberts called *your*
office one hour before he came here to
discuss the matter of illegal surveillance
with Director Ellis and Officer Corte on
Saturday. Before that phone call neither

Alberts or Senator Stevenson had any awareness that we were involved in the Kessler case."

"My office? Ridiculous."

DuBois blinked. "Actually not, sir. Here're the phone records." She opened the document and her charm bracelet tinkled like bells. She was bejeweled once again. "I highlighted the relevant portions in yellow. It's a little lighter than I would have liked. Can you see them okay? I tried blue. But that was too dark."

Chris Teasley was clutching her own notebook fiercely. Her pretty, pale face went red, the color seemingly reflected in the pearls, though that was surely my imagination. She whispered, "Alberts knew about the Kesslers. He knew the name. I just assumed . . . he only wanted to know who was running the protection detail. That's all he asked. I thought . . . I thought it was okay."

Claire duBois, bless her, kept her eyes steadily on Westerfield and didn't offer so much as a millisecond of a glance toward her unfortunate counterpart.

"Ah, yes," the U.S. attorney said slowly.

After a moment, during which the only sound in the room was that of duBois's bracelet as she slipped the documents back into her attaché case, Westerfield jutted out his lower lip. "Looks like we better get to work putting a senator *et son ami* in jail." He rose. His assistant did too. "So long, gentlemen . . . and lady." The two of them left.

My edge, apparently, trumped his.

Chapter 71

In my office I opened my safe and extracted the board game that I'd received on Saturday.

As I undid the bubble wrap and opened the lid the aroma of old paper and cardboard arose. The scent of cedar too, which was pleasing to me. One of the things I like about board games is their history. This particular one had been bought new in 1949. It could have passed through several generations of one family or moved laterally to another, thanks to a yard sale, or perhaps found its way to a New England inn, where it would sit in a bed-and-breakfast parlor for amusement on Saturday afternoons when the rain derailed the leaf viewing.

The smell of moth deterrent suggested that it had spent its recent days in a closet. The board itself was scuffed and stained—one of the reasons it had been such a bargain—and I wondered how many people had moved the markers from start to finish, who they were, what they were doing now, if they were still with us.

For all their cleverness and high-definition graphics, computer games can't match the allure of their elegant, three-dimensional forebears.

I slipped the game into a shopping bag. It was 4:00 p.m. and I was about to go home.

Across my office a small TV sat on my credenza, the sound down. I glanced up at the screen and saw on CNN a flash: breaking news. That was something that duBois might comment on: breaking news versus news flashes versus news alerts.

I read the crawl. Lionel Stevenson was announcing he was going to be leaving the Senate, effective immediately. He was under investigation, it seemed, but no details were forthcoming. Sandy Alberts, his chief of staff, had been arrested, as had the head of the political action committee that Alberts was affiliated with and a partner at Alberts's old lobbying firm.

Whatever else you could say about Jason Westerfield, grass didn't grow under the man's feet.

A voice from the doorway startled me and I shut the TV off. "I have it," my personal assistant, Barbara, said. "You ready?"

I took the document from her and read through it. It was a release order, freeing the Kesslers from our care. The letter is merely a formality; if a lifter who hadn't, say, heard the primary was in custody and made a move on our principals again, of course, we'd be there in a minute, even after the release was signed. But we're a federal agency like any other and that means paperwork. I handed the signed document to Barbara and told her I'd be back in three days, maybe four, but she could always reach me. Which she knew but I felt better saying.

"Take some time," she said in a motherly way, which I found heartwarming. "You're not looking so good."

The effects of the pepper spray were

gone, as far as I felt. I frowned. She explained, "You're still limping."

"It's just a scrape."

Then she said coyly, "You have to let that toe heal."

I laughed, thinking I never in a million years could have come up with that one. Maree and Freddy were right, I don't joke much. But I'd try to remember the heal and toe line, though I doubted I would.

I gathered the board game, my computer and gym bag of clothes and walked to duBois's office. She was on the phone when I stepped into her doorway. Her playful tone told me she was probably speaking to the Cat Man. It was the night for a romantic dinner, it seemed. She was describing to him—with typical duBois detail and digression—a chicken dish she had in mind.

I waved good-bye. She held up a wait-a-minute finger.

But I didn't want her to hang up. I whispered, "Have to go. And thanks. Good job."

The smile was faint but her eyes beamed. I remembered that when Abe

Fallow would praise me I had the opposite reaction. I'd look down and deflect the compliment. I decided that Claire duBois had it right. She joked occasionally and had her bizarre observations and she talked to herself. She was at ease measuring emotion both in and out. That was the way it should be. If I could go back in time and change things, I would have fixed that about myself.

But that's the past for you. Not only does it come back at the most unexpected, and inconvenient, times but it's set in stone.

I left her to her monologue about cooking and I went to the garage to collect my personal car, a dark red Volvo. My career may not be the safest in the world but I drive the same make of vehicle that my insurance attorney father entrusted his family's life to. Not stylish—but who needs style? It also gets pretty good mileage.

I was just driving out onto King Street when I got a text message. I paused on the apron and looked down. Gazing out the window at the Masonic Temple, I stared at the screen, debating.

Chapter 72

I found Joanne Kessler in the Galleria at Tysons Corner, the fancier of the two shopping centers joined at the hip near the tollway, close to the government building where the interrogation of Aslan Zagaev had occurred.

The Galleria features the Ritz-Carlton, DeBeers and Versace and I could never figure out how it stayed in business because, aside from Christmastime, it always seemed deserted.

Joanne, at a wobbly table, was clutching a cup of tea in the cavernous space in the middle of the mall. Starbucks again.

For a month or so after a job is over, the principals keep their cold phones—just in case. After that time, the software overwrites the codes and numbers with nonsense and they can mail them back to a post office box or throw them out. It was Joanne's text I'd received a half hour ago, asking if we could meet.

I had already called her and Ryan, and Amanda, of course, and explained everything to them. We'd said our goodbye. And with the release order signed, that was the end of the job.

Except apparently not quite.

I got some coffee and joined the somber woman.

"How are you feeling?" she asked.

Not comfortable talking about the aches and pains and the raw toe, I said briefly, "Fine. And Ryan?"

"Coming along well. He'll be home tomorrow."

"Amanda?"

"She's good. All fired up to take on corruption in Washington."

"Keep an eye on her blogs," I said. "I need to stay anonymous."

She smiled. "I've already had that conversation."

"Did you see the news? About Stevenson?"

"I did." She continued, "Look, Corte, I was feeling that none of us really thanked you properly. I was thinking about that. Everything you did. You were nearly killed. We were just strangers to you. We were nobodies."

I was silent for a moment. Awkward. I said, "You were my job."

"I thank you anyway."

But I knew this meeting wasn't just about gratitude.

A pause. "There's one thing more. I wanted to ask you something. I shouldn't but . . . I didn't know anybody else to turn to."

"Sure. Go ahead."

"It's about Maree." Joanne lowered her head. "That's something else I blew."

I waited, watching window shoppers.

"She won't talk to me. But I overheard her. She's going ahead: moving in with Andrew. I tried to talk her out of it but she shut me out completely. She grabbed her things and ran out the door. . . . He's going to hurt her again and she's going to let him." Joanne touched my arm. An odd sensation. When you treat those in your care as game pieces to be protected, you aren't used to physical contact. As Abe said, it's to be avoided.

Which thought, of course, brought to mind the kiss Maree and I had shared on the ledge overlooking the Potomac.

Joanne whispered, "Could you talk to her? Please. I know it's not your job. But she won't listen to me. She may never talk to me again. . . ."

I saw tears in her eyes. Only the second time since I'd known her.

I was uncomfortable. "Where is she now?"

"She's meeting him in an hour in Washington Park, downtown."

As I'd made clear to Claire duBois and all my protégés, a shepherd's involvement with his principals ends the minute the primary and lifter or hitter are arrested or neutralized. Therapy, divorce, tragic accidents, happily ever after—none of those possible endings has anything to do with us. By the time the Kesslers' lives began to right themselves—one way or the other—following the horrors of the past few days, I'd be in another safe house or on the road somewhere, guarding new principals.

"Please."

On the edge, I found myself thinking. I had a memory of the Potomac River's turbulent foam below me.

On the edge . . .

"All right."

The pressure on my arm increased. "Oh, thank you . . ." She wiped the tears.

I rose.

"Corte."

I looked back.

"You remember what we were talking about? Having the two lives, you know, your job guarding your principals or my job, and then having a family too? I said you can't have both. But I'm not so sure . . . Maybe you can. If you handle it right." She gave an uncharacteristic smile. "And if you want it badly enough."

I didn't know what to say to that. I nodded a good-bye and, limping slightly, walked off to find my car.

In forty minutes I was at Washington Park, not far from DuPont Circle. It was small and dated to the early days of the city. Some park benches in the city are new and, I've heard, made from recycled tires or milk cartons. That's very

green and good for humankind but I
preferred the older ones, like those here.
They looked like they'd been installed
when Teddy Roosevelt was at work
about three miles from here on Pennsyl-
vania Avenue. Black ironwork, rusty in
spots, with wooden slats to sit on, un-
even from years of sloppy overpainting.

A couple crossed through the park,
stopped once to look at a bush, a ca-
mellia, I believe, in fall bloom, and then
continued on. A moment later the park
was empty. The day was blustery, overcast. I parked in a spot where I could
have a view of all the benches and spot
Maree from any angle. I shut the engine
off and dropped the visor. I was invisible
enough. I'd tried her phone but gotten
voice mail and I suspected she'd shut it
off to avoid calls from her sister.

Then someone else approached. I
was discouraged to see it was Andrew—
Claire duBois had sent me his picture
when I'd had her check on him as a
possible primary in the Kessler job. He
was on his mobile phone, walking leisurely into the park. He looked around
and stood for a moment and then sat

on a bench. He crossed his legs. I couldn't see his expression—I was about forty feet away—but he wasn't smiling and gave off the body language of someone who's irritated. He'd be an easy opponent to defeat at a game; in addition to his temper, his mind would be elsewhere frequently.

Since he'd gotten here first there wasn't much chance of having a conversation with Maree unless I could intercept her.

But that wasn't going to happen either. Just then she arrived from the opposite side of the park. Unlike Andrew she was smiling, clearly looking forward to seeing him. There was a lightness in her step and she carried a small shopping bag from Neiman Marcus and her camera bag. The now-familiar wheelie suitcase was trailing behind her like a dog. Did the shopping bag contain a present? She'd reverted to her uncertain, childlike role, begging for the man's approval, which I recalled from the message we'd heard her leave on Andrew's phone. She was so different with him than, say, someone like me.

Mr. Tour Guide . . .

Andrew noticed her and nodded but didn't smile or end his call. I wondered if he'd made an unnecessary call as a show of power. Animals exhibit dominant behavior, like this, but they do so for survival, not out of ego. I knew that Andrew had hurt Maree in the past and I sensed too, seeing this disregard, that he was a threat to her now, as Joanne had believed.

Since my workweek was over, I'd left my Glock in my locked desk drawer. Still, I could always call 911. I watched closely, tallying up details that might be important: He was wearing gloves. He had a little stiffness in his hip, I'd noticed earlier. He carried a large backpack, which could contain, or could even be, a weapon. He was not wearing glasses, which would imply a vulnerability that can be helpful to an opponent in flight or fight. The man was clearly fit and strong.

Still, Maree seemed to notice none of the threat and was clearly pleased to be with him. Smiling still, she sat, kissed him on the nonphone cheek. He gripped her hand, ignored her otherwise for a moment or two longer then hung up. He slipped the phone away and turned to her with a smile. I couldn't hear the words but the conversation seemed harmless enough. He'd be asking where she'd been for the past few days and— I could tell from the expression of sur- prise—she told him something of the truth. He gave a brief laugh.

But whatever you think is going on, Corte, whatever it seems, *don't make assumptions. Stay attentive.*

Sure, Abe.

Andrew's grin morphed into a seduc- tive smile and he slipped his arm around her. He whispered what would be the in- vitation to head back to his apartment. I knew from duBois's research that he lived not far from here.

It was then that Maree shook her head and shrugged his arm off her shoulder. She scooted away. She was silent for a moment, took a breath and then deliv- ered what seemed to be a speech, avoiding his eyes. She seemed awkward at first but then she caught her stride and looked into his impassive face, as he took in her words.

He gestured with a gloved hand and leaned closer. He spoke a few words and Maree shook her head.

She lifted the bag and took out a framed photograph. It was a still life I'd seen at the Kesslers' house and realized that it was probably a gift that he'd given her earlier. One of his own photos maybe. She handed it back to him.

Well, interesting. She was breaking up.

He stared at the picture, then smiled sadly. He spoke to her some more, making his case. He leaned in for a kiss but she backed away further and said something else.

He nodded. Then leapt up in a fury and flung the photo to the sidewalk, where it shattered. Maree cringed, dodging the shards. The he reached out and grabbed her arm. She winced and cried out in pain. He drew back with his other gloved hand, curled into a fist.

I opened the door and stepped out fast . . .

Just as Maree too stood and slammed

her palm straight into his face. Andrew hadn't expected any aggressive moves and he was caught completely undefended. She had connected with his nose. The pain would be fierce—I knew; a panicking principal had once elbowed me accidentally.

He fell back to the bench, hunched over, raging, gripping his bloody face.

"You fucking bitch."

"I told you; it's through," she said firmly.

Now that I was out of the car I could hear them clearly.

He rose again and reached for her blindly but she calmly shoved him back, hard. Hampered by tears of pain, he stumbled and landed hard on the sidewalk, on his side. He scrambled to his feet and stepped back, digging for a Kleenex.

"You attacked me, bitch! I'm calling the police."

"That's fine," she said, the epitome of calm. "Just remember my brother-in-law's a cop. I know he'd love to talk to you about it. He and some of his friends."

I was pleased to note that, under my

care, Maree had learned about getting—and using—an edge.

She looked down with some pity, it
seemed. "Don't ever call me again."
Then she hiked up her camera bag on
her shoulder, turned and, wheeling her
suitcase behind her, walked slowly away.
I waited to see if Andrew would follow
her. He seemed to debate. He grabbed
what was left of the shattered frame and
flung it to the ground once more. Then
he strode off in the opposite direction,
his gloved hand pressed against his
bleeding nose.

I dropped back into the driver's seat
and started the car, then turned in the
direction Maree had gone. I found her
at the next intersection, pausing for the
light. She ran her hand through her hair
and leaned back, looking up into the
deepening sky. She'd be smelling what
I was, through the open window of the
Volvo, the sweet scent of autumn leaves
and the sweeter smell of a fireplace log
from a brownstone somewhere nearby.

The light changed. Maree crossed the
street and walked to the tall, glassy
Hyatt.

I eased up to the curb in front of the hotel and stopped, flashed my federal ID to a traffic cop, who nodded and walked on.

I shut the engine off.

I watched Maree walk through the revolving door. It paddled slowly to a stop. She looked around and approached the front desk, handing off her suitcase to a bellboy. She greeted the clerk and opened her purse, proffering ID and credit card.

I studied her for a moment. Then, the last of my principals finally safe, I started the engine and put the car in gear. I eased into traffic, away from the hotel, to return home.

Endgame

When driving on the job, I didn't allow myself the luxury of listening to music: too distracting, as I'd told Bill Carter.

But on my own time I always had the radio, a CD or a download playing. I liked old-time music but what I meant by that was the period from the 1930s through the '60s, nothing before and little after.

Performers like Fats Waller, Sinatra, Billie Holiday, Louis Armstrong, Rosemary Clooney, Ella, Sammy Davis, Jr., Dean Martin . . . if the lyrics weren't stupid. Words were important. That was a concept that the Beatles, say, for all their musicality, just didn't get. Great music but I always thought they would have created transcendent art if only they'd stopped and thought about what they were writing.

Now, as I sped away from the District, I was on the Sinatra channel on Sirius satellite radio, which plays a good mix of artists of that era, not just Frank. The voice coming through the speakers was that of Harry Connick, Jr.

Enjoying the music.

Enjoying the driving too.

I'd left the city behind. I'd left Maree and Joanne behind. Ryan and Amanda.

Henry Loving too.

They were all, in different ways, permanent farewells.

Other people too had ceased to exist for me—only temporarily, of course. Freddy was gone, as were Aaron Ellis and Claire duBois, who I hoped was cooking up a storm just now with Cat Man.

Jason Westerfield had departed earlier from my mental cast and crew as had the woman with the pearls.

A sign flashed past. Fifteen miles to Annapolis, Maryland.

Twenty minutes later I pulled up in front of a modest white colonial house not far from the Chesapeake Bay. The wind was tame tonight but I could still hear the waves—one of the things I liked best about the area here.

I slowed, signaled, though no one was behind me, and turned up a narrow drive, flush with leaves, which bail out earlier here than in the city. I enjoyed raking them—not blowing but raking— and would get to the task tomorrow, the start of my weekend. I braked to a stop, then climbed out, stretched and gathered my computer, gym bag and the shopping bag containing the precious board game.

Juggling these items, I made my way along the serpentine strip of concrete— crunching leaves underneath—to the front door. I started to set the suitcase down to dig in my pocket for the keys but suddenly it burst open.

I blinked in surprise.

Peggy barked a laugh. Small but strong, face dusted with freckles even into her fourth decade, the brunette flung her arms around me and, with the packages, I nearly went over backward. She steadied us both—strong, I was saying—and, her arm hard around my lower back, we walked into our house.

"You're back early." She frowned. "Should I tell my lover to get out by the bedroom window?"

"Can he cook?" I said. "Ask him to stay."

Peggy gigged me in the ribs, laughing again. Setting down the bundles, I gripped her hard. Our lips met and kissed for a lengthy moment.

"So the project finished up early?" I noted that she glanced at herself in the mirror and straightened her dark wiry hair. She hadn't been expecting me home until tomorrow. She usually got dolled up for my arrival after I'd been away. This was one of the things I loved about her. I hadn't called because I didn't want her to go to any trouble and because I liked to surprise her—like this, as well as for birthdays and anniversaries; our fifteenth was coming up in two weeks.

"What happened to your head?"

"I'm a klutz. You know that. Crawling around in a construction site."

"Hardhat," she admonished.

"I usually do." I asked, "Are your mom and dad still coming this weekend?"

"Yep. With Oscar."

"Who?"

"Their dog."

"Did I know they got a dog?" I asked. I honestly couldn't remember.

"They mentioned it."

"What kind?"

"A pick-a-poo or something. I don't know. A corga-doodle."

I looked around. "The boys?"

"Jeremy's in his room, on the phone with your brother. Sam's in bed. I'll make you some supper."

"A sandwich, maybe. Some wine. A big glass of wine."

"Come on." Peggy stowed the luggage in the hallway I'd been meaning to retile, ever since a bathroom pipe committed suicide a month ago. She led me into the kitchen and dug in the refrigerator. Before she started assembling the food she dimmed the lights and lit several candles.

She poured a French Chardonnay, a Côte d'Or, for both of us.

We touched glasses.

"How long you home for?"

"Four days."

"Really!" She stepped forward, pressed her entire body against mine and kissed me hard, her hand sliding down my back and pausing in the exact spot where my holster had been only a few hours before.

After a moment or two, when she stepped back, I said, "Did I mention I'm home for five days?"

"What do I have to do to make it a week?" she whispered, lips against my ear.

I smiled, though even with Peggy I wasn't the best smiler in the world.

A few more kisses and when she finally escaped from my arms I said, "Look what I found." I stepped into the hall, grabbed the shopping bag and pulled out the game that had been delivered on Saturday. I unwrapped it and set the box between us.

"Oh, my . . ." Peggy isn't the board game aficionado that I am but since there are more games in the house than books she's become something of an expert by osmosis. "Is that what I think it is?"

"An original."

We were looking down at a first edition of Candy Land, the simplest and
arguably the most popular of all children's board games. One I had grown
up playing with my brothers and our
friends. You draw cards and move your
pieces around a landscape that includes
a chocolate swamp and a gumdrop
mountain.

"Jer's too old, I'd guess. But Sammy'll
like it."

"No, with you, Jeremy will play."

I realized she was right.

"Now, go sit and relax," Peggy told
me. Then the smile faded. I was sized
up. "You working out or something and
not telling me? You've lost weight."

"No good fast food where they sent
me."

"Hm."

As she pulled open the refrigerator
door, I walked into the den. I eased into
my wheezing armchair, surrounded by
the 121 games on the shelves. A thought
occurred to me, a thought directed to
one of my recent principals:

You're more right than you know,
Joanne. It's *not* impossible to have the

two lives. The public, the private. The dark, the light. The madness, the dear sanity.

But that balancing act takes so very much work. Superhuman, it sometimes seems.

You have to force aside every memory and thought of your other life, your life with your loved ones when they pop into your head. If you don't, the distraction could be fatal.

You have to accept the loneliness of a secret life. Like the one I live four or five days at a time, or more, on the road, in safe houses and in the Alexandria town house, which the government subsidizes so I can be on call, near the office. Even though it's near my beloved gaming club, even though it's filled with some of the favorite games in my collection, even though it's decorated with certificates and commendations I've received from the Diplomatic Service and from my present organization, it's essentially an empty place, smelling of cardboard and paint. It just isn't home.

And, most difficult of all—if you want

to lead this double life—you must deceive.

Peggy knows I work for the government but, because of my degree in math, she thinks it has something to do with scientific analysis of secure federal facilities here and abroad. I've told her I can't say anything more and I assure her it's not dangerous, just highly classified. A lot of numbers crunching. Boring.

She understands, I think, and accepts that I have to be tight-lipped.

And, conversely, I share little about my home life with my coworkers—all but the closest, like Freddy. Buried deep somewhere in federal government human resource departments, of course, are full records about me and about Peggy, the boys, my mother—she lives in San Diego—and my three older brothers, one an insurance executive and two college professors. Those files will be relevant should benefits and retirement and beneficiary issues arise but like so much else in my life, I've done everything I humanly can to make sure facts about me are NTK.

Need-to-know . . .

To most of the people I come across in my job I'm single, childless, a resident of Old Town Alexandria and probably a widower with a tragic past (the stalker story I told Maree was true, though it didn't end as dramatically as I suggested when making my point to the young woman). I'm a stiff federal employee who doesn't tell jokes or smile much. I prefer to be called by the pretentious, one-syllable "Corte."

Gratefully, I was now drawn from these thoughts by a high-pitched shout of youthful joy from behind me. I rose, turning and smiling.

My youngest, Sammy, had awakened and stood in the doorway. "Daddy, you're home!" He was in SpongeBob pajamas and his hair was tousled and he looked adorably cute.

I immediately set the wineglass down. I knew the boy was going for a running leap. Greeting me this way had become a recent tradition. And sure enough, bare feet thumping, he sped toward me, ignoring his mother's laughing plea from the kitchen to be careful.

But I encouraged him. "Sammy, come on, come on!" I called, sounding, I'm sure, as enthusiastic as I felt. And, as he took off into the air, I braced myself firmly and made absolutely certain that my son landed safe and unharmed in my waiting arms.

Acknowledgments

Corte's strategies involving game theory and his ideas about rational irrationality come largely from *The New Yorker* writer John Cassidy and his marvelous (and sobering) book, *How Markets Fail.*

Many thanks to the folks who have made this book what it is: Sarah Hochman, Carolyn Mays, Deborah Schneider, Vivienne Schuster . . . and, as always, Madelyn, Jane and Julie.

About the Author

A former journalist, folksinger and attorney, Jeffery Deaver is an international number-one best-selling author. His novels have appeared on best seller lists around the world, including *The New York Times, The Times* of London, Italy's *Corriere della Serra, The Sydney Morning Herald* and *The Los Angeles Times.* His books are sold in 150 countries and translated into 25 languages.

The author of twenty-six novels, two collections of short stories and a non-fiction law book, he's received or been shortlisted for a number of awards around the world. His *The Bodies Left Behind* was named Novel of the Year by the International Thriller Writers Association, and his Lincoln Rhyme thriller *The Broken Window* was also nominated for that prize. He has been awarded the Steel Dagger and the Short Story Dagger from the British Crime

Writers' Association and the Nero Wolfe Award, and he is a three-time recipient of the Ellery Queen Reader's Award for Best Short Story of the Year and a winner of the British Thumping Good Read Award. *The Cold Moon* was recently named the Book of the Year by the Mystery Writers Association of Japan, as well as by *Kono Mystery Wa Sugoi* magazine. In addition, the Japanese Adventure Fiction Association awarded the book their annual Grand Prix award.

Deaver has been nominated for six Edgar Awards from the Mystery Writers of America, an Anthony Award and a Gumshoe Award. He was recently short-listed for the ITV3 Crime Thriller Award for Best International Author.

His book *A Maiden's Grave* was made into an HBO movie starring James Garner and Marlee Matlin, and his novel *The Bone Collector* was a feature release from Universal Pictures, starring Denzel Washington and Angelina Jolie. His most recent books are *Roadside Crosses, The Bodies Left Behind, The Broken Window, The Sleeping Doll* and *More Twisted: Collected Stories, Vol-*

ume II. And, yes, the rumors are true, he did appear as a corrupt reporter on his favorite soap opera, *As the World Turns*.

Deaver is presently writing the next James Bond novel, following which he will return to alternating his series featuring Kathryn Dance, who will make her appearances in odd-number years, with that starring Lincoln Rhyme, who will appear in even.

He was born outside Chicago and has a bachelor of journalism degree from the University of Missouri and a law degree from Fordham University.

Readers can visit his website at www.jefferydeaver.com.